VIKING
Mystery
Suspense

# WHOM THE
# GODS LOVE

✳

Also by Kate Ross

CUT TO THE QUICK
A BROKEN VESSEL

# WHOM THE

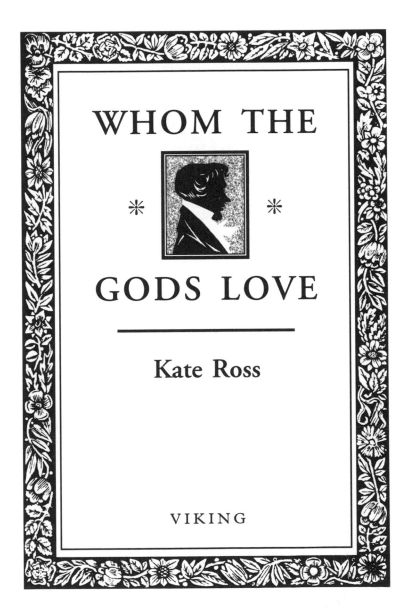

✴ ✴

# GODS LOVE

### Kate Ross

VIKING

M

VIKING
Published by the Penguin Group
Penguin Books USA Inc., 375 Hudson Street,
New York, New York 10014, U.S.A.
Penguin Books Ltd, 27 Wrights Lane,
London W8 5TZ, England
Penguin Books Australia Ltd, Ringwood,
Victoria, Australia
Penguin Books Canada Ltd, 10 Alcorn Avenue,
Toronto, Ontario, Canada M4V 3B2
Penguin Books (N.Z.) Ltd, 182–190 Wairau Road,
Auckland 10, New Zealand

Penguin Books Ltd, Registered Offices:
Harmondsworth, Middlesex, England

First published in 1995 by Viking Penguin,
a division of Penguin Books USA Inc.

1 3 5 7 9 10 8 6 4 2

LIBRARY OF CONGRESS CATALOGING IN PUBLICATION DATA
Ross, Kate.
Whom the gods love / Kate Ross.
p. cm.
ISBN 0-670-86207-X
I. Title.
PS3568.0843494W46 1995
813'.54—dc20 94-43877

This book is printed on acid-free paper.
∞

Printed in the United States of America
Set in Adobe Plantin
Designed by Virginia Norey

To Steven Come, Reed Drews, Jay Harris,
and Peter Mowschenson, without whom there
would have been no Julian Kestrel

# AUTHOR'S NOTE

The characters in this novel are fictitious. Streets, villages, and other locales mentioned by name are authentic, with the exception of Cygnet's Court, Haythorpe and Sons, and the Jolly Filly. Readers who know Hampstead may perceive that Sir Malcolm's house in the Grove (since renamed Hampstead Grove) is based, very loosely, on Fenton House. Serle's Court, where Quentin Clare has his chambers, is now New Square, and a garden has displaced the gravel, fountain, and clock.

I would like to thank Dana Young for giving me the benefit of her expertise on horses and riding. I would also like to thank the Honourable Society of Lincoln's Inn—in particular the Chief Porter, Leslie Murrell—for their kind assistance with my research. Finally, I am grateful for the help and encouragement of the following people: Julie Carey, Cynthia Clarke, Mark Levine, Louis Rodriques, Edward Ross, Al Silverman, John Spooner, and Christina Ward.

# CONTENTS

1. The Ring in the Fish      1

2. Portrait of Alexander      11

3. Letters      23

4. Last Night on Earth      31

5. Full Orchestra      52

6. Duets      67

7. Bad Blood      77

8. Argus      92

9. Breaths of Scandal      104

10. Remember Your Sister      119

11. A Sporting Proposition      131

12. The Root of All Evil      141

13. London Clay      150

14. A Tangled Web      161

15. Night Visitors      172

16. A Pair of Nails      183

17.  Abandon All Hope                          199

18.  An Alibi Shattered                         211

19.  Vance Turns Up a Trump                     223

20.  Villain or Victim?                         232

21.  A Promise to a Lady                        243

22.  Blind-Man's-Buff                           255

23.  Ghosts                                     267

24.  Let Justice Be Done                        275

25.  The House without Windows                  287

26.  Behind the Mask                            303

27.  Verity                                     316

28.  Trompe l'Oeil                              331

29.  Far above Rubies                           342

30.  The Iron Weapon                            359

31.  Endings                                    370

32.  Beginnings                                 376

# CHARACTERS

## The Bow Street Runners and their allies

JULIAN KESTREL . . . . . . . . . . . . . . . . a gentleman
THOMAS STOKES,
   known as DIPPER . . . . . . . . . . . . . his manservant
PETER VANCE . . . . . . . . . . . . . . . . . a Bow Street Runner
BILL WATKINS . . . . . . . . . . . . . . . . . a Bow Street patrol

## The Falkland family

ALEXANDER FALKLAND (deceased)
BELINDA FALKLAND . . . . . . . . . . . . . his widow
EUGENE TALMADGE . . . . . . . . . . . . . her half-brother
SIR MALCOLM FALKLAND,
   bart., K.C. . . . . . . . . . . . . . . . . . . . Mr. Falkland's father

## Mr. Falkland's servants

PAUL NICHOLS . . . . . . . . . . . . . . . . the butler
HIPPOLYTE VALERE . . . . . . . . . . . . . Mr. Falkland's
                                         manservant
MARTHA GILMORE . . . . . . . . . . . . . . Mrs. Falkland's maid
LUKE HALLAM ⎱
NELSON BEALE ⎰ . . . . . . . . . . . . . . . the footmen
JOE SAMPSON . . . . . . . . . . . . . . . . . the coachman
MIKE NUGENT . . . . . . . . . . . . . . . . . Mrs. Falkland's groom

## Sir Malcolm's servants

DUTTON . . . . . . . . . . . . . . . . . . . . . . an elderly retainer
BOB CHEEVER . . . . . . . . . . . . . . . . . the coachman
FRED . . . . . . . . . . . . . . . . . . . . . . . . a stable boy

## Guests at Mr. Falkland's party

LADY ANTHEA FITZJOHN . . . . . . . . . . . a wealthy spinster
THE HON. FELIX POYNTER . . . . . . . . . a butterfly dandy

Sir Henry Effingham, bart. . . . . . . a Member of
Parliament
Quentin Clare . . . . . . . . . . . . . . a law student
David Adams . . . . . . . . . . . . . . . . . a broker of international
loans

### Mr. Clare's family

Verity Clare . . . . . . . . . . . . . . . . Mr. Clare's sister
George Tibbs . . . . . . . . . . . . . . . their great-uncle

### People associated with Cygnet's Court

Marianne Desmond . . . . . . . . . . . . an adventuress
Fanny Gates . . . . . . . . . . . . . . . . . her maidservant
Mrs. Wheeler . . . . . . . . . . . . . . . . their neighbour
Bet . . . . . . . . . . . . . . . . . . . . . . . Mrs. Wheeler's
maidservant
Giles Underhill . . . . . . . . . . . . . . the landlord
Jemmy Otis . . . . . . . . . . . . . . . . . an urchin

### People associated with the Jolly Filly

Ruth Piper . . . . . . . . . . . . . . . . . . the landlord's daughter
Ben Foley . . . . . . . . . . . . . . . . . . an ostler

### Absent friends of Mr. Kestrel

Philippa Fontclair . . . . . . . . . . . . . a precocious twelve-
year-old
Hugh Fontclair . . . . . . . . . . . . . . her brother
Maud Fontclair . . . . . . . . . . . . . . his wife
Duncan MacGregor . . . . . . . . . . . their friend, a surgeon

### Miscellaneous

Oliver de Witt . . . . . . . . . . . . . . . a dandy and
Mr. Kestrel's rival
Alfred . . . . . . . . . . . . . . . . . . . . . Mr. Poynter's tiger
E. Ridley . . . . . . . . . . . . . . . . . . . "Proprietor"
Miss Meeks . . . . . . . . . . . . . . . . . a lady companion
Mr. Pruitt . . . . . . . . . . . . . . . . . . a youthful barrister

# WHOM THE
# GODS LOVE

✳

# The Ring
# in the Fish

*Go through the holly archway,* Sir Malcolm's letter had said, *then take the long, straight path past the church.* Well, this must be the archway, cut into a cluster of holly trees beside the church tower. The opening was narrow; Julian parted the shiny, spiky leaves with his riding whip and stepped through.

He found himself in a small, hilly churchyard, covered with a fantastic growth of foliage. There were more holly trees, great clumps of rhododendron, and shocks of unkempt grass overrun with ivy. Birds sang unseen from high branches; swarms of midges filled the air. Occasionally a bumblebee sailed by, as slow and stately as a barge. Weathered gravestones stood in disorderly ranks, some all but smothered in the rampant growth of vines and shrubs, others rising starkly above the greenery—the only dead things in a landscape teeming fiercely, incongruously, with life.

Julian glanced about in search of the path he was supposed to follow. There were so many footways swerving through the graves, around the bushes, and up and down the diminutive hills. Finally he spied a path that unfurled itself into a long, narrow lane. He set off, watched furtively by some half-dozen bystanders strolling among the graves. Despite Hampstead's proximity to London and its growing colony of artists and professional men, it was too small not to take an interest in a stranger—especially a young man dressed in the very pink of West End elegance.

The weather was typical of early May: chilly except when the afternoon sun fought its way through masses of grey and white cloud. It did so now, warming the air surprisingly swiftly, and turning the dull jade foliage a pale, brilliant green. Julian followed the path to what seemed to be the end, then it suddenly veered right, and he saw a man standing in a patch of sunshine just beyond a gnarled old tree.

He was forty-five or fifty, generously built, with a large head, broad shoulders, and sturdy limbs. His clothes were dark and sombre, and there was a wide black crape band on his hat. When he saw Julian, he waved eagerly and took a step as if to meet him. Then he checked himself, glanced down at a head-stone at his feet, and stayed where he was, as if loath to leave the grave behind.

Julian went up to him. "Sir Malcolm?"

"Mr. Kestrel!" Sir Malcolm grasped his hand. "Thank you for coming."

"Not at all. I'm glad of an opportunity to meet you. I've heard a great deal about your prowess in court."

Sir Malcolm shook his head. "Oh, it's no great matter to confuse a jury sufficiently to win a case now and then. Still, I'm relieved the world remembers me for something besides —this."

He looked down at the headstone. It was a simple slab of white marble, untouched as yet by the weather, and only just caressed at its base by the encroaching grass. The inscription read:


*ALEXANDER JAMES FALKLAND*
*born 1800, died 1825*
*WHOM THE GODS LOVE DIE YOUNG*


"We weren't sure what to do about the dates," Sir Malcolm said quietly. "We don't know if he was killed before or after midnight. In the end, I decided to leave off the months and days altogether."

*I decided,* Julian thought. Did that mean Alexander's widow had left it to Sir Malcolm to choose the inscription? Perhaps she was too overcome by grief; her husband had been murdered only a little over a week ago. Certainly that last line was more likely to be Sir Malcolm's idea than hers. He was said to be a first-rate classical scholar.

"How is Mrs. Falkland?" Julian asked.

"As well as can be expected. No—why should I put on a brave face with you? I intend you should be in my confidence. The fact is, she's in a very bad way. I mentioned in my note to you yesterday that she's been ill—a sudden indisposition, alarming at the time but, thank Heaven, it seems to have passed. It's the wound in her heart that's sapped her strength, blasted her youth. She's in despair, Mr. Kestrel. And she makes one understand that 'despair' is just what the Latin root conveys: the absence of all hope. She doesn't speak of it, but I know. She no longer believes that life has anything to offer her."

"Surely time will help assuage her feelings. No one can live long without hope—it isn't human nature."

"We live in the here and now, Mr. Kestrel. And in the here and now, she has to feel this way, and I have to see her every day, and know I can do nothing for her. And I have to grapple with my own demons: the rage, the frustration, of knowing that my son lies here, and justice goes in search of the villain who murdered him, and finds—nothing! We don't know by whom he was killed—worse still, we don't even know why! It wasn't a robbery, it wasn't a duel, it wasn't anything that ordinary human experience could school us to understand or accept. That's what makes it all so terrible—that he should have been killed, brutally murdered, for no reason!"

"For no *apparent* reason," Julian corrected him gently. "Murderers invariably have a reason for what they do. Even madmen think they have a reason, though to sane people it may make no sense."

Sir Malcolm was looking at him intently. "I believe, Mr. Kestrel, that murder is a specialty of yours. I mean, that you have a knowledge of the subject."

"I've had some experience with it. In one case, I was staying in a house where a murder occurred and found myself over head and ears in the investigation. The second time, I happened on evidence that it seemed only I could put to effective use."

"And both times, you found out the murderer when no one else could."

"I had that good fortune, yes."

"Mr. Kestrel, I'll be frank: I'd heard of your skill at solving crimes, and it's on that account that I asked to see you. Of course it was a theatrical gesture, appointing a meeting at Alexander's grave. I'm afraid every barrister has a dash of the actor in him. But I knew we could talk in private here." He glanced around this part of the churchyard, which they had entirely to themselves. "I come here every day, and no one disturbs me." He shrugged sadly. "No one knows what to say."

Julian said delicately, "Do you mean that I might be of service to you somehow?"

Sir Malcolm hesitated. "Let me begin at the beginning. You knew Alexander, I suppose?"

"We ran into each other fairly often, and I went to a few of his parties. I can't say I knew him very well. He had a great many friends."

"Yes, he made friends very easily. I don't know most of them, myself. Alexander and I moved in very different circles. My friends are all lawyers and academics. He was in his element in the fashionable world, going to routs and balls and pleasure gardens. He excelled at all the gentlemanly pursuits —riding, hunting, cards—and he always knew what to say to gratify and amuse a lady. On top of everything else, he had good looks—I can say that without conceit, since he didn't get them from me." Sir Malcolm shook his head, marvelling. "When he was a boy, I used to ask myself where he came from. He was beautiful and strange, like some exotic bird that, for reasons utterly baffling to me, had decided to nest in my house."

"What about his mother? Does he take after her?"

"Oh, no. Agnes was as shy and quiet a girl as you'd ever meet. Alexander never knew her, anyway—she died soon after he was born."

"He followed in your footsteps in one respect," Julian pointed out. "He was reading for the Bar, wasn't he?"

"Yes." A reminiscent glow lit Sir Malcolm's face. "He would have made a fine lawyer, and I would have done everything in my power to advance him. But he was also thinking about a career in politics, and that might have suited him even better."

Julian was inclined to agree. Politics would have made the most of Alexander's gifts: his charm, his verbal facility, his genius for getting on with a wide variety of people.

"Of course," Sir Malcolm went on, "a Parliamentary career requires money. But Alexander was never at a loss for that. He'd married an heiress, and, as you probably know, he had a knack for investing money. When I was his age, no gentleman would have had anything to do with the Stock Exchange, but speculation seems to be all the rage these days. Alexander conjured money out of nothing and scattered it in all directions, and everywhere it fell, something beautiful sprang up: his house, his art collection, his carriages, his entertainments.

"Of course I was proud of him, and rejoiced in his success. It's odd, isn't it? how you can read and write about a subject all your life, and never once apply it to your own experience. The great classical works are full of warnings about the danger of being too beloved by the gods. Do you remember the story of Polycrates?"

"I know he turns up in a poem of Byron's."

"He also turns up in Herodotus's *Histories*. He was the ruler of the island of Samos, famous for his power and wealth. He had an immense fleet, won every battle, filled his coffers with plunder and his enemies' hearts with fear. One day his friend

Amasis warned him that the gods are envious of success, and advised him to find a way to break his long run of luck. So Polycrates took the thing he most treasured, an emerald ring, and threw it into the sea. A few days later, a fisherman presented him with an immense fish he had caught, and when its belly was slit open, the ring was found inside. Then Amasis knew for certain that his friend would die a terrible death, and, sure enough, Polycrates was captured by a Persian official and crucified."

Julian looked down thoughtfully at the inscription on Alexander's headstone. "That suggests the gods destroy what they love, not what they envy."

"In Greek, the words 'to admire' and 'to envy' are the same. At all events, Alexander was like Polycrates: until he died that gruesome death, he simply couldn't fail. May I tell you something in confidence?"

"Of course, if you wish."

"It's not widely known, but Alexander was in grave difficulties shortly before he died. He'd been investing in South American mines, and of course some of those have been faring badly of late. A few months ago, two of his mining ventures went down the wind within days of each other. I didn't know about it at the time. He didn't talk to me much about his investments, and he always kept such a cool head about money matters that few people can have suspected he was so hard hit. He was left owing thirty thousand pounds."

Julian's brows shot up. "That's quite a considerable sum."

"Yes. But here's the most extraordinary part of the story. Alexander had borrowed the money to invest in those mining ventures, and given notes-of-hand to several men in the City. In fact, he'd been borrowing for some time before that. His investments were so successful, he was emboldened to increase them, I suppose. The life he led was very expensive. He had a reputation to keep up in society, and of course he wanted Belinda to have the best of everything."

Sir Malcolm looked at Julian belligerently, prepared to defend his son against any charges of extravagance. But Julian only said, "Of course," politely and waited to be further enlightened.

"Yes, well—" Sir Malcolm cleared his throat. "You must have met David Adams?"

"Yes, at one of your son's parties. And of course I know of him by reputation."

Adams was a dealer in securities. In particular, he was a broker of loans to the newly independent South American nations. Although only in his mid-thirties, he already had the confidence of foreign officials and English ministers alike. Julian had heard he was fiercely ambitious, a dangerous man to cross. Alexander had invested successfully in some of his projects; what was far more eccentric, he had drawn Adams into his circle of friends and invited him to his parties. No one less courted and admired than Alexander would have dared. The man was not only in trade—he was a Jew.

"Adams had been buying up Alexander's notes-of-hand at a discount," Sir Malcolm said. "Whether Alexander knew what he was doing isn't clear; certainly no one else knew except a handful of men in the City, and they kept their own counsel. By the time those two mining ventures failed, Adams held nearly all Alexander's notes. And about three weeks before Alexander died—he forgave them."

"You mean, he and your son reached an accommodation?"

"I mean that Adams cancelled the debt, the whole of it, without Alexander's lifting a finger or paying him a farthing in exchange."

"That's extraordinary." To be sure, Adams was wealthy—the commissions on South American loans were said to be immense—but even he could hardly afford to throw money away on such a scale. "I suppose he's been questioned about all this—not only why he forgave the notes but why he bought them in the first place."

"Oh, yes. He says he did it to oblige Alexander."

Julian cocked an eyebrow skeptically. "No man of business is as obliging as that. I could understand his making lenient terms with your son, but to forgive the notes outright—"

"Yes, I know." Sir Malcolm nodded glumly. "Of course, Adams doesn't pretend he did it wholly out of friendship. He says Alexander was useful to him, and I'm sure that was true. Alexander introduced him to wealthy and influential men— potential investors, members of Parliament, all sorts of people who could advance his business. Anyway, the point I'm trying to make is that Alexander led a charmed life. The one time he failed spectacularly, he was saved from the consequences. Until a little over a week ago, when some person, evil or mad or both, bludgeoned him with a poker and scattered his brains across the floor of his own study, while overhead a houseful of guests drank his wine and wondered where he was!"

Sir Malcolm clenched his fists and walked rapidly back and forth. Julian gave him a chance to recover himself, then asked, "Will you tell me now why you wished to see me?"

"I suppose you've already guessed. It was Peter Vance who suggested I write to you. He's the Bow Street Runner investigating Alexander's murder, and he's finding it uphill work. It's not his fault—this crime would baffle anyone. The murderer left nothing behind in the study. The weapon was one that anybody could have wielded. Nothing was stolen from the house, and there was no sign anyone had broken in. So the murderer was almost certainly one of Alexander's servants, or one of his guests. But there were eighty guests at the party that night, and only a few have alibis.

"Vance says our best hope is to find someone with a motive and try to connect that person with the crime. He says that with so little physical evidence, motive is paramount. But whenever he's tried to question the guests, he's been balked at every turn. People like Sir Henry Effingham and Lady Anthea Fitzjohn don't take kindly to being interrogated by a Bow Street officer. You know what the fashionable world thinks of Bow Street: an institution invented to interfere with all their wholesome amusements—drinking, gambling, knocking over watchmen's boxes, blowing each other's brains out in duels. And there's not much Vance can do to coerce them—at least not without some concrete evidence linking them to the crime.

Ordinarily, Bow Street depends on rewards to loosen witnesses' tongues, and God knows I've offered them in abundance. But Alexander's guests are above accepting money for information. They insist they're eager to help, but they won't demean themselves by cooperating with Bow Street. And these people called themselves Alexander's friends!"

He drew a long breath and went on more calmly, "That's why Vance thought of applying to you for help. He remembered you from the investigation of the murder at the Reclamation Society."

Julian nodded. That had been six or seven months ago. Bow Street had not become involved until after Julian had solved the crime, but the subsequent arrest and trial had thrown him and Vance together a good deal. "You're fortunate to have him in charge of the investigation. He's canny and efficient, and completely imperturbable in a crisis."

Sir Malcolm smiled. "He says much the same thing of you. He also pointed out that you have access to all the fashionable world. Enquiries that would be offensive from a Bow Street Runner might be acceptable, even flattering, from you. I don't suppose there's a gentleman since Brummell with your reputation as an arbiter of fashion. I'm not flattering you—it's merely what everyone knows." He added in some embarrassment, "I hope you won't take this amiss, but before I approached you, I wrote to Samuel Digby. I knew he'd backed your investigation of the Reclamation Society murder, and he's a fine magistrate and an honest man. So I asked him for—well—"

"A reference?" said Julian, amused.

"Please don't be offended. It's just that solving this crime is so important to me! I've racked my brains over it, I've pestered poor Vance, I've been twice to see the Home Secretary, and still nothing's been accomplished—"

"I understand," Julian said gently. "I'm not in the least offended."

"I'm glad to hear it. Anyway, Mr. Digby wrote back to me that you were honourable, resourceful, and shrewder than any man has a right to be at your age. So there you have it, Mr. Kestrel. I'm appealing to you as a father, as a man of law, as a British subject—Why can I never say anything simply? After twenty years at the Bar, a man forgets what plain and honest discourse is." Sir Malcolm faced Julian squarely. "Help me, Mr. Kestrel. Help me find out who killed my son."

# ✳ 2 ✳

## PORTRAIT OF
## ALEXANDER

Julian was strongly tempted. How could he resist the chance to investigate a crime already so famous, with its challenging lack of evidence and its constellation of eminent suspects? And he was far from unmoved by Sir Malcolm's grief, bewilderment, and yearning for justice. But his first experience of solving a murder, at the country house of a proud old family, had made him wary of conducting investigations within a group of intimate friends and relatives. It meant becoming privy to their secrets, turning each against another, and all of them against himself—

He said, "You must realize, Sir Malcolm, these investigations can turn up painful, even shocking, information. The fact that your son wasn't robbed suggests that the murderer killed him for some personal reason, which means he or she was very likely someone close to him—a friend, even a relation. If I accept this task, I shall have to explore that possibility. I shall rifle through your son's possessions and papers; I shall ask impertinent questions, respect no one's privacy, treat nothing as sacred, and everyone not absolutely cleared as a suspect. I don't say this to alarm you—merely to make you see that, in embarking on an investigation like this, you must ask yourself, not merely what the truth is, but whether you wish to know it."

"Yes, Mr. Kestrel," Sir Malcolm said steadily. "With all my heart, I wish to know the truth, whatever it may be. Ignorance to me is the worst of torments—the most frightening and frustrating state a man can be in. And I swear to you here and now that, whatever questions you ask, and whatever you discover, I shall never reproach you. Any pain your investigation inflicts on me will be of my own seeking—the price of my conviction that light is always better than darkness."

"And Mrs. Falkland? Is she of your mind?"

"I talked all this over with Belinda before I wrote to you. I could hardly take such a step without her consent. She agreed that we should consult you. I can't say she showed much hope or interest, but that's her state of mind. She's too sick at heart to be roused to enthusiasm about anything."

There was a pause. The sun went behind a cloud, dropping a veil of shadow around them. Julian weighed Sir Malcolm's promise, wondered if he could keep it, and decided that it did not matter. In his heart of hearts, he had known all along what his response would be. "Very well, Sir Malcolm. I accept your proposal."

"Thank you, Mr. Kestrel!" Sir Malcolm wrung his hand. "I haven't a doubt that between you, you and Vance will get to the bottom of this crime! I hope you needn't go back to London just yet? I should like to take you back to my house —there's something there I want to show you. And I'm sure Belinda will want to thank you personally for your kindness in helping us. We'd best not tax her with questions, though, till she feels more the thing."

"I should only be wasting both my time and hers, trying to question her when I know so little about the crime myself. I've spent the past fortnight in Newmarket, and though I've been following the newspaper accounts, they're one part information to three parts drama and rumour. I need to see Vance and find out what he's discovered so far, in particular about suspects and alibis." He paused, eyeing Sir Malcolm consideringly. "There's one thing I had better ask you at the outset: On the night your son was killed—where were you?"

"Where was—?" Sir Malcolm stared in bewilderment. Then his eyes filled with horror. "You can't mean—oh, I understand. You're illustrating your point, that no one is above suspicion. And you're right, of course. I want you to be thorough. I was at home that night. My servants can confirm that I never left the house, let alone went all the way to London, killed my son, and came all the way back."

"Thank you, Sir Malcolm. I realize that was an appalling question." And he did feel for Sir Malcolm, but he also intended to ask Vance if his alibi was as sound as he claimed. Because it was not beyond imagination that Sir Malcolm had killed his son, and was now conducting a zealous search for the murderer in order to divert suspicion. True, he appeared to have loved and admired Alexander, but he had also observed: *In Greek, the words "to admire" and "to envy" are the same.* It would be highly inconvenient, at the very least, to harbour suspicions of parricide against the man who had brought him into the investigation. But the possibility had to be faced.

"You'll come, then?" said Sir Malcolm.

"I should be very pleased."

"Good, good! You rode here from London, I assume?" Sir Malcolm glanced at Julian's top-boots and riding whip.

"Yes. I left my horse at a public house called the Holly Bush."

"I live quite near there, in the Grove. We can walk, if you've no objection, and I'll send a servant to fetch your horse."

They left the church grounds by a side gate and ascended a steep, narrow street flanked by handsome brown-brick houses. Holly bushes clustered thickly in the gardens and along the grass verges. Laundresses had turned some of them into drying-racks; damp white-linen sleeves waved phantom greetings in the wind.

They reached Holly Bush Hill and turned into the Grove, a narrow, curving street lined with stately houses behind high brick walls. Sir Malcolm stopped before a gilded wrought-iron gate, which bore the initials of some former owner and the

year 1705. The house beyond looked to be of about that period. It was square and solid, of brown brick, with red-brick
borders around the windows. The roof was steep, giving the
house a high-browed, thoughtful look. A small wing jutted
forward on either side, connected by a simple but elegant
white colonnade before the door.

Sir Malcolm and Julian entered. A servant met them and
took their hats. He was an elderly man, probably a retainer of
long standing, dressed in mourning like his master. Sir Malcolm told him to send to the Holly Bush for Julian's horse,
then asked where Mrs. Falkland was.

"She's in the drawing room, sir. Martha is with her."

"Martha is her maid," Sir Malcolm explained in an aside
to Julian. He turned back to the servant. "Run up and ask her
if she's well enough to receive us."

"Yes, sir." The servant bowed and went upstairs.

"I'm being especially careful with her just now," Sir Malcolm confided. "As I told you, she was very ill a few days ago.
At first I assumed she'd eaten something that disagreed with
her, but then I began to wonder—" He dropped his voice.
"It's been a great sorrow to me that Alexander left no children. I'm the last of my line, and God knows, I'm not likely
to marry again, at forty-eight. I don't suppose any woman
could tolerate my books and my solitary habits. But since Belinda's illness, I've dared to hope Alexander left something of
himself behind. It would be a great consolation both to her
and to me."

"Then I hope with all my heart you may be right."

"Thank you. I feel sure it would lift her spirits, having
something new to think about and plan for. It was easier for
her just after Alexander's death, when she had so many things
to do: looking after the servants, ordering mourning for the
household, answering letters of condolence. I was always trying to persuade her to rest, but I can see now she knew what
was best for her. Since I brought her here, she hasn't had
enough to occupy her, and it's set her brooding."

The servant returned. "Mrs. Falkland says, will you and Mr. Kestrel please come up, sir."

"Splendid! Mr. Kestrel, will you step upstairs?"

✳

The drawing room, that most feminine of precincts, had sunk into dowdiness and disuse during Sir Malcolm's long widowerhood. The furnishings were old-fashioned, with more dignity than grace. The marble fireplace was too large, the crimson wallpaper too dark. The porcelain shepherds on the mantelpiece were comically out of style. Most of the furniture stood formally against the walls, but a sofa was drawn up to the fire. Mrs. Falkland sat there, still and remote, her hands folded in her lap.

Julian knew Belinda Falkland only slightly, and could never see her without being struck afresh by her beauty. Even the pallor of illness and the strain of grief could do little to mar it. She had well-nigh perfect features: the nose straight, the lower lip a little full, the chin poised proudly above a slim white throat. Her hair was guinea-gold, her eyes pale blue, with a lustre like frost. Her black gown was cut in the latest fashion, with long sleeves full at the shoulders, a trim, belted waist, and a cone-shaped skirt. On her breast she wore an oval mourning brooch, with a red-brown, ropelike border of what must have been Alexander's hair. Inside was a sepia painting of a broken column, with a pair of scales like those carried by Justice lying crumpled at its foot. This might equally symbolize Alexander's blasted legal career or his lawless death; either way, Julian suspected that the metaphor, like the choice of inscription for Alexander's headstone, was Sir Malcolm's.

"Belinda, my dear." Sir Malcolm went to her and kissed her on the brow. "How are you?"

"I'm better, Papa, thank you."

"You know Mr. Kestrel, I think?"

"Good afternoon, Mrs. Falkland." Julian came forward and bowed over her hand. "I wish we might have met again under

other circumstances. I was very sorry to hear of your husband's death."

"Thank you. Papa said you might be persuaded to help us
find out who killed him. I take it from your coming here that
you've agreed?"

"Yes."

She glanced toward a corner of the room, where a woman
sat sewing—her maid, Martha, no doubt. Julian had expected
a pretty young soubrette, but this woman was about forty,
with a square jaw and greying, dun-coloured hair. She was
dressed in mourning like the rest of the household, her clothes
neat, spotless, and starkly without ornament.

There was no need for speech between her and Mrs. Falkland. She got up at once and brought forward chairs for Julian
and Sir Malcolm. The chairs were large and heavy, but she
lifted them without effort, as a farmer's wife might heave sacks
of grain. Country-bred, Julian thought.

Her task finished, she retired to her corner and took up her
needlework again. Mrs. Falkland looked into the fire. Sir
Malcolm seemed a little at a loss. "I'm afraid we're tiring you,
my dear. Perhaps if Mr. Kestrel were to return in a day or
two—"

"I'm not tired, Papa." She turned to Julian. "Have you
anything to ask me?"

"Only the broadest of enquiries, and they aren't urgent. I
don't wish to tax your strength."

"You're very kind, but you needn't be concerned about
that. I'm well enough to answer questions."

He decided to take her at her word. "Who do you think
killed your husband, Mrs. Falkland? Have you any theories?"

"No. I have no theories."

"Had he any enemies?"

"Not that I knew of. He was very popular. Everyone
liked him."

"Had he quarrelled with anyone recently?"

"Alexander never quarrelled. It wasn't in his nature."

"Surely everyone has disagreements?"

"A disagreement isn't the same thing as a quarrel. Alexander had differences of opinion with people, but he didn't become angry, or make them angry. You knew him—you saw what he was like."

"I saw him out in the world, at clubs and parties. Was he the same in private?"

"Yes. He never lost his temper with me. I should almost say he hadn't one to lose. There was a lightness about him. He made life very easy. Wherever he went, he was like a perfect host, making everyone around him comfortable and happy. There was no unpleasantness, ever. He found ways of smoothing it away."

"The man you describe is remarkable—hardly human."

"Yes," she said quietly. "I know."

Martha emerged from her corner and stood by Mrs. Falkland, with a mixture of deference and protectiveness. "Excuse me, ma'am, but it's time for your medicine." She spoke with the lilting inflection and guttural *r* of the West Country.

Sir Malcolm rose. "We won't trouble you anymore, my dear. Take good care of her, Martha—I know you always do. Mr. Kestrel, will you come into the library?"

Julian took leave of Mrs. Falkland. She seemed as indifferent to his departure as she had been to his coming, but he had the impression Martha was distinctly glad to see him go.

✳

Sir Malcolm's house was designed very simply. The ground floor was a square, with two rooms on each side of a central hallway. Above were four more rooms, ranged around the top of the main stairs. Sir Malcolm brought Julian down to the library, which was the first room on the right as you entered the house.

The library was clearly Sir Malcolm's sanctum: plain and oak-panelled, lined from floor to ceiling with shelves of classical authors. Bits of ancient pottery and sculpture served as paperweights or book props. The big knee-hole tables were covered with open books, ink-stained blotters, and piles of paper. It was the kind of room that would seem chaotic to everyone but its owner, who would know in some mysterious way exactly where everything was.

"A hot drink wouldn't come amiss, do you think?" said Sir Malcolm. "Rum punch, or perhaps brandy-and-water?"

"Brandy-and-water, if you please."

Sir Malcolm rang for the servant who had taken their hats. Meanwhile Julian strolled over to the fireplace—and there was Alexander Falkland.

It was a full-length portrait, large as life, filling all the space between fireplace and ceiling. Alexander stood in a standard pose yet looked quite natural, his arm resting on a mantelpiece as though he had casually laid it there in conversation. The likeness was superb. The painter had not only captured his physical traits—red-brown hair, brown eyes, slim, youthful figure—but conveyed their charm. The eyes were alight with laughter, the lips curving into their radiant, confiding smile, which seemed to draw the merest stranger into privileged intimacy. Here was a young man who enjoyed his life and made other people enjoy theirs.

Sir Malcolm joined Julian before the portrait, letting him see the father and son juxtaposed. They had the same auburn hair and cinnamon-brown eyes, but there the resemblance ended. Sir Malcolm's woolly hair and craggy features had nothing in common with Alexander's wavy locks and fine-drawn face.

"It's a remarkable portrait," Julian said.

"Yes. I'm very grateful to have it. I only wish the painter had chosen a different background. Do you realize where he is?"

Julian looked more closely. Alexander stood by a fireplace, with a reproduction of one of Palladio's architectural drawings hanging above it. Behind him was a niche displaying classical urns and marble or bronze statuettes. The walls were painted a soothing white and grey, conducive to meditation. "His study?"

"Yes. His own design, in part."

Julian nodded. "Much of the house was, wasn't it? I've only seen the public rooms, where he gave his entertainments, but I know the whole house is reckoned a *tour de force.*"

"Yes. All the rooms are in different styles: Greek, Gothic, Turkish, Chinese—"

"Renaissance," mused Julian, surveying the details of the study. His eyes came to rest on the polished steel poker propped neatly against the grate. "Is that the same poker—"

"Yes," said Sir Malcolm heavily. "The one that was used to kill him."

"Is this what you wanted to show me?"

"No, no." Sir Malcolm wrenched his gaze away from the portrait and went over to a marble-topped cabinet. "What I wanted to show you is in here. I keep them locked up. Since Alexander died, they've become my greatest treasure."

The servant brought in a tray containing a decanter, glasses, a pot of hot water, and a sugar-bowl. At a sign from Sir Malcolm, he bowed and went out. Sir Malcolm waved Julian toward the tray. "Don't stand on ceremony, Mr. Kestrel— mix yourself a glass. I'll join you in a moment."

While Julian helped himself to brandy and water, Sir Malcolm unlocked the cabinet with a key he kept on his watch-chain. He took out a pile of folded papers with broken seals and brought them over to Julian.

"Letters?" Julian asked.

"More than letters. A side of Alexander most people never saw. A little over a year ago, he told me he wanted to enroll as a law student at Lincoln's Inn. Of course I was pleased he was thinking of following in my footsteps, but I must confess, I didn't expect he'd buckle to it seriously. A good many young men get themselves admitted to Inns of Court as a sort of gentlemen's club, and since the only real requirement for being called to the Bar is to eat a certain number of dinners in Hall every year, a man can qualify himself to practise law without ever studying at all. Some do study of course—the ones who really mean to make a career of it. But Alexander was newly married, he was taken up with refurbishing his house, and he had so many friends and social engagements, I didn't see how he'd find time to pore over legal tomes.

"But he surprised me. He read—soaked up knowledge like a sponge. And not just law, but works on government, philosophy, political economy. His friends never would have guessed—he was always light and gay and amusing with them. But here"—Sir Malcolm flourished the pile of letters—"here he stored up his reflections, his ideals, his political and moral concerns. We didn't see much of each other this past year— I was often in court or away at the county assizes, and he had such a busy social life. But, through his letters, I felt closer to him than I ever had before. One of the cruelest things about his death is that I should have lost him just when we were getting to know one another—when we were becoming friends."

Julian was moved; all the same, he made allowances for a bereaved father's partiality. It was hard to believe Alexander's political and moral views could be so profound. He was not the kind of young man one thought of as having any. "Do you think these letters might shed light on his murder?"

"I don't know. I just felt you needed to know him—really know him. I wanted you to see there was more to him than the bright surface he showed the world." Sir Malcolm hesitated, then held out the letters. "I'm going to lend them to you, so you can read them at your leisure. I don't like to let them out of my hands, but there's no help for it. And, here." He went back to the cabinet and took out another sheaf of papers. "You'd better have my letters to him as well, so that you can follow the give-and-take of ideas. I took them back after he died. He'd left his papers to me—his books as well."

"*A propos,*" said Julian, "how did he leave the rest of his property?"

"Nearly everything went to Belinda. Of course, his most valuable property was the landed estate she'd brought him, and on his death that reverted to her by law. He left generous bequests to his servants, particularly his valet, a pernickety little Frenchman named Valère. And there was a conditional bequest to Eugene, consisting of some paintings and other property worth about four thousand pounds."

"Eugene is Mrs. Falkland's brother, I believe?"

"Half-brother, to be precise. Alexander was his guardian. He's staying with me now. Belinda brought him with her."

"What did you mean when you said the bequest was conditional?"

"I meant that it depended on Alexander's dying without issue. If he and Belinda had had a child, Eugene's bequest would have been reduced by about three-quarters. Alexander was fond of Eugene, but I suppose he felt he owed it to his own children to put them first."

"What if your hopes are well-founded, and Mrs. Falkland proves to be in the family way?"

"Well, if there's a live child, Eugene will be the loser. Awkward situation, but there it is."

"I can see I shall have to speak to Eugene."

Sir Malcolm eyed him uneasily. "You do know he's only sixteen?"

"I imagine he's capable of wielding a poker?"

"Well, yes."

"Was he in the house on the night Alexander died?"

"Yes. But you don't understand—Alexander was his hero! He perked up like a dog noticed by its master whenever Alexander looked his way! You can't think he'd kill him, just for four thousand pounds?"

"Men have killed each other for four pounds, even four shillings. The income from four thousand pounds would be two hundred a year—not an inconsiderable supplement to a gentleman's income. Has Eugene any money of his own?"

"Not a farthing," Sir Malcolm admitted. "His father came to a bad end, you know. Belinda's father—her mother's first husband—was a respectable country squire, who died when Belinda was a baby. A few years later his widow married Tracy Talmadge, an engaging young man, but a rake and a spendthrift. He ran through his own fortune and whatever of his wife's he could lay hands on. Luckily he couldn't touch Belinda's property—that had been well tied up by her father. In the end his friends caught him cheating at cards, he was disgraced, and cut his throat in a fit of despair. His wife was left a pauper, living on the charity of her daughter's trustees. And Eugene, who was only three, had nothing in the world but a legacy of dishonour."

"You must see, Sir Malcolm," Julian pointed out gently, "you haven't exactly made a case for his innocence."

"I haven't, have I? Well, by all means question him. Question anyone you like—I give you *carte blanche.* Where shall you begin?"

"With Vance. I shall try to arrange to see him this evening. Then tomorrow I should like to inspect Alexander's study and the rest of his house."

"Why don't I meet you there? I can let you in, introduce you to the servants, and answer any questions you may have. I'd like to watch you, see how you go about your investigation. You don't know how helpless I've felt—waiting and wondering, receiving reports from Vance, but not really knowing what's going forward, or how I might be of use."

"Very well. Shall we say ten o'clock?"

"Ten o'clock it is. I can't tell you what your assistance means to me, Mr. Kestrel. You've given me hope. Perhaps in time you'll give Belinda hope as well."

Julian thought it would take more than a solution to the murder to lift Mrs. Falkland's spirits. He did not know what was behind her dull despair—shock or grief or guilt. But one thing seemed clear: it did not matter to her who had killed her husband.

# ✳ 3 ✳

## LETTERS

"It's as I expected," said Julian, surrendering one booted foot to his manservant. "Sir Malcolm wanted to talk to me about his son's murder. Not only that—he's asked me to help Bow Street solve it."

Dipper removed the boot with one smooth tug. "You going to have a go, sir?"

"I seem to have agreed, yes."

Dipper nodded approvingly. Mr. Kestrel needed the challenge of another murder investigation. He needed it himself. He had been accustomed to live by his wits until a few years ago, when Mr. Kestrel came to London and took him on as his valet. What Mr. Kestrel had done before that, Dipper did not exactly know, but he felt sure his master had not been a mere idler—he knew life too thoroughly and took care of himself too well. Nowadays their life was too easy—or would be, if Mr. Kestrel had not developed this singular interest in murder.

Julian shifted position to let him take off the other boot. "You know all the servants' gossip. Tell me: what was Alexander Falkland's reputation below stairs? Did he stint the servants on beer money, shout at the butler, make love to the maids?"

"He was a first-rate master, by all accounts, sir. It wasn't

so much the wages he paid, though they was up to the mark.
It's that he treated his slaveys—I dunno, like they had feelings,
same as him. He said 'please' and 'thank you,' and told 'em
when they done well, and if some'ut went wrong, he'd laugh
about it, like as not, 'stead of cutting up rusty. His man—he's
a *mounseer*, his name's Valère—took it mortal hard when his
master croaked, and now he's in a stew 'coz the killer ain't
been nabbed. Says if this was France—"

"—the killer would have been found at once, and we'd all
be celebrating over *foie gras* and Chambertin. Actually, he
has a point. These investigations are haphazard affairs in
England—that's what comes of having no regular police. The
Bow Street Runners are clever and effective, for all the fashionable world's efforts to make them out buffoons, but their
force is too small and too dependent on private rewards. That
the old law-enforcement institutions go creaking on only
makes things worse: the Runners are at odds with the parish
constables, the unpaid justices of the peace look down their
noses at the paid magistrates, and the watchmen get quietly
drunk each night and ignore the whole lot of them. And whenever Sir Robert Peel attempts to bring some order to this
chaos, he meets with horrified cries that a professional police
would be the downfall of English liberties. One wonders what
the devil Parliament is thinking of—I seem to be making a
speech."

"Yes, sir." Dipper went on tranquilly laying out Julian's
evening clothes.

"I hadn't meant to. It disrupts the temperate, philosophical
frame of mind necessary for dressing. By the way, did you
know our old friend Peter Vance is in charge of investigating
Falkland's murder?"

"Is he, sir?"

"Yes. As soon as I've dressed, I'm going to write him a note,
and I want you to take it to Bow Street directly."

"Yes, sir."

"You look something less than eager. I thought you and

Vance got on tolerably well, for all that you used to be on opposite sides of the law."

"Yes, sir. It's just that it feels a bit queer, going to Bow Street o' purpose, 'stead of being pulled in. Makes me skin crawl, sir."

"I'm afraid I'm obliged to trample on your sensibilities. I want Vance to call on me tonight and bring any papers he has on the investigation. If it's any consolation, I shan't need you again until late in the evening. So have a drink or two with any servants you know who happen to be at liberty. And while you're about it, tell a few of them—in the *strictest* confidence, mind you—that I've undertaken to help Sir Malcolm Falkland solve his son's murder."

"If I do that, sir, it'll be all over town by morning."

Julian smiled. "So it will."

Dipper asked no questions. It was an article of faith with him that his master had excellent reasons for all he did, however mysterious it might seem. "You dining out, sir?"

"No. Have some cutlets and a bottle of claret sent up from the coffee-house down the street. I'm going to dine with Alexander Falkland."

"Sir?"

"To be precise, reading his letters."

✳

While he waited for dinner to arrive, Julian glanced through the evening's post. It was mostly the usual invitations and bills. But there was also a letter, addressed in a quick, surprisingly legible scrawl. No amount of governess's training would ever teach Philippa Fontclair a lady's hand.

Julian had met Philippa a year ago at her father's country house, where he had had his first confrontation with an unsolved murder. He had also become the mistaken object of her brother Hugh's jealousy, because he had befriended Hugh's distraught bride-to-be, Maud Craddock. Since then, he and Philippa had kept up a correspondence. If she had been older, her parents would probably have put a stop to it, for she was a girl of pedigree and wealth, while he was a rootless, unpropertied man of fashion. As she was only twelve, their friendship was eccentric but unthreatening. They exchanged news, anecdotes, and opinions, Julian taking care not to let too worldly or irreverent a tone creep into his letters. He felt very responsible toward her. It was almost like having family.

He took the letter into his study, broke the seal, and unfolded it. It read:

> *Bellegarde*
> *30 April 1825*
>
> *Dear Mr. Kestrel,—Thank you for the globe you sent me for my birthday. It's very handsome. I especially like the sea monsters in the oceans. Sometimes I spin it, close my eyes and touch a place, and imagine I'm there. I should like to go on a long journey and write a book about it, like Marco Polo. Pritchie clucks her tongue and says you're putting ideas into my head. Wouldn't you think a governess would approve of that?*
>
> *Now I'll tell you a secret. I'm going to be an aunt! Pritchie says I mustn't write that to you, as it's indelicate, but I think that's silly, don't you? We're all glad about it, though Hugh is rather anxious and keeps running about fetching Maud cushions and things that she doesn't want. She's very nice about it. I don't feel the least bit like an aunt, but perhaps that's why it takes so long to happen—so that people will have time to get used to it.*
>
> *I'm afraid everyone here is very cross with you. I was, too, at first. You see, Dr. MacGregor told us his old teacher Dr. Greeley was going to give up his London practice and go to live at some poky watering place, and Dr. MacGregor was thinking of moving to London and taking over his patients. He said it was you who proposed it—he would never have had such a hare-brained idea on his own. We were all very indignant that you should*

*be angling to take him away from us, when we all love him and we've had him so long. But then I thought it over and decided we were being selfish. Dr. MacGregor's lived here practically all his life, and perhaps he's quite bored—I know I should be. I think he could do to be shaken up and have the dust knocked off him, like beating a carpet. I told him so—a bit more politely than that, because everyone thinks I haven't any tact, but I do. And he said I was in league with you and you'd probably been writing to me behind his back. As if I couldn't make up my own mind, without that!*

*I must stop now, or I shan't be in time for the post. I have the honour to remain, sir, yours respectfully,*

*Philippa Fontclair.*

*Don't you like the sound of that? It's how Papa's solicitors sign their letters.*

Julian smiled, refolded the letter, and tucked it into the blotter on his desk. Then a shadow passed over his face. He had never stopped to think how he might distress the Fontclairs by trying to lure Dr. MacGregor to London—as if he had not done enough, unmasking a murderer in their midst! He had genuinely thought MacGregor might relish a more exciting life and a more varied and challenging practice. But he had been selfish, too: he liked the peppery, blunt-spoken surgeon and wanted him near him. He was so real, so truly respectable—a Rock of Gibraltar in Julian's dizzy, deceptive world.

He especially wished he had MacGregor here now. In his first two murder investigations, he had honed his ideas on MacGregor's pugnacious skepticism, like sharpening knives on a whetstone. Well, he would just have to do without him. He could hear the man from the coffee-house arriving with his dinner, and it was time to immerse himself in Alexander Falkland's letters.

✳

Even Alexander's handwriting had charm. It was graceful without being affected, easy to read but not so regular as to lack character. That much was apparent from a cursory glance at the letters; whether their content would live up to Sir Malcolm's description was another matter.

Julian arranged all the letters in order by date, Sir Malcolm's alternating with Alexander's. Then he read through the whole correspondence. And before he had gone very far, he understood why Sir Malcolm had been so impressed by the scope of Alexander's knowledge. History, classics, philosophy, government—he had a thorough grounding in them all. Some of the legal discussions were obscure: he and Sir Malcolm explored concepts like *assumpsit* and *quantum meruit* with an ardour incomprehensible to anyone not a lawyer. But Alexander was concerned about broad human questions as well. At one point, Sir Malcolm wrote cynically to him about the use of defence lawyers in criminal cases. It was not so long ago, he observed, that an accused felon could only bring a barrister into court to argue narrow points of law. Now counsel were permitted to cross-examine witnesses, sometimes even address the jury. It would not be long before they took over the prisoner's defence altogether. How would the jury gauge guilt or innocence, when a great fog of legal oratory and sleight-of-hand came between them and the defendant?

Alexander sympathized with his father's impatience but could not share it:

> *I've often heard it said that a prisoner's demeanour in court is the most reliable measure of his honesty and good faith. But only consider, sir, how often the guilty are more glib and persuasive than the innocent! Innocence stammers in shame when confronted with an accusation, while guilt anticipates blame and has all manner of fictions ready to hand. Then, too, a criminal charge carries with it such a taint of guilt that, without the aid of defence counsel, an impressionable juror may lose sight of the presumption of innocence that is a prisoner's first hope and*

*safest refuge. Every man—but above all the poorest, least educated, most vulnerable of the King's subjects—should be able to summon eloquence and wisdom to speak on his behalf, before he is deprived of liberty or life.*

Another of Alexander's letters spoke admiringly of what he called "the American adventure in democracy." In reply, Sir Malcolm reminded him that slavery, abolished in England half a century ago, still flourished in the land of liberty across the water. Alexander acknowledged this regretfully, then went off at a surprising tangent:

> *Slavery, I think, is a matter of degree, not merely of definition. To be sure, a person is a slave who works against his will in harsh conditions, without the power to leave his employer or collect the wages his labour deserves. Certainly that is the plight of the Negroes in the United States, but it's equally the condition of many men, women, and children in our factories. I think I know what you will say: the political economists have proved that government interference in the management of factories undermines the principles of free labour on which our prosperity depends. I'm afraid you'll think me naive, sir, but how can it be that, to support the nation's textile trade, a child of nine must needs work in a mill twelve hours a day? If the world is really so constituted, then I can only say, sir—the world must be changed.*

If Sir Malcolm was right that Alexander had contemplated going into politics, Julian thought, these views would not have won him many friends among the propertied interests that controlled most Parliamentary seats. Was that why he had hidden his more serious side from his friends—because he preferred not to show his true colours until he had established himself in politics?

Julian finished the last letter and sat back, musing. The correspondence was intriguing—yet, at a practical level, wholly useless. Alexander's letters shed no light on his personal life or his relationships with anyone except his father. In fact, the lack of even a glancing reference to his wife, his brother-in-law, or his many friends was curious. It was almost as if he had wanted to shut them out—to escape from the life he had seemed to enjoy so much. Julian could only conclude that there had been two Alexander Falklands. And the solution to the murder might well hinge on which of them had been the intended victim.

# ✳ 4 ✳

## LAST NIGHT
## ON EARTH

Among the criminal classes, Peter Vance was known as
Lighthouse Pete. This was on account of his nose, a large red
efflorescence that seemed to have been attached to his otherwise pleasant face by mistake. It gave him the air of a genial
drunkard, but Julian had never seen him the worse for liquor.
He was actually very domestic, with a small wife and a large
number of children tucked away in Camden Town. He was
about forty, big and beefy, with blue eyes gleaming between
narrow creased lids.

He arrived at Julian's flat in Clarges Street a little after eight
o'clock. Julian brought him into the front parlour, which was
the largest of the flat's three rooms and the one where he
usually entertained. It was sparely but elegantly furnished,
adorned with keepsakes he had picked up on his travels: a
Moorish prayer rug, an astronomical clock, a Roman head of
Venus with her nose slightly chipped. A fine pianoforte stood
open, Rossini's latest score on the stand.

Vance eased his bulk into a seat by the fire, disposed of his
hat under his chair, and laid a battered leather portfolio in
readiness on his lap. Julian went over to a table where a Ve-
netian decanter and glasses were set out. "Brandy?"

"Won't say no, sir."

Julian poured them each a glass, and they clinked rims.

Vance took a swig and grinned appreciatively. "Now this is something like, sir! It ain't every gentleman as'd have me into his parlour and give me some'ut to dip my beak in. Why, when I go to see one of your sort about a hire, sir, most times I ain't even asked to sit down."

"But I'm your colleague, not your client," said Julian, smiling. "It would hardly do for me to give myself airs."

"Now, that's very decent of you, sir—'specially seeing as how, for you, this is all sport. I mean to say, you don't make your living by it."

Julian knew what he meant: a gentleman would surely deem it beneath him to claim a share in the rewards for capturing Alexander's killer. In reality, Julian could have made good use of the money. But he could hardly compare his occasional difficulty paying his tailors with the struggle of a working man to support his family.

"You're right, of course," he agreed. "But you'll allow that, to a gentleman, sport is a very serious matter."

"And it does you credit, sir!" Vance said heartily. "Well now, sir: where would you like to begin?"

"I suggest we start with the events leading up to the murder. Assume I know nothing about it—which is very nearly true—and tell me all you've learned about Alexander Falkland's last night on earth."

"Right, sir." Vance untied the strings of the portfolio in his lap. "I've got everything here: reports of the inquest, newspaper stories, my own notes. And I've culled out the most important witness statements, so you can read 'em now and get the flavour of things. I'll set the scene a bit first, if I may. On the night of Friday, April the twenty-second, Mr. and Mrs. Falkland gave a party at their house in Hertford Street. Now, the lay-out of the house is like this: kitchens in the basement; parlour, library, and study on the ground floor; public rooms on the first floor; bedrooms on the second floor. Bill Watkins—he's the patrol working with me—he's handy with his pencil, so I had him make a sketch of the ground and first floors. Here it is, sir."

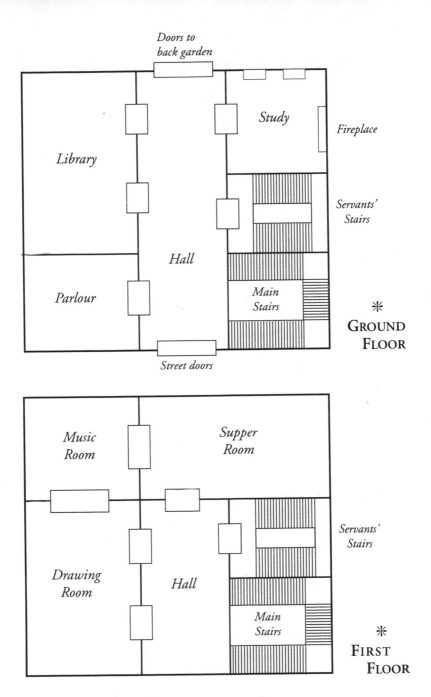

**Doors to back garden**

Study

Fireplace

Library

Servants' Stairs

Hall

Main Stairs

Parlour

✳

**GROUND FLOOR**

**Street doors**

Music Room

Supper Room

Servants' Stairs

Drawing Room

Hall

Main Stairs

✳

**FIRST FLOOR**

*Alexander Falkland's House*

Julian examined it. "I suppose the party took place on the first floor?"

"Yes, sir. Conversation and cards in the drawing room, entertainment in the music room, and a late supper in the supper room. All three rooms were got up with flowers and lights, and there were four musicians: a harp, two fiddles—violins, as *you'd* say, sir." Vance inclined his head, eyes twinkling. Hobnobbing with the Quality obviously amused him. "And a big fiddle—what's it called?"

"A violoncello?"

"Right, sir. Now, the party was to start at nine o'clock, but I'm told nobody comes to these set-outs on time."

"My dear fellow," said Julian, in his best drawing-room drawl, "punctuality is for people so vulgar as to have *appointments*."

Vance chuckled. "Anyhow, the first guests arrived around ten, and nearly all of 'em had come by eleven. There were about eighty—all swells of one kind or another. Now for the witnesses' statements. They're a bit stilted, on account of being written up from answers to questions the magistrates put, but the clerks did pretty well at taking 'em down in just the words they used. Here." He handed Julian some papers tied together with a ribbon. "You can't do better than to start with Mr. Quentin Clare."

Quentin Clare was a fellow law student of Alexander's at Lincoln's Inn. Alexander had taken a fancy to him—no one could fathom why, for they could not have been less alike. Julian knew Clare slightly from Alexander's parties: a pale, thin, awkward young man, dressed in ill-fitting evening clothes and looking as if he wished very much he were somewhere else. "His statement is quite long."

"He had a sight more to say than any of the other guests. Just happened to be on the scene for everything important that went on."

Julian cocked an eyebrow. "That strikes you as suspicious?"

"You've got his statement, sir. You can judge for yourself."

*STATEMENT OF QUENTIN CLARE, ESQ.*
*My name is Quentin Clare. I live at No. 5, Serle's*
*Court, Lincoln's Inn.*

*I attended Alexander Falkland's party on 22 April. I*
*arrived at about eleven o'clock. Falkland greeted me. He*
*seemed in good spirits. I saw very little of him after that,*
*as he had so many guests. I did not see Mrs. Falkland*
*at all. I was told she had retired from the party with a*
*headache shortly before I arrived.*

*I remember nothing unusual in anyone's behaviour,*
*apart from one episode. At about half past eleven, one of*
*the young ladies was persuaded to sing. I believe she is*
*reckoned a beauty, so there was a crush in the music*
*room, with everyone wanting to get near her. Falkland*
*and others retired into the drawing room to make more*
*room. I was feeling the heat and slipped out into the cir-*
*cular hall at the top of the stairs. That was at about*
*twenty-five minutes to twelve.*

Julian frowned. "He's very precise about the time."

"Well, he seems like that sort of young man, sir. Consci-
entious, good memory, trying to get everything right."

"Or he knew in advance he was going to be asked. It's not
the sort of thing a party guest usually thinks about."

*I was alone in the hall at first, but after a few minutes,*
*a woman came up the servants' stairs. She was about*
*forty, stockily built, dressed very plainly in a dark gown*
*with a cross around her neck. I've since been told she was*
*Mrs. Falkland's maid, Martha Gilmore. She dropped me*
*a brief curtsey and stood looking about.*

*Just then Luke, one of the footmen, came out of the*
*drawing room. Martha spoke with him in an undertone.*
*I assume she asked him to fetch Falkland, because he*
*went into the drawing room, and Falkland came out.*
*Yes, it was very unusual for a servant to summon him*

*out of a party. Ordinarily his parties ran like clockwork, and nothing interrupted them.*

*David Adams came out of the drawing room behind Falkland and stood in the doorway. I don't know Mr. Adams very well. I believe he advised Falkland about his investments.*

*Falkland went up to Martha and said something like "You asked to see me? I hope your mistress isn't worse?" Then he looked peculiar. He stared at her, his eyes widened, and his breath seemed to come quickly. But it was only for a moment. He had great self-command and regained it almost at once.*

*Martha said Mrs. Falkland still had a headache and would not be coming down again. Falkland said, a bit dazedly, "Is that all you wanted to tell me?" She said yes, curtsied, and went out through the door to the servants' stairs. Mr. Adams, who was still behind Falkland in the drawing room doorway, looked after her, then looked at Falkland malevolently. I don't know how else to describe the expression in his eyes. Falkland did not look back at him. Perhaps he did not realize he was there.*

*Falkland seemed to see me for the first time. He came forward, smiling, and asked why I was out in the hall alone. He took my arm and brought me back into the drawing room. Mr. Adams slipped in just before us. He seemed not to want Falkland to know he had been listening.*

*When Falkland and I returned to the drawing room, people surrounded us, asking what Martha had wanted and whether Mrs. Falkland was very ill. Falkland said there was nothing to worry about—she merely had a persistent headache, which would prevent her from coming down again. He ought to look in on her, he said, and excused himself. That was some time between a quarter to twelve and midnight.*

*At about twenty minutes to one, I left the party again. I'd been feeling beleaguered. Falkland hadn't come back, and people were beginning to wonder why both he and Mrs. Falkland had disappeared from their own party. Rumours began to fly about. I should rather not repeat them.*

*(Witness was pressed for an answer.)*

*If you must know, people said Falkland and his wife had quarrelled, she'd gone to her room, and he was trying to persuade her to come back. Some of the guests seemed to think I knew more about it than I let on. I don't know why, except that Falkland and I were friends, and I had overheard his conversation with Martha. Lady Anthea Fitzjohn was especially persistent in questioning me. I'm afraid it's ungracious, but I wished to get away from her. I went into the hall again, took a candle from the sideboard, and went downstairs, meaning to read in the library until the supper was served at one.*

*I walked down the central hallway toward the library, which is on the left. The study is on the right. The study door had been left half open, and as the hall was quite dark, I could see a flicker of light inside. I thought someone must have left a candle burning and went in to put it out.*

*I saw—*

*(Witness briefly overcome with emotion.)*

*I saw Falkland lying sprawled under one of the windows. His head was pushed up against the window seat, his right leg was crumpled under him, and his left leg was sticking out. There was a candle burning on the window seat above him.*

*I ran in and dropped down beside him. I was about to try to rouse him when I saw the wound in the back of his head. It was hideous. The poker from the fireplace was lying next to him. I realized that must be what had killed him. No, I didn't think about who might have done it. I was sick and dizzy, hardly able to think at all.*

*I tried to collect myself and felt for a pulse in his wrist and neck. There wasn't one, and his skin was turning cold. I ran out of the study and upstairs. I was about to go into the drawing room, but then I thought what a panic there would be among the guests. The supper room door was open, and I could see the butler and Luke making preparations for the supper. I went in and told them Falkland had been killed. I think they thought I was mad. I took them downstairs and showed them his body. The butler was horrified and sprang toward it, but I said I thought we weren't supposed to touch anything.*

Clare went on to describe how the butler took charge of everything: sent for Falkland's physician, got word to Bow Street, and appointed Martha to break the news to Mrs. Falkland. Clare returned to the party. The guests were more restless and bewildered than ever, but no one was inclined to leave till the mystery of Falkland's disappearance had been explained.

*Suddenly we heard screaming from the floor above. It sounded like "No! No!" There was consternation. Guests poured out of the drawing room into the hall. Some of them started up the stairs, and Luke had to bar their way.*

The butler restored a measure of order, Clare said. Soon after, Mrs. Falkland came downstairs and told the guests of her husband's murder.

Julian flipped back to the beginning of the statement. "He says Falkland seemed in good spirits that night, but since he also admits he didn't see much of him, he may not be any judge."

"The other guests say the same, though, sir. If Mr. Falkland thought he was in danger, he gave nary a sign of it."

Julian turned a few pages. "He says Falkland left the party between a quarter to twelve and midnight."

"Yes, sir. Most of the guests put it at just before midnight —ten minutes before at the earliest."

"What do we know about his movements after that?"

"Not a thing, sir. Except that he ended up in the study, where Mr. Clare found him. If anybody saw him in between, they ain't letting on."

"He said he was going upstairs to look in on Mrs. Falkland. Didn't she see him?"

"No, sir. Never saw him again after she left the party with a headache, which was about an hour earlier."

"Is it possible he looked in on her, but she was asleep?"

"She says not, sir. Says she was awake with her headache."

"Then we have Falkland leaving the party to go upstairs and see his wife, but instead going *downstairs* to the study. Why?"

Vance shook his head. "It's a poser, sir."

"It is indeed. Very well: the earliest Falkland could have died is ten minutes to twelve, when he left the party. What's the latest possible time?"

"Here." Vance fished out another statement. "Mr. Falkland's doctor came to examine his body that night. This is what he had to say."

Julian skimmed the physician's statement. It was full of dense medical language, but the main points were clear. Alexander's death had been caused by a severe blow to the back of the head, which must have killed him almost instantly. There was no possibility that the wound had been self-inflicted or had resulted from an accident. He was probably lying just as he had fallen, along the bottom of the window seat with his head at the left end. Most likely he had been facing toward the left when he was struck; there was a bruise on his forehead that might have been caused by his being knocked against the left-hand shutter-case. The shutter had been found drawn out; perhaps he had just closed it.

The murder weapon was clearly the poker that had been found beside the body; there were blood and skull fragments on the end. Based on his own examination and the information he had received from the butler and Mr. Clare about the condition of the body, the physician believed Alexander had been dead at least half an hour when he was found. In other words, the murder had taken place no later than a quarter past twelve.

"So he was killed some time between ten minutes to twelve and a quarter after," Julian concluded. "At least it's a narrow time frame."

"Not narrow enough, sir," Vance said ominously.

"I take it alibis are in short supply. Never mind, we'll get to them presently." Julian glanced through Clare's statement again. "This encounter he describes between Alexander and Martha may well be important, since it happened just before Alexander left the party. In fact, it gave him his excuse for leaving, since Martha told him Mrs. Falkland was still unwell and wouldn't be down again. But why should she have dragged him out of the party to tell him that? Why did he look so disconcerted when he first came out to speak with her? And, finally, why should David Adams stand by listening, then look at Alexander—how does Clare put it?—malevolently?"

"Have a look at Mr. Adams's statement, sir. It gives you his side of the story."

### STATEMENT OF MR. DAVID ADAMS

*My real name is David Samuel Abrahms. I find it convenient to call myself Adams for business reasons. I live in Bedford Square and have my counting-house in Cornhill. My business is the arrangement of loans to foreign countries, mainly in South America. I also handle foreign investments. Of what sort? The sort that succeed.*

*I arrived at Falkland's party on the twenty-second of April some time between half past ten and eleven. Falkland was flitting about from one group of guests to another as he always did. We talked, but not about anything of consequence. He seemed quite himself. I didn't see much of Mrs. Falkland. She retired with a headache soon after I arrived.*

*At about half past eleven, one of the marriageable young ladies was put forward by her mama to sing. Most*

*of the guests crowded into the music room to hear her.*
*Falkland retired into the drawing room to make more*
*space. I went with him. Young ladies showing off their*
*accomplishments set my teeth on edge.*

*One of the footmen came in and told Falkland his*
*wife's maid wanted to see him in the hall. He went. I*
*followed him to see what it was all about. The maid was*
*in the hall. So was Quentin Clare, a friend of Falkland's*
*from Lincoln's Inn. Falkland went up and spoke to the*
*maid. No, he didn't seem startled or disturbed by any-*
*thing she said or did. But since he was turned away from*
*me, I couldn't see his face.*

*The maid told him Mrs. Falkland still had her head-*
*ache and wouldn't be coming back to the party. She*
*didn't say anything more—just curtsied and went out*
*through the door to the servants' stairs. I went back into*
*the drawing room. No, I wasn't angry with Falkland.*
*Why should I be? I didn't look at him malevolently or*
*any other way. If Clare wanted to implicate me in*
*the murder, he might have thought of something more*
*original.*

Julian put down the statement. "Somehow I rather doubt
Mr. Adams made a good impression on the magistrates."

"Not by half, sir. Insolent, they said he was. 'Twixt you and
me, sir, I don't think they'd be sorry to find he was our man."

"He may have realized that. A man of business, a Jew, a
rank outsider. I should think it would be a relief to everyone
from the Home Secretary down to the lowliest gaoler to pin
the murder on him."

"He didn't help matters by talking so brassy to the
magistrates."

"He wouldn't be the first man who felt driven to bring
about the very outcome he feared." Julian leaned back in his
chair, stretching out his legs and crossing one sleekly trousered
ankle over the other. "Tell me, what do you make of this affair
of the thirty thousand pounds?"

"Very rum, sir." Vance shook his head. "Here's Mr. Adams, such a knowing gentleman in money matters, goes to all the trouble of buying up Mr. Falkland's notes-of-hand—then he turns 'em all over to Mr. Falkland and takes nary a farthing in exchange."

"How did you find out about it?"

"After Mr. Falkland was killed, I went through his ledgers. He kept close track of his money, being very took up with investing, as you'll have heard. There was an entry on the second of April, in his handwriting, crediting himself with the amount of the notes. I did a bit of digging in the City, and I found out Mr. Adams had been buying them up."

Julian glanced over the statement again. "His account of Martha's calling Alexander out of the party dovetails with Clare's, except that he denies having looked at Falkland malevolently. What does Martha say?"

Vance had her statement ready. Her name was Martha Gilmore. She had been with Mrs. Falkland for thirteen years, first as her nursemaid, then later as her lady's maid. On the night of the party, Mrs. Falkland had sent for her shortly before eleven and told her she had a headache and would keep to her room for the time being.

> *A little after half past eleven, I went to her room again to see how she was. The door was locked. I knocked, and she let me in. She was still dressed in her evening gown and looked ill. I offered to make her one of my headache remedies, but she said there was no need. She said she was going to lie down and try to rest.*
>
> *I went downstairs and stood outside the drawing room. Mr. Clare was there, but we didn't speak. Luke came out of the drawing room, and I told him to ask the master to come out and speak to me. The master came out a few minutes later. No, I don't remember him looking at me strangely. I told him my mistress was still ill and wouldn't be coming down again. No, she hadn't asked me to tell him that. I just thought he ought to know. Mr. Adams*

*stood behind him listening, but I didn't take any notice of him.*

*I went back to my room in the attic and stayed there sewing. I didn't go to bed, because I thought my mistress might need me. I was alone there till about one o'clock in the morning, when Luke came and told me the master was dead. I went down to speak to Mr. Nichols, the butler, and he asked me to break the news to Mrs. Falkland.*

*I went to her room. Her door was still locked. She opened it, and I told her what had happened. At first she had the 'sterics. She kept screaming "No, no!" and flailing with her arms. I comforted her as best I could, and soon she was calm enough to go downstairs and speak to the guests. I'd expect no less of her. If I may take the liberty of saying so, she is the bravest lady I ever knew.*

*There was a great to-do after that, but I was sent downstairs to the servants' hall and didn't see much of it. Just before two o'clock the mistress took me with her to Mr. Eugene's room to tell him about the master's death. Mr. Eugene is Mrs. Falkland's half-brother and was staying with her and the master. She tapped on the door, and when he answered we went in. He was in bed and looked as if he'd been asleep. The mistress sat by his bed and told him Mr. Falkland was dead. He looked very shocked, then asked, "How was he killed?" I don't know why he asked that.*

" 'How was he killed?' " Julian repeated. "Why not simply 'How did he die?' Well, one thing is clear from Martha's statement: she has no alibi. She might have been anywhere between ten minutes to midnight and a quarter after."

He perused her statement again. "I'm devilish curious about this headache of Mrs. Falkland's. She's not a vapourish woman. In fact, she strikes me as one of those people who think it a disgrace to be ill. When I saw her today, she was obviously worn down with grief and still recovering from a stomach ailment Sir Malcolm says she had a few days ago, but she kept insisting she was perfectly well."

"So you think there's something in the story that she left the party because she and Mr. Falkland had a row?"

"What does she say about that?"

"She didn't give a written statement. The magistrates didn't like to ask—bereaved widow, sir, you understand. But she did answer a few questions. Says she went upstairs at about a quarter to eleven and stayed there nursing her headache till she heard about the murder. Except when Martha came to look in on her, she saw nobody, and nobody saw her."

"In other words—no alibi."

"Not the ghost of one, sir."

"I'm sorry to hear that. I assume she denies any quarrel with Falkland?"

"Oh, yes, sir. Took offence at the very idea."

"So she would, if it really is a slander. But so she might equally, if it were true. Whether she had a hand in his death or not, it would be devilish awkward if he were killed an hour after she retired to her room in a temper with him."

"Mr. Poynter backs her story, sir—that's something."

Julian's brows flew up. "Felix Poynter? Is he mixed up in this?"

"I don't know as I'd say he was mixed up in it, sir. But he was the last guest to see Mrs. Falkland afore she left the party, so we had to take notice of him."

"No one can help taking notice of Felix. It's the way he dresses."

Vance eyed him cannily. "Friend of yours, sir?"

"Yes. But I'll try not to let that cloud my judgement. What does he say?"

Vance unearthed his statement:

*STATEMENT OF THE HON. FELIX POYNTER*
*My name is Felix Poynter. Actually it's Felix Horatio Poynter, but I wish you wouldn't put that in. Yes, I'm Lord Saltmarsh's son—well, one of them. The youngest.*

*I went to Alexander Falkland's party on the twenty-second of April. I can't recall anything out of the common about it. Apart from his being killed—but you knew about that, of course.*

*I'm sorry, yes, it was out of the common that Mrs. Falkland retired with a headache. She and I were talking, and she wasn't looking well, and presently she said her head ached, and she'd better go to her room and lie down. She said it was nothing to worry about, and no one should feel the need to leave on her account. She was quite insistent about that, else I should have thought it d—ced bad ton to hang about enjoying ourselves while she was feeling I-know-not-howish.*

*No, I hadn't the least reason in the world to think she and Falkland had quarrelled. I know a rumour of that sort got about, but I'm persuaded there was nothing in it. Falkland was in great spirits all evening, and she— well, she couldn't help having a headache, could she?*

"He's quick to defend her," said Julian, frowning.

"Just doing the gentlemanly thing, I expect."

"I hope that's all it is. Because you see, he was in love with her two seasons ago, before she married Falkland."

"In love with the victim's wife, sir?" Vance let out a low whistle.

"Yes. But you must understand about Felix—he falls in love cheerfully and frequently, with very little hope of having his feelings noticed, let alone returned. There's no reason to suppose his attachment to Mrs. Falkland was different from the others." He caught himself up short, with a wry smile. "How easy it is to find excuses for one's friends! You're perfectly right: Felix's old *tendre* for Mrs. Falkland gives us every reason to suspect him. Unless he has an alibi?"

"He don't, then, sir. But nor do most of the other guests." Vance dug into his portfolio and drew out a collection of sheets. "This is a list of their names and addresses. I've drawn a line through the ones with alibis. About a dozen were playing at whist or *écarté* and can vouch for each other, and there's a few young ladies who were under the eye of chaperons. Oh, and the musicians are out of it: they were playing in full view of everybody. But that leaves some three-score guests unaccounted for. They were all seen at the party between ten minutes to twelve and a quarter after, but they can't prove they were there the whole time. I mean to say, any of 'em could have nipped downstairs, killed Mr. Falkland, and come back."

"And that includes Clare and Adams?"

"Yes, sir. 'Course, I don't doubt there's more to be learned from the guests than they've told so far. Their sort ain't just what I'd call obliging, when it comes to being questioned by one of *my* sort. That's one reason I hoped you'd come in with me on this case. You know these folks; you understand what makes 'em tick. Set a thief to catch a thief—no offence meant, sir."

"None taken. Were you able to find out anything from the guests about the source of this rumour that Alexander and Mrs. Falkland had quarrelled?"

"Nearest I can tell, sir, it began with Lady Anthea Fitzjohn. You remember Mr. Clare mentioned her in his statement— said she tried to cog information out of him about where Falkland had disappeared to."

"I can imagine her doing that. She's an elderly single lady with no responsibilities and too much money, which means her only occupation in life is gossip. She's reliable, as gossips go—extremely sharp and insightful. If she thinks the Falklands had a row that night, there may be something in it. But she also likes making pets of young men and abusing their wives and sweethearts. Alexander was one of her favourites, so she may have been over-eager to believe he and Mrs. Falkland were at odds."

Vance digested this, then nodded. "Now, there's one more statement you ought to read, sir. Mind you, there's lots of others—we took statements from most of the servants and guests—but I'll leave 'em, and you can look at 'em later."

He passed over another ribbon-bound sheaf of papers. Julian read:

### STATEMENT OF MR. EUGENE TALMADGE

*My name is Eugene Talmadge. I'm sixteen years old. I don't know what my address is. My parents are dead, and now my guardian's been murdered, so I don't see that I have a right to live anywhere. At present I'm staying at Sir Malcolm Falkland's house in Hampstead.*

*Mrs. Falkland is my half-sister. We had different fathers. Mine cheated at cards and cut his throat. I expect you know about that—everyone does.*

*Yes, I was at Alexander's house on the night of the twenty-second of April. I'd been away at school, but I had measles over the Christmas holidays and had to stay with Belinda and Alexander till I was well again. No, it didn't take me four months to recover. I could have gone back much earlier, but I didn't want to, because I hate school, and Alexander was too kind-hearted to send me back against my will. In the end he did say I would have to go, but that was only because Belinda made him. It wasn't his fault at all. I was supposed to leave on 16 April, but I caught a feverish cold from staying out all night in the rain the night before. Why was I out in the rain? To catch the cold, of course.*

*So I was still at Alexander's house the night he was killed. I didn't go to the party. I stayed in my room. I went to bed at about eleven. At about two o'clock, Belinda woke me and told me Alexander had been murdered. I could hardly believe it. No, I hadn't seen or heard anything unusual. I was asleep.*

"He's very skittish about this dispute over his return to school," Julian mused. "And very keen to establish that it was Mrs. Falkland he blamed, rather than Alexander. I suppose that's a natural impulse in a suspect, innocent or guilty, though it doesn't say much for his gallantry. All in all, Eugene bears looking into. He inherited four thousand pounds from Alexander—or he will, if Alexander didn't leave a child—and he has a daring, desperate streak, to judge by his braving a rainy London night in an effort to catch a fever. And finally, it's clear he has no alibi. Alexander's family is faring badly in that regard. I hope Sir Malcolm at least is cleared of suspicion?"

"Yes, sir. His servants say he was at home all evening, and I can't see any reason to doubt their word."

"Thank Heaven for small mercies. Let's turn to Alexander's servants. Which of them can we scratch from this race?"

"The butler and the kitchen staff are out of it, sir. Between ten minutes to twelve and a quarter past, they were all below stairs seeing to the preparations for supper. The housemaids had gone to bed, and since they share a room, they can vouch for each other. Martha's got no alibi, as you'll recall, and nor does Mr. Falkland's man. Stuck-up little Frenchman, name of Valère. Says he was in his room catching a wink of sleep before he was called to wait on his master after the party. Nobody to say if that's true or not.

"The two footmen, Luke and Nelson, were on duty at the party. They'd worked out an arrangement beforehand that Luke would do the fetching and carrying from downstairs, and Nelson would keep to the first floor, so he'd always be at hand if a guest needed him. That gives Nelson a pretty good alibi: people were always calling on him for one thing or another, so if he'd ever been absent, he would have been missed. Luke's another matter. He says he left the party a few minutes after the clock struck twelve to replenish the wine supply. The butler confirms that he came downstairs for the wine, but nobody can say just how long it took him to get from the first floor to the basement and back. And now I think we've covered all the servants, sir."

"So, to sum up: Mrs. Falkland, Eugene, Mrs. Falkland's maid, and Falkland's valet have no alibi at all, and Luke the footman has gaps in his alibi, where he went downstairs and came up again. Clare and Adams were seen at the party during the crucial twenty-five minutes, but they can't prove they were there the whole time, and the same is true of most of the other guests, including my friend Felix." Julian shook his head. "That's a devil of a lot of suspects. I suppose it would be too much to hope for such a thing as a clue?"

"Watkins and I combed the study, sir, but all that's worth reporting is what we *didn't* find. There was no sign of a struggle, nothing had been ransacked, nothing was missing. And there were some choice moveables in the study: antiques and silver-topped inkstands and the like. So this wasn't a robbery —not unless the thing stolen was something nobody knew about, like a letter or a will."

"So we have a host of suspects, and nothing concrete linking any of them to the crime. Let's try to narrow the field. The murderer was probably familiar with Alexander's house and its routine, to get to and from the study at night in the middle of a party without being seen. And he or she must have known Alexander fairly well, to have had any motive at all. So the odds are, our murderer is either a member of the household or a frequent visitor. May I see the list of guests?"

Vance handed it to him. Julian ran his eyes over it. "I should say about twenty were established members of Alexander's set, including Clare and Adams. I'll make a particular point of talking with them. But first I'll see if there's anything more to be got out of Alexander's servants. I'm meeting Sir Malcolm at Alexander's house tomorrow morning—I'll have a word with them then."

"Well, I wish you luck, sir. If there's anything I can do, just tip me the wink. The way I see it, sir, you'll nose about among the swells—if you'll pardon me putting it like that—and I'll follow any leads you throw in my way and do any digging a gentleman might gib at."

"The investigation may not work itself out into such a neat division of labour. But thank you all the same. I shan't hesitate to rely on you."

"That's the ticket, sir." Vance heaved himself out of his chair. "Well, thanks for the grog. I'd best be moving on, see-

ing as it's Sunday, and I ain't been home all day, and the
missus—well, you know what women are. Or p'raps you
don't, sir, being a bachelor." He grinned tolerantly. It was
evident that he considered any unmarried man a mere fledge-
ling, even if he had solved a murder or two. "You'll have your
hands full, won't you, sir? Even whittling down the number
of suspects as you have, there's a power of people mixed up
in this."

"Yes. And to complicate things further, there's always the
possibility that the murderer was someone not known to be
in the house."

"How do you make that out, sir? We had a good look round
the house, and none of the doors or windows had been tampered with. So I don't rightly see how a sneak thief or any
such ugly customer could have got into the house."

"I don't doubt your thoroughness. But consider the arrangement of the household at about midnight on the night
of the murder. The kitchen staff were in the basement, the
party was on the first floor, Mrs. Falkland and Eugene were
in their bedrooms on the second floor, and Martha, Valère,
and the maids were in their rooms in the attic. That left the
ground floor deserted, apart from the occasional servant passing between floors. So if there was anyone there at midnight
who oughtn't to have been, it's most unlikely he or she would
have been seen."

"Except by Mr. Falkland himself, sir. *He* went down to the
ground floor at about that time."

"And we can't fathom why he did that, when he said he
was going upstairs to see Mrs. Falkland. What I'm suggesting
is that he may have gone down to the ground floor precisely
to let this unknown person in."

"Could be, sir," Vance said slowly. "This unknown man—
we'll call him John Noakes, as the lawyers do—could have
come in through either the street door or the back door from
the garden. 'Course, if he'd rung at either door, the servants
would've heard him."

"He may not have needed to ring. Falkland may have been

expecting him and let him in at the appointed hour. Midnight
is a fitting time for a secret meeting—or an assignation."

"Meaning, John Noakes might've been a Jane, sir," Vance
said, winking.

Julian frowned. "If so, it seems implausible that Falkland
would have arranged to meet her at his own house. And he
was notoriously devoted to his wife—not at all given to dangling after opera girls or keeping *chères amies*." He shrugged.
"I may well be romancing. Certainly we can't let this possibility distract us from the suspects nearer to hand. But we
ought to keep in mind that there may be an unknown element.
Mrs. Falkland said her husband had no enemies. The truth
may be that he had an enemy no one knew."

# ✳ 5 ✳

## FULL ORCHESTRA

"Are you Luke or Nelson?" Julian asked the footman who let him into Alexander Falkland's house next morning.

The footman, who had been wearing his impassive servant's mask, blinked and became suddenly human. "I'm Luke, sir."

He was about twenty-one and a fine specimen of a footman: well over six feet tall, broad-shouldered, with legs that needed no padding to set them off. For all his imposing dimensions, he had a boyish look: his cheeks healthily ruddy, his blond hair fine and curly as a child's. Ordinarily he would have worn the turquoise-and-silver livery of Alexander's household, but now he was dressed in mourning, as all the dead man's servants must be.

"I was to meet Sir Malcolm here," said Julian.

"Yes, sir." Luke took his hat, gloves, and walking stick. "If you'll follow me, sir, Sir Malcolm is waiting for you in the study."

Evidently we're not to lose any time, Julian thought. He regarded Luke with veiled curiosity. The young man was clearly ill at ease, but whether this had anything to do with his incomplete alibi, there was no knowing.

He led Julian down the broad central hallway that ran between the front and back doors. It was designed like a Renaissance loggia, with blind arches cunningly moulded and painted to give an illusion of depth and space. Medallions between the arches contained reliefs of allegorical scenes. Julian noticed one of Time unveiling Truth. With any luck, he thought.

The study was in the back right-hand corner of the house. Luke opened the door and stood aside to let Julian in. Sir Malcolm hastened forward. "Good morning, Mr. Kestrel! I thought we'd begin here, then we'd interview the servants. Have them gather in the parlour and wait for us, will you, Luke?"

"Yes, sir." Luke bowed and went out.

Julian regarded Sir Malcolm wryly. The man was obviously starved for solutions—for any information that might make sense of this seemingly senseless crime. And he himself was expected to perform the miracle—to pull insights from the scene of the murder as a conjuror produces rabbits. Well, there was nothing for it but to have a go, as Dipper would say.

He began by walking around the room, taking stock. It was about fifteen feet square. The only door was the one from the hallway. On either side of the door were satinwood cabinets, waist-high, with wheels for moving them about. They seemed identical, but when Julian opened them he found that only one was a cabinet, while the other artfully concealed a set of stairs for reaching books down from high shelves.

The bookshelves were built into the wall to the left of the door. They were filled with books on architecture and interior decoration. One of the books lay open on a long table beside the bookshelves. It was quite technical, with section drawings and elevations that no mere dilettante would have understood. Beside it was a sheet of paper with jottings in Alexander's light, elegant hand. Sir Malcolm came and looked at them over Julian's shoulder. "He was planning some improvements to Belinda's country house," he explained. "We've left his notes here, just as he'd left them at the time he died."

The wall opposite the bookshelves had two windows, with a looking-glass between them to enhance the light. In front of the windows was a writing table of mahogany, inlaid with paler woods and mother-of-pearl. It looked small and compact, but when opened, it revealed a blotting-paper surface and an ingenious array of drawers, pigeon-holes, and compartments for pens, ink, candles, and sealing-wax.

"Everything was in order here, I gather," Julian mused. "There was no sign that a search had been made among his papers, and nothing was missing, so far as anyone knew."

Directly opposite the door was the grey marble fireplace that Julian had seen in Alexander's portrait. Niches on either side held Greek red-figure vases, bronze statuettes, and fragments of classical columns. The register grate was the latest model, designed to maximize heat and minimize smoke. Propped against it in a row were the steel fire implements: shovel, tongs—and, of course, the poker, cleansed of its owner's blood and brains, and polished to a mirror-like gleam.

Julian picked it up. It was slim but surprisingly heavy. "A very efficient weapon," he observed, "no more like a bludgeon than a rapier is like a broadsword. Not much physical strength would be needed to wield it; aim would be all-important."

He crossed to the windows. Both were tall and recessed, with shallow seats and chaste white-linen curtains. The shutters were folded out of sight into cases on either side of each window—all except the left-hand shutter of the left-hand window, which had been drawn out.

"He was lying just here," said Julian, "underneath the closed shutter, face down, with his head pushed up against the window seat. The poker lay beside him, so, and the candle was on the window seat above." He ran his eyes over the shutter. "The servants say all the shutters in this room had been left open. So who closed this one? Either Alexander or the murderer, but more likely Alexander. That would explain why he was standing here when he was killed."

He went to the window and carefully folded the shutter into its case, then drew it out again by its brass knob. "Curious. If he meant to close the shutters, why didn't he close them both at once?" He closed the other shutter, then opened it again. "They're a bit difficult to manage without jerking or banging. Perhaps he thought it best to close them one at a time. But why should he have wanted them closed? Was he afraid of being spied upon from the garden?"

He looked out into the tranquil back garden, with its crescent-shaped flowerbeds, walls draped in blue clematis, and a statue of Pan playing his pipes. At the far end was a green-painted gate. Julian recalled the theory he had posited to Vance: that Alexander might have gone down to the study to meet a secret visitor. Perhaps he had stood by this window, watching for John (or Jane) Noakes to appear through the garden gate. But in that case, he would have wanted the shutters open, not closed. And why should he have closed them after the visitor arrived?

He turned back into the room. "The next question is, how did the murderer take the poker from the fireplace and carry it to the window without Alexander's noticing?"

"But that's simple—isn't it?" Sir Malcolm said. "Alexander was facing away from the fireplace, toward the window and the shutter-case. The murderer need merely have gone to the fireplace, taken the poker, and crept up behind him."

"Look." Julian went back to the left-hand window, beckoning Sir Malcolm to follow. "Alexander was standing here. In that mirror"—Julian pointed to the mirror between the windows—"you have a clear view of the fireplace and the area in between. If there were any light in the room at all, Alexander would have caught at least a glimpse of the murderer coming toward him with the poker raised. Whereas in fact he seems to have been wholly unconscious of his danger. There was no indication he turned toward his assailant, much less struggled with him.

"Of course," added Julian thoughtfully, "he wasn't facing the window directly—he was turned away from the mirror and toward the shutter-case. The murderer might have taken that opportunity to seize the poker and rush at him. But if, as seems likely, he meant to close the other shutter next, he would have been expected to turn back again in a moment. To catch him unawares in that brief interval would have taken extraordinary quickness and presence of mind. And the risk would have been tremendous."

"But there's no other explanation, surely?"

"On the contrary." Julian smiled faintly at this chance to give Sir Malcolm a little of the mental sleight-of-hand he had been craving. "We've been envisioning that Alexander was engaged in some sort of colloquy with the murderer when the murderer suddenly attacked him. But there's also the possibility that Alexander never knew the murderer was in the room."

"You mean the murderer hid somewhere and sprang out at him when his back was turned?"

"Precisely. The murderer could have come here before Alexander did, taken the poker, and hidden in a dark corner, perhaps in one of those niches by the fireplace—or, even better, behind the curtains of the window on the right. When Alexander went to the left-hand window and turned toward the left-hand shutter-case, the murderer could have jumped out and struck him from behind."

"But how could the murderer have known Alexander would come to the study in the middle of the party?"

"Because he'd appointed a rendezvous with Alexander here, at midnight. He had only to come early and hide, so that Alexander would think he hadn't arrived yet. At night, with light from only one candle, it would have been easy enough to conceal himself. I'm assuming it was Alexander who brought the candle—the one found beside the body. Even if he were going to the study for some secret purpose, it was unlikely to be a purpose he could accomplish in the dark. The murderer, on the other hand, would have had every reason to avoid attracting notice on his way to the study. He would have crept there and back without a light—which, incidentally, reinforces the notion that he knew the house tolerably well."

"Why did he leave the candle burning beside Alexander's body? It was the light coming through the half-open door that prompted Mr. Clare to go into the study. It's almost as if the murderer were courting the attention of the first person to pass by."

"Perhaps he was. He may have wanted the murder to be discovered before the end of the party, so as to multiply the number of suspects. If the body were found after the guests had gone, suspicion might have been directed more narrowly to Alexander's family and servants."

"But—but that suggests that one of Alexander's household is responsible!"

"It does seem to point that way. But there are other possibilities. The murderer may have been a guest who, for reasons not yet clear, wanted to protect Alexander's household —or someone in it—from suspicion. Then too," he added delicately, "the murderer may have hated your son so much that he wanted to be here when his body was discovered and watch the consternation that ensued."

"My God, how horrible." Sir Malcolm covered his eyes for a moment. "Are we making progress, do you think? This lying-in-wait theory—do you believe it?"

"Well, it answers two puzzling questions: why Alexander went to the study and how the murderer was able to creep up on him with the poker unawares. But there are—complications. If the murderer hid behind the curtains of the window on the right—"

He went to the right-hand window and experimented with concealing himself behind the curtains. "This would do very well as a hiding place in near darkness. But it seems an extraordinary stroke of luck for the murderer that Alexander came and stood by the other window with his back turned, like a lamb to the slaughter—if you'll pardon that image, Sir Malcolm. All in all, it's a daring and uncertain plan. Anyone who attempted it would have had to be bold, cool-headed— and desperate."

He took up his quizzing-glass—the little gold-framed magnifying glass he wore on a black ribbon around his neck—and prowled about the two window embrasures for a time, then moved on to the niches by the fireplace and other spots where the murderer might have lain in wait. "Apparently he or she wasn't obliging enough to leave stray coat-buttons or scraps of lace about for us to find. I suppose that would be making things a bit too easy. This lack of physical evidence is devilish inconvenient. No wonder Vance attaches such importance to motive."

"What you're saying is, you're as baffled by this crime as Bow Street," Sir Malcolm said sadly.

Julian perceived that solvers of crime, like physicians, are not allowed to confess to even a momentary bewilderment. This was the first time he had embarked upon a murder investigation under the eyes of the victim's distraught relatives, and it was certainly an education. He smiled quizzically. "What I'm saying, Sir Malcolm, is that our murderer was very clever, or very lucky, or both. That we'll find him out in the end, I have no doubt. But it might be rushing our fences to expect to do it in one morning."

"You're right, of course. I know I've been riding at this thing neck or nothing."

"That can be a mistake. One misses details."

"I'm sure no one could ever accuse *you* of that, Mr. Kestrel," Sir Malcolm said, smiling.

Julian had a distinct sense of missing something now. He gazed around the room, but it still eluded him. He shrugged. "Well, why don't we speak with the servants."

"Of course. Would you like to see them all at once?"

"Yes. I'll start with the full orchestra—then, as needed, move on to duets."

\*

The servants were gathered in the parlour. They made a strange picture, their stark mourning clothes set against the vivid colours around them. The parlour was Turkish: all bright ottomans and billowing cushions, mosaic-topped tables and sumptuous carpets. After the austere greys of the study, it was almost too dazzling, like being inside a plush-lined, gem-filled jewel-case.

Julian amused himself with trying to identify as many of the servants as possible before they were introduced. Luke he had already met. The other tall, strapping young man must be the second footman, Nelson Beale. He was dark rather than fair, and, unlike Luke, he seemed to be enjoying all this excitement. The dignified man, with his few remaining strands of iron-grey hair neatly lacquered to his head with pomatum, was surely Paul Nichols, the butler. Alexander's valet, Hippolyte Valère, was likewise unmistakeable: a fussily dressed little man, very like a grasshopper, with a small, triangular face, eyes made prominent by large spectacles, and wiry, tense limbs.

The remaining servants were Alexander's French chef, the rest of the kitchen staff, the maids, and the stable servants. All these were of secondary interest, since they had alibis and had played no part in the events surrounding Alexander's murder.

"There are two missing," Sir Malcolm told Julian. "Belinda's maid, Martha, is with her at my house—you saw her yesterday—and so is her groom, an Irishman named Nugent."

"These will do to be going on with." Julian turned to the servants. "Please sit down. All of you," he added, smiling, as the scullions and stable-boys hesitated and twirled their caps between their hands. They obeyed, looking bewildered at this reversal of roles. Since when did servants sit and the Quality stand before them, as Mr. Kestrel was doing now?

Julian began by going over ground that Bow Street had already covered. There was always the chance some buried memory might come to light; in any event, these familiar questions helped put the servants at their ease, while allowing Julian to study their characters and interactions. Nichols, calm and competent, acted as their principal spokesman. Valère followed the proceedings with a mixture of keen attention and inimitable French disdain. Nelson listened avidly and injected a word wherever he could, while Luke seemed determined to be taken for a marble statue. The coachman, Joe Sampson, a burly man of about forty, sat imperturbably chewing on an unlit pipe. The rest of the servants mutely followed the steady exchange of question and answer, like spectators at a tennis match.

At first the servants merely confirmed what they had already told Bow Street. They knew of no reason why Mr. Falkland would have gone to the study in the middle of the party. Nothing out of the common had happened that evening, apart from Mrs. Falkland's retiring with a headache and Martha's interrupting the party to tell the master she would not be coming back. The outside doors had remained locked all evening, and the ground-level windows bolted. No stranger had been seen in the house, and no guest had behaved suspiciously.

Did the servants know of anyone who had a grudge against Mr. Falkland? No, everyone liked and admired the master. He did not have an enemy in the world. All the servants had been on good terms with him; none was under notice or had been reprimanded lately.

Had all been well in the household? The servants looked at each other uncertainly. Then Nichols coughed and said he believed that Mr. Eugene had not wanted to return to school, but Mrs. Falkland had insisted.

"He'd been at Harrow," Sir Malcolm explained. "Alexander sent him there after he and Belinda were married. Until then, Eugene hadn't been able to attend a proper school, because he had no money of his own, and the trustees who managed Belinda's property didn't see it as part of their duty to pay for Eugene's education. Of course, after Belinda married Alexander, her income came under his control, and she was very willing he should use it to send Eugene to a good school. Unfortunately the boy took a freakish dislike to it. He was positively relieved when a bout of measles sent him home."

Julian turned back to the servants. "When did Mrs. Falkland begin urging that he go back?"

Nelson bobbed to his feet. "I heard her speak of it a month or two ago, sir. I was making the rounds of the house one evening—trimming the lamps, you know—and I caught a

word or two of a conversation between her and Mr. Falkland."

Julian saw a few of the servants roll their eyes and exchange
glances. Evidently Nelson had a reputation for just happening
to overhear things. "What did they say?"

"Mrs. Falkland said it wasn't good for Mr. Eugene to be
so idle, and he ought to go back to school, but the master
disagreed."

"Did he say why?"

"No, sir. He said she knew his reasons."

"She knew his reasons," Julian repeated thoughtfully. "So
they'd spoken of this before?"

"Seems so, sir."

"Do the rest of you know anything about this quarrel?"

"I wouldn't call it a quarrel, sir," said Luke. "The master
and Mrs. Falkland, they always seemed to get on very well."

"Naturally they would be too well-bred to show any ill will
to each other in public," Julian suggested. Luke flushed and
seemed to wish he had held his tongue.

*"Mais, c'est absurde, ça!"* Valère said scornfully. "No one
could have any cause to quarrel with Mr. Falkland. He was
*tout à fait raisonnable.* If he did not wish that Mr. Eugene return to school, there is no doubt he had excellent reasons."

"Have you any idea what they were?" asked Julian.

"No, *monsieur.*" Valère shrugged.

Julian addressed the whole group again. "I gather that Mr.
Falkland was finally persuaded to send Eugene back to school.
When did he have this change of heart?"

Nelson was on his feet again, bubbling over with information. "It was a Saturday, sir, the second of April. I remember,
'coz it was a wash day, and wash days are the first Saturday
every month. Mr. and Mrs. Falkland and Mr. Eugene were
sitting here after luncheon, and Mrs. Falkland up and told
Mr. Eugene he was to go back to Harrow in a fortnight."

"How did you overhear all this?" Nichols demanded
sternly.

"Begging your pardon, Mr. Nichols, but I was bringing

coals into the library next door and closing the blinds, and I couldn't help hearing a word now and again." He put on an injured look, as if eavesdropping on his employers were a painful necessity of his job. "Anyhow, Mr. Eugene made a great combustion—said Mrs. Falkland only wanted to be rid of him and begged the master to take his side, seeing as how he was his guardian. But the master said Mrs. Falkland was his sister, it was for her to say what was best for him, and he couldn't stand against her any longer. And Mrs. Falkland said it was all decided, and there was nothing more to be said."

"Would you say Eugene was disappointed in Mr. Falkland?" Julian probed delicately, glancing around at the other servants.

They hesitated. "Mr. Eugene was very unhappy, sir," said Nichols at last. "And I'm afraid he was quite angry with Mrs. Falkland. But I never observed him to show any rancour toward the master."

"You see, sir," put in Nelson, "he knew it was Mrs. Falkland as wanted to send him away, and she'd overborne the master. He was in a very bad skin with her after that. He'd hardly speak to her."

"Had they been close formerly?"

Nichols knit his brows. "I don't know quite how to answer that, sir. The mistress, she isn't one to make a show of her feelings, and Mr. Eugene—well, he's given to moods. I'd say they rubbed along together as well as might be expected."

Julian interpreted this to mean, as well as a boy with a disgraced father and no money could be expected to get on with a wealthy and irreproachable sister. "Did Mrs. Falkland seem to take the rift with her brother much to heart?"

Several of the servants spoke up at this. Mrs. Falkland had seemed under a strain in the weeks following the decision to send Mr. Eugene away. Not that she went about weeping or starting at shadows—she wasn't that sort. But she was pale, she held herself very rigid, and some days she hardly seemed to have slept.

"Did she continue in that state up to the night of Mr. Falk-

land's death?" The servants exchanged glances, then broke
out in nods and murmured assents.

"Had anything else happened to disturb her in the first few
weeks of April?"

The servants searched their memories. There had been a
failure to deliver flowers for a party. A banker's wife trying to
get into society had pestered the mistress with calls and card-
leaving. And a week before the master was killed, Mr. Eugene
had stayed out all night in the rain and made himself ill, so
his return to school had to be put off.

All at once Joe Sampson, the coachman, took his pipe from
between his teeth and said, "P'raps the mistress was worriting
about her friend as was took sick."

The others looked at him in surprise—all except Luke, who
froze and stared straight ahead, as if he feared his slightest
movement might give something away.

"What friend do you mean?" asked Julian.

"The one as lives near the Strand," said Joe.

"Near the Strand? Are you sure?"

"Sure as eggs is eggs, sir."

Julian tried to imagine a friend of Mrs. Falkland's living in
that neighbourhood of shopkeepers, theatres, and loose
women. "You had better tell me all you know about this
friend."

Joe pondered a short while. He was clearly not one to put
himself forward, but having once brought up a subject, he
would see it through. "Here's how it was, sir. I drove the
master and mistress out one day in the town carriage. Luke,
he rode up on the box with me. I took 'em to a shop called
Haythorpe and Sons, in the Strand. It's a hardware showroom—grates and lamps and such. Hard by it, there's a passage, very narrow, couldn't have fit the carriage through.
Don't know where it leads.

"Mr. and Mrs. Falkland was just coming out of the showroom when a young 'oman, looked like a servant, come out
of the passage. When she seed the master and mistress, she
stopped short, then she ran up and spoke to 'em. Next thing,

she and the mistress hurried off through the passage, and the master come back and told Luke and me that a woman friend of the mistress's was took sick, and the mistress had gone to see her. Said she'd send for the carriage again if she needed it. And we went home, and that's how and about it."

"What do you know about this friend?"

"Naught, sir. 'Cept that the girl was her servant. She come up to Mrs. Falkland 'coz she recognized her in the street."

"That seems a singular coincidence," Julian remarked.

Joe shrugged.

"Don't you think so?" Julian turned to Luke.

"I don't know anything about it, sir," Luke said shortly.

Julian regarded him politely, as if expecting him to say more. It was a tactic that often provoked people into nervous speech, but this time it failed. Luke shifted about in his seat, avoiding Julian's eyes, but said nothing.

"Did Mrs. Falkland send for the carriage to bring her home?" Julian asked Joe.

"No, sir."

"Then how did she get home?"

Luke spoke up unwillingly. "She came in a hackney coach, sir."

"How do you know?"

"I let her in, sir."

"When was that?"

"About an hour before dinner, sir."

"Which would make it—?"

"About six, sir."

"How long had she been gone?"

"Three hours, sir."

"You were keeping track of the time?"

Luke coloured. "No, sir."

"Then how do you know so precisely?"

"I don't know precisely, sir. It was three hours more or less."

"Why are you so reluctant to talk about this incident?"

Luke said, very clearly and carefully, "I beg your pardon,

sir. I'm not reluctant to talk about it. It's just that there's nothing to say. Mrs. Falkland's friend was took ill, so she went to see her. She came home a few hours later, and I let her in."

"Didn't it strike you as curious that Mrs. Falkland should have a friend in that neighbourhood?"

"It's not my place to be curious, sir."

"Did she say anything to you about her friend when she returned?"

"No, sir."

"What frame of mind was she in?"

"I—I couldn't say, sir."

"Was she distressed about her friend?"

"She wouldn't talk to me about it if she was!"

"See here," cut in Nichols, "that's no way to speak to a gentleman. Beg Mr. Kestrel's pardon at once."

"Yes, sir. I beg your pardon, Mr. Kestrel."

Julian inwardly wished Nichols at the devil. With the best intentions, he had interfered just when Luke was losing his self-command and might have said something interesting. "This maidservant who took Mrs. Falkland to visit her mistress—what was she like?"

A slow grin spread across Joe's face. "Prime little piece, she was. Tall, yellow-haired, with a pretty waist and ankle."

"How was she dressed?"

"Brown-checked frock, I think, sir. And a white cap, with them flaps hanging down on each side. What do you call 'em? Lappets."

Julian glanced around at the other servants. "Does any of the rest of you know anything about Mrs. Falkland's friend or her maidservant?"

They shook their heads.

"Then I have only one more question. Do you recall when this visit to the sick friend occurred?"

If Luke could remember, he clearly had no intention of saying so. But Joe nodded sagely. "It was the first of April. Sticks in my mind, 'coz the weather was sunny and showery, warm one minute and cold the next, and I said to myself, a typical April day."

April first. Julian thought back through the calendar. That had been a Friday, so the next day was that first Saturday in April when, according to Nelson, Mrs. Falkland had told Eugene he was to return to school. Something else had happened on April second—what was it? Oh, yes: Alexander had recorded in his ledgers Adams's forgiveness of his notes-of-hand. Could all these events be connected? And if they were, what might they have to do with Alexander's murder three weeks later?

"Thank you," he said to the servants. "You've been immensely helpful. I won't detain you any longer—except that I should like a few words in private with Valère and Luke."

Valère inclined his head, as if a private interview were no more than his due. But Luke stiffened and set his jaw. And Julian became more determined than ever to find out what he had to hide.

# ✳ 6 ✳

## Duets

Julian had some trouble persuading Sir Malcolm not to attend his interviews with Valère and Luke. If they had anything to say that reflected badly on Mr. or Mrs. Falkland, they would surely speak more freely out of Sir Malcolm's hearing. But it was awkward explaining this to Sir Malcolm, who could hardly credit that anyone would have cause to speak ill of his son or daughter-in-law. In the end, however, he agreed not to be present, provided that Julian would report to him anything of importance that was said.

Julian began with Valère, if only to let Luke stew for a while. The other servants dispersed, and Sir Malcolm went next door to the library. Julian wondered if he would be able to resist Nelson's habit of listening at keyholes. Probably he was incapable of that: he had a scrupulous probity rather astonishing in a lawyer.

Valère had little to say about the events leading up to the murder. That he had no alibi did not seem to cause him any concern. "I was taking a nap in my room, *monsieur*. It was very natural I should do this. At the end of the party, perhaps three o'clock or later, my master would have rung for me to attend him. This was my only chance to sleep."

"You received a bequest of fifty pounds from your master, I think."

"*Oui, monsieur.* My master was good enough to reward devoted service. I think no one will dare to say I was not devoted to him. It was a matter of great pride to me to serve a gentleman of his quality. In his dress and in his manners, he was *le parfait gentilhomme.* The *beau monde,* too, they recognized this, and flew to him as moths to a flame. Since he died, many gentlemen have done me the honour to request my services, but I will take no new post yet. I am in mourning. In a month or two, *eh bien,* I will move on. One must live, *monsieur.* But never will I see the like of Mr. Falkland again."

Julian was impressed. The little man had a quiet dignity that shone through the formality of his words. If he was not sincere, he was wasting his time as a manservant. He belonged on the stage at Drury Lane. "Tell me, who do you think killed your master?"

Valère's face darkened. "That woman Martha Gilmore, she knows much she is not saying."

"Mrs. Falkland's maid?"

"*Oui, monsieur.* She was spying upon Mr. Falkland. Always she would ask me, Where is he going? Where has he been? It was not any business of hers. And once I caught her in his dressing room! I demanded that she explain why she was there, but she would not answer. Out she walked on her flat feet without a word. *Quelle effronterie!*"

"When did she begin asking these questions?"

"It was some days before Mr. Falkland's death, perhaps a fortnight, *monsieur.*"

"Was anything missing from his dressing room after you found her there?"

"*Non, monsieur.* But things were moved. I keep—kept—all my master's things *en règle.* So I knew she had been moving them about. She was searching, *monsieur*—for what I do not know."

"Have you spoken to her about this since your master died?"

"I have had no chance, *monsieur.* She went to Hampstead with Mrs. Falkland, and I have not seen her since."

"Why haven't you told the Bow Street Runners?"

"*Voyons, monsieur*, they are not police! They work for hire, like hackney coachmen. In England you have no Prefecture of Police, no public prosecutors. And your Bow Street Runners, they have no power. The French police can enter any house upon the slightest suspicion, stop anyone for questioning, take letters from the post and read them. Your so-called police, always they need warrants. Always they cannot do this or that because your English liberties do not permit it. It is no wonder they have not found my master's murderer. They are all *amateurs!*"

"But I'm an egregious amateur myself. Why have you told me?"

Valère opened his eyes in surprise. "But you are different, *monsieur*. You have lived in France. You are an admirer of the French police. Last night I saw your valet at the Red Lion, and he told me so."

"Did he indeed?" Julian said softly. He had, of course, sent Dipper out last night to spread the news that he was investigating Alexander Falkland's murder. Trust Dipper to take that opportunity to make inroads for Julian with Valère.

"*Mais oui, monsieur*. So I know you will find out what this woman Martha is hiding."

"Have you any theories about that yourself?"

"*Non, monsieur*. But I think there is nothing she would not do for her mistress."

"Are you referring to the spying, or to the murder?"

Valère shrugged. "*Ça fait rien, monsieur*. She has nerve enough for either."

✳

"Your master's murder must have come as a great shock to you," Julian observed to Luke.

"Yes, sir."

"You were one of the first to hear of it?"

"Yes, sir. Mr. Clare told Mr. Nichols and me he'd been killed, and we went down to the study. I wouldn't have known what to do, but Mr. Clare said not to touch anything, and Mr. Nichols sent me back upstairs to wait on the guests and make sure that none of them left."

"Did any of them try to leave?"

"No, sir. I think they all knew something was amiss and wanted to know what it was all about."

"Did anyone seem skittish or afraid?"

"No, sir—leastways not till we heard Mrs. Falkland screaming. Then they all got in a taking. Some of the ladies had the vapours, and some of the gentlemen tried to run up the stairs. Then Mr. Nichols came and told them Mrs. Falkland had had bad news, and after that Mrs. Falkland came down herself."

"How did she look?"

"She looked—like an angel, sir! She was still in her sky-blue evening frock, with a black lace shawl thrown over it. Her face was as white and still as marble. And she was so brave, all the guests were ashamed of being in such a fret. She asked them to stay till the Bow Street Runners came, and they couldn't say her nay. I'm sure no one could as saw her, sir."

Julian thought wryly that Luke had left no doubt about his own feeling for Mrs. Falkland. It might be—very likely was— a guiltless passion, respectful and modest, if not entirely chaste. But love affairs between ladies and their footmen were not unknown, and Luke was a very comely young man. Such an intrigue seemed foreign to Mrs. Falkland's nature: her pride and honour would reject it out of hand. But Julian knew he must be especially stern in his judgements of her, because his tiresome chivalry would be constantly urging him to take her part.

He said, "As you probably know, Mr. Falkland was killed some time between ten minutes to midnight and a quarter after. During that time, you went down to the basement to fetch more wine."

"Yes, sir."

"Did you see or hear anyone on the stairs?"

"No, sir."

"Did you stop on the ground floor?"

"No, sir."

"Did you go near the study?"

"No, sir." Luke's wide blue eyes were clear and un-wavering.

"This visit Mrs. Falkland made to her friend who lives near the Strand. What have you been holding back about that?"

Luke's guard went up with a vengeance. "With respect, sir, I haven't been holding anything back."

"You know, you can't help her by concealing information. You can only make it appear more damning when it does come out—as it assuredly will in the end."

"I wouldn't presume to think Mrs. Falkland needs help from the likes of me, sir."

"Very pretty. But you don't believe a word of it, and nor do I."

Luke said nothing.

"My dear boy," said Julian, who was no more than five years older, "you must realize your secrecy about this episode invites the worst suspicions. You may be slandering Mrs. Falkland far more gravely by keeping silent than you could by speaking out."

"If I thought—" Luke stopped himself, shaking his head in bewilderment. "I just don't know, sir. You're cleverer than I am. I don't know what's right, and until I do, I must hold my tongue, even if I go to gaol for it."

"It won't come to that. I shouldn't like to make a martyr of you—you'd enjoy it far too much. Tell me, are you pro-tecting Mrs. Falkland because you believe she's innocent, or because you're afraid she's guilty?"

Luke said slowly, "I believe she's innocent, sir. But to me it wouldn't make any difference."

"Your loyalty to her wouldn't change a jot, even if you knew she was a murderess?"

"I don't mean that, sir. But you see, I know she'd never do anything wrong. So if it turned out she'd killed anyone, I'd think—"

"Yes?"

"I'd think, sir, he must have deserved it."

※

Julian joined Sir Malcolm in the library and gave him an account of his interviews with Valère and Luke. "So you see," he finished, "my next steps are to question Mrs. Falkland about this mysterious visit to the sick friend, and to ask Martha why she took such an untoward interest in Alexander's comings and goings. I also want to speak with Eugene. In short, if you're returning to Hampstead, I should like to go with you."

Sir Malcolm was standing before the window and did not look around. "It's beginning already, isn't it? The revelations you warned me about—the skeletons poking their heads out of closets. Martha spying on Alexander, Luke keeping secrets about Belinda—" He shook his head. "I suppose it will only get worse from now on."

"You're difficult to please, Sir Malcolm. Earlier you fretted that we weren't making progress, and now you seem distressed because we are."

"I know." Sir Malcolm came away from the window with a rueful smile. "I beg you won't listen to me. Of course you may come back with me to Hampstead. Are we finished here?"

"Not quite. I thought we might make a brief tour of the house."

"By all means. Are you looking for anything in particular?"

"I'm gathering impressions about what I believe lies at the heart of this investigation: the mind and character—the soul, if you will—of Alexander Falkland." He stepped back, gazing around the library. "This room alone expresses a great deal about him. The Gothic style is the easiest in the world to reduce to satire. People build whole houses like marzipan castles, with rooms like stage sets in a pantomime. But this has substance as well as grace. It conveys something of the medieval world as it was, not merely as Walter Scott's worst imitators have imagined it."

He walked around the room, scanning the tall, glass-fronted bookshelves. Everywhere were volumes on law, political economy, and philosophy—beautifully bound and well-kept, ornaments in themselves. But there were also books in a lighter vein. "*The Monk, The Castle of Otranto, Melmoth the Wanderer, Frankenstein*—apparently someone in the house liked horror novels."

"Those were Alexander's. Belinda doesn't like novels much."

"No," mused Julian, "I suppose she wouldn't. She's prosaic, for all her ethereal look—the sort of woman who inspires poetry but doesn't read it. Whereas Alexander had, if anything, an excess of imagination. In all this room, nothing is so characteristic of him as this."

He went to a bookshelf in a corner, away from the direct light of the windows. Close examination revealed that books and shelves were an illusion—a mere painting on the wall.

"He seems to have delighted in this sort of effect. Imaginative, as I said. That may explain the political views he revealed in his letters to you. People of intense imagination are apt to sympathize with the poor and despised—they envision themselves in the same plight, and the picture is so real and horrifying, it impels them to action. I daresay that's why so many of our best poets have flirted with Radicalism: Byron, Shelley, Wordsworth."

"You're a very imaginative young man yourself," Sir Malcolm pointed out, smiling.

"But neither political nor poetic," said Julian lightly. "Shall we move on?"

They had seen the entire ground floor: parlour, library, and study. Sir Malcolm suggested they visit the basement next. They went down the servants' stairs, which were concealed behind a door next to the study. Julian observed that they reached from the basement all the way to the attic. A conveniently clandestine route for the murderer, provided he did not encounter any of the servants on the stairs.

The front basement room was the kitchen. It boasted the latest combination boiler and coal-fired range, with a roasting jack that turned the meat by clockwork. Overhead, brilliantly burnished copper pots and kettles dangled from hooks. The servants' hall next door was large and airy for a basement room, with bright chintz curtains, pretty worktables for the women, and cribbage boards for the men. All in keeping with Alexander's reputation for treating his servants well.

They returned to the ground floor and moved toward the front of the hallway. On a table beside the street door was a salver overflowing with this season's visiting cards. Julian leafed through them, knowing he would see many of the oldest, most eminent names in the kingdom. To move in such circles was no slight achievement for the son of a landless baronet, of no very ancient or distinguished family. Having a beautiful wife must have helped, but still, the primary achievement was Alexander's.

They ascended Alexander's superb "flying staircase," springing up from the floor with no visible means of support. The steps were marble, the handrail of polished mahogany. The gilded wrought-iron balusters were adorned with angels ascending and descending. The walls above were pale blue and bare of ornamentation, to enhance the impression of Jacob's Ladder rising to the sky.

The first floor Julian knew already: the scene of Alexander's entertainments. The drawing room and music room were adjacent, with doors that could be thrown open to make them virtually a single room. They were furnished in the latest style, with dazzling yellow walls and curtains, black marble fireplaces, and striped scroll sofas. The supper room was Chinese. Its most striking feature was its shutters, which were delicately painted with oriental scenes. At night, by the flickering light of candles, they made the windows appear to overlook a moonlit Chinese landscape.

All these rooms were spacious, but Julian knew that, with

eighty guests sidling in and out of groups, fetching glasses of negus, slipping onto balconies for breaths of air, no one would remain under any one person's observation for long. Little wonder that few of the guests could establish alibis for the entire period in which Alexander might have been killed.

The second floor was given over to bedrooms. Alexander's was surprisingly spartan; he seemed to have reserved his artistic feats for rooms other people would use. Yet he clearly valued comfort and convenience. He had gone to the expense of having running water laid on all the way to the top of the house, and his bath was equipped with an ingenious shower, as well as a frame to hold newspapers and breakfast dishes.

The spare bedroom, which had been Eugene's, was decorated in a Roman style, with wallpaper reminiscent of the paintings at Pompeii. Mrs. Falkland's bedroom was Greek, in shades of blue, white, and gold to complement her eyes, complexion, and hair. Even the dressing-table ornaments were classical: an ivory scent-bottle, a pottery vase, a bronze mirror mounted on a figurine of a goddess holding a dove. Above the bed was a lively marble frieze of a Greek hunting scene. The central figure was a beautiful young woman in drapery kilted up to her knees, with a bow in her hand and a quiver of arrows slung over her shoulder.

"It's a compliment to Belinda," Sir Malcolm explained. "Diana, the goddess of the chase. You must know Belinda is a fearless rider to hounds."

Julian did know, but all the same he thought it a strange image for Alexander to place over his wife's bed. After all, Diana was a virgin goddess, who had once had her dogs tear a man to pieces for watching her while she bathed.

He looked around the room, his brows knit. "Don't you think it curious, Sir Malcolm, how little Mrs. Falkland's influence shows in this house, even here in her own room? A tenant in a set of furnished rooms leaves more of a mark than she has."

"She was glad to leave that sort of thing to Alexander. She admired his taste. Everyone did."

"No doubt."

"What's troubling you, Mr. Kestrel?"

"I was thinking that your son was a phenomenon, Sir Malcolm. And I was wondering what it was like for Mrs. Falkland, being a phenomenon's wife."

"She and Alexander were very happy!"

"How do you know?"

"You saw them together! There was nothing he wouldn't do for her. 'So *loving, he might not beteem the winds of heaven visit her face too roughly.*' That's how he was."

"It's tempting to quote back to you from the same play: '*These indeed seem, for they are actions that a man might play.*' "

Sir Malcolm fairly bristled. "Why should you think my son was anything but genuine in his behaviour toward his wife?"

"I pray you won't take offence. I don't suggest that any particular thing about him wasn't genuine—only that it seems impossible that everything could have been. He was a mass of contradictions. He surrounded himself with fine furnishings, food, and servants, and yet wrote passionately about the sufferings of factory workers and accused felons. His library is made up of legal and philosophical works and horror novels. He made himself the darling of society's *corps élite*, yet he took as his particular friends a shy, awkward fellow like Clare, and David Adams, a man of business and a Jew."

"What are you trying to say?" asked Sir Malcolm, with something like fear in his eyes. "Where is all this leading us?"

Julian relented. "At the moment, I think it's leading us to luncheon. And, after that, to Hampstead."

# * 7 *

## BAD BLOOD

"Of course I know what you're thinking," said Eugene Talmadge.

"Do you?" Julian lounged back in his chair and surveyed him with lifted brows. "What a remarkable faculty. I usually find it enough of a task sorting out my own thoughts, let alone trying to read anyone else's."

Eugene stared. However he had expected their interview to begin, it was not like this.

"What is it you suppose I'm thinking?" Julian asked.

"The same thing everyone is."

"Evidently this talent you have for divining thoughts has a fairly wide reach. And for perhaps the first time in the history of human intellect, we find an entire population thinking precisely the same thing."

The boy flung up his head. "Sir Malcolm brought you here to ask me questions, not to laugh at me!"

"I have time for both," Julian assured him.

Eugene's eyes fairly started from their sockets. Shock, bewilderment, indignation struggled on his face. It was not a bad face, though unfinished—a rough sketch of the comely young man he might be in a few more years. Certainly the high, wide brow and expressive blue eyes were promising. More sleep and less tautly strung nerves would help; so would soap and water.

"Now then," said Julian, "what do you believe that every-one, including me, is thinking?"

"You may pretend you don't know if you like. But I think it's rather shabby. People might at least come out and admit it to my face. Bad blood, that's what they're saying. My father ran through all his money and cheated his friends at cards, and when they caught him at it, he cut his throat with a razor. So why shouldn't I have killed my sister's husband? He left me money, after all."

"Did you know he would?"

"You wouldn't believe me if I said I didn't."

Julian smiled. "Conversation with you is extremely restful, Mr. Talmadge. You not only read my mind—you make it up for me. I could nod off to sleep, and you could conduct this entire interview by yourself."

"I think you're extremely rude! And you're doing it on purpose!"

"Of course. One should never be rude except on purpose."

Eugene's defences dropped abruptly. He looked at Julian with shy curiosity. "Why?"

That one syllable told Julian more about Alexander Falk-land than all his father's praise, his servants' loyalty, or his own eloquent letters. Alexander had been Eugene's brother-in-law and guardian for a year and a half, had lived under the same roof with him for months—and he had taught him noth-ing. Eugene's unkempt state, his skittishness, his ignorance of the most elementary rules of how one gentleman addresses another: they were all faults that brotherly guidance could have smoothed away. And no one was better able to give such guidance than Alexander, who had been the epitome of charm and taste. Everyone said Eugene had worshipped his brother-in-law. If that were true, how could Alexander have given so little back?

These thoughts washed over Julian swiftly, making no change in his face or manner. He answered, "Because one should never appear to do anything without intent. It's the secret of poise."

"I shouldn't have thought it could ever be right to be rude."

"It depends on the circumstances. In a man of wealth and power, it's unsporting. He has advantages enough."

"Well, you have power. Everyone knows you're a famous dandy and tell everybody how to dress and behave."

"I don't tell anybody how to do anything. Some gentlemen choose to emulate me."

"Why?"

"Because I give the impression I don't care a fig whether they do or not."

"But that doesn't make sense."

"Not much in society does."

Eugene's face fell. He looked as if he were being sent down from Mount Sinai without the Commandments.

Julian could not leave him in this state. "People suppose what I do must be right, because I do it with conviction. A true dandy ought to be able to walk down Pall Mall with an upturned bucket on his head, and have every young blood in London scrambling for one just like it. It's all conviction—sheer effrontery, if you prefer. A kind of philosophical conjuring trick: *I believe in myself, therefore I am*—"

He broke off. Every now and then the outrageousness of his achievement startled even him. But he knew the first rule of keeping one's balance at a great height is not to look down. "We're wandering from the subject. I asked you if you knew before Alexander died that you would be remembered in his will."

Eugene cast about confusedly, as if he were trying to rebuild his defences but found some of the pieces missing. "He hinted something about it," he said at last. "It was over the Christmas holidays. He said he particularly wanted to do something for me, as he hadn't any children of his own."

"Did you interpret that to mean he intended to leave you money?"

"I didn't think about it. I just thought he was trying to cheer me up, because I'd had measles and was still a bit low. I wasn't going about wondering if people would leave me money. I've never had any. I didn't expect I ever should."

"Now it appears you'll soon have four thousand pounds—assuming Alexander didn't leave any children."

"You mean, Belinda might be—" It appeared the idea had never occurred to him. "Wouldn't she have said something?"

"I'm not an expert in these matters, but it's possible she doesn't know yet."

Eugene started walking—back and forth, like an animal caught in a trap. "I don't want to think about it. If Belinda is—in the family way—it's nothing to me, I don't care. I never believed in the money, anyway. I've never had anything of my own."

But of course he must care desperately, Julian thought. Four thousand pounds would yield him a substantial income or launch him in a gentleman's profession: the Bar, the army, the Church. To be sure, his sister would probably do as much for him and more. But wouldn't it mean a great deal to this dispossessed child to do it for himself?

"How did Alexander come to be your guardian?" Julian asked.

"My mother died two years ago, and my father killed himself when I was three. Neither of them had any close male relatives. Mother was fond of Alexander and asked him to get himself appointed my guardian. He did, through some sort of petition to the Court of Chancery."

"How did you feel about him?"

"I thought he was wonderful."

"In other words, you liked him?"

"Liked him?" Eugene looked puzzled. "You don't understand about Alexander. It's like asking if I liked the King, or the Tower of London. They're splendid, and they're *there*. Alexander was top of the tree, a non-pareil. He used to come to my room and talk to me sometimes before he went out in the evening. He'd be dressed in his evening clothes, and he'd talk about who he might meet and what they'd do. He was like a hero in a novel. He looked perfect, and everything he said and did was perfect. When he wasn't there, it was hard to believe in him. I mean, that he could be real."

"Do you miss him?"

"I can't believe he's dead."

"You've just said you couldn't believe he was real to begin with."

"Well, if someone isn't real, how can he be killed? What I mean is, I can't imagine someone coming up to him and striking him down, breaking his head—as if he were just anybody. I would have thought he'd have only to smile, and the poker would turn into a feather and not hurt him. I suppose that sounds mad."

"No. I think I understand."

There was a pause. Eugene walked back and forth, biting his nails. The house was very quiet: no sound but the muffled footsteps of servants and the occasional spitting and crackling of the fire. Sir Malcolm had given Julian his study for this interview and gone for a walk—his daily visit to the churchyard, Julian supposed. Mrs. Falkland had gone out riding before Sir Malcolm and Julian arrived.

"I should like to ask you about the night of the murder," Julian said. "You went to bed at eleven?"

"Y-yes."

"And you didn't awaken until your sister and Martha came to tell you about the murder shortly before two?"

Eugene shook his head.

"You didn't hear your sister screaming about an hour earlier?"

"I heard something like 'No, no.' I think I thought it was a dream."

"When you heard Alexander was dead, the first thing you asked was 'How was he killed?' How did you know he'd died by violence?"

"Well—people his age don't just die. Someone or something kills them. Or they kill themselves, as my father did."

"You seem rather fond of reminding people of that."

"People don't need reminding! Everyone knows, and no

one ever forgets. At school they were always taunting me with it. They tied me up and waved a razor under my chin and asked me if I wanted to play cards. You don't know what it's like. I don't suppose anything like that ever happened to you when you were my age."

"Nothing quite like that, no."

Eugene regarded him curiously. "Where did you go to school?"

"I was privately educated." And that's enough on that subject, Julian thought. "I take it this is why you didn't want to return to school?"

"I *hate* school. Belinda and I had an enormous row about it. I don't know why she was so set on being rid of me. I hadn't done anything wrong. And lots of fellows my age are educated at home. But she *would* send me away, and Alexander had to give in to her in the end."

"Were you angry with him about that?"

"I wouldn't have killed him on account of it!"

"Be so good as to answer the question I asked."

"I was disappointed. I thought he was on my side. But he said it was up to Belinda, as she was my sister, and she'd known me much longer. I was mostly angry at her, not him. But that's past. I can't quarrel with her when she's feeling so wretched. And besides, after Alexander died she said I needn't go back to school before the autumn. I'm hoping she'll give up the idea altogether by then."

"You'll have to face the world sooner or later, you know. Unless you were planning to live out your life in a bandbox."

"That's easy enough for you to say. Look at you. Anyone who can tie a neckcloth as you do doesn't have to worry about facing the world."

Julian regarded him thoughtfully. Then he rose and began drawing off his gloves. "Come here."

"Why?" asked Eugene, alarmed.

"Because my arms don't stretch like India rubber."

Eugene approached him haltingly. Julian twitched off the

boy's neckcloth, held it between forefinger and thumb, and surveyed it wryly. "I highly recommend cleanliness. It pleases women and annoys men, which are two excellent ways to get on in society. However, we'll make the best of what we have. This is called *Trône d'Amour*. It's extremely simple. It has one dent in the centre and no collateral creases, and it ties in a knot in front—so. The neckcloth ought to be starched, but no matter."

Eugene went to look in a mirror, then gazed at Julian in awe. "But—but I could never tie it like that."

"You might consider wearing a black stock instead. It's much easier to keep neat, and if it isn't clean, no one will notice. It's very stiff, but that will be useful for learning to hold up your head—a trait you haven't been noted for up to now."

"You're very hard."

No, thought Julian, far too soft. I may have just given a lesson in sartorial elegance to Alexander Falkland's killer. And if that's so, how can I tie a cravat round his neck one moment, and a noose around it the next? The devil!—I'm becoming *involved*. And that's precisely what I expected to escape in this investigation.

He said, "This is a murder inquiry, and you're a suspect without an alibi, who profited signally by the victim's death. You can hardly expect to escape a few uncomfortable moments."

"There! I knew you suspected me!"

"I do suspect you. I also suspect Mr. Clare, Mr. Adams, and a number of other people. You haven't broken out of the field yet. If you do, I'll let you know."

"I think you're beastly cold-blooded. You've probably been trying to win my confidence in order to make me confess. Next you'll be thinking I killed that woman, too! If I bashed my brother-in-law on the head, why not her?"

"What in the devil's name are you talking about?"

"That woman who was found in the brickfield near here.

Her face was all smashed with a piece of brick, till it was just a wet, muddy pulp. I saw the place where they found her. It was horrible. I wished I hadn't gone."

"The Brickfield Murder," said Julian slowly. "I'd forgotten about that. It was in all the newspapers while I was in Newmarket—till Alexander's murder crowded it out. It hasn't been solved, I suppose?"

"No. No one even knows who the woman was, because she hadn't any face—"

The door opened. Eugene started and spun around. Mrs. Falkland came in, still in riding dress, with a colour in her cheeks that made her look far healthier than she had yesterday. With one hand she held up the skirt of her black habit, which was cut overly long to hang becomingly from a side-saddle. In her other hand was an open letter.

"I have to speak with you, Eugene— Oh. Mr. Kestrel. I didn't know you were here."

"Good afternoon, Mrs. Falkland." Julian bowed over her hand. "I'm glad to see you looking so well."

"Thank you. This is the first day I've been well enough to ride."

"You ride on the Heath, I suppose?" He made conversation at random, wondering all the while why she seemed braced for some great effort. He did not think it had anything to do with him.

"Yes. I prefer to ride in the morning, but this morning it rained. But I'm afraid I interrupt you—I know you have things to ask Eugene."

"Don't go unless you'd rather. I believe Mr. Talmadge and I were finished." He glanced at Eugene.

Eugene was searching his sister's face. He fairly quivered with alertness, like an animal sensing danger. His eyes came to rest on the letter in her hand. "Something is wrong."

"No," she said levelly. "I merely wish to talk to you, but it can wait until later."

"Tell me now."

"You will please refrain from making a scene before a guest."

"I know what it is!" he cried. "You looked just so when you told me I was to go back to school!"

She said nothing.

"But—but you promised! You said I needn't go back to Harrow before the autumn!"

"I'm not sending you back to Harrow. It's too late in the year for that, and anyway, I know you dislike it. So I've chosen a private school for you. I think you may be happier there. It comes very well recommended, and, as it's quite small, perhaps your—your father's history won't be so well known."

"It will all come out in the end! It always does. You can't get 'round your promise just by sending me to a different school. You gave your word, and you've broken it!"

"If I led you to believe you could neglect your education till the autumn, it was in a moment of weakness and confusion after Alexander died. I ought not to have made that promise —but you ought not to have asked it of me at such a time. You can't expect I should let you remain here, in the midst of a murder investigation. You're too morbid as it is. Surely now that Mr. Kestrel has had a chance to question you, he can have no objection to your going."

They both turned to Julian, Mrs. Falkland's gaze coolly expectant, Eugene's eloquent with appeal. Julian knew it was not for him to meddle. If Alexander had left it up to Mrs. Falkland to make decisions about Eugene's education, then he, a complete stranger, could hardly interfere. "I have nothing further to ask Mr. Talmadge at present. That may change, in which case I shall require him to return."

"I'm willing to take that chance," Mrs. Falkland said.

"Where am I to go?" Eugene asked grimly.

"The school is in Yorkshire—"

"Yorkshire! I know about those Yorkshire schools! Boys are sent there when no one ever wants to see them again. They haven't any holidays, and nobody cares what becomes of them—"

"It isn't that sort of school! Listen to me, Eugene. This is all for your good. You're too idle here. You do nothing all day but walk on the Heath and brood."

"Then I'll study!" he pleaded. "Sir Malcolm has heaps of books—"

"I've made my decision. Nothing you can say will alter it. I've arranged with the proprietor of the school for you to leave the day after tomorrow." He started to protest, but she held up her hand. "The last time I tried to send you back to school, I gave you too long to think about it, and you went so far as to make yourself ill to keep from going. I shan't make that mistake again. The day after tomorrow, early in the morning, you leave by post-chaise. There's nothing more to be said."

"There is something more." Eugene was very pale. "I just want you to know, I'm not deceived about why you want to send me so far away. You think I killed Alexander. Perhaps you want everyone else to think so, too. You've always been ashamed of me! Alexander was kind to me, but you're cold and hateful!—"

"Oh, Eugene," she said wearily. Then her back straightened. "You've made a spectacle of us both before Mr. Kestrel. You will please beg his pardon and then go to your room."

"I beg your pardon, Mr. Kestrel. But I did warn you, I'm a bad lot, just as my father was. You can't expect anything better of me." He started to leave, then turned to face his sister. "You won't be able to tell me what to do much longer. I have money of my own now—or I will, as soon as I'm of age. Alexander did that for me. He gave me what I wanted most in the world—he made me free of you!" He ran out.

Mrs. Falkland made a strange movement with her shoulders, like a porter adjusting the load on his back. That was just how she seemed: braced, determined, tired, like someone carrying a burden a long distance with no hope of relief. "I'm sorry you had to see that quarrel, Mr. Kestrel. It's a very old one. Eugene has always disliked school. He lived a retired life with Mama until a few years ago. After she died, and I married Alexander, he was thrown into the world quite suddenly. Harrow was too large and worldly a place for him. This new school may be better."

"From the standpoint of the investigation, it would be more convenient if he remained here."

"Why?" She looked him directly in the eyes. "Do you suspect him?"

He looked at her just as directly. "I suspect everyone, Mrs. Falkland."

"I see." She said nothing for a moment, then: "My brother doesn't wish to live in the world. I understand his feelings, but I can't indulge them. You've seen how odd and ill-mannered he is. The longer he lives like a hermit, the more settled in those ways he'll become. I have a duty to him, even if he can't understand or appreciate it. My mother left him in my charge. Almost her last words to me were that I should look after him. I shall do as she asked—even if he hates me for it."

Just for an instant, her voice quavered. Julian said delicately, "Perhaps if he knew it cost you an effort to send him away, he might be more willing to go."

"If he knew it cost me an effort, he might be deluded into thinking I would change my mind. That would be more cruel than my present hardness. I must ask you, Mr. Kestrel, to accept that I know what must be done."

"To be sure, Mrs. Falkland. It isn't my affair." Though it will be quickly enough, he thought, if it proves to have something to do with the murder. "I'm glad of this opportunity to speak with you. I should like to ask you a few questions."

She inclined her head and sat down. The skirt of her habit made a pool of black around her on the floor.

"Were you conversant with your husband's financial affairs before he died?"

"Not really. He sometimes told me when an investment he'd made had fared well."

"What about when an investment had fared badly?"

"I don't think any of his investments did, until those mining ventures failed a few months ago."

"Did he tell you about that when it happened?"

"He mentioned it."

"Were you worried?"

"No. I never doubted he would set things right."

"Did he tell you how he did that—set things right?"

"I believe he reached an accommodation with Mr. Adams, who'd bought up his notes-of-hand."

"The accommodation amounted to Mr. Adams's forgiving the notes outright—thirty thousand pounds' worth. Did your husband tell you that?"

"No. You must understand, Mr. Kestrel, I never concerned myself with money matters. Alexander was well able to handle them without my help."

"What did you think about his friendship with David Adams?"

"I didn't think anything about it. I hardly knew Mr. Adams. He came to our parties occasionally, but for the most part Alexander saw him without me. He wasn't the sort of person I was accustomed to associate with, but as he was Alexander's friend, I paid him every courtesy."

Julian studied her face. It was white and cold and expressionless. "I should like to ask you about another matter. It concerns a visit you made about a month ago, to a friend who lived near an ironware showroom in the Strand."

A moment ago, he would have thought it impossible she could become more white and still. Now she seemed set in marble. "Yes?"

"Who was this friend?"

"She was Mrs. Brown, a former tenant of my father's at our estate in Dorset. But I didn't actually see her. She wasn't there."

"Perhaps you had better begin at the beginning."

She inclined her head in assent. It interested Julian that she did not pause to ask what this had to do with Alexander's murder. She had expected to be questioned about this visit. And she had her answers ready.

"Alexander and I went to a shop in the Strand called Haythorpe and Sons. He wanted to look at grates. When we came out, a girl came up to us in the street. She said she was Mrs. Brown's maidservant, and she remembered me from my visits to Dorset. I didn't remember her, but of course I would have been more conspicuous to her than she was to me. She said Mrs. Brown had moved to London and was living nearby, and that she was very ill. I didn't stop to think, but said I would go to her. I was raised to believe I had a duty to servants and tenants. In my father's day, they had looked to him for help and protection; now it was only right they should look to me.

"I told Alexander I wished to go to Mrs. Brown at once. He wanted the carriage to wait for me in the Strand—it couldn't fit through the passage where the girl was taking me. But I knew he had another engagement, and I didn't know how long I might be. So I suggested he take the carriage away, and I would come home in a hackney coach."

"And he agreed to that?"

"Not at once. But I persuaded him."

"Forgive me, Mrs. Falkland, but I find it hard to credit that he let you venture into a questionable neighbourhood, with only a strange maidservant for escort."

"He couldn't go with me. I told you, he had an engagement. I don't remember what it was."

"Why didn't he send Luke with you?"

"It all happened quite quickly. There wasn't time to think of such things. I'm not accustomed to anticipate danger. I thought only of my father's old tenant and my duty to look after her."

"Very well. Please go on."

"The maidservant brought me through the passage into a narrow court. There were half a dozen grey-brick houses there, most of them in disrepair. Then it turned out Mrs. Brown didn't live there at all. The maidservant had left her service some time ago and only brought me there to beg for money. I was angry at being lied to and went away. A hackney coach brought me home."

"Luke says you didn't come home for three hours."

She caught her breath. "What else did he tell you?"

"What were you doing all that time?" he countered.

"Walking. Shopping."

"Alone?"

"Alone." She breathed hard, as if through a knot in her throat.

He paused. He knew he should not give her any respite, but bullying women was not his forte. "This maidservant: what was her name?"

"I don't know. I told you, it was she who recognized me, not the other way round."

"What was she like?"

"She was blond and slender, pretty in a doll-like way." Her gaze strayed beyond him. "She was like one of those papier-mâché heads used to display hats: long, dark lashes, and great, vacant blue eyes."

"Vacant of intellect?"

"Vacant of soul," she said quietly.

"She seems to have made a profound impression on you."

Her head snapped round at him. "She tried to impose on me. I try to be generous to dependents and the poor, but I don't care to be tricked or taken advantage of. Yes, she made an impression on me, and it was an unpleasant one."

"I see. I take it that, as Mr. and Mrs. Brown were your father's tenants, their names would appear on the rent rolls of your estate?"

"I—I don't know. They may not have been tenants, strictly speaking. They may have had a freehold."

"If I went to your estate and looked through the records— if I spoke to neighbours, tenants, the local clergyman—would I find any trace of these Browns at all?"

She drew a long breath and closed her eyes. "Very likely not, Mr. Kestrel."

He asked, gently but inexorably, "Who was this blond girl with the vacant eyes you remember so vividly, Mrs. Falkland? And why did you go with her?"

"I've given you my explanation. If you're not satisfied with it, you must do whatever you deem necessary." She rose. "Is there anything more you wish to ask me?"

"Not at present. I do have some questions for your maid, if you'll be good enough to send her to me."

"Very well. Good afternoon, Mr. Kestrel."

He started to open the door for her, then paused with his hand on the knob. "You know, telling the truth is always the best course in these investigations. It comes out sooner or later, and in ways you can't predict or control."

Her frost-blue eyes looked up at him steadily. "Have you ever been to Hell, Mr. Kestrel?"

He stared. "Not recently."

"Then you can't advise me. You can't even find me, where I am now."

# ✳ 8 ✳

## ARGUS

Martha Gilmore stood very straight, hands clasped over her stomach, elbows thrust out. "Please sit down," said Julian.

"No, thank you, sir, I'd rather stand."

"As you wish. You've been in service with Mrs. Falkland's family for some years?"

"Yes, sir. I was taken on as nursemaid after Mr. Talmadge—Mr. Eugene's father—died. My mistress was seven, and Mr. Eugene was three."

"At that time the family lived at Mrs. Falkland's estate in Dorset?"

"Yes, sir."

"Your speech suggests you're from Dorset, or somewhere close by."

"Yes, sir. I come from Sherborne."

"I don't suppose you've ever met a Mr. or Mrs. Brown—former tenants on Mrs. Falkland's estate?"

"Not so as I can recall, sir."

Julian nodded. He did not believe anyone had met, or ever would meet, the Browns. "You've known Mrs. Falkland longer than anyone I've talked to so far, except Eugene. She seems to be in great torment. Have you any idea why?"

"She was very devoted to Mr. Falkland, sir. That would account for it, to my mind."

"That would account for her grief. But I believe she suffers from something more—something that gnaws at her from within, like jealousy or guilt."

"I wouldn't know anything about that, sir."

He smiled and asked frankly, "Tell me, after this interview, shall you repeat everything I've said to your mistress?"

"That depends, sir. If I think she ought to know it, yes. If it would bring her more pain than profit, no. But whatsomever I do, sir, it will be for her good—not yours, nor Sir Malcolm's, nor Bow Street's. And so I tell you plainly, sir."

"That's tolerably plain, yes. Would you go so far as to lie for her?"

"If I would, sir," she said imperturbably, "I'd hardly admit it to you."

He was impressed, and rather puzzled. It was hard to know how to come at her. She was too dour to charm, too stubborn to persuade. And too brave to overawe: this woman was afraid of no one, servant though she was. To lift a poker against her master would not daunt her. And she had ample physical strength for it, to judge by her broad shoulders and sinewy arms.

He said, "It was you who broke the news of the murder to Mrs. Falkland?"

"Yes, sir."

"At about one o'clock in the morning?"

"A little after, sir."

"Was she asleep when you came to her room?"

"I believe so, sir. I had to knock loudly to make her hear me."

"Why didn't you simply go in?"

"The door was locked, sir."

"Was that unusual?"

She paused. "Mrs. Falkland didn't usually lock her door, no, sir."

"Why did she lock it now?"

"I don't know, sir."

"She heard you knocking, came to the door, and let you in?"

"Yes, sir."

"She was still in her evening gown, I believe."

"Yes, sir."

"If she didn't mean to come back to the party and had gone to sleep, why was she still dressed?"

"I don't know, sir. She'd have rung for me if she wanted to undress. I can't say why she didn't."

"When had you last seen her?"

"A little after half past eleven, sir. I looked in on her to see how she was and offered to make her an herbal drink for her headache. She said no, she'd just lie down and try to sleep."

"Did she ask you to tell Mr. Falkland she wouldn't be returning to the party?"

"No, sir."

"Then you took it on yourself to interrupt the party and give him that message?"

"Yes, sir." She met his gaze squarely. "I didn't think it right for him to be larking with his friends while she was poorly. I thought he ought to go up to her."

"But she told Mr. Poynter she wanted the party to go on in her absence."

"That's as may be, sir. No doubt she wouldn't wish to spoil the master's pleasure. It was like her to put him first. But to me, *she* was all in all. And I thought he ought to go to her."

"So you sent Luke to fetch him from the drawing room. And when he came out, you told him Mrs. Falkland still had her headache and wouldn't be coming back to the party. Did you say anything more?"

"Not so as I can recall, sir."

"Mr. Clare says he looked taken aback while speaking to you."

"Happen he did, sir. I can't remember."

"Was there anything in your conversation to startle him?"

"No, sir. Unless he was worried about the mistress."

"He went back to the party and told the guests he was going upstairs to look in on her. But instead he went downstairs to his study. Have you any idea why?"

"No, sir."

The woman was a brick wall, Julian thought. He might beat on her for hours without getting the slightest response. "Where did you go after speaking with him?"

"Up to my room in the attic, sir."

"By the servants' stairs?"

"Yes, sir."

"That was at about a quarter to midnight. What did you do then?"

"Needlework, sir."

"How long did you remain there?"

"About an hour, sir. Then Luke came and told me the master'd been killed, and Mr. Nichols said I was to break the news to Mrs. Falkland."

"Did anyone see you in your room during the first half hour you were there?"

"No, sir."

It was odd, thought Julian, that none of the servants without alibis—Luke, Valère, and Martha—showed the slightest concern about it. "How do you get on with M. Valère?"

"Not very well, sir. I don't hold with his stuck-up French ways, or his being a Papist. I will say this for him: he was very attached to the master."

"Perhaps that's why he's so indignant about your spying on him."

"Spying on him, sir?"

For the first time, she was evasive. This was promising. "Asking questions about his comings and goings. Poking about his dressing room."

"I did go once into his dressing room. And I sometimes asked Mr. Valère where he was going. I wouldn't call that spying, sir."

"But you didn't merely go into his dressing room—you searched it. Valère says he found things moved about."

"It's true I had a look around." She was picking her way now, weighing each word. "I thought the master wasn't spending enough time with the mistress. I wondered what had got his attention away from her."

"Had you any idea what it might be? A business matter? A *chère amie?*"

"I didn't know in the least, sir. That's why I was keeping my eyes open and asking questions."

"Did Mrs. Falkland ask you to do that?"

"No, sir. She didn't know anything about it."

"Had she and Mr. Falkland quarrelled?"

"I couldn't say, sir."

"Couldn't you? If I were married, Martha, I have no doubt my manservant would know precisely the state of my relations with my wife at any time—not because he's inquisitive, but because he and I live in each other's pockets, and he's observant. As I'm sure you are as well."

"I never saw any sign they'd quarrelled, sir. I just thought the master had other things on his mind than the mistress. And I didn't think that was right."

"You seem to feel a great responsibility to protect Mrs. Falkland, without her asking or expecting it of you."

Martha looked back at him stolidly. "When I know the right thing to do, I do it, sir. As a Christian woman should."

✳

Julian was not inclined to tell Sir Malcolm any more than he could help about his interviews with Eugene and Mrs. Falkland. His witnessing their quarrel over Eugene's return to school could only embarrass Sir Malcolm, while his impulsively playing mentor to the boy rather embarrassed himself. He did pass on Mrs. Falkland's very inadequate explanation of her encounter with the maidservant in the Strand. Sir Malcolm could not imagine what had possessed her to go away with the girl. Julian could think of several explanations, but as none of them reflected credit on Mrs. Falkland, he kept them to himself.

He was more forthcoming about his interrogation of Martha. "Have you any idea why she would feel the need to keep track of Alexander's movements or search his rooms?"

"Not the least in the world," said Sir Malcolm.

"I wonder if she found anything," Julian mused.

"I thought Valère said nothing was missing from Alexander's dressing room."

"There might have been something there he didn't know about. But, more to the point, I doubt if Martha's spying was confined to Alexander's dressing room. If she searched there, she probably searched other rooms as well: his bedroom, and his study."

"Do you think he caught her searching his study that night?" asked Sir Malcolm eagerly. "And she panicked and hit him with the poker?"

"It's possible. But she doesn't strike me as the sort of woman to panic easily. And if there was a direct confrontation between them, it's hard to see how she could have crept up on him from behind. Finally, there's still the question of why he went to the study in the first place."

"True." Sir Malcolm sighed. "Well, I know Alexander thought she was very sharp-eyed. He nicknamed her Argus, after the hundred-eyed servant of the goddess Hera. He was eternally vigilant, because only fifty of his eyes slept at any time."

"Do you think Alexander knew Martha was watching him and felt uneasy about it?"

"I've no idea. I didn't see much of him during the last few weeks of his life, though we went on writing to each other as usual."

"And unfortunately his letters tell us nothing about his life, or his worries, if he had any." Julian took a turn about the room. "Sir Malcolm, what do you know about the Brickfield Murder?"

"The Brickfield Murder? Why do you ask?"

"Eugene brought it up. It piqued my curiosity—I suppose because it happened so recently, and so near here."

"It was a very distressing crime, especially in a small community like this. Of course, we're only four miles from London, so I suppose we have to expect its thieves and ruffians to overflow into our back gardens from time to time. And that brickfield was always an unsavoury spot. It fell out of use and became a lurking ground for runaway apprentices, gipsies, all sorts of flotsam and jetsam. Still, there'd never been a violent crime there before that murder."

"When exactly did it happen?"

"It was a week before Alexander's murder—the night of April the fifteenth. I remember there was a torrential rain that night: we woke up to find the cistern overflowing and branches blown off trees. Then suddenly everyone was saying a woman had been murdered in the brickfield. Nobody knew who she was, and she'd been so brutally beaten about the face, her own mother wouldn't have recognized her. There were no reports any woman had gone missing, and no one came forward to claim her, so the parish buried her. We still know nothing about her, except that she looked to be in her forties and wore plain woollen clothes."

"What about the murderer? Is anything known about him?"

"Not so far as I know. The rain washed away any traces he might have left in the brickfield—footprints and wheelmarks and such. And there were no suspicious characters seen in the neighbourhood—at all events, none who couldn't account for their whereabouts on the night of the murder. It's widely believed he must have been a madman; in fact, there were enquiries at all the local hospitals and private madhouses, to see if any patients had escaped. None had, but it's easy to see why people's thoughts turned that way. It was such a senselessly brutal crime. Even if the murderer had robbed her, or raped her—her body was so smothered in wet and mud, the surgeon couldn't tell about that—where was the need to kill her so— so *thoroughly?*" His voice dropped to bitter sadness. "We know from Alexander's murder that a single blow can snuff out a life. So why go to all the additional trouble of smashing her face?"

"Some men enjoy brutality for its own sake. Although you'd expect such a man to have beaten her thoroughly and indiscriminately. His concentrating on smashing her face suggests that he sought exactly what he achieved: the suppression of her identity."

"But why?"

"I haven't the remotest idea. I suppose we ought to return to the murder at hand. Tomorrow I mean to see Quentin Clare. What can you tell me about him? You and he belong to the same Inn of Court."

"Yes, but I don't know him very well. Benchers aren't thrown together with the students much. Mind you, I like to get to know them: I don't think we give them nearly enough guidance. Dining in Hall with them for a few weeks, four times a year, is hardly what I'd call a legal education. It's like throwing a young man into the sea and saying you've taught him to swim. Clare seems very well-behaved—never has to be reprimanded for holding drunken parties in his chambers or running about at night stealing door knockers or any of the other nonsense the students get up to. Otherwise, I don't know anything about him. He's very shy—seems to have nothing to say for himself. I hope for his sake he doesn't mean to practise—there's no room at the Bar for the self-effacing."

"What do you think Alexander saw in him?"

"I don't know. I saw them together on occasion, but Clare always kept in the background and let Alexander talk for them both. I think Alexander was sorry for him. He was generous to men who were disadvantaged socially, like Eugene or Adams. I should be sorry to think any of them repaid his kindness with murder."

"That remains to be seen," said Julian noncommittally. Sir Malcolm's praise of his son grated on him, but why? That he himself did not trust Alexander to be all he seemed should not prevent him from acknowledging the man's real and visible generosity to Clare and Adams. And yet—

"I suppose you'll be questioning a good many people," said Sir Malcolm. "The guests at Alexander's party, and anyone else in society who knew him at all well."

"I shall want information from them, naturally. But I shan't question them. That would be the worst possible line to take."

"Then how will you find out what they know?"

"Precisely by not asking them. The only way to accomplish anything in the *beau monde* is to do precisely the reverse of what you intend."

"I don't understand."

"Let me give you an example. When I came to London from the Continent three years ago, I knew almost no one, and almost no one knew me. I rode in Hyde Park every day at the fashionable hour, cutting a figure but not attempting to talk to anyone or courting anyone's notice. Eventually a few people who'd met me in Italy made a point of showing off that they alone knew who I was. Soon it became *de rigueur* to know me. I was invited everywhere and went almost nowhere. Sometimes I received three invitations for one evening, declined them all, and stayed home and read or played the piano and left everyone wondering where I was. The trick of it is that the *ton* are so desperately bored, and so sated with being admired and sought after, that they fawn on anyone who appears to have no use for them. That was Brummell's secret, but few people learned the lesson he taught, and fewer still can put it into practice.

"So my plan, Sir Malcolm, is simply to appear in public and let Alexander's acquaintances come to me. They know I've undertaken to solve his murder—I had my manservant kindle that rumour last night, and it should be a rare conflagration by now. Tonight I'm going to the theatre, and then to a rout: one of those parties great hostesses give for three or four hundred intimate friends, where people stand about on a hot, crowded staircase and wonder why they're not enjoying themselves. Alexander's friends will be expecting me to approach them about the murder, and I shan't so much as touch on the subject. They'll feel slighted and set out to prove how valuable their opinions and observations are. In short, by asking no one for information, I shall be inundated with it. And though much of it may be worthless, there's bound to be a grain or two of wheat amidst the chaff."

"I don't mean to doubt you, Mr. Kestrel, but are you sure about all this?"

"I know these people, Sir Malcolm. They're the element in which I live."

Sir Malcolm looked at him more closely. Julian saw the next question coming: *Why? What possesses you to spend your life with people you have to train like spaniels, amuse like children, manipulate like pieces on a chessboard? A man of your abilities—*

He said quickly, "Where will you be over the next few days, if I need to speak to you?"

"I'd as lief stay close to home. I feel my place is here just now, with Belinda. But it's Easter term, the courts are humming, and there's a deal of administrative business at Lincoln's Inn. So I'll be in chambers for at least part of each day—Number 21, Lincoln's Inn Old Square. If I'm not there, you can leave a message with my clerk." He smiled ruefully. "It's awkward appearing in King's Bench these days—the jury hang on my words, but for the wrong reasons. They're far more interested in me than in my argument. How is the murdered man's father bearing up? Whom does he suspect?"

"Whom *do* you suspect, Sir Malcolm?"

"The people I know least, I suppose: Clare and Adams and the other guests at the party. Or even that mysterious maidservant who accosted Belinda in the Strand. *She* seems to have been up to no good. Do you suppose we'll ever find her again?"

"We'll try, Sir Malcolm. And, what's more, we'll begin this very night."

＊

When he got home, Julian wrote two notes. The first was to Quentin Clare:

> 35, Clarges Street
> 2 May 1825
>
> Sir,—As you may have heard, Sir Malcolm Falkland
> has asked my help in solving his son's murder, and I've
> agreed to do what I can. To that end, I should like very
> much to speak with you. I shall do myself the honour to
> call on you tomorrow morning at ten, and shall hope to
> find you in.
>
> Believe me, sir, your obedient servant,
> Julian Kestrel

The second note read:

> My dear Vance,—Will you be so good as to send me any
> information you have about the Brickfield Murder? I'm
> afraid you'll think me fickle, flitting from one crime to
> another like this, but I assure you I haven't abandoned
> Alexander Falkland. I merely feel the need to know more
> about the Brickfield Murder, and would gladly tell you
> why—if I knew myself.
>
> Yours, with thanks, J.K.

He gave Dipper the notes to deliver. "And when you've
done that, I have a task that's rather more in your line. There's
a certain maidservant I should like to know more about, and
as she's young and pretty, I know I can count on you to make
an exceedingly thorough investigation."

Dipper received this as he did most of his master's sallies,
with the wistful air of one labouring under unjust accusations.
It was a look that must have served him in good stead in his
pickpocketing days.

Julian told him about the mysterious maidservant who had
lured Mrs. Falkland down a passage near an ironware showroom in the Strand. "Mrs. Falkland says it leads to a narrow
court of grey-brick houses, most of them in disrepair."

"That'll be Cygnet's Court, sir."

"You know the place?"

"Oh, yes, sir. Me and me pals, we used to duck in there sometimes when we was playing at bo-peep with the watchmen. 'Course, in them days none of the houses was fit to live in, but since then the ratcatchers has been in, so somebody must mean to furbish 'em up."

"Have a look around the place, and try if you can to find the girl. She's tall and slender, with blond hair and large, doll-like blue eyes. She was wearing a brown and white checked dress and a white cap with lappets."

"If I smokes her out, sir, what should I do?"

"Strike up an acquaintance. I know you're more than equal to that. If you can't find her, find out all you can about her in the neighbourhood. I want to know who she was and what her business was with Mrs. Falkland."

"What do you think it was, sir?"

"Most likely something that doesn't reflect credit on Mrs. Falkland, or she wouldn't be keeping it dark. She may have been meeting with a cent-per-cent about a loan. She may have been conducting an *affair de coeur*, with the maidservant as go-between. She may have been blackmailed. And, of course, she may have been arranging her husband's murder. The trouble with all these explanations is—why would she have gone off with the girl on business of that kind, right under Alexander's nose?"

# ✳ 9 ✳

## BREATHS
## OF SCANDAL

Dipper felt more at home in the Strand than anywhere else
in London. As a child, he had lived in many different places:
rookeries like Chick Lane and Seven Dials, where his family
was squeezed into a single room; flash houses where appren-
tice pickpockets learned their trade; doss-houses where boy
and girl criminals slept a dozen to a bed. But he had worked
most often in and around the Strand. Here people of all classes
came to search the shops for bargains, go to the waxworks,
see the five-ton elephant at Exeter 'Change, or pick up one of
the girls who walked the pavements in scanty silk gowns and
gaudy bonnets. Everyone carried bulging pocketbooks, and no
one was keeping a close eye on them. It was a pickpocket's
paradise.

It was eight o'clock by the clock at St. Clement Danes, one
of the two little white churches incongruously islanded in the
busy street. The shops were still doing a brisk business, but
the pastry cooks were putting out trays of stale tarts at half
price, the last clerks in their rusty black suits were hurrying
home, the coffee-houses were emptying, and the gin-shops
filling. Carriages clattered over the cobblestones, speeding
theatre-goers to Covent Garden and Drury Lane.

Dipper walked jauntily along the pavement. Knowing his

old colleagues' habits, he thrust his hands in his trouser pockets and looped his coattails over his arms, to keep the tail-pockets under his eye. He passed cook-shops reeking with roast meat, drapers' warehouses awash in colourful linens, a man dressed up as an enormous boot to advertise blacking. At last he reached the broad windows of Haythorpe and Sons, with their dazzling display of polished grates and fire irons. Just beyond was the passage into Cygnet's Court.

He went through. The court was much as he remembered it: narrow and dark, with two grey-brick houses on each side and one at the far end. But now two of the houses—the smallest and the largest—had been refurbished. The smallest was just to the left as one entered the court. It had white dimity curtains in the windows, a red and blue woven mat at the door, and smoke curling up from the chimney. The largest house, at the opposite end of the court, was dark and still. As Dipper drew nearer, he saw a "To Let" sign in one of the windows.

All at once he had a tickly feeling down his back—the preternatural sense that he was being watched. He turned just in time to see a face peeking out at him through the window of the smallest house. It was an elderly woman, who darted behind the curtains when he saw her. He went up to her door and knocked.

A maidservant answered. She was not the one who had accosted Mrs. Falkland. This girl was raw-boned and ungainly, with carroty hair and a wall-eye. Dipper suspected she was none too well furnished in her upper story.

He said, slowly and distinctly, "I'd like to speak to your missus, if I might."

She stared at him dully with her good eye. The wall-eye gleamed white, with just a few flecks of brown iris.

The old lady he had seen at the window came hobbling forward, leaning on a cane. "Out of the way, you silly girl! Don't mind her, young man, she's worse than useless. You're worse than useless, Bet, do you hear?"

Her tone was not angry; it was even affectionate. And Dipper supposed the tone was all the girl really understood. "Yes'm." She nodded inanely.

The old woman peered out at Dipper, a little anxious but more curious. She was plump and comfortable, with a broad face, two dimples, and three chins. She wore a blue calico gown and a white cap that looked like the dome of St. Paul's broken out in lace.

" 'Evening, ma'am," said Dipper, doffing his hat.

"Good evening." His neat appearance and manners seemed to reassure her somewhat.

"I seen you watching me just now—well, you was bound to, wasn't you, living tucked away like this, and not expecting to see a stranger hanging about—"

"Oh, yes, that's all it was. I didn't mean to be inquisitive, mind. Only Bet and I live quite alone, and I do worry about burglars."

"You might not want to be a-telling strangers you lives alone," Dipper suggested. "That's the kind of thing that warms a burglar's heart."

"I'm sure you're right. But you seem such a nice young man. Did you want something?"

"I'd like to ask you some'ut, if I might."

"Oh, do come in! I was just sitting down to evening tea, and you're more than welcome to share it. There's toasted cheese and gooseberry jam, and there might—I'm not certain, mind, but there *might*—be some pickled walnuts."

"Thanks, ma'am, I'd like that."

She waddled briskly down the hall, Dipper following. They went into a tiny back parlour, with a crackling fire that kept it almost too hot, for all the evening chill. The old woman clearly did not get many visitors. Her parlour was furnished for preservation rather than use, with green druggets on the carpet, brown Holland covers on the chairs, and paper mats on the tables. A musty smell, as of windows seldom opened, mingled with the fragrance of dried flowers in a bowl. Two cats, one white and one tawny, lounged on the hearth-rug.

"This is Snowflake, and this is Amber," the old lady introduced them. "And I'm Mrs. Wheeler."

"How d'ye do, ma'am? I'm Tom Stokes." This was Dipper's real name, but it served him as well as an alias, since no one ever called him by it.

While he made friends with the cats, Bet fetched the tea things, and Mrs. Wheeler made the tea. When it was ready, Dipper sat down opposite Mrs. Wheeler and helped himself to gooseberry jam. It was very good, and he told her so.

"You've got a sweet tooth," she said.

"Yes, ma'am, uncommon."

"My eldest girl—that's my married daughter, Millie—had such a sweet tooth, you can't think. You won't have a tooth in your head by the time you're twenty, I'd tell her, and how will you find a husband then, I'd like to know? But all my worriting was for naught—she married a law-stationer in Holborn and has three fine boys, and every Friday I go to visit her in the morning and stay till Saturday. 'Course, I have to bring Bet with me, since the poor thing's off at the side and can't be left alone. I wish Mr. Wheeler'd lived to see his grandchildren grow up so bright and bobbish. He was a glovemaker, with a shop quite close to here. When he died, I didn't want to leave the neighbourhood, so I took this little house, as it's quiet, and the cats can run about without being trampled by horses or teased by those hateful boys."

"Bit of a lonely place, though, ain't it?"

"Well, I used to have a neighbour, in that big house on the other side of the court. But *she* was worse than no neighbour at all. Bless me, you wanted to ask me a question, and I forgot all about it. What is it?"

Dipper would have liked to hear more about the neighbour and resolved to make his way back to her as quickly as possible. "I was looking for an old friend of me ma's—me godmother, she was. We hadn't heard from her in so long, me ma asked me to find out if she was all right. I had an idea she lived here, but it seems I was all out."

"Indeed you were. No one's lived in Cygnet's Court these

twelve months and more except me and Mrs. Desmond—
that's the woman I was telling you about. And *she* was never
your mother's friend, I'll be bound!"

"Wasn't she, ma'am?"

"Mercy on us, no. Too young, and not the sort to be anybody's godmother. Not that I ever knew her, to speak to. She
gave herself such airs, she'd never have wasted a morning call
on such as me. Not that I'd have received her if she *had* come
a-calling—knowing what I know. Mrs. Desmond—humph! If
she was ever Mrs. anything, I'd be much surprised."

"No better than she should be, was she?" Dipper asked
confidentially.

"Well, of course, I wouldn't know—not for a fact. But I've
got eyes. She moved in about a year ago, lived all alone except
for a maid-of-all-work, and a man called on her often, and
always at night! I never got a good look at him—the court's
too poorly lit. I only saw what you'd call his silhouette. He
was young, though—I could tell by his spare, straight figure,
and the way he walked. Dressed like a gentleman, too. Now
what was I to make of that, except the very worst?"

"Sounds like a rum go," Dipper owned.

"And she never had any proper callers. Just tradespeople:
mantua-makers, milliners, and upholsterers. It seemed she
had nothing to do but put fine clothes on her back and fine
furnishings in her house. And she never went to church! Oh,
it was a dreadful thing, Mr. Stokes, living almost next door to
a woman like that. I can't tell you how relieved I am she's
gone." She sighed disconsolately.

"Her maid went to church, though," she resumed. "Poor
thing, she seemed like a God-fearing soul. She must have been
troubled in her mind about working for a bad lot like Mrs.
Desmond. P'raps that's why she was so shy and timid,
wouldn't talk much, and 'specially would never say a word
about her mistress, nor her mistress's gentleman friend. I'd
often see her passing in and out of the court and invite her in
for a dish of tea, but the poor thing never would stop."

Dipper tried an experiment. "I think I seen her once—the

maid, I mean. I come here once before—the first of April, I
believe it was." That was the date the maidservant had
brought Mrs. Falkland into Cygnet's Court, and Mr. Kestrel
thought dates might be important. "She was blond and pretty,
wasn't she?"

"Who, the maid? Not at all. Drab and thickset, and forty
at least."

"The gal I seen was blond and light-timbered, with big
blue eyes and a brown checked dress, and a white cap with
lappets."

"Ain't that curious! Fanny, the maid, dressed just like that.
But the blond, pretty girl—why, she sounds like Mrs. Desmond herself."

"You think she might've put on her maid's togs?"

"Lord save us! Why should she do such a thing? Still, I
wouldn't put anything past her. What a pity I missed seeing
what she was about! Not that I'd want anything to do with
such goings-on, you understand."

" 'Course not."

"I just think, if people are going to dress up in their servants' clothes—well, respectable people ought to keep an eye
on them, and see they don't do anything to disgrace the
neighbourhood."

"That's the ticket," said Dipper encouragingly. "You has
to think of the neighbourhood."

"To be sure. Stop a moment: did you say it was April first
you saw her? Why, there you are!—that was a Friday, so I'd
have been at Millie's. What a pity! Now we'll never know what
deviltry she was up to, seeing as how she's gone away Heaven
knows where, and Fanny with her."

"When did she pike off?"

"A little over a fortnight ago, sudden-like. Just whistled off
one night, and as it was a Friday, I didn't see her go."

Apparently everything hole-and-corner that Mrs. Desmond
did was timed for a Friday—the one day in the week when
her inquisitive neighbour would be gone. Mrs. Wheeler was
clearly the kind of old woman who liked things just so: an

orderly house and an unshakeable routine. Her comings and goings would be utterly predictable, and Mrs. Desmond would soon learn all about them.

"I thought at first she'd done a moonlit flit," Mrs. Wheeler went on. "Her fancy-man had cast her off, and she had to run from her creditors. But the bailiffs haven't been in, so p'raps it wasn't that, after all. And it seems she didn't take anything that didn't belong to her—which you might have expected of one of her sort, seeing as how the house was let furnished. But the landlord's man came and took inventory a few days after she left and said there was nothing missing."

"Who's the landlord?" Dipper asked casually.

"He's Mr. Giles Underhill, of Clapham. He used to be a banker, but he's retired now, and prodigious lazy. He let these houses go to rack and ruin for years afore he furbished up mine and Mrs. Desmond's, and Heaven knows when he'll make the other three fit to live in."

Dipper thought a moment. "Did you ever see Mrs. Desmond with a gentry-mort—a real lady, that is—tall and golden-haired, a reg'lar stunner?"

"Lord-a-mercy, no! Mrs. Desmond never had anybody respectable to call on her." She added in a hushed, conspiratorial voice, "She did bring young women home with her once in a way. She'd go out during the day and come back with some pretty girl, and at night her gentleman friend would come, then the girl would leave a few hours later. Well, what was I to think of that, Mr. Stokes? What was anyone to think?"

"Was it al'ays the same gentleman?"

"I'm sure it was. I knew his shadow and his step, though I never saw his face."

So Mrs. Desmond was not a bawd, thought Dipper, or not in the usual sense. It looked as if she had been pimping for one particular man, for whom her own charms were not enough. Lord knew, there was plenty of choice in this neighbourhood: high-fliers sporting fine jewels and coaches, actresses making ends meet between roles, draggle-tails who would stoop to anything for the price of their next drink. But what could Mrs. Falkland have to do with such people? Could it be Mrs. Desmond's gentleman friend had fancied her and put Mrs. Desmond up to approaching her on his behalf?

That might explain why Mrs. Falkland was so secretive about her visit to Cygnet's Court. Whether she had accepted or spurned the man's advances, she would want to keep the episode dark. After all, once people knew a lady had been involved in any intrigue, they were quick to believe the worst of her. And suppose Mr. Falkland had found out? Gentleman fought duels about such things. If Mrs. Desmond's fancy-man saw a duel in the offing, might he have sought to ward it off by striking first?

※

At the theatre that evening, Julian found he was an object of more interest than the actors. Of course he was used to being stared at. Strangers to London pointed him out as they might Carlton House or the Tower of London. Aspiring dandies took note of how many seals he wore on his watch-chain (never more than two) and whether he approved of coloured cravats in the evening (he did not). But tonight he attracted a particularly rapt, nervous attention, especially from those who had been guests at Alexander Falkland's last party. Gentleman peered at him through quizzing-glasses. Ladies whispered about him behind their fans. He kept his eyes on the stage, making one of an eccentric minority in the dress boxes who actually came to the theatre to watch the play.

During the interval, he joined the crowd in the crush room, where he chatted with female friends about the actors' abilities and with male friends about the actresses' ankles. He helped remove a tipsy acquaintance to the open air and fetched lemonade and negus for ladies who dared not run the gauntlet of flash-girls in the refreshment rooms. All the while, he did not so much as mention the word *murder* or Alexander Falkland. People were relieved, then disappointed, then chagrined. And before the interval was over, Alexander's acquaintances began sidling up to him, whispering that he might wish to talk to them later. "Indeed?" Julian would reply, lifting his famous eyebrows, as if challenging them to have anything useful to say. Then they would bridle and hint at portentous revelations they might make. Was he going to the rout at Lady Gillingham's later that night? Good—they would have a word with him there.

After the performance came the ritual of standing about in the crush room, waiting for carriages to pull up before the theatre one or two at a time. An insinuating voice spoke at Julian's elbow: "How clever you are, Mr. Kestrel!"

He turned. It was Lady Anthea Fitzjohn, magnificently gowned in purple satin, with diamond earrings sparkling through the glossy black curls around her face. Her real hair was tucked into a turban-like headdress adorned with ostrich plumes.

"My dear Lady Anthea, you overwhelm me."

"Overwhelm *you?*" Her wicked little black eyes danced. "Oh, surely not, Mr. Kestrel! I shouldn't think armed dragoons could accomplish that."

"What are armed dragoons to a word and a smile from you?"

"Oh, I do like it when young men flatter me. Of course it's all flummery, but a harmless enough pleasure—less expensive than cards and far better for the complexion than Madeira. I'm perpetually waiting for one of you young gallants to marry me for my money. I'm frightfully rich, you know, and I've led such a very *respectable* life that I'm surely entitled to a little excitement and heartbreak at my age. Don't you think?"

"Lady Anthea, I am the happiest of men. Only name the day, and I shall place an announcement in the *Morning Post.*"

"Odious man!" She laughed, making creases in her dry, rouged cheeks. "As if I'd give up the fun of making my relatives guess what I mean to do with my money. Shall you bring an action against me for breach of promise, I wonder?"

"Can you doubt it? When the jury looks on you and sees what I've lost, the damages will be tremendous."

"Brazen creature! I take leave to tell you, I know perfectly well what you're about."

"I beg your pardon?"

"Keeping so silent, and shooting out your little penetrating glances. You mean to drive us all to distraction—those of us who were at the Falklands' party, I mean. We know you're looking into the murder, and we can't make out if you brush us aside because you suspect us, or because you think our observations of so little value."

"My dear Lady Anthea, what a relief someone has finally noticed. I was beginning to worry for people's wits. I hope you don't mean to give me away?"

"And miss seeing you torment all my dear friends? Not for worlds! On the contrary, I mean to play into your hands—"

A servant's voice boomed out: "Lady Anthea Fitzjohn's carriage stops the way!"

"How vexatious!" she declared. Then she brightened. "Are you going to Lady Gillingham's?"

"Yes."

"Splendid—so am I. Allow me to take you in my carriage. We can talk quite privately there." She sighed. "If only I were younger, or you older, what a scandal we might cause!"

✳

There was an immense snarl of traffic outside the theatre. Julian and Lady Anthea entered her carriage, drew the curtains, and settled in for a long chat. Julian began by asking her opinion of Alexander.

"Oh, I thought the world of him! Present company excepted, he was quite the most agreeable young man I knew. So attentive and polite, so amusing, always knowing when to talk and when to listen. Never rowdy in public, never boring, and never bored. And then, he had such exquisite taste! His house is a positive work of art. I do hope Mrs. Falkland doesn't make a mull of it, now he's gone."

"Do you think that's likely?"

Lady Anthea leaned toward him confidentially. "Well of course, everyone knew the house was all his handiwork. In fact, everything the Falklands achieved—their entertainments, their popularity, the admiration they commanded—was his doing. I grant you, she's good-looking enough. But that merely shows his collector's instinct extended to people as well as things."

"You're suggesting he chose a wife as he might an Aubusson carpet, to decorate his house?"

"Well, not precisely. An Aubusson carpet hasn't an estate in Dorset with an income of ten thousand a year."

Julian was not sure how seriously to take these gibes. He knew how spiteful Lady Anthea could be toward the wives of young men she liked. "You don't think he was as much in love with her as he appeared?"

"I think he was bored to distraction by her. What does she know about except horses? At heart she's merely a country miss, while he was a highly cultivated young man with a wealth of interests."

"Tell me about his last party. Did you see much of him?"

"I saw him quite frequently. You know how he always managed to be everywhere at once. But we hadn't any opportunity for a *tête-à-tête.*"

"Do you know if there was any trouble between him and Mrs. Falkland's maid?"

"Heavens! I heard she was a forty-year-old spinster, and positively *muscular.* You don't say she'd been making sheep's eyes at him?"

"No, hardly. But he seems to have been unpleasantly startled when she called him out of the party."

"He was probably worried about his wife. She'd retired with a headache, you know. Such a curious thing, her falling ill like that! She didn't look at all unwell when the evening began."

"I'm told you were especially solicitous in asking after her."

"Oh, come, let's be quite candid. I knew what must have happened. She and Alexander had quarelled, and she'd retired in a pet. Or else that awful boy, her brother, was having a fit or some such thing. But I thought a quarrel far more likely."

"Are you still of the same mind?"

"Now if I say yes, you'll think I mean to accuse dear Mrs. Falkland of killing her husband. Which of course I *never* would." She smiled archly.

"After Falkland left the party, you questioned Clare closely about where he'd gone and what he was doing. Why?"

"My dear Mr. Kestrel, because I thought he knew. He and Alexander were such close friends, though I'm sure I can't think why, poor Mr. Clare being so desperately awkward and having nothing to say for himself. Alexander was gone from the party so long, and of course now we know why, but at the time it was quite mysterious. The house was becoming a positive Gothic castle, with people disappearing right and left— first the mistress, then the master."

Yet another witness who did not seem disturbed by her lack of alibi, he thought. For of course Lady Anthea, in common with most of the other guests, could not fully account for her whereabouts between ten minutes to twelve and a quarter after. "Did you see anything of David Adams?"

"Oh, yes. He looked particularly dark and dangerous. I've always thought he had something of the corsair about him. He would make a superb villain."

"Don't you think him rather too obvious a scapegoat?"

"Oh, don't mistake me. I don't believe for a moment he killed Alexander. Hitting a man with a poker isn't his sort of crime at all. He would be far more likely to knock his adversary down—or, better still, ruin him financially. No, whoever killed Alexander was weak but clever: subtle in design, but passionate in hatred. In short, Mr. Kestrel—this was a woman's crime."

✳

It was nearly three in the morning when Julian got home from Lady Gillingham's. He had learned little of interest there. Not that Alexander's friends were reticent. If anything, they were too prodigal in their recollections—too inclined to twist ordinary incidents into omens of the violence to come. Then, of course, anyone who had been observed to envy or criticize Alexander was at pains to explain that he liked him very well, had never wished him any harm, and so on. And there was a great deal of finger-pointing, especially at David Adams. As Julian had foreseen, many of Alexander's acquaintances resented his thrusting Adams upon them and thought he had paid the price for befriending a tradesman and a Jew.

Dipper's account of his interview with Mrs. Wheeler was more promising. It seemed likely that the mysterious maidservant who had accosted Mrs. Falkland was Mrs. Desmond dressed in her maid's clothes. But what was her business with Mrs. Falkland? If they were meeting for some illicit purpose, why would Mrs. Falkland have brought Alexander, only to fob him off with the feeble excuse of a sick friend? Yet the rendezvous must have been planned, or how had Mrs. Desmond known Mrs. Falkland would be in the Strand at that hour, so near the entrance to Cygnet's Court? Perhaps Mrs. Falkland had meant to go alone, but at the last minute Alexander proposed to go with her, and she dared not refuse.

Mrs. Desmond and her maid must be found; Julian would write to Vance about it in the morning. The best thing he could do now, he supposed, was sleep. But something was nagging at his mind. It was the calendar: the sequence of seemingly disconnected events leading up to Alexander's murder. He could not rest until he had written them down; on paper they might make more sense. He knew he was really too tired to think this out; he also knew he would not sleep until he did.

He exchanged his evening coat and waistcoat for a dressing gown. Dipper made him coffee laced with brandy, a drink he enjoyed not only for the taste but for the pleasing effect on his head—both soothing and stimulating. He sent Dipper to bed and took the steaming cup into his study. Tying back the ruffles on his cuffs to keep them from trailing in the ink, he wrote:

## CHRONOLOGY OF EVENTS
## LEADING UP TO ALEXANDER'S MURDER

*March 1825*
*Two mining investments of Alexander's failed.*
*Mrs. Falkland urged Alexander to send Eugene back to school. He refused, telling her she knew his reasons.*

*Friday, 1 April*
*Alexander and Mrs. Falkland went to an ironware showroom in the Strand. Mrs. Desmond approached them, dressed in her maid's clothes. They talked, then Alexander departed in the coach, telling the coachman and Luke that Mrs. Falkland was going to visit a sick friend. Mrs. Falkland went with Mrs. Desmond into Cygnet's Court. Luke says she came home about three hours later. Both he and Mrs. Falkland are concealing something about the episode.*

*Saturday, 2 April*
*Alexander recorded in his ledgers Adams's forgiveness of his notes-of-hand.*
*Mrs. Falkland and Alexander told Eugene he was to return to Harrow in a fortnight. Eugene accused Mrs. Falkland of wanting to be rid of him and appealed to Alexander. Alexander said he had been obliged to accede to Mrs. Falkland's wishes.*

*First half of April*
*Eugene hardly spoke to Mrs. Falkland, who was seen to be under a strain.*

*Night of Friday, 15 April*

The nib of Julian's quill split, leaving a little star-shaped smear. While he repaired it with a penknife, he thought over the events of the night of 15 April. There were three, and their juxtaposition took him aback. What, if anything, could they have to do with one another?

> *Mrs. Desmond and her maid disappeared from Cygnet's Court.*
> *Eugene stayed out all night in the rain.*
> *The Brickfield Murder.*

He stared at the three events. How might they be linked? The first two had occurred in London, the last near Hampstead, but Hampstead was only some four miles away. A good horse could cover the distance in half an hour, especially between midnight and dawn, when traffic was sparse. But what conclusions followed? That Eugene was the Brickfield Murderer? That Mrs. Desmond or her maid had been the victim?

He finished off the chronology:

> *Night of Friday, 22 April*
> *Alexander was murdered.*

> *Sunday, 1 May*
> *I met Sir Malcolm at Alexander's grave and agreed to take part in the investigation.*

He blotted the sheet, then lay back in his chair and closed his eyes to think it all out.

He was back in the churchyard in Hampstead, making his way toward Alexander's grave. Trees loomed up before him, creepers caught at his feet, paths tied themselves into inextricable knots. At last he saw the grave ahead, bathed in light just as on the day he met Sir Malcolm there. But this light was white and cold, and as he drew nearer, he saw that the figure beside the grave was not Sir Malcolm. It was Alexander himself, dressed in evening clothes and looking quite at his ease. *No one can identify me,* he explained, smiling, *because my face has been destroyed.*

Julian woke up. The fire was dying, his candle was burnt out, and a cold grey dawn was breaking. He went to bed.

# ✳ 10 ✳

## REMEMBER
## YOUR SISTER

In the morning, a messenger arrived from Vance with a file on the Brickfield Murder. Julian sent back a letter thanking Vance, explaining briefly what Dipper had learned from Mrs. Wheeler, and asking Vance to find Giles Underhill, the landlord of Cygnet's Court, and sound him about Mrs. Desmond.

The reports on the Brickfield Murder made gruesome breakfast reading. The victim was found at about eight o'clock on the morning of 16 April. She was thought to have been dead about six hours. She was lying on her back, her clothes and hair and the remains of her face all smeared with wet, clayey mud. There was no evidence of a struggle. She seemed to have lain quite passive while her face was smashed; perhaps she had been drunk or unconscious. There was little to identify her. Her age was estimated at forty or forty-five. She was about five feet five inches tall, with a stocky figure and brown hair going grey. She wore a drab, buff-coloured gown, cheap boots, and woollen stockings.

The inquest resulted in a verdict of willful murder by a person or persons unknown. Subsequent enquiries proved vain. Then the news of Alexander Falkland's murder all but drove the Brickfield Murder from people's minds. Julian could not but contrast the assiduous hunt for Alexander's killer with the rather perfunctory investigation into the brickfield woman's death. It was inevitable, of course: Alexander had been a darling of the *beau monde,* while the brickfield victim was apparently a nobody, and her murder was important chiefly to the labouring classes, who might have to walk alone through abandoned brickfields at night. No one had associated the two crimes. And why should they? Julian thought. What could the sordid beating of an unknown woman have to do with Alexander Falkland, beloved of the gods, struck down in the flower of his youth and promise?

Except, of course, that both crimes were connected with Hampstead. Except that they happened just a week apart, and in each case the victim was fatally bludgeoned with an object conveniently to hand: a piece of brick from the brickfield, and the poker in Alexander's study. Coincidence? Perhaps. But if it was not, then for the third time in his career of solving crimes, Julian would have to identify an unknown female victim and try to fathom who had had reason to kill her.

\*

From the window of his hackney coach, Julian gazed out at legal London in the bustle of term-time. Black-clad solicitors with tightly furled umbrellas and blue bags held whispered colloquies with clients. Ink-stained clerks rushed about with menacing sealed documents or sat hunched over desks at dingy windows. Even the local shopmen were cogs in the legal machine: booksellers, robe-makers, law-stationers.

Julian got out of his hackney in Carey Street, at the gateway to Lincoln's Inn. Shabby-genteel men in dirty neckcloths and patched boots shuffled out of his way; presumably their business was with the Insolvent Debtors' Court down the street. He passed through the gateway and asked the porter to direct him to Quentin Clare's chambers in Serle's Court.

Serle's Court was a neat, gravelled square with a fountain and a diminutive clock tower in the centre. Rows of handsome brown-brick houses ran along three sides; the fourth was open to give a view of the gardens beyond. Julian ascended the creaky wooden stairs of No. 5 and found Clare's chambers by the name painted on the door. He knocked.

A door opposite opened, and a spindly young clerk in green spectacles looked out. "Mr. Julian Kestrel?"

"Yes."

"He's expecting you. He arst me to tell you he was called away, but he'll be back directly. Go on in if you like—he won't mind."

Julian was not sorry to have an opportunity to look around Clare's chambers in private. He thanked the clerk and went in.

The chambers consisted of a parlour and bedroom. The parlour was sparsely but comfortably furnished, remarkable only for its enormous quantity of books. They ranged over every shelf, cluttered up the mantelpieces and window sills, and stood in rows along the skirting-boards. Most were worn with reading; some of the bindings had been broken and lovingly tied or glued together. Julian opened a few at random and found that many passages were underscored, and notes had been written in the margins in a neat, light hand.

Not surprisingly, legal tomes occupied a prominent place: Blackstone's *Commentaries*, a forbidding treatise called *Principles of Pleading*, and a variety of books on trials, evidence, and the criminal law. But there were also political economists like Smith, Ricardo, and Malthus; historians from Herodotus and Livy to Gibbon and Guizot; Greek and Roman philosophers and their modern counterparts, including Hegel (in German) and Saint-Simon (in French). Traditional political thinkers like Burke and Locke stood cheek by jowl with the utilitarian Bentham, the evangelical Wilberforce, the radicals Godwin and Paine. And there were dramatists and poets in numerous languages, both living and dead.

Evidently Clare was far more of a scholar than the Bar required, or his tongue-tied manner revealed. Here might lie the explanation for the friendship between him and Alexander, which had surprised so many of Alexander's worldly friends.

Perhaps Clare had appealed to Alexander's intellectual side—the side that devoured books on law and political economy, wrote long philosophical letters to his father, and worried about the plight of factory workers.

One book in particular caught Julian's eye: Mary Wollstonecraft's *Vindication of the Rights of Woman.* He had read it some years ago in Paris, in a contraband French translation; the restored Bourbon monarchy did not look kindly on such revolutionary sentiments. In England the book was not absolutely proscribed, but no respectable woman would read it, and most men regarded it as scandalous rubbish.

He took it down and leafed through it. The binding was frayed and faded, the pages so brittle it was hard to turn them without the corners dropping off. Like the other books, it had notes in the margins, but the handwriting was different: quick, firm, impetuous. One sentence had been circled in blue ink and studded with exclamation points:

> *I love man as my fellow, but his sceptre, real or usurped, extends not to me, unless the reason of an individual demands my homage; and even then the submission is to reason, not to man.*

The same hand had written *"Yes, yes, yes!"* beside the passage:

> *. . . if fear in girls, instead of being cherished, perhaps created, were treated in the same manner as cowardice in boys, we should quickly see women with more dignified aspects. It is true, they could not then with equal propriety be termed the sweet flowers that smile in the walk of man; but they would be more respectable members of society, and discharge the important duties of life by the light of their own reason. "Educate women like men," says Rousseau, "and the more they resemble our sex the less power they will have over us." This is the very point I*

*aim at. I do not wish them to have power over men; but over themselves.*

As Julian was closing the book, it fell open to the flyleaf. There the bold blue pen had dashed off:

*My dearest Quentin,—I want you to have this, my best-beloved book, so that when you're reading and writing and dreaming about the rights of men, you'll remember the wrongs of women—those thousands of human souls who have no voice in Parliament and no status in law. But, most of all, remember your sister, who loves you more than all the world,*

*Verity*

"Mr. Kestrel," said a quiet, rather husky voice.

Julian turned. "Good morning, Mr. Clare."

Clare started to speak again—then he saw the book in Julian's hand. His eyes dilated, and the words died on his lips.

"I beg your pardon for taking this down from the shelf." Julian spoke lightly, affecting not to notice his discomfiture. "It's so rarely seen and has such an infamous reputation, I couldn't resist the opportunity to look at it. I hope you're not offended at my reading the note on the flyleaf?"

"Not at all, it's quite all right."

"I wasn't aware you had a sister."

"She—she doesn't live in London."

"I'm sorry to hear that. I should have liked to meet her—she seems a remarkable woman."

"Yes—she is."

"Where does she live?"

"In Somerset, with our great-uncle. I'm sorry to have kept you waiting—I was called away briefly. Please sit down."

"Thank you."

"I'm afraid I haven't anything to offer you to drink. I could send to a public house—"

"You needn't on my account."

"Oh. Thank you. I mean—" Clare did not seem to know what he meant. He hung his hat on a peg and sat down opposite Julian, twisting his fingers together.

He was in his early twenties, pale, with a narrow face and fair, straight hair that tended to fall into his eyes. They were fine eyes, grey and serious—his one claim to good looks. He was thin and rather delicate. As if to hide this, he wore loose, ill-fitting clothes: a black frock coat and trousers, a buff waistcoat, and a white cravat wound thickly around his neck. Julian, who was accustomed to learn a good deal about people by how they dressed, observed that his clothes were country tailoring, serviceable but without style.

"I want to thank you, first, for agreeing to talk with me so readily," Julian said. "You make my task far easier. I should like to ask you some questions about the night of the murder, and about your relationship with Alexander Falkland."

Clare shifted in his seat. "Of what importance is my relationship with him?"

"It's merely background. How did you meet him?"

"We were both students here. He didn't live in chambers, being married, but he was obliged to dine in Hall a certain number of times per term—keeping term, we call it. We dined in the same mess."

"When did you first meet?"

"A little over a year ago, when Falkland started here."

"You were here already?"

"Yes. I started the previous term."

"How did you and he become particular friends?"

Clare looked away, pushing the unruly hair back from his brow. "Last year, in Easter term, I was taken ill at dinner. I think I may have eaten a bad oyster. Falkland offered to help me back to my chambers. I tried to dissuade him, because there's a rule that if you leave Hall before the final grace is said, you lose credit for that day's attendance, and I didn't want him to forfeit the dinner on my account. But he insisted, and I was too ill to prevent him. After that—" He paused and seemed to choose his words carefully. "An intimacy grew up between us. He would come to my chambers, and I would go to his parties. He was good enough to introduce me to his friends."

"What sorts of things did you and he talk about?"

"The sorts of things you'd expect. The practice of law, trials we'd seen, social engagements."

"What did you see in him?"

"What do you mean?"

"Why did you like him? What made you choose to be his friend?"

"I think it was he who chose me."

"Why?"

Clare hung fire, then said quietly, his eyes on the carpet, "I don't know."

"Let me be frank with you, Mr. Clare. What I find most enigmatic about this crime is Alexander himself. There's a great deal I don't understand about him. And I have an idea that you knew him extremely well—better than his father, perhaps even better than his wife. I'm afraid I distress you?"

Clare had risen and was shading his eyes with his hand. "This is—very painful—very difficult—"

"He was as dear to you as that?"

Clare buried his face in his hands.

Julian gave him a moment to recover. When he lifted his head, he was flushed, but his eyes were tearless. "I'm sorry. Please go on. You said you thought I knew Falkland better than those closest to him. I hope you're mistaken. I should be sorry to think I'd usurped a greater share of his confidence than his family."

There was a pause. Then Julian asked, "Do you look at your watch very frequently?"

"I don't think so," Clare said, surprised.

"In your statement to Bow Street, you said that on the night of the murder you left the party at twenty-five minutes to twelve and went into the hall for a breath of air. At twenty minutes to one, you went downstairs and saw the light in the study. Why were you keeping such close track of the time?"

"Because I intended to go home after the supper was served at one, and I wanted to see how near to that time it was."

"Why were you planning to go home at one?"

"Because it was the earliest I felt I could leave without being discourteous." Clare got up and began to stir the fire. "I don't like parties. I feel very out of place at them."

"Yet you went to a great many of Alexander's."

"He asked me."

"Were you in the habit of doing everything he asked?"

Clare's hand shook, causing the poker to clatter against the bars of the grate. "No." After a moment, he added more steadily, "He liked me to come to his parties. He took great pride in them. And he thought it would advance my interests to meet people of consequence. I'm afraid I didn't make very good use of the opportunity. I never know how to put myself forward, or what to say in company."

"When you left the party the first time, you observed a conversation between Falkland and his wife's maid, Martha. She told him Mrs. Falkland wouldn't be down again that evening. And, according to you, he looked peculiar."

"Yes. Taken aback, disconcerted. I don't know why."

"You're certain she said nothing more to him than you've reported?"

"Quite certain, yes."

"You said David Adams was standing behind Falkland, and after Martha left he looked at Falkland malevolently. I believe that was your word?"

"It may have been."

"You must realize that if Adams was angry with Falkland that night, it tells heavily against him."

Clare pushed his hair back from his brow again. "I don't wish to implicate Mr. Adams. I hardly know him. I'm only reporting what I saw."

"Adams withdrew into the drawing room, and Falkland went over to you and took your arm to lead you back there as well. So there must have been a short period when you and he were alone in the hall?"

"Yes."

"Did he say anything to suggest he was about to go downstairs to his study?"

"No."

"Are you certain?"

Clare showed his first sign of impatience. "In light of what happened afterward, I shouldn't be inclined to forget it if he had."

"Did he tell you he was going upstairs to see his wife?"

"He didn't tell me specifically. He told everyone, after we'd gone back into the drawing room."

"Lady Anthea thinks he and Mrs. Falkland had quarrelled, and that was why she retired from the party."

"Yes, she hinted as much to me."

"She followed you about, I believe, trying to pump you for information."

"Yes. That's why I went downstairs—to escape from her questions and insinuations."

"Was there some basis for them? Had Falkland quarrelled with his wife?"

"I have no idea."

"Would he have been likely to tell you if he had?"

"Probably not. He rarely spoke to me about Mrs. Falkland."

"Lady Anthea told me she thinks this was a woman's crime."

Clare winced.

"Do you have a theory about who the murderer was?" asked Julian.

"No."

"If you did, would you tell me?"

"That would depend." Clare walked back and forth thoughtfully before the fire. "I don't think a mere theory worth very much. I would have to have concrete proof before I accused anyone of murder. A charge like that is apt to take on a momentum of its own. It's so much easier to plant a suspicion than it is to remove it."

Julian stared—surprised, then searching. Could it be? No, it was too outrageous. And yet it would answer so many questions—or, rather, it would reveal that the wrong questions were being asked.

He put it out of his mind. An idea like that could not be let loose without proof to back it. "It was you who found Falkland's body."

"Yes." Clare stopped walking and stood very still.

"What went through your head?"

"Horror. Disbelief. Repulsion. He looked ghastly. He would have hated that—to be an object of disgust. But I don't think that struck me until later. I wasn't capable of reflection at the time. I only knew I had to do something, summon someone. So I found the butler and footman and brought them down to the study."

"You showed great presence of mind, telling them not to touch anything."

"I suppose I did. I'm not sure how I knew about that. I must have read it in accounts of crime in the newspapers."

He sat down again, fairly collected now. Julian had the impression that, little though he cared to talk about the murder, he would rather discuss it than his relationship with Alexander. But there was one subject he would probably like even less. "Did Alexander ever meet your sister?"

Clare started. "No, I don't think so."

"You don't seem certain."

"I am certain. I mean, I feel sure my sister would have mentioned it, especially since Falkland's murder."

"She writes to you frequently, then?"

"No." He got up, scraping his chair. "No, not lately. May I ask—what has my sister to do with this?"

"Nothing that I know of. But you seem unwilling to speak of her, and in a murder investigation, anything people are reluctant to talk about becomes madly interesting. A really clever murderer would talk volubly about whatever seemed most likely to incriminate him. That would virtually ensure that no one took any notice of it."

"My not wishing to talk about my sister has nothing to do with Falkland's murder. You see, she—isn't very happy. You'll have gathered from looking at that book"—he gestured at the *Vindication*—"that she has unconventional views about the rights of women and their social role. It makes her discontented, keeps her from marrying or settling anywhere. I worry about her, but it seems I can't do anything to help her. I feel very responsible toward her. Our parents are long dead. She has no family except me and our great-uncle, who was our guardian."

"You say she lives with him in Somerset?"

"Yes." Clare's gaze slid away from Julian's. He went to the mantelpiece and leaned an arm on it, staring into the fire.

Julian followed and laid a hand on his shoulder, which went rigid under his fingers. "What are you afraid of, Mr. Clare?"

"I'm not afraid."

"You're very young, and you're out of your depth. You need a confidant."

"Please—"

"Whatever burden you're carrying, it's too heavy to bear alone. Let me help—"

"No!" Clare broke away from him. "You—you don't know what you're saying. No one can help me—" His voice cracked like a boy's. He swallowed hard and pressed his hands together. "There's nothing more I can tell you. I didn't kill Falkland. I don't know who did. I wish—"

"What do you wish?"

"That I'd never seen him. That I'd never come to this place. That's what I meant when I said you couldn't help me. Unless you can turn back the clock, roll back the calendar, there's nothing you can do."

"I hope you'll change your mind and confide in me, while you still have the luxury of doing it of your own free will." Julian put on his hat, then paused and picked up the Wollstonecraft book. "May I borrow this? I'll take good care of it, as it's a keepsake from your sister."

"What do you want with it?"

"I have an idea it has something to tell me. If nothing else, it will educate me about the rights of women. I shouldn't think your sister would object to that?"

"I don't think she'd object to anyone's being enlightened on that subject," Clare sighed. "Yes, you may borrow it if you wish."

"Thank you."

Julian took his leave, wondering if the book really did have something to tell him. That Verity Clare was important, he had no doubt. Clare was obviously afraid for her. He might have been telling the truth when he said she never knew Alexander; certainly she was not at the party at which he was killed. But the possibility remained that Alexander had let an unknown person into the house. The hypothetical John Noakes—who might have been a Jane.

# ✳ 11 ✳

## A SPORTING
## PROPOSITION

In keeping with his policy of appearing frequently in public
and letting the Quality approach him with information, Julian
betook himself to White's Club. As he entered the morning
room, he saw a group of young men with their betting books
out. The London beaux laid wagers on everything—not only
racing, boxing, and cricket, but anything with an uncertain
outcome: elections, love affairs, illnesses. When there was
nothing else to bet on, they invented wagers, the more absurd
the better. One young lord had recently sported two hundred
pounds that he could hop on one foot the length of St. James's
Street before a friend had finished reading a page of the *Morning Post* aloud.

When they saw Julian, they fell silent and cast him sidelong
glances. He had no difficulty guessing what they were betting
on now. He strolled up to them. "Well, gentlemen, what odds
have you given me?"

They looked at each other, some amused, others a little
nervous. At last one spoke up. "I've laid a hundred pounds
that you'll solve Falkland's murder in a fortnight."

"Only a hundred?" Julian lifted his brows. "I'd back myself
for five hundred, if I thought anyone would take me up."

"I'll take that bet." It was Oliver de Witt, a dandy who had
lately set himself up as a rival of Julian's. He was a wizened

young man with a pinched, patrician face and a long nose that seemed designed to be either turned up or looked down.

"I shouldn't if I were you, de Witt," warned one of the others, laughing. "After all, Kestrel holds all the cards. Only he knows what he's found out about Falkland's murder and can say when he's likely to turn up a trump."

"I don't believe he's found out anything to the purpose," de Witt retorted coldly. "As I understand it, the Bow Street Runners have been baffled by this crime for days. There's no evidence, and not the merest *soupçon* of a motive."

"What a great deal you know about the case," Julian marvelled. "You didn't kill him yourself, by any chance?"

"Must I remind you, I wasn't at his party."

"No, that's true," said Julian. "I'd forgotten how select it was."

De Witt glared. "Mr. Kestrel, I shall be delighted to take your wager, with one slight modification. I'll stake five hundred pounds against your solving Falkland's murder in—not a fortnight, but seven days."

"Done," said Julian promptly.

They entered the wager in their betting books: the murder to be solved by noon on Tuesday, the tenth of May. A flurry of subsidiary betting broke out among the other men.

Felix Poynter sidled out from among them and took Julian's arm. "My dear fellow, I've been pining to talk to you. Come into the coffee-room."

Felix was about Julian's age, the son of an autocratic peer from the bleak northeastern counties. Julian suspected that the grey, barren landscapes of his childhood accounted for his taste in clothes, which certainly needed excusing. Today he was wearing a canary-yellow tailcoat, white trousers, and two waistcoats, the inner of scarlet satin, the outer with black and white stripes. His neckcloth was a cherry-coloured India print, splashed with blue and yellow flowers. A bunch of gold seals, all shaped liked chessmen, dangled from his watch-chain. He had an amiably rangy figure and curly brown hair that tended to stand on end.

The two young men sauntered into the coffee-room and sat down at a corner table. A waiter brought them coffee, biscuits, and freshly ironed newspapers. Felix moved the newspapers aside, taking care not to let the ink rub off on his gloves. "You must be quite close to finding out who killed Falkland."

"Must I?" said Julian pleasantly.

"To make a wager like that, yes."

"Are you angling for a tip? That would hardly be sporting."

"Of course not, my dear fellow. I just wondered how you were getting on. I'm a bit involved in it all, you know. I was at Falkland's party."

"Yes, I read your statement to Bow Street."

"Did you?" said Felix, interested. "Did I say anything coherent? I was in an awful fret, what with the magistrates glaring at me, and the clerks snickering and picking their teeth with penknives, and a gaoler rattling his keys as if he'd made up his mind to lock *somebody* up, and I would do nicely."

"You were tolerably clear. You said you and Mrs. Falkland were talking, and she told you she had a headache and was going upstairs to lie down. I gather you thought the headache was genuine, and not simply an excuse to leave the party?"

"Oh, yes. She looked quite green about the gills."

"Did you see Falkland leave the party about an hour later?"

"No. I was with the crowd in the music room." Felix's eyes went dreamily out of focus. "Miss Denbigh was singing."

Julian regarded him with tolerant exasperation. "I take it she's your latest *grande passion?*"

"You must admit, she's a regular stunner!"

"I admit she has a head very like a china doll's: pretty to look at, and probably stuffed with sawdust, to judge by her conversation."

"You're too demanding, my dear fellow. When a girl has a face like that, I don't ask for conversation."

"You don't ask for anything. Don't you ever tire of languishing at women from a distance?"

"Not at all. I like it excessively. It's the only thing I've ever shown any talent for. Ask my father."

"You've had practice, at all events. Before Miss Denbigh, there was Miss Somerdale—and before her Miss Warrington, afterwards Mrs. Falkland."

Felix looked at him more closely. He had very round, light-blue eyes, which tended to give him an expression of child-like surprise. "Do you mean something by that, old fellow? Am I—*under suspicion,* is that the right term?"

"I must own, I find it hard to imagine you creeping up with a deadly weapon on anything more sentient than a roasted fowl. I've seen you turn green at a cockfight, and whenever I hear you've been hunting, I suspect you of giving aid and comfort to the foxes. All the same, you were at Falkland's party, and you can't set up an alibi for the period between ten minutes to twelve and a quarter after."

"Well, of course not, my dear fellow. Who in the world goes to a party thinking about a thing like that? Only conceive of it: 'Good evening, Duke. Devilish good champagne, isn't it? Shall you be entering your horse in the Derby this year? Well, must toddle off and pay my respects to Lady Thingummy. Oh, and could you please remember we talked at precisely six minutes after twelve? Just in case you should be asked to give evidence about it later.' "

"Very amusing. But the fact remains you haven't an alibi, and you once had a *tendre* for the victim's wife."

"You could say the same of half the fellows at that party. Remember what a smasher Belinda Warrington was when she came out? She took the shine out of every other female that season. Scores of fellows wanted to marry her. Why, they used to come to blows over who would dance with her."

That was true, Julian thought. He himself had admired Belinda Warrington in those days, although he had never been in any danger of falling in love with her. There was something about her that put him off. The image of Diana, the virgin goddess, suited her all too well. Even her present grief and despair were on an Olympian scale: bleak and tragic, without tenderness. A man who really loved her might find it rough going. How did one penetrate armour like hers? Alexander had evidently charmed his way in—but there were few men like Alexander.

"Of course," Felix was saying, "from the moment she met Falkland, no one else had a chance with her. She fell to him like spoils to the victor."

"Did you mind that very much?"

"He gives me his owlish look," Felix informed an imaginary audience. "And of course I break down and confess that I've been brooding over Falkland's luck for months and waiting for a chance to knock him on the head with a poker. Oh, my dear Julian." Felix gazed at him in amused remonstrance. "Everyone could see that the match between her and Falkland was bound to be. Her beauty and wealth and his charm and talent belonged together. I wasn't likely to break my heart over that. It doesn't break in any event—it bounces. Else I should have nothing left of it by now."

Julian eyed him thoughtfully. "Do you know a Mrs. Desmond, by any chance?"

"Why? Is there a Mrs. Desmond who says she knows *me?* More important, is there a Mr. Desmond, and does he want my blood? It's really too bad, when I don't remember anything about it. I must have been in my cups—"

"My dear Felix, you're babbling."

"I know." Felix sighed. "This conversation is giving me rather a turn. It's all very well to make light of the murder, and bet on it and that sort of thing, but still, it *is* a murder."

"Yes. Tell me, did you like Alexander Falkland?"

"Of course. How could anyone help but like him?"

"I mean, was he your friend? Shall you miss him?"

"Seriously? No, I suppose not. What I think about Falkland is that he was spread too thin. Do you see what I mean? He was all things to all people, and nothing important to anybody. In a twelve-month, nobody will remember him—or if they do, it will only be for the way he died."

"I think that may be the profoundest and saddest thing anyone has said about him."

"I shall give us both a fit of the dismals in a moment. Let's change the subject. What do you think of my new coat?"

"I think the buttons will be very useful if we should happen to break any of the saucers."

"I wonder you can bear to be seen with me," said Felix sympathetically.

"It's a great advantage to be seen with you. You make every gentleman around you seem a model of taste and restraint."

He spoke lightly—then his thoughts took a serious turn. Why does a man surround himself with unprepossessing friends? An awkward, uncultivated boy like Eugene, a shy bookworm like Clare, a scorned outsider like Adams: what did they have in common that had appealed so strongly to Alexander? That they were all disadvantaged and needed his help? Or was it that they could never be his rivals—that his splendour shone all the more brightly, set against their flaws?

※

Felix left soon after. Julian remained in the coffee-room, appearing to read a newspaper but keeping an eye on on the gentlemen drifting in and out. For a while there were no likely prospects; then a promising fish swam into his net. Sir Henry Effingham, his bristly black hair combed into a crest, his long bluish chin thrust out above a stiffly starched cravat, came in and sat down with his back to the wall—a politician's instinct, Julian supposed. He snapped open a newspaper and ran his eyes swiftly up and down the columns, probably looking for a mention of his name.

Julian went to work. He peered over his newspaper at Sir Henry with what Felix called his owlish look. When Sir Henry caught him at it, he affected to be absorbed in the paper again. He repeated this manoeuvre several times. Finally, when the ebb and flow of men had left the room unusually empty, Sir Henry rose and stalked over to him. "Did you wish to speak to me, Mr. Kestrel?"

"I should be delighted to speak to you, Sir Henry, but I had no particular wish to do so."

"You were looking at me very persistently."

"I beg your pardon, but I don't believe I was. It's far too early in the day to be persistent about anything."

Sir Henry struck an attitude, one foot before him, hands grasping his lapels. "If you have anything to say to me, Mr. Kestrel, I should prefer you to say it straight out."

"I should be glad to oblige you, Sir Henry, if I had anything to say."

They met one another's gaze, giving no ground. They both knew that Sir Henry had been at Alexander's last party, and that, like most of the guests, he had no alibi for the crucial twenty-five minutes. Julian did not need to question him about that—Bow Street had been over it thoroughly. What he wanted to know was what Sir Henry would feel driven to say by his silence.

"May I sit down?" said Sir Henry, with awful politeness.

"By all means."

He took a seat, his hands folded on the table before him. Julian felt like a committee about to be addressed. "Mr. Kestrel, it's common knowledge that you're attempting to solve Alexander Falkland's murder. Naturally you wish to know my opinion on the matter. Falkland and I were acquainted; I might go so far as to say that we were friends. I had the greatest respect for him. Of course he was young and untried. I think no one can deny that."

"I wouldn't dream of denying it, Sir Henry."

"And it must be owned, he was given to dissipation, which was only to be expected in one so young, whose head had been a little turned by admiration. Still, he had considerable abilities. Whether he would have had the discipline to make good use of them, I'm not prepared to say."

"He seemed to make rather good use of them in money matters."

Sir Henry's mouth tightened. His own financial straits were well known. He had a tuft-hunting wife, a bevy of children, and an estate that was out at elbows. On top of all that, his Parliamentary seat had been fiercely contested, which had compelled him to spend even more on beer and bribery than the usual election required. Of late he had turned to the investment market to recoup his fortunes, so far with disastrous results.

"I grant you, he had talents in that line," Sir Henry allowed. "Of course, he was very lucky. And he had that Jew businessman behind him."

"You think Mr. Adams was responsible for his success?"

"Well, he certainly let him into a number of good things. I don't know why—usually those people stick pretty closely to their own kind."

"Surely Adams benefited by Falkland's introducing him into society. And by all accounts, they were friends."

Sir Henry smiled faintly and began to toy with one of the coffee cups. "Does Mr. Adams say so?"

"Why? Have you any reason to doubt it?"

"What if I were to tell you that Falkland didn't invite Adams to his party—the one where he was murdered? Adams invited himself, and Falkland wasn't altogther pleased."

We come to the root of it, Julian thought. This is what he came over here to tell me. But can he be trusted? He has no alibi for the murder, and every reason to implicate someone else. And who better than Adams, whom he despises for everything but his financial success, which he envies bitterly?

Still, there was no harm in hearing what he had to say. "You intrigue me, Sir Henry. Please explain."

"If I do, will you undertake to keep my name out of this? I don't care to have it bandied about the police courts. I assume that what I say to you as one gentleman to another will be held in confidence?"

"Insofar as possible, Sir Henry."

Sir Henry smiled sourly. In his walk of life, he must be used to noncommittal answers. "I take that to mean that, unless you are compelled to reveal the source of this information, you will not do so?"

"Precisely."

"Very well. The day before Falkland's party, I went to the sale at Tattersall's." Tattersall's was an auctioneering house where sporting gentlemen bought their horses and carriages, settled their racing debts, and hung about talking of hunting and the turf. "You know that little circle of columns with a statue in the middle? I was standing on one side of it, and Falkland was on other. I hardly noticed him till Adams came up and accosted him. Being hemmed in by groups of people, I was obliged to overhear a good part of their conversation."

And to pick up any investment tips they happened to drop, Julian thought. "How very awkward for you."

"Yes, it was. I don't think they saw me. They were absorbed in what they were saying. I don't remember it exactly, but I know Adams as good as invited himself to Falkland's party the following evening. He was quite peremptory about it, as if saying 'I want to come' were enough to command an invitation."

"How did Falkland respond?"

Sir Henry knit his brows. "He seemed surprised. He said 'Really?' or some such thing, and then 'Do you think that's wise?' Then Adams demanded to know if he was invited or not."

"Was he angry?"

"He was—impassioned. His voice shook a little. I think that may be why I remember the conversation so well. It naturally seemed of little importance at the time. But Adams's intensity surprised me. I suppose there was money involved—that's the only thing those people care desperately about."

Julian did not consider this worthy of a response. "Please finish your story, Sir Henry."

"As I said, Adams demanded to know if he was invited. Falkland was quite unruffled. He laid his hand on Adams's shoulder for a moment, in a friendly way, and said 'My dear fellow, since you ask so graciously,' or something of that sort. And he went off."

Julian frowned thoughtfully. The story sounded true to him.

If Sir Henry were lying in order to implicate Adams, he would surely have invented something more damning than this. So the next step, clearly, was to see David Adams and ask why he had wanted so badly to be at the party where Alexander met his death.

# ✻ 12 ✻

## THE ROOT
## OF ALL EVIL

David Adams's office was in Cornhill, in the heart of mercantile London. It was a world apart from the West End. The men here wore rusty black frock coats, carried umbrellas rather than walking sticks, and never strolled when they could hasten. The women were all plump tradesmen's wives and skinny maids of all work—no ladies, and no ladybirds. Street entertainers did not waste their time here; the only colourful sights were the Turks and East Indians in native dress around the Bank and the Royal Exchange. As for greenery, there was none to be seen, except through the rusty railings of churchyards.

It was strange, thought Julian, that one could move so quickly from the leisured world of White's to this dirty, noisy, energetic hive. The *beau monde* took pride in knowing nothing of this part of town; even Alexander Falkland, for all his love of speculation, had probably rarely been to Adams's office. What most struck Julian about the transition from west to east was the diminishing scale. The City was a labyrinth of little spaces: tiny courts, dark covered ways, dabs of shops, and dingy cubbyholes of offices. But perhaps it all seemed small to him in part because it had once looked so much larger, when he ran about these close, teeming streets as a child.

D. S. Adams and Company occupied an old brick building,

with a jutting, half-timbered garret that threatened to topple into the street. Julian enquired for Adams in the counting-house, which was the front room on the ground floor. Here half a dozen clerks sat on high stools and scribbled at little tilted desks, while a spotty-faced boy in the chimney corner sharpened quills and tended the fire. How they had gotten to their perches Julian had no idea, since they seemed hemmed in on all sides by leatherbound ledgers, stacks of blotting-paper, steel strongboxes linked together with chains, and a hodgepodge of inkwells, bits of sealing-wax, and hanks of string. A sheep-like smell of mutton-fat candles mingled with the dust and soot that flew about whenever a drawer shut or a pile of papers rustled. Tacked up on the walls were maps of unfamiliar nations, pages torn from almanacs, and pamphlets touting the latest foreign investments.

Julian's arrival brought a superior clerk in a green eyeshade out of a little back office. He greeted Julian civilly and took his card upstairs. Soon after, he returned to say that Mr. Adams would be glad to speak with Mr. Kestrel in quarter of an hour, as he was presently engaged with some Bolivian gentlemen. Julian said he would take a short walk in the meantime. Cramped spaces made him restless, and the dogged, slightly frantic activity here reminded him of his landlady, Mrs. Mabbitt, on one of her dreaded laundry days.

He returned just as the Bolivian gentlemen were leaving. Their intricately ruffled shirts and magnificent side-whiskers made vivid splashes of black and white in these grey surroundings. Adams saw them out, taking leave of them in fluent Spanish. Then he turned to Julian with his faintly ironic smile. "Mr. Kestrel. I expected you."

"Thank you for seeing me so readily. I hardly dared hope I would find you at liberty."

"You haven't. I've had to cry off from another appointment. But I knew I'd have to see you sooner or later, and I'd as lief have it over. Please come upstairs."

Adams's private office made a striking contrast to the counting-house below. The mahogany furniture was more suited to a gentleman's library than to a place of business. The inkstands were of Sèvres porcelain, the fireplace of porphyry. The walls were covered in red velvet and hung with paintings of ships and country landscapes. An elegant silver coffee service was set out on a table. The clerk with the green eyeshade came in and removed the urn and cups. "He'll bring us a fresh pot," said Adams. "I hope you don't object to coffee rather than tea?"

"No, I prefer it."

"So do the Bolivian gentlemen you just saw. They're looking to raise money to build a railway in their country. I don't think anyone in England is likely to bite. We don't know if we can make a success of a railway here, let alone on the other side of the world. Wait till the one between Liverpool and Manchester is finished—then we'll see."

"Do you think it will answer?"

"Too early to say." Adams smiled noncommittally. "Please sit down."

He gestured toward a pair of leather armchairs by the fire. He himself took the one facing the window, as if to show he had nothing to hide from its light. He was about five-and-thirty, with a lean, sharply chiselled face and a high brow. His hair and eyes were dark, his skin a fine, pale olive. He sat back, one long leg thrown over the other, his thin, rather beautiful hands resting easily on the arms of his chair.

"First," said Julian, "I should like to know why you demanded an invitation to the party at which Alexander Falkland was murdered."

Adams looked meditative, faintly intrigued, as though the matter were interesting but hardly important. Yet Julian saw how his hands tightened briefly round the arms of his chair. "I wasn't aware anyone knew about that."

"I have sources Bow Street doesn't."

"Evidently. I wished to attend the party for the same reason I was always looking to penetrate Falkland's world. I made connexions through him. More important, I picked up gossip. In my line of work, political and social news are of the first importance. The fate of a burgeoning industry or a foreign loan may hinge on whether some scented lordling is out of temper with his mistress or has just lost money on a horse. It seems absurd, but this is England, where the people who know least about business have the greatest sway over it. Not that Falkland's friends went out of their way to pass on news to me. But I learned a good deal by hanging about and listening—eavesdropping, if need be. Of course I wanted to attend his party. Though I hadn't expected it to be quite so exciting as it turned out."

"The source of my information says you were very insistent about going—that you seemed agitated, and your voice shook."

"Then your source is confused, or fanciful, or would like to see me dangling in a noose. Which means he or she could be very nearly anybody."

"Are you so unpopular?"

"I'm successful, which comes to the same thing. Naturally one has to step on a number of people and offend a good many more. I'm honest, Mr. Kestrel. What I say, I stand behind, and what I promise, I fulfill. I don't think many in the City can say as much. But I give no quarter, and I have scant patience with foolish or faint-hearted people. So I make enemies."

"What you're saying is that you had no desire to attend the party, other than your usual reasons for mixing with Falkland's set?"

"Exactly."

"When you told him you wanted to come, he asked, 'Do you think that's wise?' What did he mean?"

Adams's fingers tapped tensely on the chair-arm. "I don't recall his asking that."

"My source says he did."

"I say he didn't."

They locked gazes, giving no ground.

At length Julian said, "Tell me how you came to know Alexander Falkland."

"I met him about a year and a half ago. A mutual acquaintance recommended him to me as a possible investor. He went in with me on a financial scheme that turned a large profit. After that there were several others. Sometimes he asked me what I thought about speculations he was considering."

"Did he ask you about those two mining ventures that failed a few months before he died?"

"Oh, yes, he asked." Adams smiled sardonically. "I told him they weren't sound, and he'd be mad to risk his money. But he'd got out of the habit of listening to me. He asked my advice but didn't take it. There was nothing more I could do. He was my protégé, not my puppet."

He sat back, braced for Julian's next question. No doubt he expected it to be about the thirty thousand pounds. But Julian preferred to keep him off balance. "Did Falkland ever write to you?"

"On business matters, yes."

"Did you keep his letters?"

"I believe we have half a dozen or so in a drawer somewhere."

"I should like to borrow them."

"You can have them. I'm not sentimental."

The clerk with the green eyeshade brought in the coffee urn and two fresh cups and saucers. Adams told him to hunt up any correspondence from Alexander Falkland and give it to Mr. Kestrel when he left. The clerk kept an impassive face. If he was curious about his employer's involvement in a notorious murder, he was too well-trained to show it.

After he had gone, Julian praised the coffee, which was excellent, then returned to the matter at hand. "You arrived at the party at a quarter to eleven. Soon after, Mrs. Falkland withdrew on the plea of a headache. Have you any idea why she did that?"

"I assume, because she had a headache."

"Some people thought she and Falkland had quarrelled."

"Some people are busybodies."

"That's undeniable. But I should like to know what you think."

"I think it's a waste of time to ask me. I know nothing whatever about Mrs. Falkland's headache, or her reasons for leaving the party."

"You seem unnecessarily vehement."

"It may astonish you, Mr. Kestrel, but I don't relish talking about a lady of Mrs. Falkland's quality as if she were a light-skirt accused of kicking up a row with her fancy-man."

Julian's brows shot up. "Chivalry, Mr. Adams?"

"Hardly!" Adams laughed mirthlessly. "But thank you for crediting me with one of the gentlemanly virtues."

He looked into the fire, his profile hard as granite. Julian regarded him thoughtfully, then proceeded, "About an hour after you arrived at the party, you witnessed a brief conversation between Falkland and his wife's maid, Martha. She told him Mrs. Falkland wouldn't be returning to the party. Do you know of any reason her words or manner should have disconcerted him?"

"No. I know Mr. Clare says he looked taken aback. But I don't regard him as a particularly reliable witness, since Bow Street told me he also says that after she left, I looked daggers at Falkland."

"And that was a lie?"

"It wasn't the truth. Whether it was deliberately false, I couldn't say. There must be an overwhelming temptation to make me the villain of this piece. Perhaps Mr. Clare was indulging in a little wishful thinking."

Julian thought Clare might well be lying about a number of things, but this was not one of them. "When those two mining ventures of Falkland's went to smash, he was left owing some thirty thousand pounds. You bought up his notes-of-hand, and about three weeks before the murder, you forgave them unconditionally. Why?"

"You mean, why such generosity in one of my race?"

"Such generosity would be astonishing in anyone, Mr. Adams."

"Why shouldn't I have done him a good turn? Surely that's not a ground for suspecting me of murder?"

"On the contrary, Mr. Adams, it raises two disturbing possibilities. One is that he paid you for the notes in some fashion the two of you couldn't or wouldn't put on paper. The other is that he held something over your head to make you forgive his debt. Either way, you must see the affair needs explaining."

Adams's eyes glinted. "When you put your cards on the table, Mr. Kestrel, you don't do it by halves! But you don't seem to understand how important Falkland's friendship was to me. A business like mine stands or falls on its reputation. People are very chary whom they trust with their money— they want to know you're sound, and that you can offer them something your rivals can't. To hobnob with lords and MPs gave me that advantage. What I actually learned from them about trade or taxes wasn't half so important as giving the *impression* I knew about those things. I had Falkland to thank for that—and for a certain amount of amusement as well."

"Amusement?"

"A window on his world. A chance to peep through the bars of exclusivity at the *societé choisie* enjoying their *recherché* amusements."

"While you remained an outsider?"

"I'm a realist, Mr. Kestrel. I never deluded myself that Falkland's friends would accept me on equal terms. One day, perhaps, I'll be so rich they can't afford to despise me. You don't see people sneering at Nathan Rothschild—at all events, not to his face! Meantime, I was willing to bear with the contempt of Falkland's friends and use them for my own purposes."

"What about Falkland himself? Were you using him?"

"If I was, it was a fair exchange. He got exactly what he wanted out of our association: money."

"Was that so important to him?"

"Important!" Adams shot up out of his chair and walked rapidly back and forth. "It was essential. Falkland loved money. Or, rather, he loved the things it would buy: ornaments, enjoyments, power, people. That's why he sought my advice about his investments—and why he stopped taking it in the end. My business was too tame for him. I take risks, but they're well considered; in gentlemen's parlance, I don't bet on long odds.

"It wasn't only that he had a lust for money. He liked speculation: its ups and downs, its dangers, its prospects of great gains from little investments. He was bound to dish himself in the end—that's what happens to investors who treat the Stock Exchange like a gambling house. I warned him. I enjoyed warning him, because I knew he wouldn't listen—"

He stopped walking and clenched his fists. When he could speak more calmly, he finished, "So I just want you to know, I didn't lure him into making rash investments. Those mining ventures were entirely his own affair."

"It would be rather an expensive sport," Julian agreed, "inciting him to run up debts, then buying up his notes and presenting them to him tied up with a ribbon."

"I bought them at a discount, you know. I didn't pay the full thirty thousand."

"It's still an extravagant gesture—for a man you hated."

"Hated, Mr. Kestrel?" Adams opened his eyes in mock horror. "Falkland and I were friends."

"Indeed?"

"As surely as my name is David Adams."

But it was not David Adams, Julian recalled. His witness statement said he had changed it from Abrahms. An empty, ironic gesture, since he made no secret of his Jewishness. But irony was Adams's lifeblood. "What do you mean me to infer from that?"

"That facts are nothing, and appearances everything. You say I hated him—very well. You can't prove it. I was his friend, I salvaged his fortunes. I had the highest regard for him—such a charming, talented, open-hearted, principled young man!"

"In short—whom the gods love die young?"

"Whom the gods love die young." Adams broke into harsh, bitter laughter. *"But not young enough!"*

# * 13 *

## LONDON CLAY

When Julian left Adams's office, the clerk in the green eyeshade gave him a neat paper parcel containing Alexander Falkland's letters. He read them on his way home in a hackney coach. They were all short, written on monogrammed note-paper in Alexander's elegant hand. Most consisted of requests to buy or sell securities and enquiries about particular investments. The earliest dated back about a year; the most recent had been written this past March. They were all courteous and informal, more like notes to a friend than orders to a man of business. Alexander had had a knack for charming his subordinates—though Adams clearly had not succumbed to his spell.

One letter was a little longer than the others. It had been written last November from Mrs. Falkland's house in Dorset. It began with the usual enquiries about business matters, then continued:

> *This is a charming house—a sort of fairy cottage on a grand scale, all over gables, with great wooden window casements and a myriad of dwarfish doors. All the floors are a bit crooked; the sugar bowl tends to creep slowly down the table as breakfast progresses. All agreeably rural and idyllic, but the very devil for getting any news of*

*town. So be a good fellow and write to me about what
goes on at the Stock Exchange. I believe I miss it more
than all the clubs and theatres combined.*

Julian read the letter through twice. The idea that had first
flashed across his mind in Clare's chambers became a cer-
tainty. He would need proof, of course. But he knew how and
where to find it.

✳

When Julian got home, Dipper told him Vance had called
and had asked that Mr. Kestrel look him up at Bow Street as
soon as convenient. Julian set off.

The Bow Street Magistrate's Court consisted of a pair of
narrow brick houses hard by Covent Garden Theatre. Julian
arrived just as the prisoners arrested that day were being pa-
raded out, handcuffed in pairs, to be taken to their various
gaols. They were the usual thieves, prostitutes, and vagrants,
many no older than eighteen. Some were putting on a brave
show, others looked dull-eyed and indifferent, and a few hid
their faces in shame. A girl of about twelve, her rouge mottled
by tears, was dragging the hem of a grown woman's pink silk
dress along the dusty pavement. The entire neighbourhood
seemed to have turned out to goggle at them. Julian wondered
irritably if they had nothing better to do than watch the children of the poor on their dreary progress toward prison, transportation, or death.

He threaded his way through the crowd and went inside.
Vance had once assured him the Bow Street office was regu-
larly cleaned, but it always looked unutterably dingy, with
grime caked into the mouldings and paint peeling off the walls.
The hallway was packed with the angry or dolorous people
who always seemed to hang about here. Julian picked out a
Bow Street patrol by his scarlet waistcoat and asked him to
find Peter Vance.

"Mr. Kestrel." Vance pushed his way through the crowd.

"Hope you didn't mind me taking the liberty of sending for you, but I didn't want to lose any time."

"Not at all. What have you found out?"

"You remember you asked me to hunt up Mr. Underhill, the landlord of Cygnet's Court? Well I found him, and we had a confab, and it ended with him giving me the key to the house Mrs. Desmond used to live in. I thought we'd hoof it over there and have a look round. Though if you don't mind me saying so, sir, I don't quite see why you take such an interest in Mrs. Desmond and her doings."

"It may be all a mare's nest. My friend MacGregor says I'm too prone to spin extravagant theories about trifles. But it's certainly curious that a woman of Mrs. Desmond's character should have any dealings with Mrs. Falkland, that Mrs. Desmond should disappear a fortnight later, and that Alexander Falkland should be murdered a week after that."

"It *is* a bit rum, when you put it that way, sir. Anyhow, no harm in nosing around the house and seeing if there's aught to be found."

They set off for the Strand. On the way, Vance told Julian about his interview with Underhill. "He's a banker, retired, lives in Clapham. The houses in Cygnet's Court came into his hands through some relative's will. He complains they're nothing but bother. I wish some relative'd bother *me* like that—don't I just! He had two of the houses furbished up, but the others didn't seem worth the trouble. Nobody plump in the pocket'd want to live there. The court's too little and dark, and the entrance is too narrow to let in anything bigger than a gig. There's a story the place was going to be called Swan's Court, but it was reckoned to be too small."

Underhill did not know much about Mrs. Desmond, Vance said. He had only met her once and considered her "common"—probably somebody's bit of muslin discreetly tucked away. But he did not much care how his tenants got their living, as long as they paid their rent and gave no trouble.

"Did he have any idea who her protector was?" asked Julian.

"No. Though he thinks it must have been the man who wrote him this note after she hooked it."

He handed the note to Julian. It said simply that Marianne Desmond had permanently vacated the premises at Cygnet's Court, and that a month's rent was enclosed in lieu of notice.

Julian examined it more closely, turning it over once or twice. "Written on plain paper, in the kind of anonymous hand clerks use, and anyone can imitate. If Mrs. Desmond's lover wrote it, he obviously wanted to keep his identity dark. What do we know about him? Only what Mrs. Wheeler told Dipper: that he was young and dressed like a gentleman and only visited Mrs. Desmond at night. Quentin Clare is a possible candidate; so, unfortunately, is my friend Felix. Eugene is probably old enough, and Adams young enough. We can even envision Luke or Valère in borrowed evening dress. And then again, the whole affair may have nothing to do with Falkland's murder."

He gave Vance a brief account of his interviews with Clare, Felix, Sir Henry, and Adams. Vance chuckled. "I knew you'd loosen the bigwigs' tongues. Though what we're to make of what they've said is more than I can tell."

"I'm more interested in what they haven't said." Julian frowned thoughtfully. "Mrs. Falkland, Clare, and Adams are very different people and seem to have no connexion with one another except through Alexander, and yet they have one thing in common: they're all tormented. Adams is eaten up with hatred of Alexander. Clare is frightened and seems guilty or remorseful as well. And Mrs. Falkland asked me if I'd ever been to Hell, with the air of one who knew the place intimately. The one thing missing was grief. I wonder if anyone really loved Alexander except his father and his valet— Is this the place?"

They had reached a narrow passage leading off the Strand. Vance nodded and waved him through. The court within was just as Dipper had described it: dark and close, with Mrs. Wheeler's little house by the entrance, Mrs. Desmond's more opulent one at the opposite end, and three more falling to ruin in between. The curtains of one of Mrs. Wheeler's windows parted a crack as Julian and Vance entered. Apparently she was still keeping an eye on all the court's comings and goings.

They crossed to the house that had been Mrs. Desmond's. Vance let them in with his key. "Mr. Underhill gave me an inventory of everything as was here when she moved in. That way we'll know what was hers and what wasn't. Seems the house was let furnished, but she added things of her own, and when she went, she left some of 'em behind. Mr. Underhill don't know what to do with 'em, so he's left 'em where they were. Which is a good thing for us, sir, since the place is just as Mrs. Desmond and her maid left it. Only the kitchen's been cleaned, to keep out the rats."

The house was built to the standard London design: a front and back room on each floor and a slender, zigzagging stairway. The kitchen and scullery were in the basement. On the ground floor were a dining room and parlour, and a back door leading to a small walled yard, accessible only from the house. The first-floor front was the drawing room; the back had been Mrs. Desmond's bedchamber.

Julian soon saw that they would not need the inventory to distinguish Mrs. Desmond's additions from the furniture belonging to the house. Each room was an incongruous mixture of homely, rather worn furnishings and attempts at a tawdry elegance. The drawing room was hung with prim silhouettes of people in powdered wigs, faded aquatints of Bath in its heyday, and engravings of long-dead members of the royal family. In violent contrast, Mrs. Desmond had added a large, splashy daub of Europa and the bull, which made up in lewdness for its lack of artistic merit. Her other conspicuous addition to the drawing room was a dainty pianoforte encrusted with gilt decoration. Julian found it dirty inside and egregiously out of tune.

All the rooms had large gilt mirrors and garish curtains—Mrs. Desmond's taste again. Several contained old books: collections of essays by clergymen, guidebooks to watering places, a volume on etiquette that explained how to sit down gracefully while wearing a sword. Their musty state showed they had not been opened for some time. Mrs. Desmond preferred a different sort of reading: protruding from under the drawing-room sofa was a clumsy translation of the kind of French novel that made English moralists cringe.

Vance pounced on the writing desk and looked through it, only to shut it regretfully. "No papers, only blank sheets."

"The papers are here—or, rather, what's left of them." Julian pointed to the grate, which was full of blackened shreds. They had been raked about with the poker to make sure they were thoroughly destroyed.

They moved on to Mrs. Desmond's bedroom. The bed was one of the original furnishings, plain and graceless, with thick posts like swollen legs. Mrs. Desmond had ludicrously swathed it in purple curtains festooned with tassels. She had also gilded the stolid bedroom chairs and upholstered them in yellow silk; they looked like sedate spinsters tricked out as opera girls. The old-fashioned wardrobe was empty except for a pink silk button and a scrap of lace.

The washstand was of inlaid wood, with hidden compartments for soap, tooth-powder, water jug, and glass. The top opened into a mirror bordered with gilt dolphins. It did not belong to the house, nor did it look like Mrs. Desmond's taste, Julian thought. Perhaps it had been a gift from her protector.

The maid's room was in the garret. It was tiny, with a meagre bed that turned up during the day. There was a small washstand, a table, and a narrow, rather tipsy deal wardrobe. The only sign of recent occupation was the coal ash in the grate and the remains of a tallow candle congealed on the table.

Julian and Vance had now been through the whole house. They stood reflecting a moment. Then Vance said with decision, "Dustbins!"

They retraced their steps room by room, searching through all the dustbins. Julian smiled to think what his friends at White's would say if they could see him now. By the time they reached the basement, they had garnered a collection of dead nosegays, bits of tissue paper and ribbon of the kind used to wrap purchases from ladies' shops, half-eaten sweetmeats, an empty bottle of curaçao, a torn white lace stocking, and some crinkled fair hair that looked as if it had been cleaned out of a hairbrush.

Julian regarded the little heap quizzically. "Not very informative, is it?"

"Not half, sir," Vance agreed.

"Well, we've learned one thing: Mrs. Desmond took herself off in a tearing hurry. She left the vases unemptied and the grates unswept, and packed only what she could fit into a portmanteau. You can see spaces where small knick-knacks have been removed, or pictures taken down from the walls."

"Left some fine things behind, too, didn't she? That piano, for one—her fancy-man must've forked out a good bit of blunt for that."

"A cart big enough to transport it wouldn't have fit through the entrance to Cygnet's Court. After taking all the trouble to move out at night, on the one day of the week when she knew her only neighbour would be away, she wouldn't want to be seen loading a pianoforte into a cart in the middle of the Strand."

Vance knit his brows. "Do we know she left at night, sir?"

"I'm assuming she did, to avoid attracting notice. But I know how we might find out. We could look in the front hall for signs that people went in and out loading a carriage in the rain."

"How do you know it rained that night, sir?"

"Because it was the same night Eugene stayed out in a rainstorm to make himself ill. It was also the night of the Brickfield Murder, when the rain washed away any footprints or cart tracks the murderer might have left."

"You're right at that, sir! Let's have a look."

They began prowling around the front hall. Sure enough, there were splotches of mud, all but invisible against the dark-patterned Persian carpet. Julian bent down and felt them. "It's quite dry, but it must be fairly fresh, since it hasn't been trampled into the carpet. And we clearly didn't track it in; we wiped our feet at the entrance, and in any event the streets are dry today."

"Nobody tracked this in," said Vance. "There ain't any footprints."

"No, that's true. It looks as if someone dripped rain and mud from something he was wearing, or carrying."

Vance went into the dining room and parlour, stooping to look at the carpets. "No mud in here."

"There are a few spots on the stair carpet. Whoever it was must have gone upstairs."

They followed the trail up to Mrs. Desmond's bedroom. Here they found a few more spots of mud on the carpet and one on the bed-curtains. Vance went to look in the drawing room and the maid's room. "No mud there," he reported.

Julian scraped a little off the bedroom carpet and scrutinized it, frowning. "This doesn't look like mud. It's too red—more of a deep plum colour, really."

"That's London clay, sir. My pa was foreman at a brick-works, he used to track it home all the time—"

He broke off. They stared at each other.

"Well, carry me out and bury me decent," Vance said softly.

They hastened downstairs and took samples of mud from the front hall carpet. It was the same purplish colour. Vance wrapped it in his handkerchief for safe-keeping. "This is London clay, sure as eggs is eggs. I take my hat off to you, sir: it was you as first thought to link Mr. Falkland's murder to the Brickfield Murder. And now we come here looking for a clue to who killed Mr. Falkland, and instead we stumble on brick-earth where no brickearth ought to be."

Julian waved away his praise. "Murder isn't so common, thank God, that we should be surprised to find two such brutal killings linked. Especially when they occurred only a week apart, and the methods were so similar."

"But what link could there be between a gentleman like Mr. Falkland and the poor soul found in the brickfield?"

"I have no idea. And there's one glaring contrast between the two murders: one obliterated the victim's features, while in the other the victim's identity is the most startling aspect of the case. Of course, this brickearth we've found, coupled with the disappearance of Mrs. Desmond and her maid on the night of the Brickfield Murder, strongly suggests that one of them was the victim."

"It couldn't have been Mrs. Desmond. The brickfield victim was at least forty, and Mrs. Desmond by all accounts was a chit of a girl. But the maid's a possibility."

"Yes. Mrs. Wheeler told Dipper she was a drab woman of about forty. What else did she say about her? Her name was Fanny, she was a churchgoer, and she seemed afraid of her mistress and unwilling to talk to strangers." He frowned. "But why should the murderer have killed her in a brickfield near Hampstead, then come all the way back here and dripped mud and clay on the floor? Do you suppose it was Mrs. Desmond who killed her, and that was why she took herself off in such a hurry that same night?"

"It might have been her fancy-man who did it, and she took fright and made herself scarce. I'll tell you what, sir: we have to find Mrs. Desmond. I'll start asking questions round the neighbourhood."

"Capital. But you know, this neighbourhood harbours some dubious people: beggars, nymphs of the pavement, thieves. I think we also need someone to speak to them in their own language."

"I get your drift, sir," Vance said, grinning. "You want to set Dipper on them."

"Precisely. Should you mind?"

"Not at all, sir. The more the merrier. You'll talk to the gentry in their lingo, Dipper'll patter flash to the cross-coves, and me—why, I'll talk to everybody else."

✳

When Julian got back to his flat that evening, he found a group of sharp-faced men with pencils behind their ears lounging against the area railings. They saw him and came crowding around.

"Mr. Kestrel!" cried one. "Has anyone been arrested for the murder?"

Julian smiled. "You gentlemen keep such close track of events at Bow Street, I should think you would know better than I."

"Who do you think killed Mr. Falkland?" called out another.

"I should say it was most likely a journalist, in the hope that it would make a good story."

"Seriously, Mr. Kestrel, have you any leads?"

"None that I care to see blazoned in the *Times*. Good evening, gentlemen." Julian extricated himself and went inside.

That evening, he dined with Felix Poynter and some other male friends. There was a good deal of talk about the murder, but none of it was of any interest. After dinner, he declined an invitation to a gaming hell. Instead he went to Alexander's house and told Nichols, the butler, that he wished to make some investigations in Mr. Falkland's library. Nichols showed him in. An hour or two later, he emerged more than satisfied with the results.

Next morning found him back at Quentin Clare's chambers. Clare seemed less than overjoyed to see him. "Mr. Kestrel. Please come in."

"I've brought back your book." Julian held up the *Vindication of the Rights of Woman*.

"Oh. Thank you, that's very good of you."

Clare held out his hand for the book, but Julian pretended not to notice. "I found it most instructive. I particularly enjoyed your sister's comments in the margins. Writing in books seems to run in your family: I noticed when I was here last that you'd annotated some of yours. You even underlined a sentence in this book and wrote 'How true!' beside it. I believe this is your handwriting rather than your sister's?"

Clare looked at the page apprehensively. "Yes. I did write that."

Julian read: " *'Yet truth is not with impunity to be sported with, for the practised dissembler, at last become the dupe of his own arts, loses that sagacity, which has been justly termed common sense.'* Tell me, Mr. Clare, when you marked this passage, were you thinking of Alexander Falkland or yourself?"

"What—what do you mean?"

Julian smiled quizzically. "I see you're going to make this difficult. Very well." He glanced around the room at Clare's vast array of books. "You seem extremely well-read. And to judge by your library, you're fluent not only in Latin and Greek, but in French, Italian, and German."

"I grew up on the Continent. I could hardly help but pick up a number of languages."

"You're too modest, Mr. Clare. It doesn't follow that you should have read everything from French drama to German philosophy. Some English people spend years on the Continent and never learn how to order dinner. When I first perceived what a scholar you were, I thought that might explain the friendship between you and Alexander. His letters to his father show an extraordinary grasp of law and literature. But you would know that, of course."

Clare froze. "I had no occasion to read Falkland's letters to his father."

"I didn't suppose you'd read them. I think you wrote them, Mr. Clare. And I should like to know why."

# ✳ 14 ✳

## A TANGLED WEB

Clare's eyes closed, and he stood white and silent. At last he dragged open his eyes and asked, "What makes you think I wrote Falkland's letters?"

"I've been doubtful about them from the first. They were so unlike Alexander. The style was wrong, to begin with. His real style showed clearly in a letter he wrote to David Adams: light and amusing, like his conversation. The substance of the letters was even more incongruous. Alexander wasn't a Radical—probably had no politics at all. He had taste, not convictions. If he really did mean to stand for Parliament, I'm persuaded it was only because he wanted a new world to conquer—a fresh sphere in which to shine.

"At first I could only conclude he had a scholarly, philosophical side no one knew about. The idea that he didn't write the letters at all never occurred to me—till I met you.

"Do you remember when I asked you yesterday if you had a theory about who killed Alexander? You were eloquent in your refusal to accuse anyone without firm proof. What I heard then was the authentic tone of the letters—particularly the one where Alexander defended the right of a prisoner to have a lawyer in court.

"That set me thinking. Last night I went to his house and

hunted about for the books discussed in the letters. He had most of them; his library is impressively large and handsome. But nearly all the books are in virgin condition, with uncut pages and unbroken spines. The only books in that house that aren't purely decorative are the ones on art and architecture and the horror novels. You, on the other hand, have a good many of the books mentioned in the letters, and to judge by their condition, they've been thoroughly, ardently read and reread. Am I correct so far?"

Clare looked away. "Yes. You're quite correct, Mr. Kestrel."

"When I got home, I went through the correspondence between Sir Malcolm and Alexander and compared the dates. None of Alexander's letters was written less than a week after the one from his father that preceded it. That stands to reason: he needed time to give you Sir Malcolm's letter, obtain your answer, and copy it over in his own hand. He copied it verbatim, without censoring your political views—without even troubling to add a few words about what he'd been doing lately or how Mrs. Falkland was. No wonder we thought the letters impersonal. Well, Mr. Clare? Do you deny it?"

"No. No, I wish I could."

"So I ask you again: why did you do it?"

"He asked me to."

"Forgive me, but you must see, that's a very inadequate response."

"It's the only response I can give. He asked it as a favour, and I agreed."

"What reason did he give for wanting you to impersonate him on paper?"

"He was very busy. He was refurbishing his house, he went out very often and gave a great many parties. He hadn't time to study as much as I did or to write long letters. At first he merely asked me to note down some things he could write to his father, but soon it became simpler to have me write the letters myself."

"Why did you agree?"

"I've told you, we were friends."

"I have friends, too, Mr. Clare, and there's a great deal I would do for them, but not at the expense of my honour."

A flush spread slowly over Clare's face. "You're right to despise me. I despise myself."

"Very pretty, Mr. Clare. But even as a despicable character, you don't make much sense. If Falkland were paying you or doing you some service, I could understand your falling in with his scheme. But the only thing he ever did for you was to invite you to his parties, which you disliked, and introduce you to important people, whom you made no effort to cultivate. You've told me social graces aren't your forte, but no one could deny that you have formidable intellectual gifts. You might have cut a dash among your fellow students and impressed barristers and solicitors whose patronage could advance you in your career. Instead, you chose to stand in Alexander Falkland's shadow. Why? How did he threaten you, to extort such a sacrifice?"

Clare's eyes dilated. "He—he never threatened me. I—I—"

"Your hesitancy does you credit. You hate to lie, don't you, Mr. Clare? I wonder why you do it."

"I can't tell you anything more." Clare went to the window, gripping the frame as a prisoner might rattle the bars of his cell. "I ought not to have taken part in a fraud. I'm ashamed of having done so. But it has nothing to do with Falkland's murder."

"Then why have you kept it a secret?"

"Just for the reason I said—because it was a private matter, nothing Bow Street need be concerned about."

"That isn't for you to say. Bow Street needs every scrap of information about irregularities in Falkland's life. And I should say that a tortuous deception of his father, lasting some eighteen months and serving no apparent purpose except to gratify his vanity, was a signficant irregularity."

"There's something else." Clare lowered his gaze, his colour mounting. "I didn't want Sir Malcolm to find out Alexander didn't write the letters. He seemed to take such pleasure in them—or at least I had that impression from his letters to me—I mean, to Alexander. I thought he might set some value on them as a remembrance of his son. How could I reveal that Alexander didn't write them, that he never cared enough—" Clare brought himself up short. "Anyway, I thought that, cruel as it had been to deceive Sir Malcolm, undeceiving him would be worse, now his son was dead and could never explain or atone for what he'd done."

"You're very eloquent, Mr. Clare. Remarkably so, in pleading the cause of the man you've wronged. Might his being a bencher of Lincoln's Inn have anything to do with your wanting to conceal how you'd made a fool of him? He could have you cast out and dish your legal career before it begins."

Clare waved his hand, as if to say that was the least of his worries. "You'll have to tell him now, I suppose?"

"Of course. There can't be any question of keeping this dark."

"Not even for Sir Malcolm's own sake?"

"Sir Malcolm is desperate to understand what happened to his son. He's told me he's prepared to face any knowledge, no matter how bitter, rather than remain in ignorance. I think he has too high a regard for truth to wish to perpetuate a lie, however comforting or convenient."

Clare turned his face away. The unruly lock of hair fell across his brow, shading his eyes.

Julian regarded him wryly. "You make it very difficult to help you, Mr. Clare. You've been less than candid about why you wrote the letters, and why you concealed the fact after Falkland's murder. You must realize, this duplicity casts doubt on everything else you've said. If I've offended you, you may send a friend to call on me. But I don't believe you will. You have too much conscience to risk your life, or mine, to defend a lie."

Clare leaned his arm against the window. He looked exhausted. Julian decided to let his conscience rack him for a while. He took up his hat and stick and departed.

✳

As long as he was at Lincoln's Inn, Julian thought he might as well look in on Sir Malcolm. He had a good deal to tell him. He crossed Serle's Court and asked a pug-faced laundress to direct him to No. 21, Old Square. A sooty rain was beginning to fall; he turned up his coat-collar to protect his cream silk cravat.

Old Square was aptly named: its cluster of red-brick buildings with pointed gables must date back to Charles I. Julian mounted the narrow, curving stair of No. 21 and found a door neatly painted with Sir Malcolm's name. Inside was an elderly clerk bent over a writing table, his grey head islanded amid bundles of papers tied up with red tape. On seeing Julian, he thrust his quill behind his ear, a habit that would account for the blue stain on his side-whiskers. "Good morning, sir."

"Good morning. I should like to see Sir Malcolm."

"I'm afraid he isn't in, sir."

Julian knew that eminent barristers were never in. One of their clerks' principal tasks was to keep them in magnificent isolation, turning away anyone who presumed to come without an appointment. "If you'll be so good as to present this card, I think you'll find him miraculously returned."

The clerk looked at the card, and his stern face relaxed. "Mr. Kestrel! Bless my soul, he's been hoping to see you." He opened a door behind him and called, "Mr. Julian Kestrel, sir."

"Mr. Kestrel!" Sir Malcolm appeared in the doorway. "Come in, come in! Sit down, and tell me everything you've been finding out. I feel starved for news."

Julian waited till the door had closed behind them, then warned, "I'm afraid some of what I have to say will be painful."

"Then tell it quickly." Sir Malcolm sat down at his desk,

sweeping aside a litter of opened letters and blue bags bulging with papers. A cloud of powder flew from his wig, which hung on a wooden block beside him.

Julian got through the cruelest part of his story first. When he had finished, Sir Malcolm stared at him, dazed and incredulous. "All of them? Clare wrote *all* the letters?"

"All the ones you gave me to read, yes."

"But how could Alexander—why—" He pressed his fingertips to his brow, thinking feverishly. "He—he was trying to please me, of course—trying to make me proud of him. He went about it badly, but he meant well. It's just as Clare told you: Alexander hadn't time to study, and Clare did, so Alexander—well, he took credit for Clare's industry."

"Not only for his industry," Julian reminded him gently. "For his thoughts, his understanding, his ideals."

"He ought not to have done it. I know that. But it was an error born of love—a schoolboy's effort to impress his father."

But Alexander wasn't a schoolboy, Julian thought. What may be a prank in a child is deceit in a man.

He said, "For my purpose, why Alexander wanted Clare to write the letters isn't so important as why Clare agreed. Both he and Adams did Alexander extraordinary favours: Clare supplied him with legal insights at the expense of his own career, and Adams forgave him a vast amount of debt. Even Alexander couldn't have won all that by charm alone. Either he had something valuable to offer those two men, or he threatened them somehow. And since it doesn't appear he was helping Clare in any way, we have to ask whether he had it in his power to harm him."

"You forget, my son is the victim of this crime!" Sir Malcolm flushed angrily. "He was viciously, brutally murdered! Now you seem more concerned to uncover his crimes than the murderer's!"

"The two are inextricably bound. If we don't find out who Alexander angered or wronged, how will we know who had a motive to kill him?"

Sir Malcolm jumped up and walked back and forth, clenching and unclenching his fists. At last he halted and drew a long breath. "You're right, as usual. Forgive me. But you didn't see him lying there that night, with his beautiful head all broken—the work of four-and-twenty years dashed away in a moment! A pile of bones and bleeding flesh that used to talk and laugh and—" He covered his face.

"My dear sir." Julian went to him and laid a hand on his shoulder. "Won't you sit down? Shall I ask your clerk to fetch us a drink?"

"No, you're very good, but I'll be all right." He let Julian lead him back to his chair and finished more quietly, "Now you tell me the young man I knew and loved wasn't real— that he deceived me, perhaps blackmailed his friends—that I'm not even entitled to a memory. This is hard—harder than I dreamed it could be."

"I'm sorry."

"I know." Sir Malcolm patted his shoulder. "You haven't done anything I haven't asked you to do. Let's proceed. I'll show you how calm and business-like I can be. You say my son may have had some power to harm Mr. Clare. In what way, do you think?"

"My guess is it had something to do with Clare's sister. Clare gets into a funk whenever I speak of her, and though he denies she ever knew Alexander, I hardly think he's proved himself a pattern of truthfulness."

"What do you know about her?"

"Only that she lives with her great-uncle in Somerset, and that she's an ardent disciple of Mary Wollstonecraft."

"Rights of women, eh? I know the book—it's a bit hysterical, but much of it is right. Plato, you know, saw no reason women shouldn't be Guardians in his ideal republic. He said it made no more sense to exclude them than it would to have only male watchdogs to protect your house. There's no reason a woman shouldn't learn and study and reason, just like a man. Except of course that they don't," he added regretfully. "Which is why I never know what to say to them."

Julian was glad to let him talk, since it helped him get his equanimity back. When he seemed ready to absorb more information, Julian gave him a brief account of his conversations with Lady Anthea Fitzjohn, Felix Poynter, Sir Henry Effingham, and David Adams. He went on to explain that the maidservant who had accosted Mrs. Falkland in the Strand was really a woman of uncertain reputation named Mrs. Desmond, who for reasons unknown had disguised herself in her maid's clothes. He described how she and her maid had fled on the night of the Brickfield Murder, and how he and Vance had found traces of brickearth in her house. "So you see," he finished, "I need to question Mrs. Falkland about her again."

"I can't imagine what Belinda could know about a woman of that character, much less about the poor creature who was killed in the brickfield."

"Nor can I, but I can't blink away that Mrs. Falkland is keeping something back about her encounter with Mrs. Desmond. It may not have anything to do with either of these murders, but I won't know that for certain till I know what it is."

"Well, of course you're welcome to come to Hampstead and question her again. But can it wait till tomorrow? She had a stormy leave-taking with Eugene this morning, and it's left her shaken."

"So she made good her resolve to pack him off to school?"

"Yes. We were all afraid he'd do some freakish thing at the last minute, like staying out all night in the rain. But we got him off safe and sound. He must be well on his way to Yorkshire by now."

"I'll call tomorrow morning, then."

"Belinda rides every morning at ten, unless it pours."

"Perhaps she'll allow me to ride with her." That would suit his purpose, Julian thought. Mrs. Falkland loved to ride and might well be at her most relaxed and unguarded on horseback. Of course, he might find it hard to keep his mind on the investigation. Belinda Falkland on horseback was one of the sights of Rotten Row—a joy to any admirer of fine horsemanship or feminine grace. "One more thing, Sir Malcolm: I should rather you didn't repeat to her anything I've told you about Mrs. Desmond.''

"Do you mean to imply that she might concoct some lie if she were forewarned?"

"Let's say rather that I'd like to gauge her reactions for myself."

Sir Malcolm's face relaxed into a smile. "Mr. Kestrel, you must be the most tactful man in London."

"Tact and tactics, Sir Malcolm, are the stuff of which investigation is made."

✳

In the afternoon, Julian went home for a session with his tailor. His hobby of detection could not be allowed to interfere with his profession of dress. The tailor measured him for some sporting garments for the autumn and made yet another attempt to persuade him to pad his coats. "The very latest fashion, Mr. Kestrel!" he pleaded.

"My dear man, if I *followed* the fashions, I should lose any power to lead them. And not for you nor anyone else will I consent to look like a pincushion with legs."

"Of course I didn't mean to imply you *need* it, sir. Not like that Mr. de Witt." The tailor was not above disparaging one dandy to another. "He's one that would benefit from some padding here and there."

"De Witt's thinness suits him. He looks like an elongated sneer."

"You won't change your mind then, sir?"

"On no account."

"As you wish, sir." The tailor sighed and bowed himself out.

Peter Vance arrived soon after. He had been making enquiries about Mrs. Desmond in the neighbourhood of Cygnet's Court. "And I don't mind telling you, sir, it's been to no more purpose than to give a goose hay. The neighbours—shopkeepers, mostly—never knew aught about her. Kept herself to herself, it seems. Some folks remembered her maid,

Fanny Gates, because she used to make purchases for her mistress or fetch her hackney coaches. She was a plain, drab woman, by all accounts, square-faced and stocky, and timid as a mouse. Looked as if she'd been knocked about the world a good deal and bore the bruises. She usually wore the clothes Mrs. Desmond had on when she approached Mrs. Falkland: a brown and white checked dress and a white cap with lappets."

"Those aren't the clothes the brickfield victim was wearing. But I can't think whoever went to so much trouble to obliterate her face would leave her lying about in her usual dress."

"She may have had a better one for Sundays."

"Or she may not have been the brickfield victim at all."

Vance shrugged. "One thing all the neighbours agreed on: she was afraid of her mistress and anxious to keep on her good side."

"Yes, that's what Mrs. Wheeler said."

"She's a rum customer, *she* is!" Vance chuckled. "I went to see her first thing and nearly had my head talked off. If ever a woman's tongue ran on wheels, hers does! But she couldn't tell me any more than she told Dipper. And that maid of hers is so soft-headed, I couldn't get anything out of her at all. In the ordinary way, she'd have been our best witness. Maids always make common cause in neighbourhoods like that and know all each other's secrets."

"Cygnet's Court does seem an ideal place to hide a *chère amie*. In fact, any amount of immoral or illegal things could go on there without anyone's finding out, particularly on Friday nights when Mrs. Wheeler is away. That's all the more reason not to neglect the criminal classes. Last night Dipper bought drinks for half the thieves and light-skirts in the neighbourhood, without learning anything to the purpose. I shall send him out again tonight and see if he fares any better."

"Hard life, being your servant." Vance grinned.

"It does have its compensations."

"What'll you do in the meantime, sir?"

"Wednesday is the weekly ball at Almack's, so I shall go

and dance with debutantes and become as elevated as one can on weak cherry cordials. And of course I shall see if there's anything more to be gleaned about Alexander Falkland." He pondered. "I wish there were some way we could find out more about the brickfield victim. I have a strange conviction we'd unravel this whole mystery if we only knew why it was necessary to destroy that woman's face."

# ✳ 15 ✳

## NIGHT VISITORS

That evening, while Julian was at Almack's dancing with debutantes and drinking cherry cordials, Sir Malcolm was alone in his library, remonstrating gently with the portrait of Alexander.

"Why did you do it? Why did you feel you had to deceive me? Did you think I expected—did you think the world expected—you to be perfect? That you had to be a brilliant lawyer as well as a skilled art collector, a devoted husband, a charming host? Didn't you know I'd rather have had a flesh-and-blood son, with all his faults, than a sublime, exotic creature I couldn't hope to understand?

"I suppose you thought I'd never find out. My poor boy, how could you know death was waiting for you round the next corner, and all your secrets were about to be dragged out into the light? I wish to Heaven I could see you just once more and ask you—tell you—"

He broke off helplessly. The truth was, he could never have had this conversation with the living Alexander. Something about Alexander had set intimacy at defiance. He had been like an ever-shifting kaleidoscope: too many colours, too many facets, nothing one could fix on for long at a time. Who knew what had lain beneath that surface? There might have been anything, or nothing—

"Sir?"

Sir Malcolm spun around, hoping Dutton had not heard him jabbering to a painting. I must keep my wits together, he thought. We can't have the neighbourhood saying I'm going queer in my upper story.

Dutton brought in a salver with a card on it. Sir Malcolm read the card and looked up, startled. "What does he want?"

"He's asked to see you, sir."

Sir Malcolm took a turn about the room, running his fingers through his hair. "I suppose you'd better show him in."

Dutton bowed and went out. He returned a moment later with Quentin Clare, who halted just inside the doorway, hat in hand, to signal that he did not mean to stay. Sir Malcolm motioned to Dutton to leave them.

They stared at each other across the room. Sir Malcolm felt confused, indignant, shy. What do you say to a man you hardly know, to whom you've been pouring out your deepest thoughts and ideals for months, in the belief that he is somebody else?

"I was afraid you'd refuse to see me, sir," said Clare. "I wouldn't have blamed you if you had."

"I couldn't see turning you away. But, frankly, I don't know what we can have to say to each other."

"You can have nothing to say to me, sir. And what I have to say can be said very quickly—then I'll go. I only want to tell you how sorry I am for deceiving you as I did."

"Why did you do it?"

"At first, just because Alexander asked me. You'd tried a case of forgery in the Spring Assizes that involved a dispute over hearsay evidence. Alexander asked me for some ideas on the subject, so he could seem knowledgeable about it when he wrote to you. You wrote back to him in such detail that he said he had no notion how to respond. He asked me to write a letter for him. I agreed. I didn't know he would want me to go on doing it. And I never counted on—" He looked down, colouring.

"On being found out?" said Sir Malcolm ironically.

"No, sir." Clare lifted clear grey eyes. "On enjoying the correspondence so much. I began it for Alexander's sake; I continued it for my own. I had no one to talk to about what I was reading and thinking. My father was a barrister, but he died when I was very young. I haven't many friends. Most of the time I don't mind that. I prefer to be alone. But writing to you—it got under my guard somehow. I looked forward to your letters. I forgot how wrong it was. I forgot deliberately, because I wanted to go on doing it—" He swallowed hard. "Please believe me, sir, I was stupid and selfish, but I didn't mean to hurt you. I hope you can find it in your heart to forgive me. Goodnight, sir."

"Wait!" Sir Malcolm sprang forward and caught his arm. "You can't make a speech like that and then take yourself off! And the way you look now, I'd be afraid of your making a hole in some river. There's no call to make such a tragedy of this. You were very wrong, but I forgive you. I'm always forgiving people. It's a constitutional infirmity."

He drew Clare to the fireplace, sat him down, and tugged on the bell-pull. Dutton appeared. "Bring us a bottle of port, will you, Dutton?"

"Yes, sir. May I suggest, sir, if Mr. Clare means to stay for any length of time, his horse ought to be taken round to the stable. It's tethered to the front gate at present."

"To be sure, yes," Sir Malcolm agreed. "You can't leave a horse there—the street's not wide enough. See to it, Dutton."

Clare was looking so dazed and bewildered that Sir Malcolm could not help smiling. But he said nothing more until they were settled with their port. "You know, you remind me of myself at your age: bookish and solitary and taking everything too seriously. I wanted to be a don, you know. I meant to live out my life at Oxford, immersed in study."

"Why didn't you?" Clare ventured.

"My uncle died suddenly and left me a baronetcy that had got separated from the landed property that went with it. I had to live up to the title, and that meant achieving some worldly success. More important, my uncle had left his daughter alone and unprovided for. I hadn't planned to marry—a fellow of a college can't, of course—but I had to look after Agnes. So we were married, and I left Oxford and began to study for the Bar. But Agnes died a few years later, and I was thrown back on my old monkish habits. Looking back, I can see I was wrong to live that way. At your age, a man should be getting to know live people as well as dead languages. You should go to the theatre and the Cider Cellar, practise boxing at the Fives Court, and get into scrapes with girls. Am I being too personal?"

"No, sir. I should say you were entitled, after—well, everything that's happened. But I don't like those things."

"There's time enough to live the life of the mind once the body is wearing out."

"The life of the mind is the only life I should ever care to live."

"Have you tried the other?"

"In a way, yes, I have." Clare looked steadily into the fire. "And I've learned that the mind is the only safe place—safe because the world can't see inside, and mock or demean what it sees."

"You know, you're a very strange young man."

"Oh, sir." Clare smiled suddenly. "You have no idea."

"Well, as long as you're here, and I can't persuade you not to bury yourself in books, I should like to ask what you meant in your last letter when you said you thought Helen got the best of the debate with Hecuba in *The Trojan Women*."

They began to talk about Euripides. From there they progressed to Greek drama in general, then to Greek history. They compared Herodotus with Thucydides, and both of them with Tacitus. They debated questions no one would ever be able to answer, such as whether Plato or Xenophon had drawn the more accurate portrait of Socrates, and what had really gone on at the Eleusinian Mysteries. They were refighting the battle of Salamis, using inkwells and sealing wax for ships, when the clocks in the house began to chime midnight. They looked at each other incredulously.

"I never meant to stay so long," said Clare. "I had no idea how late it was."

"Nor I."

Clare hunted about for his hat, then turned to Sir Malcolm and held out his hand shyly. "Well—goodbye, sir. I hardly dared hope you'd forgive me, much less be so kind as you've been. Thank you."

"See here, Mr. Clare. You haven't yet atoned for what you've done."

"What—what do you mean? What can I do?"

"Come and see me again. Come whenever you can. We'll talk about Greek, the law, your future. You've chosen a very competitive calling—you'll need guidance, patronage, if you're to make the most of your talents. I can help you."

Clare's eyes stretched wide with astonishment. "Sir, I don't know what to say. I couldn't ask anything from you, after—"

"Now let's not hear any more about that. If you won't think of yourself, think of me. I've lost my son twice over. First he was taken from me in the flesh, then the man I thought he was—the man who'd written me those letters—turned out to be an illusion. I'm all at sea. I don't know what other lies he may have told—what else about him may not have been real."

"But why me?"

"Because you wrote the letters. You're the living embodiment of that spirit I thought was Alexander's. Only you can restore to me something of what I've lost. Mr. Clare, you have no father, and I have no son. What more natural than that we should fill each other's need?"

"I think," said Clare in a low voice, "Mr. Kestrel suspects me of killing your son."

"Mr. Kestrel suspects everyone. That gives me the luxury of suspecting only those I choose. Now what do you say? Is it a bargain?"

Clare drew a long breath. "It's a bargain, sir."

They shook hands, then Sir Malcolm rang for Dutton to light Clare to the stable. After he had gone, Sir Malcolm found himself face to face with the portrait again. But now he was more at peace, his loneliness relieved. And he suddenly knew it was a very old loneliness, going back much further than his son's death. He had never been more alone than when he was with Alexander.

✳

Almack's was more than usually slow. Julian found out nothing of use to the investigation. Alexander's acquaintances were all eager to know how it was progressing—a subject on which Julian remained enigmatic—but they had nothing new to offer beyond wild, often malicious speculation. Among the sporting set, the betting had branched out from whether and when Julian would solve the crime to which of the suspects would turn out to be guilty. Adams was the favourite. Valère came second, perhaps because some of the gentlemen thought their own valets would be likely suspects if they themselves were murdered.

The dancing continued late into the night, but Julian went home at about one. Dipper let him in and relieved him of the bicorne hat he carried under his arm. Almack's imposed an absurdly outdated dress code on men: tight pantaloons resembling knee-breeches, silk stockings, and folding *chapeau bras*. The Duke of Wellington had once been turned away from the door for wearing trousers.

Julian was surprised to find Dipper at home. "I thought you'd be out standing drinks for the raffish population of the Strand."

"I was, sir. But I got to chaffing with some kids there, and I found one as seen some'ut rum at Cygnet's Court, so I brought him home for you to ask him about it."

"Where is he?"

"In the parlour, sir. I tipped him some hot punch so he wouldn't cut and run before you come home. He's a bit knocked by all this, sir—didn't half want to come at all."

They went into the parlour. A boy of about ten was kneeling so close to the fire that he risked scorching his face. When he saw Julian, he clambered to his feet and stood clutching his cap in one hand and his cup of punch in the other. He had a small, smudged face, big, hollow eyes, and a shock of unkempt hair. His bony wrists and ankles looked as if they would snap like twigs. He wore the remnants of a grown man's clothes, made over clumsily to fit him. His tattered coat was buttoned up to his chin, probably to hide the lack of a shirt.

For Julian, the transition from Almack's to this was sobering. "Good evening," he said gently. "What's your name?"

"Jemmy, sir. Jemmy Otis."

"Sit down, Jemmy. It's good of you to come and talk with me like this. I shall make it worth your while."

The boy gaped at him uncomprehendingly. Dipper rubbed his fingers and thumb together to signify money. Jemmy brightened, still wary and confused, but willing to cooperate.

Julian asked him a little about himself. He lived in St. Giles with his mother, who "saw company," as he put it. He went out at night so as not to be under foot when she brought the company home. Sometimes he knocked up larks with other boys, but mostly he had to earn money; his ma did not make very much. He scavenged in the streets for rags, bones, and bits of iron to sell, ran errands, took messages, or walked on his hands to amuse the passersby. "See?" he said proudly, holding out his heavily callused palms.

His favourite work was anything to do with horses. He stood guard over carriages of gentlemen calling on ladybirds in Covent Garden, fetched hackney coaches for people coming out of the "h'opera" on rainy nights, and helped the drivers clean the hackney coaches when they were not in use. This came as a surprise to Julian, who had never ridden in a hackney that looked as if it had been cleaned by anybody.

"Do you know where Cygnet's Court is?" Julian asked.

"Yes, sir."

"Dipper tells me you saw something unusual there."

"Y-yes, sir." Jemmy's forehead puckered. He was clearly not used to telling stories; perhaps he was rarely encouraged to talk at all. "There was a man in a gig," he offered at last.

"Yes?" said Julian encouragingly. "Did you see him at Cygnet's Court?"

"I seed him in the Strand, sir. I followed him, 'coz I thought he might need to have his horse held. He stopped outside Cygnet's Court."

"What happened then?"

"He got down from the gig. I says, like I al'ays does, 'Want your horse held, sir?' He give me the bridle and says, 'Here's a shilling, and when I come back, I'll give you another.' " Jemmy looked awed. "Most coves only ever gives sixpence."

"What was he like, this man?"

"I dunno, sir."

"Was he tall, short, young, old?"

"He was young. And he wore a topper and a black cloak." Jemmy thought hard, then added, "He was a gen'l'man, sir."

"How could you tell?"

"He talked very swell—like you, sir."

"I see. Jemmy, have you any idea when all this happened?"

Jemmy looked utterly confounded. Julian had expected as much—what could a boy like this know of times and dates? "It weren't last night," he said cautiously, "nor the night afore."

"Was it spring yet?"

"Yes, sir." A spark of recollection came into his eyes. "And it rained—it rained mortal hard. Not when I seed the gen'l'man, but later. I know, 'coz I had plenty of blunt to buy hot gin-twist arter I was caught in the rain."

Julian and Dipper exchanged glances. It could have been the night Mrs. Desmond and her maid left Cygnet's Court— the night the rainstorm washed away any trace of the Brickfield Murderer. "What time of night was it?" Julian asked.

"I dunno, sir."

"Well—had people begun to leave the theatres?"

"No, sir. It was about the time the half-price customers starts coming. That's what I thought *he* was at first."

"About nine o'clock, then. So he gave you a shilling and asked you to hold his horse. What happened next?"

"He went through the passage into Cygnet's Court."

Julian turned to Dipper. "That's curious. The Falklands' town carriage wouldn't fit through the passage, but a gig would be small enough."

"Yes, sir."

"Then why didn't he simply drive the gig into the court?"

They both looked at Jemmy. "I dunno, sir," the boy said blankly.

"Perhaps he didn't want it to be seen there," Julian mused. "Suppose it was the same night Mrs. Desmond disappeared, and suppose the driver of the gig was Mrs. Desmond's protector. The description of him as a young gentleman in evening clothes fits, so far as it goes. He was familiar enough with Cygnet's Court to know that, since it was a Friday night, Mrs. Wheeler and her maid would be away. So the only people he could have been meaning to hide the gig from were Mrs. Desmond and Fanny."

He turned back to Jemmy. "Please go on."

"I held the horse till the gen'l'man come back. He was carrying a lady."

"Carrying her? What do you mean? Was she ill?"

"He said she was asleep. 'Hush!' he says, 'she's asleep, and I don't want for to wake her.' And she moaned a bit and moved about, as if she was dreaming."

"What did she look like?"

"I dunno, sir. I only seed her by the carriage lamp, and she had on a cloak and bonnet, and her veil was pulled down. I seed her shoes, though, when he put her in the carriage. They was white and shiny, with gold thread on 'em. A lady's slippers, they was."

"You think she was Mrs. Desmond, sir?" asked Dipper.

"More likely Mrs. Desmond than her maid, certainly. Although if Mrs. Desmond could dress up in her maid's clothes,

I suppose the maid could wear Mrs. Desmond's. Then again, she could have been someone else entirely. Mrs. Wheeler said Mrs. Desmond sometimes had female visitors on the nights her protector came to see her."

Jemmy had little more to tell. The "gen'l'man" had lifted the woman into the gig and tucked the carriage rug around her. He gave Jemmy the promised shilling, climbed in himself, and drove away.

Julian walked back and forth, pondering. "Well, what have we learned? A woman is carried out of Cygnet's Court, perhaps on the night of the Brickfield Murder. We have no idea who she was, or who the gentleman was who took her away. If she was the brickfield victim, why was she taken all the way from the Strand to a brickfield near Hampstead? What became of her white slippers with the gold thread? And assuming the gentleman took her to the brickfield, smashed her face, and went off with her slippers in his pocket, why in God's name would he return to Cygnet's Court and drip wet clay through Mrs. Desmond's house?"

Jemmy was looking at Julian in some alarm. "We're playing a sort of game," Julian explained. "We're attempting to solve a puzzle, and you've been very helpful." But I wish to God you could tell us something more, he thought—anything that would give us a hint where to pick up this gentleman's trail.

He made one last effort. "Can you remember anything about the gig and horse?"

Jemmy turned up an alert, intelligent face. "The gig was painted black, sir, with the wheels and shafts picked out in white. It was sturdy enough, but the springs was starting to go; it could be a bone-setter on a rough road. The horse was a roan, with a snip on his left nostril, a bit long in the tooth, and ewe-necked, with a splint on the near foreleg."

Confound me for an idiot! Julian thought. How could I have waited so long to put that question to a boy so besotted with horses? "Jemmy, you've been invaluable. Here." He emptied his pocket of coins. "Here's something on account. If the information you've given me proves as useful as I think it will, you'll come in for a much larger reward.''

While Jemmy goggled at his newfound wealth, Julian took Dipper aside. "Take him home and mark where he lives—we may need him again. Meantime, I'll write to Vance and ask him to move Heaven and earth to find out what's become of that gig and horse.''

# ✳ 16 ✳

## A Pair of
## Nails

Next morning Julian rode out to Sir Malcolm's house in Hampstead. Sir Malcolm received him in the library. "I couldn't bring myself to go to my chambers today," he said. "I want to be at hand when you question Belinda."

"Is she expecting me?"

"No. You asked me not to tell her what you'd learned about Mrs. Desmond, so rather than stray onto forbidden ground, I haven't mentioned you or the investigation at all."

"Thank you. I realize it must be awkward for you to keep secrets from her." He added curiously, "Hasn't she asked you how the investigation is progressing?"

"No. I think she's too overcome by Alexander's loss to take much interest in finding out who killed him. But she's beginning to plan for a future without him—that's a good sign, don't you think? Yesterday she sent Martha to London to have the rest of her belongings packed and brought here or sent to her house in Dorset. Martha was very loath to leave her, but Belinda'd set her mind to it. She wants to sell the London house. She can't be rid of it quickly enough, after what happened there."

He rang for Dutton and asked where Mrs. Falkland was. Dutton said she was in her room getting dressed for riding.

"Ask her to stop in and see us when she comes down," said Sir Malcolm. Dutton bowed and went out.

Sir Malcolm said hesitantly, "There's something else I ought to mention to you. It will seem very odd, I know. Mr. Clare came to see me last night, to beg my pardon for deceiving me about the letters. And I don't quite know how it happened, but he stayed for three hours."

"It must have been a rather long apology."

"No, but you see, we got to talking about other things— the classics, mostly. He has a very singular grasp of trochaic metres."

"Indeed?"

Sir Malcolm looked rueful. "Did I do wrong, making a friend of him?"

"I wouldn't say you did wrong, Sir Malcolm. But I think you did so at your peril."

"Well, let it be on my head. I like Mr. Clare, and I don't think he's a bad lot. He was just—misled."

"By Alexander?"

"Yes," said Sir Malcolm steadily. "That my son was foully murdered doesn't make him a saint. He behaved very badly over those letters. I have to accept that. Mr. Clare behaved badly as well, but he was younger than Alexander and had far less knowledge of the world."

Julian thought Sir Malcolm was hardly one to talk about knowledge of the world. His naiveté in taking Clare under his wing was as exasperating as it was touching. Clare was engaging, for all his awkwardness; he proved that the very reverse of charm could itself be oddly charming. But that only put Julian more on his guard against him. If Clare tried to take advantage of this kind, lonely man, he would have Julian to reckon with.

"You wanted to see me, Papa?" Mrs. Falkland appeared in the doorway, her austere black riding habit setting off her white and gold beauty to perfection. She inclined her head coldly toward Julian. "Good morning, Mr. Kestrel."

"Good morning, Mrs. Falkland." He bowed. "I came hoping to talk with you about some discoveries we've made in the investigation. Will you allow me to accompany you on your ride?"

For a moment her eyes looked resentful, trapped. He could feel her resistance across the room. But at last she said, "As you wish."

Sir Malcolm hovered about her, as if unwilling to let her out of his protection. "Goodbye, my dear. If you need me, I'll be here when you return."

"Thank you, Papa." She turned toward him, then looked quickly away. Julian saw what had stung her gaze: not Sir Malcolm, but the laughing-eyed portrait of Alexander on the wall beyond.

She took Julian's arm, and they went out the back door to the stable yard. The gate, which led to a winding back road, stood open in readiness. Julian's black horse, Nero, had been brought round. Beside him was Mrs. Falkland's fine chestnut, Phoenix. He was a full sixteen hands, spirited for a lady's mount, but she managed him superbly.

One of the stable boys held Nero's head while Julian mounted. The other boy would have given Mrs. Falkland a leg up, but her groom, Mike Nugent, shooed him away. Nugent was nearly as well known in Rotten Row as his mistress. He was a wiry little Irishman with a brown weathered face and snapping black eyes, who would allow no one to attend to Phoenix but himself. He spread out his hands for Mrs. Falkland to step on, and she sprang lightly into the saddle. He started to tighten the girth.

Phoenix's head came up with a jerk, eyes wild, nostrils flaring. He reared, threw Mrs. Falkland from the saddle, and bolted for the gate. Her foot caught in the stirrup. She was dragged along the ground.

Julian spurred his horse and cut off Phoenix at the gate. Phoenix veered round and would have dashed off in another direction, but Nugent got hold of the reins. "Take the saddle off him, for the love of Jesus!" he roared at the stable boys. "Can't you see that's what's driving him mad?"

Julian dismounted and ran to assist Mrs. Falkland. He loosed her skirt from the stirrup, carried her a safe distance away, and laid her on the ground. She was white and insensible. Her hat was gone, and her bright gold hair straggled down, streaked with dirt.

Sir Malcolm's coachman heard the commotion and came running out of the stable. Julian called, "Is there anything we can use for a litter?"

"There's an old door. I could cover it with canvas."

"Good. And bring a blanket, and some spirits, if you have any."

The stable boys had gotten Phoenix's saddle off. The horse was calmer now, though he still trembled and pawed the ground. Nugent murmured soothingly to him, stroking his neck and muzzle.

The coachman and stable boys brought out the makeshift litter, a blanket, and a bottle of brandy. Julian tucked the blanket around Mrs. Falkland and gently lifted her head and shoulders, supporting her on his arm. Holding the bottle to her lips, he got her to take a few swallows. She coughed, her eyelids flickered, and her face convulsed with pain.

Julian looked up swiftly at the stable boys. "Fetch a doctor."

They gaped at each other for a moment, then one dashed off.

"Do you feel well enough to be carried into the house?" Julian asked Mrs. Falkland.

She closed her eyes and nodded jerkily. Julian and the coachman lifted her carefully onto the litter and bore her inside. The remaining stable boy ran ahead to open doors and alert the household.

Sir Malcolm met them in the hallway. "My poor girl! Belinda, dearest— Oh, God, she's fainted! Quick, bring her in here!"

Julian and the coachman carried her into the library. Sir Malcolm helped them ease her from the litter onto a leather sofa. Then they all gasped, staring at the litter. In the middle of the canvas that covered it was a large, sticky red stain.

Sir Malcolm beckoned frantically to two women hovering in the doorway—the cook and housemaid, Julian supposed. "Come here! Find out where she's hurt!"

The men turned their backs while the women looked under Mrs. Falkland's clothes. Their search confirmed what Julian had feared. This was no ordinary wound. It was Sir Malcolm's hope of a grandchild draining away.

The housemaid ran to fetch clean linen, hartshorn, and hot water. Julian asked Sir Malcolm, "Where is Martha?"

"She hasn't returned yet," Sir Malcolm said bleakly. "You remember, I told you she went to London to have Belinda's things packed up. We don't expect her back till the afternoon."

All at once there was a commotion in the hallway. Dutton's voice rose in agitation: "I tell you, you can't see Sir Malcolm now, he's looking after Mrs. Falkland."

Sir Malcolm turned a harried face toward the door. Julian said, "I'll go," and went out to see what was the matter.

He found Dutton with Mike Nugent, who was holding Mrs. Falkland's side-saddle. When he saw Julian, he strode up to him, turned the saddle upside down, and dropped it at his feet. "There now! I ask your honour, was there ever such wickedness?"

Julian felt a prickly sensation at the back of his neck. He dropped on his haunches and peered closely at the saddle. For a moment he saw nothing amiss. It looked like the underside of any saddle: thickly padded, except for a narrow groove running down the centre from front to back. Then he saw two long, ugly nails, all but invisible against the dark brown leather, driven through the central groove so that their points barely protruded beyond the wads of padding on either side. It was a simple, effective trap. As long as the saddle rested lightly on the horse's back, he would not feel the nails. It was only when the rider's weight came down on his back, and the girth was tightened, that the points would jab into his flesh.

Julian looked up grimly at Nugent. "Who discovered these nails?"

"Sure, it was meself and no other, your honour. As soon as Phoenix was calm enough to be left alone, I went to have a look at the saddle—for I knew, sure as Shrove-tide, that he never would have got the Devil in him as he did unless there was something wrong with his saddle. A sweeter-tempered animal you never saw, your honour—gentle as a lamb, for all his high spirits, and loves the mistress like a mother—"

"I'm fully prepared to absolve him of any wrong-doing. Now, about the saddle—"

"Aye, your honour. I says to meself, somebody's tampered with it, for isn't it I that cleans and inspects it every day after the mistress's ride? And I swear to your honour, when I set it on the saddle-bracket yesterday, so clean and polished a lady could look into it to dress her hair, there was nothing wrong with it, at all at all!"

"What time was that?"

"I'd say, between noon and one o'clock, your honour."

"And when was the next time you handled it?"

"This morning, your honour, when I set it on Phoenix's back, about half past nine. I wish I had cut off me arms before I did so! But I never had a notion those nails were there. I'd have had to look close at the saddle, and that I never thought to do. No one had any call to touch it since yesterday." He scowled and shook his fist. "Bad luck to whoever did—tormenting a poor animal that never did anyone any harm, making him the instrument of hurting his mistress—"

There was a brisk knock at the front door. Dutton let in the surgeon and showed him into the library. Sir Malcolm and the coachman, cook, housemaid, and stable boy spilled out into the hall. Sir Malcolm would have dispersed the servants, but Julian asked that the stable staff remain. Sir Malcolm blinked at him, distracted and miserable. "Why?"

"I have something to tell you, Sir Malcolm. I'm afraid it will come as a shock. But first, will you please ask Dutton to make sure no one leaves the house until you give leave—in particular, that no one goes into the stable yard?"

"Very well. Do as Mr. Kestrel says, Dutton."

Julian took Sir Malcolm into the study and broke the news that Mrs. Falkland's fall had been no accident. Sir Malcolm was beside himself. "My God, who would do anything so barbarous? Who could have hated Alexander enough to want to kill not only him but his child?"

"I don't think we should be too quick to assume that the same person committed both crimes."

"For God's sake! You can't be suggesting there are *two* vicious criminals stalking my family?"

"That's extremely unlikely. I only mean that it's never wise to take anything for granted in these investigations."

"But surely this is Alexander's enemy striking again—a kind of blood feud, running into the next generation?"

Julian cocked an eyebrow at him. "Did you know Mrs. Falkland was in the family way?"

"No. She never told me."

"Well, if even you didn't know, Sir Malcolm, how do you imagine the person who tampered with the saddle knew?"

Sir Malcolm stared. "I have no idea." He dropped into a chair, shaking his head. "I feel all at sea. What should we do now?"

"Have a glass of spirits, I think, and then question the stable staff."

✳

The stable staff were waiting in the parlour. On their way there, Sir Malcolm and Julian ran into the surgeon in the hall. "How is she?" Sir Malcolm asked eagerly.

"She'll be all right. No hope of saving the child, but she's young, she'll have others—" The surgeon broke off, recalling too late that Mrs. Falkland had lost her husband, too. "She'll be in some pain for a day or two. Her ankle's sprained, and she's had a bad knock on the head. I've bound up the ankle, and she's not to try to walk on it for at least a week. Her other hurts aren't serious, except that with head injuries you have to watch the patient carefully for the first day or so. If she loses consciousness for any length of time, send for me at

once. Otherwise there's nothing to be done but keep her quiet
and in bed. If she turns feverish, bathe her forehead with vinegar and water. If the fever persists, I'll bleed her. She wants
to go up to her room, and I don't see why she shouldn't be
carried there a little later, when she's more rested."

"Is she capable of answering questions?" Julian asked.

"If she feels up to it, she should be encouraged to talk. It
will help keep her conscious and distract her from brooding
about the child. You'd best wait a bit, though. She needs to
rest."

Sir Malcolm thanked the surgeon and saw him out, then
went to look in on Mrs. Falkland. He came out shaking his
head gravely. "She's in a bad way—more dead than alive.
This has well nigh broken her heart. And just when she was
starting to get her health and spirits back! I tell you, Kestrel,
when we find whoever did this, don't let me near him! I'm
beginning to understand what could make a man commit
murder."

Sir Malcolm told Dutton to have the cook or housemaid sit
with Mrs. Falkland, and to send for him immediately if she
took a turn for the worse. "And bring more blankets, and
pillows, and anything else she needs to make her comfortable."

"Yes, sir."

Sir Malcolm and Julian went into the parlour. The stable
staff were standing about awkwardly, unused to being in the
house. They consisted of the coachman, Bob Cheever, the two
stable boys, and Nugent. "Is this the whole staff?" Julian
asked.

"Yes," said Sir Malcolm. "I've never felt the need to keep
a large establishment. I have two carriage horses, a travelling
chaise to use when I go on circuit, and a phaeton that I drive
myself."

"And how many indoor servants are there?"

"There's Dutton, who acts as both butler and footman, and
the cook and housemaid. Oh, and a man who looks after the
garden, but he doesn't live here."

Julian turned to Nugent. "You say you cleaned Mrs. Falkland's saddle at about noon yesterday, and it rested on a saddle-bracket until half past nine this morning, when it was put on Phoenix. So the nails must have been driven into the saddle between noon yesterday and half past nine this morning. Have I understood you correctly?"

"Faith, and your honour's grasped what I had to say, entirely."

"Where in the stable is the saddle-bracket?"

Cheever spoke for the first time, in a voice surprisingly mild for such a large, burly man. "In the saddle room, sir, next to the horses' stalls."

"Is that room kept locked?"

"No, sir. It hasn't even a lock on the door."

"What about the stable itself?"

"I lock it myself every night, sir, about nine o'clock, and unlock it again about five the next morning."

"And the stable-yard gate?"

"I lock and unlock that at the same times, sir."

"Did you follow that routine last night and this morning?"

"Yes, sir."

"Who else has keys to the stable and the gate?"

"Mr. Dutton keeps a set, sir."

Sir Malcolm nodded. "Dutton has keys to every door on the property, inside and out."

"Where does he keep them?"

"I believe he carries the ones he uses most often in his pocket," said Sir Malcolm. "The rest he keeps hanging on pegs in the butler's room in the basement. I'm afraid we're not very vigilant about that sort of thing—but how could we know anyone in the house was in danger?"

"You couldn't," Julian reassured him. "Is the butler's room kept locked?"

"I don't believe so. So I suppose someone could have taken the key to the stable and sneaked in last night."

"But, sir," objected Cheever, "he'd have had to go by the stalls, and that would have startled the horses. And the boys and me would have heard if they took fright—we sleep above the stalls."

"Couldn't someone the horses knew have come in without disturbing them, if he were careful?" Julian suggested.

"Happen he could, sir. But I sleep very light, and I think I'd have heard if anybody was moving around down there."

"Very well," said Julian, "we'll take it as highly unlikely that the saddle was tampered with between nine o'clock last night and five in the morning. That leaves us with yesterday between noon and nine o'clock, and this morning between five and half past nine. During those periods, was anyone in the stable or stable yard other than the four of you?"

"The mistress came out to see Phoenix," said Nugent. "She comes every evening, God bless her, and brings him a basket of apples."

"There was a gentleman, too," said Cheever. "But he didn't come till later, after the stable was locked up. His horse had been brought round just after dark, and later he come to fetch it. Fred here stayed up to look after it." He jerked his thumb at one of the stable boys.

"That was Mr. Clare," said Sir Malcolm slowly.

"What time did he leave?" asked Julian.

"Shortly after midnight," said Sir Malcolm. "I rang for Dutton to light him out to the stable."

"How did Dutton get into the stable? Did he use his key?"

"Must've, sir," said Cheever, "since I wasn't called to let him in."

"Then we know his key wasn't stolen." Julian turned to Fred. "Did Mr. Clare come into the stable?"

"Yes, sir."

"How long did he remain?"

"I dunno, sir," stammered Fred, confused at finding himself suddenly the centre of attention.

"What did he do there?"

"Nothing, sir, 'cept waited for me to fetch his horse. And I did, and he rode away."

"Dutton was with him all that time, I suppose?"

"No, sir. Mr. Dutton went to unlock the gate."

"Were you watching Mr. Clare the entire time he was in the stable?"

"What are you suggesting, Mr. Kestrel?" Sir Malcolm broke in sharply.

"I'm not suggesting anything, Sir Malcolm. I'm merely trying to explore every possibility."

"I wasn't watching him all the time, sir," Fred owned. "Boreas, he got fractious, and I had to go to his stall and quiet him."

"Could Mr. Clare have gone into the saddle room and come out again while you were occupied with the horse?"

"Dunno why he couldn't, sir."

"Where would he have got the nails from?" Sir Malcolm demanded. "Do you suppose he carries them about in his pocket in case of an opportunity to tamper with somebody's saddle?"

"He wouldn't have to, sir," Cheever pointed out timidly. "There's nails in the saddle room, just like the ones that was drove into Mrs. Falkland's saddle."

Sir Malcolm asked in a dangerously soft voice, "So you're all suggesting that Mr. Clare wandered into the saddle room, saw the nails lying about, and thought it might be rather a lark to cause my daughter to have an accident?"

Julian cut short the cross-examination. "I repeat, Sir Malcolm, I'm not suggesting anything. I'm merely gathering information. Mr. Clare had the means and opportunity to commit the crime. You can't expect we should blink that away?"

"No. No. Never mind, please go on with your questioning." Sir Malcolm paced back and forth, working off his irritation.

Julian set about pinning down alibis. The stable staff had none: any of them could have slipped into the saddle room between noon yesterday and half past nine this morning. Moreover, they would be particularly adept at tampering with a saddle. It was hard to see what motive they would have for harming Mrs. Falkland. But in dealing with servants—the lowest paid and least respected of working people—one always had to consider the possibility that they could be bought. Sir Malcolm volunteered that all his servants had come to him with a character, and none had ever shown any sign of dishonesty or violence. But this was not conclusive. It merely meant the bribe would have had to be large, to tempt a habitually honest servant into betraying his master.

At Julian's request, Sir Malcolm sent for Dutton, the cook, and the housemaid. He himself went to sit with Mrs. Falkland while Julian questioned them. They all professed to know nothing about the nails in Mrs. Falkland's saddle; indeed, apart from Dutton's taking Clare to retrieve his horse, none of them had gone near the stable between noon yesterday and half past nine this morning. On the whole, Julian gave them long odds as suspects, if only because of the risk they would have run in laying the trap. The stable was not their province, and if anyone caught them there, they would be hard put to think of an explanation.

Julian asked the house and stable staffs if they had seen any strangers about the house lately. They all said positively that they had not.

The next step, he decided, was to have a look around the stable. He asked that Cheever accompany him and that the rest of the servants remain in the house. They went out the back door to the stable yard. It was a walled enclosure, roughly rectangular. The only means of entry were from the house or through the gate that opened on the road. Against the far wall was the stable, a brown-brick building that resembled a substantial cottage, except for the carriage-sized doors. At one end was a large space for Sir Malcolm's chaise and phaeton. At the other end were the horses' stalls, with the saddle room beside them.

Julian went into the saddle room. It was cramped and ill-lit, full of the usual stable accoutrements: brushes, scissors, lanterns, buckets, blankets. There were three saddles standing on racks and a fourth rack vacant. "Is this where Mrs. Falkland's saddle was kept?" asked Julian.

"Yes, sir," said Cheever.

"There are no other side-saddles," Julian mused. "That means whoever set the trap knew exactly whom he meant to harm. Where are the nails kept?"

Cheever pointed out a box lying open on a nearby shelf. It contained nails of all sizes, including some of the same type and length as those that had been driven into Mrs. Falkland's saddle.

Another simple, flawless crime, thought Julian, like the Brickfield Murder and the murder of Alexander. The criminal takes advantage of whatever lies to hand—a brick, a poker, a box of nails—and leaves only as much damage and disarrangement as are needed to snuff out a life. Except that the Brickfield Murderer had also destroyed his victim's face. That made it all the more likely he had a reason to blot out her identity. Assuming all these crimes were by the same hand, this was a very economical felon—one who did the minimum needed to achieve the desired effect.

Julian closely examined the saddle room but found no clue to the culprit's identity. He widened his search, but to no avail. All he was able to determine was that none of the stable entrances had been forced.

"I suppose," he said to Cheever, "there must have been abundant opportunities for someone to slip into the saddle room without being noticed, either yesterday afternoon or early this morning."

"I expect so, sir. The boys and me, we had our work to do, cleaning the carriages and taking the horses out for an airing. There was plenty of times when nobody had the saddle room under his eye."

Julian surveyed the horses' stalls. "Which is the horse Fred had to quiet when Clare came to retrieve his horse?"

"That was Boreas, sir." Cheever pointed out his stall. "He's the one as gives all the trouble. Zephyr's as mild as milk."

Julian went over to Boreas's stall. "Fred wouldn't have been able to see from here if Clare went into the saddle room. All in all, a good opportunity for Mr. Clare."

He thanked Cheever for his help and went back into the house. The stable staff had been released from the parlour and sent down to the kitchen for some refreshment. "They can return to the stable now," Julian told Dutton, who met him in the hall.

"Yes, sir. And sir, Sir Malcolm asked if you'd join him in the study directly you came in."

Julian went in and reported to Sir Malcolm the scant results of his search. Then he asked after Mrs. Falkland. Sir Malcolm said she was fully conscious now and able to converse a little. "She asked again to be taken up to her room, and I said she should rest a bit longer first. Then she wanted to know how Phoenix was. She seemed worried about him—he isn't given to freakish fits. I thought I'd better tell her what had happened—about her saddle having been tampered with."

"What did she say?"

"She didn't say anything for a long time. Then she said, 'My poor boy.' I think she was talking about the horse, but it was hard to be sure. She closed her eyes as if she wanted to blot it all out, and I didn't like to press her further."

"'My poor boy,'" Julian repeated to himself. Then, abruptly, "What time did Eugene leave for his new school yesterday?"

"You can't think—her own brother, a boy of sixteen!—"

"I hope not, Sir Malcolm. But the fact remains, he's the only person who has something obvious to gain from Alexander's dying childless. His inheritance depends on it."

"Yes, that's true," Sir Malcolm admitted. Then he brightened. "But he left too early. I put him in the post-chaise myself, at nine o'clock in the morning."

"Then he's out of the running." Julian was relieved. He liked Eugene and would have been sorry to find he had planned such a cold-blooded, treacherous crime. "Now, what about Martha? When did she leave for London yesterday?"

"At about ten in the morning. I drove her myself, then went on to my chambers at Lincoln's Inn."

"Scratch Martha, then. That leaves you, Sir Malcolm.

Where were you between noon yesterday and half past nine this morning?"

"I realize you have to do this," said Sir Malcolm, through gritted teeth. "But your methods keep coming as a shock to me. How you can ask— Very well. I was in chambers from about eleven o'clock until mid-afternoon—you know, you saw me there. Then I met with some other benchers on Inn business and dined in Hall. I got home some time between eight and half past. Mr. Clare called about half an hour later, and I was with him until midnight. Then I went to bed. So I hadn't much opportunity to tamper with Belinda's saddle. But this morning I was up at seven and not under any sort of close scrutiny. I might have managed to creep out to the stable."

"Thank you, Sir Malcolm." Julian was becoming rather tired of being rebuked for his thoroughness. What had Sir Malcolm promised, just a few short days ago? *Whatever questions you ask, however brutal you're forced to be, I shall never reproach you—* So much for good resolves.

He said, "I think we're both a little overwrought. We might be the better for some luncheon and a chance to let everything we've discovered so far sink in."

Sir Malcolm smiled. "What you're saying, in your inimitably tactful way, is that *I'm* a little overwrought and need food and rest. And you're perfectly right. Just tell me: have you any idea at all who made this attack on my daughter?"

"Well, the field of suspects is narrow at first glance—your servants, Mrs. Falkland's groom, Mr. Clare, and yourself— but we have to take into account that one of the servants may have been suborned. Then, too, the gate and the stable were unlocked yesterday afternoon and this morning. Someone might have slipped in from the street while the stable staff were absent or occupied."

"In other words, virtually anyone could have done it!"

"I wouldn't go so far as to say that. Whoever caused the accident—we'll call him X—would have had to know a good deal about Mrs. Falkland's habits: what time she was accustomed to go riding, where her saddle was kept, and when

Nugent would be finished cleaning it and could be relied on not to go near it again. And assuming X's aim was to cause her to miscarry—which is by no means certain; he may simply have wanted to do her a mischief—he had to have known she was in the family way. So one of the first questions we need to ask Mrs. Falkland is whether she told anyone she was expecting a child."

He frowned thoughtfully. "You know, I feel I've gone about this enquiry in the only possible way—I've asked the right questions and searched in the right places—and still, I'm wide of the mark. I've investigated too much and thought too little. There's a pattern here, but I'm standing too close to see it. What I need is perspective."

Sir Malcolm laid a hand good-humouredly on his shoulder. "What we both need is luncheon."

There was a flurry of noise in the hallway: doors, footsteps, voices. Then a woman's furious cry: "Where is she? Where's my mistress? I should never have left her! If I'd been here, they'd never have dared!"

Julian and Sir Malcolm hastened out into the hallway. They found Martha tugging off her bonnet and shawl and thrusting them at Dutton, who must have just broken the news of the attack on Mrs. Falkland. With her was Luke Hallam, the tall, blond footman who had seen Mrs. Falkland approached by Mrs. Desmond outside Cygnet's Court. Luke was staring at Dutton in horror—and not only horror, Julian thought. If ever a young man looked stricken with guilt, it was he.

# ✳ 17 ✳

# ABANDON
# ALL HOPE

"Where is Mrs. Falkland?" Martha demanded of Julian and Sir Malcolm.

"She's in the library," said Julian in an undertone. "We ought to move a little further down the hall, so as not to disturb her."

They all complied, although Martha seethed with impatience at being held back from going to her mistress. Luke seemed too distraught to notice where he went or what he did.

"I should like to ask you both a few questions," said Julian. "Do you know of anyone who might wish to hurt Mrs. Falkland?"

Martha bridled. "If I thought anyone would harm a hair of her head, sir, do you suppose I would have left her?"

"Had she quarrelled with anyone recently?"

"That she had!" Realization glittered in Martha's eyes. *"That boy!"*

"Eugene? He can't have been responsible for the accident. He left far too early yesterday to have set the trap."

"Well, he's the only person that ever ran rusty with my mistress. If he's not responsible, I don't know who is. But if so be the ruffian ever falls into my hands, I'll know how to deal with him!"

Julian turned to Luke. "What about you? Do you know of anyone who had a grudge against your mistress?"

"No, sir," Luke croaked. He cleared his throat and repeated a bit more strongly, "No, sir."

Sir Malcolm looked at Julian as if to say, *He knows something!* Julian nodded briefly but did not pursue it now. If Luke felt guilty about something to do with Mrs. Falkland, he would confess it more freely once Martha and her avenging fury were out of the way.

"Did you know your mistress was in the family way?" Julian asked Martha.

"She never told me, sir, but I guessed."

"Do you know if she told anyone else?"

"I wouldn't know, sir."

"Did *you* tell anyone?"

"No, sir. I was never one to tittle about my mistress's affairs."

"Pardon me for pressing you, but you must see, this is of the greatest importance. Are you quite sure you said nothing to anyone?"

"As sure as I was born, sir. I never said a word."

"Luke, did you have any idea your mistress might be in the family way?"

"*No*, sir." Luke seemed scandalized that anyone could suppose he knew such an intimate thing about Mrs. Falkland.

"Has there been any talk of it among your fellow servants?"

"Not that I ever heard, sir."

Julian had no further questions for Martha. Sir Malcolm dismissed her, and she hurried off to her mistress.

The moment she was gone, Luke's head came up. He looked tired, his eyes red-rimmed, his usually ruddy face a little pale. "I have something to tell you, sir."

"I thought as much," said Julian. "Why don't we go into the study."

Sir Malcolm went with them, first giving Dutton orders to have luncheon prepared. Finding Luke nervous and tongue-tied, Julian began with some fairly innocuous questions. It was necessary to establish which of Alexander's servants had alibis for Mrs. Falkland's accident, and to that end Julian asked Luke what they had been doing between noon yesterday and half past nine this morning.

"We were all very busy, sir. Martha'd come to pack up Mrs. Falkland's things and sort out which were to be brought here and which were to go to her house in Dorset."

Martha had enlisted nearly all the servants to help her, Luke explained. The maids had pressed and folded her clothes and swathed the furniture in Holland covers, while the footmen blacked boots and carried heavy boxes and furnishings.

"I hope nothing in the study was disturbed?" said Julian.

"No, sir, Mr. Nichols said we weren't to touch anything there."

This morning some of the furniture had been sent to Dorset in a van; the rest Mrs. Falkland intended to sell. Her clothes and small belongings had been packed into the Falklands' town coach, which had brought Martha and Luke to Hampstead. Luke was here to help with the unloading and return with any messages Mrs. Falkland cared to send to London.

"In short," said Julian, "none of you had an opportunity to slip off to Hampstead between noon yesterday and this morning?"

"Mr. Valère could have, sir. He didn't help us much—said it was beneath him to move furniture or handle ladies' clothes. But the rest of us were well nigh run off our feet all day and most of the night. It all had to be done in a hurry, because Martha wanted to be back in Hampstead today."

"Why was that?" asked Julian.

"I think she didn't like to be away from Mrs. Falkland any longer than she could help, sir."

Julian pondered this. Almost the first words Martha had spoken on learning of Mrs. Falkland's accident were, *If I'd been here they'd never have dared!* Did it mean something that the attack had taken place during the twenty-four hours she was away? Why should the culprit have feared her? What could a lady's maid do to prevent an act of foul play in the stables?

"Now then," said Julian, "will you come out and tell us what's disturbing you, or must we play at questions?"

"It—it's what you asked me about before, sir. You remember how a maidservant came up to Mrs. Falkland in the Strand, and Mrs. Falkland went away with her, and the master said she'd gone to visit a sick friend?"

"Yes." Julian's heart leaped, but he kept his voice cool and measured.

"Well, sir, everything I told you was true, but it wasn't the whole truth. I meant all for the best!" He looked pleadingly from Julian to Sir Malcolm. "I thought it was something private that might shame her if it came out. Not that I thought she'd done anything wrong, but sometimes people get mixed up in scandals without being able to help it. And now all I can think of is that someone's hurt her, and if I'd told what I knew it might not have happened. You might have found out she was in danger and saved her—"

"Look here, my boy," said Sir Malcolm, "what's done is done. All you can do now is make a clean breast of things, so we'll be forearmed against anyone's trying such a trick again."

"Yes, sir. It was when she come home, sir, after she'd gone away with the maidservant. She'd been gone for three hours, and I was getting worried. The Strand's not the sort of place I cared to think of her left alone. The master, he'd dressed for dinner and gone out, and I said to myself, if he ain't worried, why should I be? But all the same I was. I thought there might be things he didn't know. Not that she'd lie to him—not without a good reason—"

"We understand you're not accusing her of anything," Julian said.

"I never would, sir. Anyhow, I watched for her at the door and the front windows whenever I could, till finally she came home. And—and she acted very strange."

"In what way?" asked Julian.

"Afraid, sir. Haunted. She shrank away from me, wouldn't let me take her shawl—wouldn't even lift the veil on her bonnet. But I could see her eyes through the gauze, and they looked—I can't describe it. As if she was in a nightmare and couldn't wake up."

"My poor girl!" said Sir Malcolm softly.

"Go on," said Julian.

"She asked where Mr. Falkland was, and I said he'd gone out to dinner. Then she said she didn't want any dinner, she wasn't hungry, she only wanted to go up to her room. I asked if I should send Martha to her, and she said no. 'I want to be left alone,' she said, and she went upstairs."

"When was the next time you saw her?" Julian asked.

"Next morning. She looked white and tired, but she was herself again. I mean, she didn't have that terrible look in her eyes." Luke looked down, blushing a little. "There's one thing I haven't told you. She was wearing a new dress that day—a silk dress the colour of lilacs—and her shawl was all embroidered with flowers and leaves. She was clutching the shawl round her shoulders when she come home, and I was going to help her off with it, but she started away, and it slipped down, and I saw that her dress was torn. One of the sleeves was all but ripped away at the shoulder."

Julian's brows shot up. "Did she tell you how that happened?"

"No, sir. She didn't say anything about it at all. I think she knew that if she didn't speak of it, I wouldn't—not to her or anyone else. But I wish now I had. Do you think, sir, it would have made a difference?"

"I don't know," said Julian. "I hope from now on you'll answer questions unreservedly, without any misplaced efforts to protect people?"

"Yes, sir," Luke said miserably.

Julian smiled faintly. "Then I won't upbraid you any further—not when you're making such a first-rate job of it yourself. You might show yourself a little mercy on the ground of good intentions. To be led astray by loyalty isn't the worst of crimes."

Dutton announced that luncheon was ready. Sir Malcolm sent Luke down to the servants' hall for his meal. He and Julian sat down to steaks with oyster sauce, cold fowls, and a bottle of Sir Malcolm's excellent port. By tacit agreement, they said nothing about Mrs. Falkland's accident for a while. This gave Julian a chance to review the facts in his mind and try to find the pattern he felt sure was there.

"The crucial question," he told Sir Malcolm, when they had reached the fruit and coffee stage, "is whether the attack was intended to be against Mrs. Falkland or her unborn child. In other words, were you right to assume that this was Alexander's murderer striking at him again by destroying his child, or is there someone who wanted to harm Mrs. Falkland, to whom the fact of her expecting a child was unknown, or incidental?"

Sir Malcolm frowned intently at the orange segment on his fork, as if it might hold the answer. "Luke's story suggests that Belinda had a very ugly encounter at Cygnet's Court. I don't like to think of it, but perhaps she got into a struggle with someone—the man who was keeping Mrs. Desmond, perhaps?—and since then he's had a grudge against her. For that matter, Mrs. Desmond herself might have driven those nails into the saddle. You said no one knows where she is, so she could be well nigh anywhere. And you also said a stranger might have got into the stable without being noticed."

"The stranger would have had to know a good deal about the stable's routine and Mrs. Falkland's habits. Still, it's possible. Mrs. Desmond and Mrs. Falkland seem to have been engaged in some intrigue—perhaps they fell out, and Mrs. Desmond sought revenge. On the other hand, if Mrs. Desmond is the woman Jemmy Otis saw being spirited away from Cygnet's Court by the gentleman with the horse and gig, she may be a victim herself, and in no position to play malicious pranks on anyone else."

"Hmm." Sir Malcolm poured himself another cup of coffee. "Are you going to question Alexander's servants again?"

"I daresay someone should. But I think it's unlikely any of them tampered with Mrs. Falkland's saddle. If Martha kept them as busy as Luke says, they couldn't very well have stolen off to Hampstead. But there's Valère to consider: according to Luke, he refused to help the other servants pack up Mrs. Falkland's things. We ought to find out what he was doing instead. Though I find it hard to imagine that fastidious little Frenchman soiling his hands with saddles and nails.

"In short," he summed up, "both Luke and Martha have alibis for the accident, but not for Alexander's murder. The same is true of Eugene. You're the opposite case: you have an alibi for the murder, but not for the accident. Clare is the only one we know of so far who could have committed both crimes. The remaining suspects—Valère, Adams, Felix, the other guests at the party—have no alibi for the murder, and it remains to be seen if they can produce one for the accident."

"I don't know how you keep it all straight in your head. It makes me giddy."

Julian smiled. "I shouldn't have thought it any more difficult than Latin verbs or legal concepts."

"And it's a great deal more useful, you're probably thinking. I can't say I disagree!" Sir Malcolm grew serious again. "Shouldn't we report this attack on Belinda to the authorities?"

"I'll speak to Vance when I return to London. And I suppose you should swear out an information before one of your local magistrates. We can at least find out if the neighbourhood watchmen saw any suspicious characters lurking about."

"You haven't much faith in conventional law enforcement, have you?"

"I think the authorities mean well, but with the best will in the world they can't make the present system work—at all events, not when a serious crime occurs, and the culprit is unknown. The people charged with solving crimes have no experience—there are no qualifications for becoming a magistrate other than to have a sufficient income to make one proof against bribery. The constables are tradesmen chosen by lot who couldn't find anyone to serve in their place, and the watch is merely a way to support invalid or drunken old men without having to put them on parish relief. But the worst of the problem lies in the methods employed. Criminal detection ought to be active and systematic, whereas our approach is passive and haphazard. The magistrates put out advertisements, offer rewards, and wait for information to drift in. The Bow Street Runners are diligent and inventive, but there are only a handful of them, and they can't be everywhere. The solution is to establish a full-fledged professional police, but of course the opposition to that is tremendous."

"People ought to have more sense!" fumed Sir Malcolm.

Julian shrugged. "For many people, crime isn't a real concern until they become victims themselves."

"That's true. I can't say I ever gave it much thought—and I actually try criminal cases." Sir Malcolm smiled sadly. "It always seemed like the sort of thing that happened to somebody else."

Dutton appeared in the doorway and spoke to Sir Malcolm. "Mrs. Falkland's maid would like to see you, sir."

"Send her in," Sir Malcolm said.

Martha entered. "Mrs. Falkland is feeling better, sir, and says if Mr. Kestrel has questions for her, she's ready to answer them now."

Julian glanced toward Sir Malcolm, who nodded assent. "Thank you," he said to Martha. "Please tell Mrs. Falkland I'll be with her directly."

✳

The first thing that caught Julian's eye when he entered the library was the blank space on the wall. Alexander's portrait had been taken down and turned back side out. "I asked Martha to do that," Mrs. Falkland said quietly. "Those eyes were driving me mad."

She was half sitting up on the leather sofa, a quilt drawn up to her waist. Her bound foot made a bulge at the other end. She had exchanged her black riding habit for a white night-dress and a soft blue cashmere shawl. Her hair was unbound, and tiny gold strands floated, freshly brushed, like a halo around her head.

Julian sat down facing her. She did not look at him, but into a cup of tea she was slowly, monotonously stirring. He asked, "Are you sure you're well enough to talk to me?"

"Yes. What do you wish to know?"

He hesitated, suddenly appalled at the task before him. How did one question a woman about a wound so fresh, a loss so agonizing? Yet it had to be done. She had asked for this interview; he would have to take her word for it that she could endure it.

"First," he said gently, "if you'll forgive an ignorant question from a bachelor—did you know you were going to have a child?"

"Yes."

"Did you tell anyone about it?"

"No."

"Was there some reason for that?"

"Yes. I said nothing about it because I didn't think the child would live."

He was taken aback. "Do you mean you expected something like this to happen?"

"Expected? No. But if you'd been through what I have, you wouldn't think anything good could happen, or anything wholesome or beautiful could thrive, ever again."

He remembered how she had asked him if he had ever been to Hell. And he thought of the inscription over the gateway: *Abandon all hope ye who enter here.*

"Mrs. Falkland, have you any idea who did this?"

"No."

"Has anyone threatened you or been angry with you recently?"

"No. Other than Eugene, and Martha says you told her he couldn't have done it."

"No, he left too early yesterday. Have you cause to suspect any of Sir Malcolm's servants?"

"No. I've found them all to be trustworthy and good. I'm sure none of them would harm me."

"What about your groom, Nugent?"

"Nugent is unfailingly honest and loyal. He couldn't possibly be guilty." She added, "Even if he could bring himself to hurt me, he would never hurt Phoenix."

That rang true, Julian thought. "Mr. Clare had access to your saddle last night. Has he ever shown any ill will toward you?"

"No, never."

"How well do you know him?"

"Not very. I believe he's shy, especially with ladies. But he's always been civil and courteous to me."

Julian pondered. "Have you noticed anyone suspicious hanging about the stable lately, or watching you while you were out riding?"

"No."

"Nugent mentioned you went to the stable yesterday evening with a basket of apples for Phoenix. Have you any idea whether your saddle had been tampered with at that time?"

"No. I had no reason to look at my saddle."

Julian felt he was getting nowhere. "Think back. Did you see anything out of the common in the stable last night?"

"I can't think of anything. But I imagine whoever did this would make sure I saw nothing suspicious. That would be easy enough. I visit Phoenix at the same time every night. Someone who knew the house would have known that."

He pointed out gently, "But you've just absolved everyone in the house."

"I can't solve that riddle. I thought you were here to make sense of such mysteries."

"I am," he said ruefully. "But I haven't been quick enough about it. This happened on my watch, and I'm more sorry for it than I can say."

"Please don't blame yourself," she said wearily. "You only make things harder. Have you anything more to ask me?"

"There's one thing we haven't touched on: Mrs. Desmond."

"Mrs. Desmond?"

He searched her face. He would swear she had never heard the name in her life. "Mrs. Desmond is the young woman who inveigled you into Cygnet's Court."

Her fingers tightened around the tea-cup. "Really? I never knew her name."

"Mrs. Falkland, Luke was very upset when he heard of your accident. He was afraid that, by keeping back information about you, he'd exposed you to danger. So he's told us the truth about your return from that encounter at Cygnet's Court. He says you came home terrified, unwilling to lift your veil, and with one of the sleeves half torn from your dress."

She looked at him like a cornered animal. "Well?"

"Well—what was it that frightened you? And how did you tear your dress?"

"I tore my dress on a park paling. And I wasn't frightened, merely tired. I'm tired now. Please go away."

"If you have an enemy, for God's sake, tell us. Whoever it is may strike again—"

"What do I care? What have I left to lose? My husband is dead, my child is dead! I have only my life, because God won't have me, God won't let me die!"

She flung up her hands to her face. The tea-cup overturned, spilling tea down the side of the quilt. Her shoulders heaved; sobs tore at her throat.

He sprang up, took away the cup and saucer, and gave her his handkerchief. She pressed it to her face. "Please—I want Martha—"

He hastened to the door, thinking Martha could not be far. She was waiting in the hall and came at once. Seeing her mistress's state, she threw him a furious glance and rushed to her side. She gathered her in her large, strong arms and rocked her like a child.

He went out, closed the door behind him, and leaned back against it. His shock at Mrs. Falkland's outburst of grief had died down, but a deeper shock took its place. The pattern he had sought was emerging at last. And it was horrifying.

# ✳ 18 ✳

## AN ALIBI
## SHATTERED

Julian returned to London late that afternoon and stopped at Bow Street. He was lucky enough to find Vance in. Vance shook his head sombrely when he heard of the attack on Mrs. Falkland. "Seems it wasn't enough for our man to kill Mr. Falkland—he had to serve out Mrs. Falkland, too. And that's too bad, sir—taking it out on a lady, or a babe not even born."

Julian had his own ideas about this, but as they were only half formed, he kept them to himself. "I suggested to Sir Malcolm that he report this to the local authorities and ask them to make the initial enquiries in the neighbourhood—for strangers, suspicious characters, that sort of thing."

"I'm glad to hear it, sir. We've enough to do to handle the investigation in London."

"Have you made any progress with the gig and horse?"

"Not much, sir. It's been a busy day, what with a parcel of banknotes being stolen off a mail coach and a gang of footpads kicking up a shine on the Hounslow road. Still, you don't need to hear all that, do you, sir? I'll tell you what I *have* done: I sent Bill Watkins out to nose around Long Acre. That neighbourhood's full of coachmakers, and it's just the other side of Covent Garden from Cygnet's Court. If anybody'd remember a particular gig and horse, it'd be folks in the business of selling carriages, wouldn't you say?"

"That's a good thought. And you know, that neighbourhood would have been an ideal place for the driver to be rid of the gig and horse—by selling them to a coachmaker, for example."

"Assuming he had reason to be rid of 'em, sir."

"Well, Jemmy says he used them to take an unconscious lady out of Cygnet's Court on the night of the Brickfield Murder. There are traces of brickearth in Mrs. Desmond's house, and both Mrs. Desmond and her maid are missing. It's hard to avoid the conclusion that that man, and that gig and horse, were mixed up in something very rum."

"Well, if anyone in Long Acre has 'em, we'll find 'em, sir. And maybe if we're lucky we'll get a description of the driver."

"Maybe." Julian shook his head wryly. "But somehow I think our gentleman knows a trick worth two of that."

✳

Dipper met Julian at the door of his flat. "You've got a visitor, sir. Mr. Talmadge."

"Eugene? He's supposed to be in Yorkshire!"

"He couldn't very well be, sir," said Dipper reasonably, "on account of his being here."

"An unassailable piece of logic." Julian gave Dipper his hat, gloves, and riding whip and asked grimly, "Where is he?"

"In the study, sir. I tipped him some grub and a plug of malt from the coffee-house, 'coz he was dead-and-alive when he come here. Looked as if he'd been knocking about the streets since lightmans. And he ain't wearing the boots for it."

"Hell and damnation. What is that troublesome cub doing two hundred miles from where he ought to be?"

"Sleeping, sir. Leastways he was last time I looked."

"Then he's in for a rude awakening. He's certainly given me one."

Julian went into the study. Warm air and an aroma of beef and beer assailed him. The fire was burning so brightly, the little room had grown hot and close. Eugene was still asleep, sprawled in an armchair by the fire. He looked much cleaner than he had when Julian last saw him. In place of the limp, soiled neckcloth, he wore a glazed black stock so high and stiff he must be completely exhausted to be able to sleep in it.

Julian relented a little, seeing his own advice carried to such zealous excess. "Mr. Talmadge."

Eugene stirred, blinked, scrambled to his feet. "Mr. Kestrel—I—you must be wondering what I'm doing here—"

"That's merely a faint echo of my sentiments." Julian crossed the room and opened a window. The rush of cold air made Eugene shiver.

Julian motioned him to sit down again and took a seat opposite. "Let's begin at the beginning, shall we? Yesterday Sir Malcolm put you on a post-chaise to Yorkshire at nine in the morning. Is that correct?"

"I—I think so," stammered Eugene. "I don't remember the time exactly."

"We'll call it nine. Now I wish to know exactly where you were and everything you did from that time until you came here."

"But why?"

"Allow me to ask the questions for the present. Believe me, you're in no position to make terms."

Eugene looked at him uncertainly. At last he drew a long breath and commenced, "I didn't want to go away to school. I especially didn't want to go to a school in Yorkshire, because whatever Belinda says, those schools are for boys nobody wants, and horrible things happen to them there—much she cares! I saw there was no changing her mind, so I decided to run away. I didn't know what I would do, or where I would go—I only knew I couldn't face the boys and the masters. They'd all know about my father, and worse still, they'd know about Alexander. They'd say I killed him. They might even try to hang me. I know the sorts of things they do.

"I didn't really have a plan when I set out yesterday. But the third time we stopped to change horses, I saw a London-bound stagecoach stopping too. So all at once I made up my mind. I paid off the post-boy and lugged my portmanteau over

to the coach. I talked to the guard, and he talked to the coachman, and they let me have an outside seat.''

Julian was not surprised. Taking up a passenger not on the
waybill—"shouldering," as it was called—allowed the coachman and guard to divide the fee between them, instead of
passing it on to the coach proprietor. "Go on."

"So I climbed up on the roof and had to sit next to a man
who chewed tobacco and kept spitting it off the side of the
coach, only sometimes it landed on my coat, and there was a
woman with a baby that cried all the way to London. But the
view was smashing from up there. I'd never ridden on top of
a coach before. We got into London and stopped at an inn
called the Belle Savage—"

"What time was that?"

"About six o'clock. Everyone got off the coach and went
about their business—but I didn't have any business. I didn't
know what to do, and the portmanteau was confoundedly
heavy to lug about. So finally I took a room at the inn and
had dinner. After that I was fagged out and went to bed."

"Did anyone see you at the inn that evening?"

"Don't you believe me?" Eugene stared at him in bewilderment. "Why would I lie?"

"Be so good as to answer my question. Did anyone see
you?"

"I think, sir," said Eugene, with careful politeness, "that
your question is rather insulting. But as I haven't anyone else
to turn to, I suppose you may ask what you like. Yes, people
saw me in the coffee-room, but I don't know who they were.
The waiters saw me. And a maid came to my room just before
I went to bed and took my boots away to be cleaned."

"What time was that?"

"I don't know! It might have been nine o'clock, or a little
after. I know it was early, because I woke up at dawn. Everything looked grey and dismal. I went out—you want to
know what time, I suppose; I think it was about six—and I
stopped at a street breakfast for coffee and bread and butter. After that I just wandered around. I watched the clerks

coming to work in the City. Some of them were younger than I am, and I thought how lucky they were to have a place to go—"

"They were probably thinking how lucky you were not to have to go anywhere."

"Yes, but they have work, they earn their own money, they're independent! I have to go where people tell me, even if it's to a beastly school in Yorkshire. I wondered if I might get work, but I don't know how to do anything, and I don't have a character. I don't think you can get work without a character, can you?"

"It depends on how fastidious you are about keeping within the law, or the bounds of decency."

Eugene nodded. "I was afraid of that. Anyway, I just kept walking, and I liked seeing parts of town I hadn't seen before, but my feet got sore, and I was more and more worried about what would become of me when my money ran out. Finally I was so desperate, I decided to come to you."

"You've put that rather inartfully."

"I didn't mean it that way. I meant that I know I haven't any claim on you, and you've no reason to help me, but I thought since you're a man of honour, you'd at least respect my confidence and not give me away. And you know the world—you might be able to advise me. I feel so lost. You don't know what it's like to be my age and feel everyone is against you, and you have nowhere to go except home, and you'd rather die than go there."

"Actually," said Julian quietly, "I know exactly what it's like."

Eugene looked at him respectfully. "I believe you."

"That's very gratifying." Julian nipped the subject in the bud. "But we digress. Have you anyone who can vouch for your whereabouts from six o'clock this morning until half past nine?"

"No. I was just walking about the City. Why are you asking me all these questions?" he pleaded. "What have I done?"

"What you've done, you exasperating infant, is pitched

yourself into a devil of a mess." He added, watching him, "I have some grave news for you. Your sister was in an accident this morning."

"An accident! Is she all right?"

"She twisted her ankle. And she lost the child she was carrying."

"Oh, poor Bel! Is she very ill? Will she get well?"

"The surgeon thinks so."

"How did it happen?"

"She was thrown from her horse."

"But she's never thrown! She's a bruising rider!"

"This time she had help. Someone drove two nails into her saddle."

"You mean—to make her fall? But that's monstrous! Who would do a thing like that to her?"

"Some people may want to know if you have any ideas about that."

"I—I don't understand—"

"Then I'll put it more bluntly. Your inheritance was conditioned on Alexander's dying childless. Now he has."

"Oh, no," Eugene whispered, shaking his head. "Oh, no."

"So you see, you're in an awkward spot."

"But—but—I didn't—I wouldn't! I'd never have hurt her like that! I wouldn't do anything so mean and base to anyone, let alone my sister! I didn't even know she was in the family way! She never told me."

"She was ill when I saw her last Sunday. You might have deduced from that that she was going to have a child."

"I never even thought of it. She said she must have eaten bad food. And that was exactly how it seemed."

"Yes," said Julian, nodding, "that would fit quite well."

"Fit what?"

"Never mind. I was thinking aloud."

"You do believe me, don't you? You don't think I drove those nails into her saddle?"

"You had ample opportunity. You could have stolen off to

Hampstead early this morning, set the trap, and returned to London at your leisure."

"Well, perhaps I could have, but I didn't!"

"Surely a young man with your bad blood would think nothing of playing a trick like this?"

"Look here, I know I said the other day I had bad blood, but—but that was—well—"

"Self-indulgent rubbish?"

Eugene lifted his chin. "Yes. Yes, it was. I may have been an ass then, but I'm not a liar now. I didn't hurt Belinda, and I didn't kill Alexander. I swear it."

Julian regarded him for a short time in silence. "What do you mean to do now?"

"I don't know." Eugene collapsed into childhood again. "What do you think I ought to do?"

"There's only one course open to you. You must go back to Hampstead at once."

"To—to Sir Malcolm's house? I can't! Everyone will suspect me, Belinda will hate me, she'll think I killed her baby!"

"What were you proposing to do instead? Disappear? You might as well sign a confession of guilt and be done with it."

"But she'll look at me, and I'll know she's thinking: *Did he do it? Is he a murderer?* And what will I say?"

"Anything is better than staying away and letting your absence speak for you. Who do you think is going to believe in your innocence, if you haven't the courage to proclaim it yourself?"

Eugene was silent. At last he swallowed hard and asked, "Will you come with me?"

Julian felt he owed him that. He could not pitch him into the lions' den and then leave him to fight it out alone. Besides, he wanted to see how Eugene was received in Hampstead. "Very well," he said, rising.

"Must we go now?"

"Of course if you'd rather hang about here brooding and imagining how it will be—"

"No!" Eugene shuddered. "No, sir," he amended politely.

They went out into the hall. Julian glanced wryly at his reflection in the looking-glass, but decided that in this emergency he could permit himself to go out in the evening in riding dress. Eugene, too, stole a look in the glass and gave a few tugs to the formidable black stock around his neck.

"It's a distinct improvement," Julian told him. "But you know, you needn't wear it *à la guillotine*."

"It *is* a bit high," Eugene admitted. "But you said I ought to learn to hold my head up."

"You seem to be making progress."

"I could hardly help it, wearing this."

Julian smiled. "I wasn't talking about your neckwear."

✳

It was nearly sunset by the time they arrived in Hampstead. Shadows of trees and gaslamps stretched like pointing fingers along the streets. Eugene sat up tense and taut in the hackney coach. Julian had an idea he would resound like a tuning-fork if touched.

Sir Malcolm received them in the library. Mrs. Falkland had been carried up to her room, and Alexander's portrait was back on the wall, looking out with laughing eyes on the troubles and torments of his family.

Julian left it to Eugene to explain how he had run away and returned to London. Eugene flushed and stammered a little but got through his story fairly bravely. At the end, he drew a long breath and said, "I should like to see my sister."

Sir Malcolm took Julian aside. "I don't think we should let him see her. You said yourself he had the most obvious reason to want her to lose her child. Now we know he had an opportunity to tamper with her saddle. She's bound to realize that herself, and it might upset her terribly."

"It might upset her more if she heard he'd returned, and he seemed ashamed to face her."

"There's something in that," Sir Malcolm owned. "I suppose we could at least go up and find out if she's awake and well enough to see him."

The three of them trooped upstairs and knocked at Mrs. Falkland's door. Martha opened it, then stopped dead, staring. "Mr. Eugene!"

"I've—I've come back, Martha."

"So I see, sir." She came out and shut the door behind her, looking grimly at Julian as if to say, *So much for his alibi!*

"Martha?" called Mrs. Falkland from her room. "Who is that with you?"

They all hesitated and looked at each other.

"Martha!" Mrs. Falkland's voice rose urgently. "Who is it? Not Eugene!"

Martha reluctantly opened the door a crack. "It *is* Mr. Eugene, ma'am. He's come back unexpectedly."

"No! He can't have! *No!*"

That was too much for Eugene. He turned about and started to flee, but ran straight into Julian. They looked at each other, Eugene's eyes pleading, Julian's remorseless. Eugene swallowed hard, turned back, and opened Mrs. Falkland's door.

She was half sitting up in bed, her shawl fallen off her shoulders. Her eyes, large and bruised-looking in her white face, stared across at him. "How long have you been here? Why aren't you at school?"

"I ran away. I've been back since yesterday." He took a few halting steps into the room. "I didn't do it, Bel!"

She struggled up into a sitting position. "Come here."

He hung back an instant, then went to her. She looked beyond him to Sir Malcolm, Julian, and Martha in the doorway. "Please come in, all of you. I have something to say. My brother is innocent of this crime." She took Eugene's hand and looked fiercely at the others. "I don't care how circumstances may tell against him. No one will ever convince me he did anything to harm me or my child. Whoever accuses him insults me, and will answer to me."

She lay back against her pillows. "I'm tired now, and I wish you all please to go away—except Eugene. Will you stay a little," she asked him, "and just sit quietly by my bed?"

"Yes, of course," he said huskily.

There was nothing for the others to do but bid her goodnight and go out. Martha was fuming. "Loyal to a fault, is Mrs. Falkland! Putting her trust in that boy!"

"Have you any reason to doubt him?" Julian asked.

"Doubt him? It's plain as a pikestaff it was him that caused her accident!" She stood, hands on hips, and looked at him challengingly. "Who else had anything to gain by it?"

✱

"Who else had anything to gain by it?" repeated Sir Malcolm, when he and Julian had retired to the library. "There's no getting round it: Eugene was the only person with a motive to destroy Alexander's child."

"That's true, so far as we know. But I don't believe he's guilty."

"You don't? Why not?"

"Well, first, because I'll lay any odds he knew nothing about the accident until I told him of it. I don't believe he's a good enough actor to counterfeit such shock and concern. But principally, I don't think he drove those nails into Mrs. Falkland's saddle—because I think I know who did."

"Who?" asked Sir Malcolm excitedly.

"I should rather not tell you just yet."

"What? Why not?"

"Because I haven't yet determined whether the same person killed your son."

"But surely that's overwhelmingly likely!"

"On the contrary, I can easily imagine the two crimes being committed by different people. For example, suppose Luke loved Mrs. Falkland with more than a servant's devotion and killed Alexander in a fit of jealousy. The very motive that made him commit that crime would forbid his doing anything to harm Mrs. Falkland. But let's say someone close to

Alexander—his friend Mr. Clare or his loyal servant Valère—found out the reason for his murder and blamed Mrs. Falkland? That person might have tampered with her saddle in order to punish her—might not even have known she was in the family way. In fact, if he *had* known, he might have spared her for the sake of Alexander's child."

Sir Malcolm clasped his head in his hands. "This certainly has got complicated! We haven't yet solved Alexander's murder, and now we have two crimes to investigate!"

Three, thought Julian—we still don't know how the Brickfield Murder fits in. But this did not seem the best time to remind Sir Malcolm of that.

"All you've said makes sense," Sir Malcolm admitted. "But I still don't see why you shouldn't tell me who you think caused the accident. It will drive me distracted, not knowing."

"You'll agree that, until we know if the same person killed your son, it's important to keep my suspicions dark?"

"I suppose so."

"Well, if I tell you who I think caused the accident, can you meet that person, talk with him or her, as though you knew nothing of my suspicions?"

"No. No, I couldn't possibly. You're right, you'd better not tell me. But wait—how do we know Belinda isn't still in danger? If the attack was directed at her, and not solely at her child, the attacker may strike again."

Julian pondered this, then shook his head. "It wouldn't help her to voice my suspicions. In fact, it could only increase the danger, if there is any."

"How can that be?"

"Will you take my word that's it's so? Believe me, I wouldn't hazard her safety." He paused. "All the same, I should keep a close watch on her. We know she has at least one enemy near at hand."

"Who?"

"Herself. She's a very strong woman, but her despair may be stronger. I shouldn't leave her alone."

"We won't," Sir Malcolm said fervently. "But, Mr. Kestrel,

there has to be a limit on this secrecy of yours. The surgeon says Belinda won't be able to walk on her ankle for another week. If you haven't found Alexander's murderer by then, I think you should tell me whom you suspect of causing her accident. I don't want her up and about, perhaps running into the villain without knowing it."

"Very well." In reality, Julian knew he had less time than that. He had bet Oliver de Witt five hundred pounds that he would solve Alexander's murder in a week, and there were only five days left. The contest was useful, since it distanced him a little from the investigation, and distance was the essence of perspective. Of course, he would like to win. Five hundred pounds was a large sum to gain—or lose. If de Witt won, he would be insufferable; he would dine out on his victory for weeks. Julian would not give him the chance. Five days might not be long—but it would have to be long enough.

# ✳ 19 ✳

## Vance Turns Up
## a Trump

Julian dined with Sir Malcolm and returned to London quite late. In the morning he considered what his next move should be. It was all very well to have a theory about who had caused Mrs. Falkland's accident; he had to make sure the facts would bear it out. There were stories to verify, whereabouts to check—

The street door-bell rang. Dipper went down to answer it and returned with Peter Vance. "Good morning, sir!" Vance greeted Julian, taking off his hat with a flourish. "And a fine morning it is, too!"

"You seem in high feather."

"Well, as I say, sir, it's a fine day. Such a fine one, you might like to come outside with me and see how I got here."

Intrigued, Julian accompanied him downstairs. Waiting in the street was a rickety gig painted black and white, drawn by an old roan horse with a snip of white on his left nostril and a splint on his near foreleg.

"My dear Vance," marvelled Julian, "you excel yourself! Next time I want a miracle worked, I shall come to you at once. Where did you find them?"

Vance rocked back and forth on his heels, grinning. "Well now, sir, I told you I was going to nose about among the coachmakers in Long Acre and see if our gentleman tried to palm off the gig and horse on any of them. The third one I visited got into a pucker as soon as I started asking questions. So I pressed him, and he admitted he'd found just such a gig and horse. Said he was keeping 'em on his premises till the owner came to claim them. 'Course, he wasn't doing nix-my-doll to find the owner, but he wouldn't, would he, sir? If nobody claimed the gig and horse, he could sell 'em and pocket the money. They ain't much to look at, but they've got a few good years left. Lucky for us, though, sir, the coachmaker hadn't the pluck to sell 'em straightaway. He thought he'd wait for a bit and make sure the owner didn't turn up. So there they were, sir, just waiting for me in his stable.''

"You've certainly turned up a trump. How did the coachmaker find them?''

"He says he got up one morning and saw 'em in the street. He lives in Long Acre, next door to his workshop and stables. At first he and his men took no notice of 'em. It was raining —had been for hours—and he thought the driver must've left 'em in the street and gone inside somewhere to get warm and dry. But as the morning went on and nobody came to collect 'em, he decided to take 'em in himself—for safe-keeping, so he says.''

"It had been raining for hours, you say? Then it may well have been the morning after the Brickfield Murder.''

"May have been? Bless you, sir, it was! The coachmaker knew the date: Saturday, the sixteenth of April. I expect he was keeping track of how much time had gone by, thinking he'd sell the gig and horse if the owner didn't turn up—say, in a month.''

"It was devilish clever of our gentleman, abandoning them like that," said Julian. "We thought he might try to sell or store them in Long Acre, but this was far simpler. He didn't have to make terms with anyone—he simply stopped the gig, jumped down, and walked away. If it were still dark, no one would have got a good look at him. Even if dawn had broken, in a heavy rain people aren't looking about them—they cover themselves with shawls or umbrellas and walk with their heads down. Besides, there's always a bustle in Covent Garden at that hour, with the market gardeners bringing their produce into town, and the libertines skulking off home. If our gentleman was implicated in the Brickfield Murder, he couldn't have found a better time or place to be rid of his means of transport."

"I'd say he was more than implicated, sir—he was in it up to his ears. Look'ee here."

Vance beckoned Julian closer to the gig. The wheels, the upholstery, and the broad apron where the driver put his feet were all caked with old, dried mud and traces of reddish clay. "That's brickearth, that is, sir. It's a mercy the coachmaker never cleaned it off. He was so afraid he'd be accused of trying to disguise stolen goods, he didn't lay a finger on the gig except to bring it indoors. You'd think that, once news of the Brickfield Murder got out, he would've tumbled to it that there was something rum about a gig with brickearth spattered on it, abandoned on the very morning after the murder. But some folks never see past the ends of their noses. I expect all he thought about was what the gig might mean to him in profit."

Julian walked slowly around the carriage, peering closely at the splotches of mud and clay. "This certainly gives our gentleman some explaining to do—if we could find him." He went around to inspect the horse and patted its neck in some amusement. "If you could only talk, my dear fellow, you would now be our most valuable witness."

He turned to Vance. "Let's take stock. What do we know about our mysterious driver? We know that at about nine o'clock on the night of Friday, April the fifteenth, he drove this gig to the entrance to Cygnet's Court. He went into Cygnet's Court, leaving Jemmy Otis holding the horse. He came out carrying a sleeping or unconscious woman, dressed in a cloak and bonnet and white slippers decorated with gold thread. He put her into the gig and drove off with her. That same night, Mrs. Desmond and her maid, Fanny, disappeared from Cygnet's Court, and a woman about Fanny's age was murdered in a brickfield near Hampstead. In the morning, the gig was found covered in mud and brickearth, and traces of brickearth have turned up in Mrs. Desmond's house. All of which suggests, first, that our gentleman spirited away either Mrs. Desmond or Fanny; second, that he was involved in the Brickfield Murder; and, third, that Fanny was the brickfield victim."

"S'pose our gentleman did take Fanny all the way to Hampstead and do for her there, sir. Why did he come back here and track mud and clay through Mrs. Desmond's house? We most likely never would've made the connexion between the Brickfield Murder and Mrs. D. if it hadn't been for that."

"I've been wondering about that myself. Perhaps he came back to remove Mrs. Desmond's things, to make it appear she and her maid had simply moved away of their own free will."

"What would Mrs. D. have been doing all that time?"

"I don't know. It depends very much on whether she or Fanny was the woman Jemmy saw taken away in the gig. Logically it ought to have been Fanny, since she fits the description of the brickfield victim. But why would she have been wearing gold-threaded slippers? And given that the Brickfield Murder was committed between two and eight in the morning, and even this super-annuated horse could have reached Hampstead in under an hour, what was the driver doing for anywhere from four to twelve hours between his departure from Cygnet's Court and the murder?"

He peered into the gig again and shook his head. "I'm wrong in any case. The driver couldn't have come back to remove Mrs. Desmond's things, because the mud stains haven't been disturbed by any large objects being packed in here. There are only the driver's footprints on the apron and the smear of mud and clay where he sat—"

Julian held up a finger. "Why, Vance, that may be why he went back to Mrs. Desmond's house. If the gig was splashed and soiled to this extent, imagine the state the driver must have been in. His clothes would have been soaked with mud and clay—blood too, if it was he who committed the Brickfield

Murder. Smashing a woman's face must make an appalling mess. I'll lay you any odds he returned to Mrs. Desmond's house to clean himself, perhaps change his clothes. And the reason he went straight up to her room is that the washstand is there."

"I believe you're in the right of it, sir!" Vance clapped Julian on the back, then drew away, embarrassed but amused. "I beg your pardon, sir. My feelings got the better of me."

"My dear Vance, I shan't have you up for an assault. I should like—in fact, I should be honoured if you would treat me as a colleague and not make these differences between us."

"I'm much obliged, I'm sure, sir. But you see, though you may treat me as familiar as you like—in a gentleman that's being what you call mag-nanimous—if I was to be familiar with *you*, that'd be imper'ence. And a man in my place as don't know the difference is asking to be blowed up."

"I beg your pardon. I never meant to overturn the social order."

"That's all right, sir," said Vance indulgently. "Gentlemen like you don't have to pay much heed to the social order. A mountain don't get in the way of a man as lives on the top."

"Why, Vance, I believe you're a Radical."

"Who, me, sir?" Vance's eyes danced. "Just a working man as knows my place."

"And knows how to put me in mine."

Vance grinned, then his brows came together. "We're learning heaps about the Brickfield Murder, sir, but it's Mr. Falkland's murder we're supposed to be a-solving. You think we're getting anywhere with that?"

"Yes, because I'm certain the two crimes are connected. Mrs. Falkland had a suspicious meeting with Mrs. Desmond just two weeks before the Brickfield Murder, and a week after it Alexander was killed. You realize what that means? We must find out who the gentleman was who drove this gig. Because Alexander may have known who he was and guessed he was involved in the Brickfield Murder. And that would have given the gentleman a compelling motive to kill him."

"If Mr. Falkland knew who'd committed the Brickfield Murder, sir, why wouldn't he have gone to the authorities?"

"He may have lacked proof, or been reluctant to betray a friend. But there's another possibility."

Julian paused. He was not superstitious about speaking ill of the dead, but he felt it was a thing one ought not to do lightly—especially when the living would bear the brunt of the suffering and shame. "Alexander had a knack for making people do him favours. He induced Clare to take part in an elaborate deception of his father. He prevailed upon Adams to forgive a debt of thirty thousand pounds. Why would a man of Clare's intelligence, or Adams's strength of will, act so drastically against his own interest?"

Vance nodded cannily. "Blackmail, sir?"

"Precisely. It looks as if Alexander had quite a talent in that line. So if he learned that a gentleman of his acquaintance had committed a murder, would he report it to the authorities? Or would he hold it over the culprit's head for his own purposes?"

They exchanged an understanding look. Then Vance said, "It looks to me, sir, as if we'd better find the gentleman as drove this gig."

"You'll put out advertisements?"

"I'll blanket the city, sir. If there's anyone between here and Hampstead as knows aught about this gig, I'll find him.— What's this? You seem to have company, sir."

A handsome town chaise, painted black and scarlet and drawn by a pair of well-matched bays, was drawing up behind the gig. Julian thought it curious that the carriage bore no crest. A man of good family would blazon his coat-of-arms on the doors; even a wealthy parvenu would buy or invent some heraldic device. But the owner of this carriage kept its shiny black doors almost defiantly bare.

"I'll lay you any odds," said Julian softly, "it's David Adams."

A footman in black and scarlet livery jumped down from behind the carriage and opened the door. Adams stepped out, raking the street with his gaze as if seeking a particular house. All at once he caught sight of Julian and Vance. He bore down on them swiftly. "Mr. Kestrel! I must see you at once."

"If you'll allow me a moment, Mr. Adams. Vance, I believe we're finished? Unless you can help us," he added, turning back to Adams. "We're attempting to identify this gig."

Adams cast an impatient glance over it. "I know nothing about it."

No, thought Julian, I don't believe you do. Which means that, whatever else you may have done, you're not our mysterious nocturnal driver.

Vance took his leave and drove the gig away, saying he would find a safe place to store it. Julian brought Adams inside and upstairs to his parlour. "Now then, Mr. Adams, how may I be of service to you?"

"Is it true? About Mrs. Falkland?"

"What exactly do you wish to know?"

"It's all over the City that she's been in an accident, miscarried of a child, and that someone deliberately brought it about. Is it true?"

"Yes. She was thrown from her horse, and her groom discovered two nails driven into her saddle. We're attempting to find out who was responsible."

"How badly hurt is she?"

"She's sprained her ankle and had a bad knock on the head. And as you've heard, she suffered a miscarriage."

Adams started pacing back and forth as if the Devil were at his heels. Suddenly he spun around and looked at Julian. "I'm afraid this is my fault."

"What do you mean?"

"I mean that I might have prevented it. I tried, but not hard enough. Tell me: does she still have a woman waiting on her—large, fortyish, with a square jaw and a West Country accent?"

"Her maid, Martha Gilmore. Yes."

"Damnation!" Adams resumed his headlong pacing. "I

tried to warn her about that woman. I should have been more direct. If it turns out her maid did this to her, how shall I—how can I ever—?" He clapped a hand to his brow.

"Mr. Adams, why do you believe Martha caused the accident?"

"Because she's not to be trusted! I saw her—" He stopped.

"You saw her where? Doing what?"

Adams forced out, his voice heavy with repugnance, "At the house of a woman named Marianne Desmond."

"My dear Mr. Adams," said Julian softly, "you touch on a subject very near my heart. How do you know Mrs. Desmond?"

"I wouldn't say I knew her. I met her once."

"At her house?"

"Yes."

"How did you happen to go there?"

"I was invited."

"By Mrs. Desmond?"

"No."

"Come, we shall make better progress if you expand your answers beyond monosyllables. If Mrs. Desmond didn't invite you, who did? The gentleman who supported her?"

Adams looked at him strangely. "Are you playing cat and mouse with me?"

"Why should you think so?"

"Well, you obviously know who Mrs. Desmond is. So why do you speak of 'the gentleman who supported her' in that roundabout way?"

"Because, Mr. Adams, regrettably, I don't know who that gentleman is."

Adams stared. Then he threw back his head and laughed. "No, of course you don't! You wouldn't, would you? How could you possibly have guessed?"

"Then tell me. If you really wish to help Mrs. Falkland—"

"Oh, yes, I'll tell you! With the greatest pleasure! Have you met Mrs. Desmond? No? Well, she's utter rubbish—a tawdry little jade who would do anything, sell anyone, for the price of a new pair of gloves. And who was keeping this nasty little piece of goods? The last man you would have suspected— and the first one you ought to have! Her lover was Alexander Falkland."

# ✳ 20 ✳

## VILLAIN
## OR VICTIM?

While Adams savoured the effect of his words, Julian took a turn about the room. He needed to think this out. It might not be true—but if it was, it cast a whole new light on Alexander. That he had kept a mistress was not surprising in itself. Many men of fashion, married or not, took a *chère amie* as a matter of course. But Alexander had always played the devoted husband. Yet wasn't that part of his pattern—to run with the hare and hunt with the hounds? In society, he posed as the charming, light-hearted host, while his letters to Sir Malcolm made him appear a serious and thoughtful scholar. In the same way, he married a virtuous woman and won laurels for his constancy—all the while keeping a low adventuress as his mistress.

If it were true, Julian reminded himself. But why would Adams lie? He obviously hated Alexander and took delight in savaging his reputation. But in order to expose Alexander's connexion with Mrs. Desmond, he was obliged to reveal he had met her himself, and that could only draw him more deeply into the investigation—perhaps even implicate him in Alexander's murder. No, it looked very much as if he were telling the truth. And that meant facing the ugliest implication of all.

He pictured that encounter between the Falklands and Mrs.

Desmond outside Cygnet's Court. Mrs. Desmond, dressed in her maid's clothes, took Mrs. Falkland into Cygnet's Court, and Alexander told the coachman and footman she was going to visit a sick friend. Until now, Julian had believed the two women deceived Alexander with this story. Now it seemed Alexander knew perfectly well who Mrs. Desmond was. There was no plot between Mrs. Falkland and Mrs. Desmond against Alexander. The plot, if any, was between Alexander and his mistress against his wife.

Julian said at last, "This is the first I've heard of a love affair between Alexander and Mrs. Desmond. He seems to have been remarkably successful at keeping it dark."

"Well, that was important to him. He liked cutting a romantic figure—the young lover dancing attendance on his beautiful bride. The reality was that virtue bored him. I told you last time we talked that he liked speculation because it was exciting. He liked other kinds of excitement as well. He spared me the details—I didn't want to know them. But I don't doubt Mrs. Desmond gave full satisfaction in that line."

Julian recalled that Mrs. Desmond was said to have brought young women home to meet her protector. It looked as if Alexander had made her his procuress as well as his mistress. "Why should he have told you about her, when he seems to have told no one else?"

Adams paused, as if feeling his way. "I daresay he wanted to show her off. He liked showing off his acquisitions. He hardly counted it worth owning a thing, if there was no one to admire it."

"That does sound like him."

"Then you're beginning to understand him. I've understood him for a long time—better than anyone, I think. He couldn't help showing his venal side to me. I handled his money, and that's the next thing to being a man's confessor. So he probably felt he had little to lose by letting me know about Mrs. Desmond. He knew I was already—skeptical—about his reputation as a virtuous youth."

"You say you only visited her once. When was that?"

"Oh, early in April. I don't remember exactly."

"I should have thought you were the sort of man to keep close track of his appointments."

"This wasn't an appointment. It was an impromptu visit. Mrs. Desmond's house was a convenient place for Alexander and me to duck in and discuss business. I didn't exchange more than a few words with her."

"Then how do you know enough about her to despise her so thoroughly?"

"Her character was apparent enough. And Alexander dropped hints. I don't remember exactly what he said."

Your memory is convenient, thought Julian. Faces but not dates, character but not conversation. It won't wash, Mr. Adams. You must have had a very personal experience of Mrs. Desmond, to loathe her as you do now.

He said, "Tell me about Martha. You say you saw her at Mrs. Desmond's?"

"Yes. Very briefly. Mrs. Desmond let me in, and I saw another woman behind her in the hall. I didn't know then who she was—I'd never seen Mrs. Falkland's maid. I assumed she was a servant of Mrs. Desmond's. Mrs. Desmond sent me into the parlour, saying, Never mind about her, I'll get rid of her. And I suppose she did, because I didn't see her again."

Julian repeated musingly, " 'Mrs. Desmond let *me* in, Mrs. Desmond sent *me* into the parlour.' Are you quite sure Alexander was with you on this visit?"

Adams's head came up. Julian could see the tension run through him, all the way to his fingertips. "Yes, Mr. Kestrel. Of course he was."

"I think your memory may be a trifle foggy on that point. But we'll let it pass for now. When did you find out the woman you'd seen was Mrs. Falkland's maid?"

"On the night of Alexander's party—the night he was murdered."

"Yes, of course. Martha called him out of the drawing room to tell him Mrs. Falkland wouldn't be coming back to the party, and you went with him."

"Yes. And I recognized her at once: same broad shoulders, square face, and heavy jaw. Even the same cross around her neck. So I knew they were up to something—she and Alexander. Why else would his wife's maid be visiting his mistress?"

"Perhaps on Mrs. Falkland's behalf. Martha had been spying on Alexander for several weeks before his death: searching his rooms and pestering his valet about his comings and goings. Perhaps she found out about Mrs. Desmond and went to see her, hoping to make her break off with him. She's very protective of Mrs. Falkland."

"Then why has she kept dark what she knows about Alexander and Mrs. Desmond?"

"She may have wanted to spare Mrs. Falkland the knowledge of his infidelity. Or she may have feared we would suspect her of killing him to avenge his wife's wrongs." As perhaps she did, he thought. "This does explain one thing. You've always dismissed with scorn Clare's story that you looked daggers at Alexander after his conversation with Martha. Now it appears that seeing her gave you a most unpleasant jolt. Do you think perhaps Clare was telling the truth?"

"It's possible," said Adams, through clenched teeth. "I suppose this is exactly what you needed to fasten the murder on me. Yes, I was angry when I realized the woman I'd seen at Mrs. Desmond's was Mrs. Falkland's maid. I'm not softhearted, and I've no illusions about human nature. But I don't think loyalty is too much to expect of a servant—or a husband. I hate treachery, and Martha was treacherous. So was Alexander."

Julian asked quietly, "Does Mrs. Falkland know you're so protective of her?"

"Protective? Are you mad?" Adams walked about wildly. "If you only knew!—"

"Yes, Mr. Adams? If I only knew—what?"

Adams stopped walking, clenched his hands till the knuckles whitened. "I thought Mrs. Falkland was being betrayed by the people closest to her. I was sorry for her on that account

—nothing more. And after Alexander was killed, I was afraid she might be in danger. I knew her maid wasn't to be trusted. She'd been up to something hole-and-corner with Mrs. Desmond—perhaps had a hand in killing Alexander. I thought I should warn Mrs. Falkland against her, but I wasn't sure how to go about it. In the end, I wrote her a letter."

"She never told me that."

"I can't account for what she did or didn't tell you. I wrote it and had it delivered—that's all."

"What did you write?"

"I remember exactly, because I was a long time deciding what to say. *'Mrs. Falkland. Beware of your maid. She's betrayed you and may have done worse to your husband.'* That was all— I didn't sign it."

"Why not?"

"Because—" Adams hung fire a moment. "Because I knew she didn't like or trust me. I thought if she knew the warning came from me, she wouldn't heed it."

"She doesn't seem to have heeded it in any event."

"No."

"I wonder you think she dislikes you," said Julian, watching him. "To be frank, I had the impression she gave you no thought whatsoever."

Adams's face twisted, became a mass of pain. "Why should she?"

Julian let it go. Interrogation was one thing, torture another. There was only one more question he needed to ask, and it was critical. "How can you be sure it was Martha you saw at Mrs. Desmond's? Did you get a good look at her?"

"Of course I did! Do you suppose I'd kick up such a dust over a mere fancy? I only saw her briefly, but she was standing by the street door, and there was sunshine streaming in on her through the fanlight. It was Martha, no question about it."

"Thank you, Mr. Adams." Julian rose. "You've been extremely helpful—more than you know."

"What do you mean?" asked Adams sharply.

"Surely you must realize you've given yourself away?"

"I don't know what you're talking about! I didn't kill Falkland!"

"That remains to be seen. In any event, I hardly think you're to be congratulated for not numbering murder among your crimes."

Adams whitened. "I don't know what you're hinting at, or what you think you know. But I won't stay to be taunted and insulted. I have enough of that from your kind as it is. I came because I thought I had a duty to tell you what I knew about Mrs. Falkland's maid."

"I can set your mind at rest on that score. It wasn't Martha who tampered with Mrs. Falkland's saddle. She has an unshakeable alibi for the time in which that might have been done."

Adams sat down slowly. "What you're saying is, I've told you all this for nothing. And you let me do it—you even egged me on. What a cold-blooded devil you are."

"I needed your information. You ought to have given it long since. By the way: we haven't accounted for *your* whereabouts at the time the accident might have been caused. Where were you and what were you doing on Wednesday from noon to nine o'clock, and yesterday from dawn until half past nine?"

"Yesterday morning I was at home, then I went directly to my counting-house. My servants and clerks can vouch for that. On Wednesday—" He paused. "I was meeting with clients all afternoon, then I went to dinner at Garraway's. After that I went back to my counting-house and worked for several hours."

"Can anyone give you an alibi for that time?"

"No. So you may believe if you like that I went to Hampstead and drove nails into Mrs. Falkland's saddle. But I don't see how that fits with your theory of my so-called protectiveness toward her."

"I shan't detain you with explanations." Julian went with him to the door. "One more thing: I hope you won't attempt to leave the country before these crimes are solved."

"My God, are you threatening me? Do you think I'm so easily frightened?"

"I think, Mr. Adams, that you're frightened now. And I think you have reason to be."

⁂

Julian sent for his horse and set off for Hampstead. The weather was damp without being rainy, which in London meant that yellowish mists curled around the chimneys, and the air hung heavy with the smell of soot and horses. But as the houses thinned and gave way to fields, there came a sweet scent of earth and grass, and even a faint spring breeze. Julian turned his horse off the main road and made for the Heath, which was a little out of his way but irresistible on a day like this.

The chief advantage of Hampstead Heath, Julian had always thought, was that it was not fashionable. You ran into no one you knew; there were no ladies expecting to be flirted with and no gentlemen trying to outshine you. A man could actually ride in peace and quiet under the trees. Julian had no great hankering for bucolic retreats; he was inclined to agree with Samuel Johnson that a man who was tired of London was tired of life. But there was much to be said for a sylvan spot when there was reflection to be done.

He saw his way clearly now through parts of the Falkland mystery. His theory of who had caused Mrs. Falkland's accident remained unshaken; moreover, he thought he knew why Adams had forgiven the thirty-thousand-pound debt. But all manner of enigmas remained. They might be unimportant, but how would he know that until he had worked them out? Why was Quentin Clare so secretive about his sister? Why had he written those letters for Alexander? Was Fanny Gates the brickfield victim? And what had become of Mrs. Desmond?

Above all, had Alexander been the driver of the gig? Did the fact that he had been Mrs. Desmond's lover mean he was mixed up in her disappearance—perhaps in the Brickfield Murder? More than ever, Julian felt sure Alexander's character lay at the heart of this mystery. Was he villain or victim? Or both?

✳

Julian stopped at the Flask for a roasted fowl and a pint of ale, then rode on to Sir Malcolm's house. He asked for Sir Malcolm and was shown into the library. Sir Malcolm was seated by the fire with Quentin Clare. Martha was roaming about, taking books down from their shelves.

Julian greeted Sir Malcolm and Clare, then asked after Mrs. Falkland. "She's a little better in health," said Sir Malcolm, "but no better in spirits."

Clare rose. "I'll take my leave of you, sir. I expect you and Mr. Kestrel have a great deal to talk about. Thank you for having me to luncheon."

"You needn't run off just yet." Sir Malcolm glanced meaningfully toward Martha, conveying that they could not discuss the investigation as long as she was here. He added to Julian in an undertone, "She's looking for something Belinda might like to read. I haven't many books that would interest her—she likes gardening and horses—but Martha wanted to have a look all the same."

There was an uneasy silence. Sir Malcolm broke it. "Mr. Clare and I were just talking about the significance of names. I named Alexander after the ruler and conqueror, and there are times when I feel a kind of superstitious guilt about that, because Alexander the Great, too, died so young, in the flower of his success."

"I think, sir," Clare said gently, "you would rather blame yourself than have no one to blame at all. It's a way of imposing some sort of order—of feeling less helpless in the face of violent death."

Julian looked at him with interest. His usual shyness had eased, and he sounded like one of his letters: thoughtful, sensitive, astute. But the letters were part of an elaborate deception. Was Clare in earnest now?

"You're right, my dear boy," Sir Malcolm said. "The murder gives me sick fancies sometimes, and they ought not to be encouraged. As we were saying: one wonders why some parents choose the names they do. For instance, Mr. Clare's Christian name means 'fifth,' though he's one of only two children."

"What about your sister?" asked Julian. "Does her name suit her?"

"Not exactly," Clare said slowly. "Verity values truth, but she values other things more."

"What things?" asked Sir Malcolm.

"Right. That isn't always the same as truth. Often it isn't," he added, after a pause. "Verity has her own notions of right and wrong, and they aren't the same as other people's."

"I should like to meet her some time," said Sir Malcolm.

"That's kind of you, sir. I'm not at all sure you would like her."

"Don't be silly, of course I should. I don't mind if she has odd ideas. It's better than having none at all."

Clare smiled.

"Is she older or younger than you?" asked Julian.

"Older—by a matter of minutes."

"Twins!" said Sir Malcolm. "You never told me that."

"I didn't think to mention it, sir."

"But I think twins are immensely interesting. I suppose you're very close."

"Oh, yes," Clare said quietly. "One is closer to a twin than to anyone in the world. There's nothing Verity and I wouldn't do for each other."

"I believe you mean that," said Sir Malcolm.

"I do. We've always had an understanding that each of us would do anything the other asked. However difficult, however dangerous, it would have to be done if the other wished it. We didn't abuse the privilege—hardly ever took advantage of it. But, once exercised, it was absolute. Nothing was exempt."

"You speak of it in the past tense," Julian observed. "Don't you and your sister have this understanding anymore?"

"Yes." Clare did not meet his eyes. "But we haven't seen each other for some time."

"You must miss her," said Sir Malcolm.

"Yes, sir. Very much."

Martha was coming toward them on her way to the door, her arms full of books. Clare looked at her with concern—or perhaps he was merely eager to change the subject. "You can't carry so many books yourself."

She stopped before him and looked at him. Her face softened; she spoke with a gentleness Julian had never heard from her before. "That's kind of you, sir. I'm strong enough."

"Why don't I ring for Dutton to take them upstairs," said Sir Malcolm.

Julian and Clare relieved Martha of the books and put them on a table. Clare said shyly, "I hope you'll convey to Mrs. Falkland my—my regrets for her accident."

"I will," said Martha warmly. "Thank you, sir."

Dutton came in answer to Sir Malcolm's ring. After he and Martha had gone, Julian asked Clare, "Have you known Martha before?"

"No, I—" Clare stopped short, his colour rising. "I—I don't think so. I can't recall having met her. I did see her once, at Alexander's last party. She came to tell him Mrs. Falkland still had her headache and wouldn't be down again."

"Her manner toward you was strikingly familiar," said Julian. "Ordinarily she's very stolid and self-contained."

"I don't know why she should feel that way about me. I don't know her at all." Clare looked from Julian to Sir Malcolm, spreading out his hands helplessly.

Julian thought a moment. "Where exactly in Somerset do your uncle and sister live?"

"Why do you want to know that?" Clare said, startled.

"Mrs. Falkland's country estate is in Dorset. I thought that if your family lived near the Dorset border, you and the Falklands might have visited back and forth, and Martha might remember you from there."

"Uncle George does live near the Dorset border—a village

called Montacute. But I never visited the Falklands at their country place. I don't think Alexander liked it much. He wanted to improve it—redesign the house and grounds."

"That's true," Sir Malcolm confirmed.

Julian nodded. The Dorset connexion had been only a guess. But it had got him the information he wanted: he knew now where Verity Clare lived. And he would make good use of the knowledge.

## * 21 *

# A PROMISE
# TO A LADY

After Clare had gone, Julian told Sir Malcolm what he had learned from Adams: how Adams had seen Martha at Mrs. Desmond's and sent Mrs. Falkland an anonymous warning against her. Sir Malcolm was shocked at the revelation that Mrs. Desmond was Alexander's mistress. "But if that's true," he faltered, "then Alexander must have recognized her when she came up to Belinda in the Strand."

"Yes. He probably arranged the whole thing with her beforehand."

"But why on earth would he let his mistress take his wife away for a *tête-à-tête?* Look here, Kestrel, couldn't Adams have been lying about all this?"

"It's possible. If it were he and not Alexander who was keeping Mrs. Desmond, it might be very convenient to claim that her lover was a man who is dead and can't defend himself. But in that case, why volunteer the information at all? He had nothing to gain, and everything to lose, by revealing his link with Mrs. Desmond. I don't know why he should have done so, if not to tell the truth."

"But even if Alexander was Mrs. Desmond's protector, it wouldn't mean he was the gentleman who drove the gig? It wouldn't mean he had anything to do with the Brickfield Murder?"

"Not necessarily," Julian said gently. "One thing we know: Adams wasn't the driver of the gig. I'd stake all Lombard Street to ninepence he'd never seen it before today."

Sir Malcolm walked about distractedly. "This is—very hard. When you warned me the investigation might rake up unpleasant things, I assumed you meant things about Alexander's friends or servants. I didn't know there might be such rot dredged up about Alexander himself. He deceived me about the letters, he deceived Belinda with Mrs. Desmond. How do we know what else he may have done? I feel afraid to go forward. Anywhere I step from now on, the ground may give way under my feet."

"Alexander was what he was. It's too late to change him now. And you weren't responsible for him. He had a mind and soul of his own."

"I was his *father*, Mr. Kestrel. His mother died when he was a baby. Who was responsible for what he became, if not I?"

"I'm inclined to think," said Julian slowly, "that people are responsible for themselves. I know a father's influence is far-reaching. I'm very much the product of my own father's up-bringing. But I think, as Shelley said, a man must rule the empire of himself. Alexander had every advantage needed to bring out the best in him: birth, means, education, good looks, a kind and encouraging father. If, in spite of all that, he contrived to go to the bad, the fault was his."

Sir Malcolm sighed heavily. "What do you mean to do next?"

"Is Mrs. Falkland well enough to see me? I should like to ask her about Adams's anonymous letter."

"Don't you want to ask her about Mrs. Desmond?"

"No," said Julian quietly. "I don't think that's necessary. And I know it wouldn't be wise."

✳

Julian brought Sir Malcolm with him to question Mrs. Falkland. He could not with any propriety go to her bedchamber alone; besides, he thought Sir Malcolm's presence would soothe and reassure her. He wanted to avoid upsetting her as he had yesterday.

Eugene was reading aloud to her from one of the books Martha had brought. She was in bed, half reclining against her pillows, listening with closed eyes. She wore a black shawl over her nightdress, fastened on her breast with the brooch that contained a lock of Alexander's hair. Julian thought it like her to resume her mourning even while on a sickbed. No one could accuse her of falling short in the public duties of widowhood.

Julian told Eugene they needed to speak with her alone. He left reluctantly, promising to stay close by in case he was needed. He was fast developing a protective instinct, Julian thought. That would do more for his character than all the schools in England.

After a few polite preliminaries, Julian asked Mrs. Falkland about the anonymous letter. "I remember it," she said. "It came a day or two after Alexander died. It said Martha had betrayed me and hinted she'd killed my husband. I didn't give it a moment's credence. I know her. She's been with me for years, first as my nurse, then later as my maid. She has my most complete trust. I thought whoever had sent the letter must be either mistaken or malicious. So I burnt it."

"Why didn't you tell Bow Street about it?" Julian asked.

"Because I thought they might take it seriously. I didn't believe Martha had done anything wrong, and I didn't want her unjustly suspected."

"Did you tell her about it?"

"No. I didn't see any need."

"We've found out who sent it."

"I assumed you had, or you wouldn't have known about it." She hung fire a moment, then asked, "Who was it?"

"It was David Adams."

She sat very still. Only her hands moved, tightening round the book Eugene had left. "How singular."

"You had no suspicion he'd written it?"

"No."

"Would you have felt differently about it if you had known?"

"No. I wouldn't have credited the accusation, whoever made it." She paused, then asked, "Why did he tell you about the letter?"

"He'd heard about your accident and was worried about you. He was afraid Martha might have had a hand in it."

"I don't know why he should interest himself in my affairs to that extent."

"Don't you?"

She froze, staring back at him.

"You don't know that he's in love with you?"

Sir Malcolm started. Mrs. Falkland gripped the book till her nails bit into it. "Did he say so?"

"In everything but words."

She drew a long breath. "I wish you would tell Mr. Adams that I'm obliged to him for his concern, but I would prefer him to have no further communication with me or about me. Our acquaintance came about because of his friendship with Alexander. Alexander is dead, and the acquaintance is over."

"Those are hard words for a man in love to hear."

"I didn't ask for his love! I didn't ask to have it inflicted on me! Am I a doll to be picked up and put down by any man who professes to love me? Have I no right to any feelings of my own?"

"My dear!" Sir Malcolm went to her, prying her hands gently away from the book and holding them in his. "You mustn't upset yourself this way. No one was suggesting you should have anything to do with Mr. Adams. Mr. Kestrel, I really think this line of questioning has gone far enough."

"I beg your pardon, Mrs. Falkland. I won't pursue it further."

"Just tell me one thing," she whispered. "Why is Mr. Adams suspicious of Martha?"

Julian took a moment to frame his answer. "He claims to have seen her at the house of a woman of ill character."

"That's ridiculous." She rallied a little, as if feeling herself on firm ground. "Martha would never have anything to do with a woman whose character was in any doubt. She's extremely religious and has the highest moral standards."

"Yes," said Julian thoughtfully, "that was my impression, too." He added, "How much do you know about her? What sort of life did she lead before she entered your service?"

"She came to Mama with unexceptionable references. I believe she'd been a nursemaid in another household. Beyond that, she never talks about her early life. I've always assumed her family were all dead."

"Do you know of any connexion between her and Mr. Clare?"

"Mr. Clare?" she said in surprise. "No, none."

"I saw them together a little while ago, and she spoke to him with unusual gentleness—almost with affection."

"I can't imagine why. She's never mentioned him."

Julian rose to take his leave. But there was one last question in his mind. "Why do you find the portrait of your husband so distressing?"

She lay back against her pillows, her eyes weary and remote. "He looks so happy," she said at last. "That's what I can't bear."

✳

"I don't know any Mrs. Desmond, sir," said Martha. "I've never been to her house."

"You don't recall having visited a grey-brick house in Cygnet's Court, early in April?"

"I don't know where Cygnet's Court may be, sir."

"It's a little courtyard off the Strand, with half a dozen brick houses, all but two in disrepair."

"I don't know the place, sir."

"A witness claims to have seen you at Mrs. Desmond's."

"Your witness is lying or mistaken, sir. I was never there."

"Are you certain?"

"On my honour as a Christian woman, sir."

Julian was puzzled. Could Adams have been lying, after all?

It was hard to see what motive he could have to traduce Martha. Yet her answers were so confident. And she had taken an oath that a religious woman would not care to profane.

He said, "I should like to speak to you quite frankly on a distasteful subject—one likely to distress anyone as loyal to Mrs. Falkland as you. Have you any idea who Mrs. Desmond is?"

"No, sir."

"We believe she was living under Alexander Falkland's protection not long before he died."

Her face hardened. "I'm sorry to hear it, sir."

"But not surprised?"

"I own, sir, I'd feared something of the sort."

"Why?"

She hesitated. "Only that young men about town do keep their harlots. And Mr. Falkland was often out at night and took less notice of the mistress than he had before."

"Is that why you took to searching his things and asking Valère about his comings and goings?"

"I didn't trust him, sir. That's the best I can say."

"I'm wondering, Martha, if in your zeal to protect Mrs. Falkland, you went so far as to track down your master's *chère amie*—not for any dishonourable purpose, but in order to induce her to break off with Alexander?"

"I might have done, sir, if I'd known about her. But I didn't know. And so I've told you, sir."

"So you have," he acknowledged wryly.

"Who is it that claims to have seen me at her house, sir?"

"It's Mr. Adams."

"That man!" she said scornfully. "His word isn't worth a straw—*he* can't swear on his honour as a Christian, after all. Somebody ought to ask what he was doing at her house, instead of believing his slanders about me."

"Can you think of any reason why he should tell such a lie about you?"

"No, sir," she admitted.

Julian was obliged to dismiss her, although he was far from satisfied with their interview. Not for the first time in this investigation, he felt he had been asking what ought to be the right questions—and yet they were not. But what should he have asked instead? What had he overlooked?

He left Sir Malcolm's house in this unquiet state and rode toward the Heath. The sun was out in patches, throwing stencil patterns on the grass. Children were sailing toy boats and skimming stones on the placid ponds. Nursemaids ran after them when they strayed too far, for there were smaller ponds, curtained round with willows, where a child could vanish and not be found for hours, even days. Julian passed near one such pond and could see how it might be enticing: the pale blue shimmer of water through the drapery of leaves.

He left the Heath at its southern tip and made for the London road. Along the way there were scattered cottages and outcroppings of industry: an ironmonger's, a distillery—a brickworks. Julian bethought himself of where he was and asked a bystander the way to the brickfield where the murdered woman was found.

The bystander responded as if he were used to being asked. He must have directed a good many ghoulish sight-seers there lately. Julian found it easily enough, but there was nothing much to see. The kilns had long since vanished; only the sparse vegetation, fragments of brick, and scarred reddish earth showed there had ever been a brickworks here. The place seemed largely a repository for rubbish, and even that was scarce. Anything of the slightest use or value would have been confiscated by the gipsies and tramps Sir Malcolm said camped here nowadays. There was no sign any had stopped here lately; even the most destitute wanderers must have a superstitious horror of the place.

What could have brought the murderer and his victim here? Were they on their way to or from Hampstead? Why? To see someone? Who in Hampstead had any connexion to Mrs. Desmond, her maid, or Alexander? Julian could think of no one but Sir Malcolm. And Sir Malcolm could have nothing to do with the Brickfield Murder. Could he?

✳

Julian was back in London in time for the Grand Strut: the late afternoon parade of the *beau monde* and their hangers-on in Hyde Park. As always, Rotten Row was crowded with carriages and riders. Ladies of birth but not wealth tried desperately to keep up appearances; ladies of wealth but not birth angled for an acquaintance with people of rank. Sporting ladies drove ponies in brightly coloured harness; would-be bucks struggled to manage spirited mounts. Dandies surveyed the scene through quizzing-glasses, ogling the women and exchanging cutting quips about the men. Everyone competed for admiration—and yet, under cover of it all, political alliances were forged, assignations made, duels arranged.

Then there were what Julian thought of as the waifs of Rotten Row—young squires' wives, fresh from the country, gamely riding out in open carriages day after day, in the hope that some lady of fashion would relieve their loneliness with a bow or a smile. Usually they were disappointed: the *corps élite* could not let in every stray who tapped on their doors. Julian occasionally took one of these women under his wing, knowing that a little attention from him would catapult her into fashion. He would do it more often, but he was not at all sure he was doing them a favour. So many embarked on their first seasons so eagerly, only to flee London dunned by dressmakers, fleeced by gamblers, ruined by rakes.

Julian had not been to Rotten Row for some days, and his reappearance caused a stir. He discussed Mrs. Falkland's accident with no one, but of course everyone discussed it with him. He had the satisfaction of coming away with more information than he gave, but none of his spoils seemed of much value.

At about six o'clock the crowd began to thin, as people hastened away to dress for dinner. Julian was about to follow suit when he heard a familiar voice: "My dear fellow! Stop a moment, will you?"

It was Felix Poynter, resplendent in a sky-blue coat, a yellow waistcoat, and lilac gloves. He was driving a smart cabriolet, painted cherry-red and drawn by a handsome bay. Behind him rode his tiger: a diminutive groom in amethyst satin livery, complete with silk stockings, powdered wig, and tricorne hat trimmed with silver lace.

Julian rode up to them. "So this is your new set-out." He ran his eyes over the cabriolet and tiger in some amusement. "At least we shan't have any trouble finding you in a fog."

"There is that advantage," Felix agreed distractedly. "I say, I've been trying to get near you an hour and more. How is Mrs. Falkland?"

"A little better."

"I'm glad to hear it." Felix bit his lip, then asked abruptly, "Will you walk with me a little? Alfred will look after your horse."

"Yes, if you like." Julian regarded him more closely but asked no questions as yet. Dismounting, he gave the reins to Felix's tiger, who took charge of both horses in a condescending manner, his nose in the air. Felix shuddered as he and Julian walked away. "He was only a stable boy a fortnight ago," he confided. "But since I put him into that livery, he's grown so grand, he'll hardly speak to me."

They struck out across the park toward Kensington Gardens. Here there were no acquaintances to interrupt them—only nursemaids, children, dogs, and a pair of elderly army officers out for a constitutional. They all looked curiously at Julian and Felix, no doubt wondering what two young beaux were doing in this unfashionable part of the park. Still, it was not a bad spot for a *tête-à-tête*. In such a broad open space, no one could come near enough to listen without their knowing it.

Felix ran a hand through his curly hair, causing it to stand even more determinedly on end. "It's awful about Mrs. Falkland. Beastly. Have you any idea who did it?"

"I have all manner of ideas. That isn't the same as having evidence."

"I wouldn't know. But I hope you find whoever it was. I mean to say, attacking a woman, and in that cowardly fashion—"

"It's monstrous, I agree. But it's had one good effect. When there was only Falkland's murder to investigate, witnesses felt justified in holding things back; after all, they couldn't bring him back to life by telling what they knew. But since there's been a violent crime against Mrs. Falkland, everyone who's been hoarding a secret is coming forward."

"Oh," said Felix unhappily, "are they?"

Julian stopped walking. "My dear fellow, not you, too?"

"It's just a trifle—probably of no importance! I would have told you about it long since, but I'd made a promise to a lady."

"What lady?"

"Mrs. Falkland," Felix admitted reluctantly. "And I still don't feel right about breaking my word. She trusted me, put me on my honour. But when I heard how someone had tampered with her saddle, made her lose her child, I thought, what if she's still in danger? And what if next time it's worse? How can I set my honour against her life?"

"Exactly so. You must tell me what you know."

Felix nodded resignedly. "It was the night of the party— the night Falkland was killed. You remember what I told Bow Street—that I was talking with Mrs. Falkland when she said she had a headache and excused herself? That was true, so far as it went. She hadn't looked well all evening. When she was in a strong light, you could see she was pale and tired—fragile, like a wavering flame. You wanted to cup your hands around her, to keep her from going out.

"All the same, she was putting on a brave face, talking with me about one thing and another, and keeping half an eye on the door, so she could greet late arrivals when they came in. All of a sudden she stared, and her face went dead white. She swayed, and I had to catch her.

"She hadn't fainted, quite. She clung on to me, and I knew somehow that she didn't want anyone to know what was happening. Because nobody'd noticed—it all happened so fast, and there was such a crush of people around us. I looked around frantically, wondering if I should call for help, and that was when I saw him—David Adams. He'd just arrived and was standing in the doorway, shooting that hawk-like gaze of his around the room. I realized it was the sight of him that had made her all but lose her senses.

"Next thing I knew, she'd detached herself from me and was plying her fan very fast. You'd never have known anything was wrong, except that she was still pretty white, and there were beads of perspiration on her brow. Adams was looking right at her now, and I thought he might try to come over to her, and I'd have to stop him, which I wasn't looking forward to, because he frightens me into fits. But he didn't come near her, and she didn't look his way.

"She started speaking to me, and her voice was so calm and cool that if you couldn't hear her words, you'd never have guessed she was saying anything out of the common. All the while she kept waving her fan slowly back and forth, as if she were keeping time to music. She thanked me for looking after her and asked if she could count on me to say nothing about her dizzy spell. I said she could count on me for anything, but I was worried she might be ill. She said she wasn't, she'd be all right in a moment, but she was going to leave the party. She said, 'I have a headache. If anyone should ask you, will you tell them I had a headache—and nothing more?'

"I said I'd do anything she asked. But I wasn't happy about it, and I suppose she could see that, because she said she hoped I meant what I said—especially if I'd guessed why she felt faint just then. I got flustered and said I wouldn't presume to guess at such a thing, I was sure I should be wrong in any case, and so on. And she said—well, never mind that, it isn't important—"

"You must let me be the judge of that," said Julian.

"Oh, it was just some flummery." Felix waved his hand as

if to blow it away. "She said she thought I noticed a great deal, but unlike anyone else she knew, I didn't repeat anything that was uncharitable. The truth is, I can't keep anything in my head long enough to gossip about it."

"Oh, yes," murmured Julian, "I'm sure that's all it is."

Felix eyed him uncertainly. "Well, anyway, she said she didn't know of any other gentleman she could trust to conceal what I'd just seen, but she did trust me. Well, that finished me, I can tell you! I swore she could trust me, upon my life. But how could I keep my word, once I heard she was in danger?" He went a little pale. "I say, do you think if I'd spoken sooner—"

"Believe me, it wouldn't have made any difference. The seeds of Mrs. Falkland's accident were sown long before those nails were driven into her saddle. There was nothing you could have done to prevent it."

Felix drew a long breath and nodded. "Why do you think seeing Adams at the party gave her such a turn?"

"I suspect, because she didn't know he was coming. He wasn't invited initially. He demanded an invitation of Falkland, and Falkland acceded, but perhaps he never told his wife."

"Do you think Adams had reason to kill Falkland, and Mrs. Falkland knew it, and that was why she came over queer on seeing him—because she was afraid of what he might do?"

"There's something in what you say," Julian mused. "But I think it's only part of the answer."

✳

When Julian got home, he found his evening clothes laid out as usual. "I won't be needing them," he told Dipper. "Send to the White Horse Cellar and order a post-chaise and pair—no, make it four horses. We've no time to waste."

"Where are we going, sir?"

"Somerset—a village called Montacute. I want to meet Miss Verity Clare."

## ✳ 22 ✳

## BLIND-MAN'S-BUFF

Before leaving for Somerset, Julian dispatched a note to Vance, telling him briefly that he was going away for a day or two to pursue a lead. He deliberately sent no word to Sir Malcolm, because he was not sure how far he could trust him to keep secrets from Clare. He did not want Clare warned of his intention to see his sister.

As he changed into travelling clothes—a thick wool frock coat and a greatcoat with a short cape attached—he pondered how long the journey would take. It was now Friday evening; absent any mishap on the road, they might cover the hundred and thirty or so miles to Somerset in about ten hours. With luck, they could be back in London before dawn on Sunday. It was a costly investment of time, since he only had till noon on Tuesday to win his bet with de Witt. But there was some mystery surrounding Quentin and Verity Clare, and Julian believed it was the sister, not the brother, who held the key. Someone had to go Somerset and see her; it might as well be he.

Dipper carried out all their preparations with his usual efficiency. By ten that evening they were ready to set out. They made good progress: the roads from London to the West Country were the best in England, and tonight they were quite dry—though the cloud of dust in Julian's eyes and nose soon

made him pine for a little rain. The changes of horses were
so swift, the travellers hardly had time to get out and stretch
their legs before their luggage was tossed into a new chaise,
they themselves were more or less tossed in after it, and the
chaise dashed madly away. Sleeping was difficult, but they
managed it in fits and starts, helped by a liberal supply of
brandy.

Julian consulted a county map of Somerset and decided to
put up in Yeovil, a town four or five miles from Montacute.
He was not sure what sort of accommodation a small village
like Montacute might offer; moreover, his arrival by post-
chaise would attract attention, and he wanted the advantage
of surprise. He had an idea Miss Clare would be anything but
pleased to see him—might even try to conceal herself or leave
her home until he was gone.

In Yeovil, he found a pleasant old inn that, in time-
honoured fashion, was full of labyrinthine passages and inex-
plicable stairs. There was even a stair running straight through
Julian's bedchamber; he had to be mindful of it in crossing
the room to keep from falling on his face. He slept for an hour,
Dipper having first inspected the bed for "colonists," as he
called them. Then he washed, shaved, changed his clothes,
and went down to the coffee-room for breakfast, leaving Dipper to sleep or eat or amuse himself, as he saw fit.

After breakfast, he hired a trap and a burly, laconic driver
to take him to Montacute. It was a lovely day, the landscape
idyllically green and washed with sunshine. All the buildings
—farms, mills, churches—were of the same honey-coloured
stone. It was obviously local; Julian saw hunks of it "growing
wild" along the road. Whole villages gleamed gold in the
morning light, the houses half hidden among green trees and
splashes of bright flowers.

Montacute was one such gold and green village. It was laid
out in an orderly fashion, with two straight streets meeting at
a right angle. Looming over it was a woodsy hill crowned
with a lone tower. It looked medieval, but Julian's driver said

it was only a folly, put up by the local squire some half a century ago.

Julian left the driver at an inn, with enough money to keep him well supplied with liquid refreshment, and strolled into the village. Seeing a stationer's shop with a sign reading POST-MISTRESS, he went in. There were several customers, who all stared at him, then edged a little nearer to overhear his conversation with the woman behind the counter.

"Good morning," he said. "Would you be good enough to tell me where Miss Clare lives?"

"Miss Clare? There be no Miss Clare hereabouts, sir."

"She doesn't live in Montacute anymore?"

"She never did, sir."

"Are you certain?"

"I've lived here twenty year and more, sir, and never saw hide nor hair of any Miss Clare."

Julian looked blank. Did Clare lead me a dance, he thought, telling me his sister lived in Montacute? It's a devilish long way to come to find a mare's nest—

"Mr. Tibbs has a niece and nephew, name of Clare," volunteered a boy of about twelve, who looked to be the postmistress's son.

His mother and the customers eyed him disapprovingly. They seemed to think strangers, even gentry folk, ought to have to work a little harder to extract information from honest country people.

"Mr. Tibbs's niece doesn't live with him?" Julian asked the boy.

"No, sir."

"Do you know where she does live?"

"Aye, sir. Mr. Tibbs do say she's a companion to a lady on the Continent."

"On the Continent?"

"Aye, sir, the Continent," the boy said positively.

Julian thought a moment, then asked, "Where does Mr. Tibbs live?"

"Close by, sir. Just t'other side of the church."

"Will you point out the house to me?"

The boy glanced toward his mother, who nodded curtly. Julian thanked her, and he and the boy went out.

They skirted the Gothic tower of the church and followed a sun-dappled footpath. "How long has Mr. Tibbs lived in Montacute?" Julian asked.

The boy frowned, thinking. "He come last year, just after Plough Monday."

January of last year, thought Julian—that was about the time Clare joined Lincoln's Inn. "Have you ever seen Mr. Tibbs's nephew?"

"Aye, sir. He's a legal gentleman and lives in London. He come to stay with Mr. Tibbs last Christmas, and for a fortnight at harvest time."

"But you've never seen his sister?"

"No, sir." The boy stopped walking. "This here is the place, sir."

He pointed to a large, well-kept cottage built of the local golden stone. It had a broad front and very small windows, which would have given it a peering, suspicious look but for the nosegay of red and white flowers it wore at one window. In front was a garden bounded by a low stone wall, over which flowering shrubs spilled with impunity.

An old man was hunkered down in the garden, weeding. He wore a worn coat of grey-green wool, leather gaiters, thick gloves, and an old hat with the brim turned down to shield his face from the sun. Hearing Julian and the boy approach, he glanced up, then came to his feet. His gaze fixed on Julian—intrigued, speculative, oddly unsurprised. "Well, well. What have we here?"

He was tall and spare and carried his years extraordinarily well. His face was seamed with wrinkles, but he had such an air of health and vigour, they seemed merely the result of smiling too much or squinting in the sunlight. His eyes were dark and brilliant, his salt-and-pepper hair thick, his voice a full, mellow baritone. Julian was in no danger of mistaking him for a servant. He had the accents and assurance of a gentleman; if he did his own gardening, that was a matter of choice.

"Gentleman to see you, sir," said the boy.

"How do you do, Mr. Tibbs?" Julian came forward, extending his hand. "I'm Julian Kestrel."

"Julian Kestrel!" Tibbs marvelled. "I'm honoured." He drew off an earth-stained gardening glove and shook hands. "Don't tell me you came all the way from town merely to see me?"

"Not precisely. But now that I'm here, I should like very much to speak with you."

"I should be delighted. Please come in." He opened the wicket gate into the garden.

Julian thanked the boy and gave him a coin. The boy would have left, but Tibbs stopped him with a graceful gesture of his hand. "Take that round to the back, will you, Sim?" He pointed to a small wheelbarrow he had filled with weeds and stones. "Then tap on the kitchen window and tell Mrs. Hutchinson I said to give you some hardbake."

"Aye, sir," Sim said with alacrity.

Tibbs ushered Julian into the cottage, first scraping the dirt from the garden off his boots. "My housekeeper makes her own hardbake—treacle and almonds, brutal on the teeth, mine wouldn't stand it. But the children like it. I make a point of cultivating children—they're such a good audience."

"Audience for what?"

"Oh, a man my age, especially one who's travelled as much as I have, accumulates a fount of stories. And mine are all true—though embroidered a bit, of course." He smiled. "Children have a great appetite for amusement, and it amuses me to satisfy it. A thoroughly agreeable arrangement all round. The parlour is this way."

He waved Julian into a large, sunny sitting room, spanning the length of the cottage front to back, with gleaming oak panelling and chintz curtains in a turquoise and yellow print. The back window looked out on a small greenhouse. Tibbs brought Julian over to look at it. "This is my pride and joy. I had it built after I took this house. I've been seized by a passion for gardening since I came to live in the country. I never would have expected it—I'd lived in cities all my life. The front garden is purely decorative, but here I've contrived to grow grapes and peaches. And my cucumber frames, if I may be allowed to say so, are nothing short of magnificent."

He turned to Julian, his brows raised in amused enquiry. "Why this penetrating gaze, Mr. Kestrel? Have I said something exceptionally profound?"

"I was wondering if there's any possibility that we've met before."

"Met before?" Tibbs's eyes opened wide. "I don't see how that's possible. If I'd ever had the honour of your acquaintance, I'm sure I would have remembered."

Julian saw that, beneath his genial, puzzled surface, Tibbs was laughing at him. This was a duel of wits, and he himself was fighting it blindfold. It was disconcerting, but exciting, too. Here was an opponent worthy of his steel.

He said, "It isn't so much your face as your voice. I have an ear for voices—I remember them better than faces and names. And yours is singularly familiar to me."

"I wish I could help you, Mr. Kestrel, but I know of no occasion when we could have met. I've lived on the Continent for much of the last twenty years."

"So have I, for much of the last ten."

"Indeed? Then I daresay we might have run into each other in some European capital. But I can't recall it at all. Still, I'm nearly seventy-four—perhaps my mind is playing tricks on me."

"I hardly think any tricks are being played on *you*, Mr. Tibbs."

Tibbs smiled broadly. "My dear Mr. Kestrel, I can't tell you how delighted I am that you've come! I've been starved for civilised conversation."

"I'm happy to oblige you, but I must confess it wasn't you I came to see. Your nephew told me his sister lived here with you. Now I find that she doesn't and never has. I wonder if you have any idea how her brother could have been so mistaken?"

Tibbs smiled ruefully and walked back and forth, running a hand through his hair. "You mustn't blame the boy. He was only trying to protect his sister's reputation."

Julian's brows shot up. Tibbs was being extraordinarily candid—why? "If I've stumbled on a family secret, I'll guard it to the extent I can. The last thing I wish to do is imperil a lady's reputation. But this isn't a matter of idle curiosity. I'm engaged in helping the Bow Street Runners solve a murder."

"Yes, I know. My nephew's been writing to me all about it. In his last letter, he told me you'd become involved and had questioned him twice. I hope you're finished with him now—this has been mortally hard on him."

"How much has he told you about his part in the investigation?"

"That he found the body. That he's been questioned about the events leading up to the murder, and about his friendship with Alexander Falkland." For the first time, Tibbs looked wholly serious. "Do you suspect him?"

"Yes."

"May I ask why?"

Julian decided not to tell him about the letters to Sir Malcolm. Clare might have kept that from him, and revealing it would only put him on his guard against compromising his nephew further. "Because there are a number of matters on which he's been evasive, and some on which—pardon my frankness—he's lied outright. He said his sister lived with you; the villagers say she's a companion to a lady on the Continent. Is that another story told to salvage her reputation?"

"It's partly true. She's on the Continent, but not as a companion. She's alone."

"Forgive me, Mr. Tibbs, but when a respectable family attempts to conceal a young lady's whereabouts, it's rarely because she's alone."

"A point well taken. And I wish I could tell you a lurid story of her elopement with an Italian music master, but that would be far too conventional a scrape for Verity. She's a follower of Mary Wollstonecraft, you know. She believes with all her heart that if a man and a woman have equal intelligence and equal virtue, there's no reason the woman should be subservient. You can imagine the scandal she'd stir up, going about saying things like that in London—or, worse still, in a country village like this. The tide of public opinion is against her—ebbing away from the ideals of the American republic and the French revolution, and flowing towards family life, domestic bliss, and placing women on pedestals. Imprisoning them there, so my niece says.

"While we lived on the Continent, she had a good deal of freedom. She wasn't so circumscribed by proprieties as she would be here. So when Quentin opted to return to England and study for the Bar, and I decided to live out my last days on my native soil, Verity refused to come with us. She knew she couldn't play the demure debutante—she'd only make a spectacle of herself and damn Quentin by association. So she keeps away. But she won't stand to have a duenna, and though I'm not easy in my mind about her living alone, I can't control her. She's three-and-twenty, she has control of her income, and no power on earth can rein her in when she's made up her mind to something."

"She seems very different from her brother."

"Oh, yes. Quentin was never a whit of trouble. From earliest childhood, he was just what you see now: a shy, contemplative, studious lad, with a conscience almost crippling in its acuteness."

"It seems to have dulled somewhat. At all events, he's managed to reconcile himself to several blatant deceptions."

"I don't know what deceptions you're referring to, other than his telling you Verity lived with me. And that was for her sake, because it would be excessively awkward revealing the sort of life she's living. People would be outraged at a young unmarried woman travelling alone in foreign parts—if they even believed she was alone, which they quite likely wouldn't. Depend upon it: everything he's said or done that might not seem strictly honest can be put down to brotherly love and loyalty. Verity is the chink in his armour, you see. His conscience is wax in her hands.''

"He told me they would each do anything the other asked, if the other wanted it badly enough.''

Tibbs smiled. "Quite true. And for Quentin it's a very bad bargain, because while he would never demand anything base or dangerous of her, she isn't so scrupulous. Not that she would be venal or selfish—she wouldn't ask him to steal her a necklace, or anything of that sort. But if she got it into her head that it was right to do a thing—even if no authority on earth or in Heaven would agree with her—she would stop at nothing to do it and might look to Quentin to help her.''

"Suppose she decided it was right to kill Alexander Falkland. Would her brother help her with that?''

"Frankly, yes, I expect he would. But why should she decide such a thing? She's never even met him.''

"How can you be sure? You say you haven't seen her since you came here a year and a half ago.''

"That's true. But as I told you, she's been on the Continent. And I know Mr. Falkland was in England—Quentin mentioned him from time to time in his letters.''

"I should be interested to see those letters.''

"Sadly, Mr. Kestrel, I don't keep letters. They have a way of coming back to haunt the writers—it's like holding a bit of a person's life hostage. And that seems rather unfair. So I burn them.''

Julian smiled quizzically. At least Tibbs's evasions were entertaining. "Granted that Falkland was in England for the past year and a half, how do you know Miss Clare never returned to England during that time?''

"Because her letters were always postmarked from the Continent.''

"Which of course we can neither prove nor disprove, because you don't keep letters.''

"Alas, no.''

"You're having a game with me, Mr. Tibbs.''

"With *you*, Mr. Kestrel? I wouldn't dare. At the moment, you represent the majesty of the Law."

"You seem in no danger of being over-awed."

"Ah, well, I suppose I've lived a vagabond life too long. When you've seen as much of the world as I have, you become at once too cynical and too forgiving. You think it absurd that anyone seriously believes the law can force people to be virtuous, and you feel sorry for the poor wretches who are whipped and imprisoned and hanged merely for being the imperfect humans we all are."

"Murder seems rather more than an imperfection."

"You are right, of course." Tibbs bowed, conceding the point with grace.

Does he mean any of what he's saying? Julian wondered. Or is he merely amusing me, as he amuses the local children? "May I ask what you did before you lived abroad?"

"I was a tailor. And I take leave to tell you, as a professional, that you far surpass all the newspaper and magazine accounts of your magnificent taste in clothes."

It was Julian's turn to bow. "I'm honoured, Mr. Tibbs. May I say in return that I've never met a tailor who could approach you in gallantry or wit?"

Tibbs bowed again—and again Julian was stabbed with recognition. Where in the name of Heaven had he known this man before?

"Ah," said Tibbs, "but I'll lay you odds you never met a tailor who lived for years on the Continent, with nothing to do but improve his mind and polish his manners."

"You must have been remarkably successful, to retire so early, and so comfortably circumstanced."

"I did do rather well, I admit. And then, I've been guardian to the twins since they were six years old, and their father left a tidy sum for their maintenance. They never wanted for anything that his money or my ingenuity could provide."

"Why did you take them to live abroad?"

"I'd always wanted to travel," Tibbs said casually. "I'd never married, had no family of my own—nothing to keep me in England. The twins had no ties here, either, after their parents died. There was no reason we shouldn't light out for foreign parts."

"Where did you go?"

"For the first few years we had to dodge the wars on the Continent. We spent a good part of that time in Switzerland. But after Waterloo we travelled everywhere: France, Italy, Austria, the Rhineland. An unconventional sort of life for children. But I don't think a traditional English upbringing would have answered. I couldn't have sent Quentin to public school. He's too gentle—the other boys would have eaten him alive. And Verity had too much intellect and too strong a will to sit about sewing samplers and painting firescreens. Living abroad, with no Mrs. Grundy to shake her finger at us, I could manage their education as I liked. We had a private tutor who travelled about with us. Verity studied everything Quentin did, even Latin and Greek. She was resolved to have the laugh of people who said the ancient languages were too difficult for frail female minds."

Julian considered. "What does Miss Clare look like?"

"Why do you ask?" Tibbs countered pleasantly.

"I hope to have the honour of meeting her one day. And I shouldn't like to miss an opportunity through failing to recognize her."

"She's not unlike Quentin: fair and light-eyed. Tall for a woman, and very slender."

"Pretty?"

"My dear Mr. Kestrel, that's so utterly in the eye of the beholder, I couldn't presume to say."

"I take it she hasn't warts or a squint or a crooked back?"

"No," said Tibbs, smiling, "nothing of that sort."

"Have you any idea how I might go about finding her? She must have friends on the Continent you're acquainted with—assuming for the sake of argument that she really is there."

"It's very good of you to assume, even for the sake of argument, that I am not an egregious liar." Tibbs's eyes twinkled. "And I would be happy to give you the names and directions of her friends in Paris, Vienna, and so on. Only give me a few minutes to write them down."

Yes, you'd like that, wouldn't you? Julian thought—to see me ramble all over Europe raking up one mare's nest after another. "I shan't put you to the trouble. Thank you for being so obliging as to talk with me."

"You're not going so soon? I hoped you'd stay to luncheon."

Julian smiled wryly. "That's good of you, but cat and mouse is a tiring game, and I have other calls on my energies. Your servant, Mr. Tibbs."

＊

He returned to the inn where he had left his driver. Finding him still reasonably sober, he sent him to fetch the trap. As they jogged back along the road they had come by, he wrestled with the enigma of Tibbs. His face, his voice—even, strangely, the name Montacute—all hovered on the brink of his memory, yet they eluded his grasp. He felt sure Tibbs could unravel the mystery if he chose. But how to make him speak?

At least he knew now that Verity Clare was missing, and her uncle and brother were concealing her whereabouts. But why? Had she been seduced, ruined, left with a child? Was she ill, or dead? Had she committed a crime—and could that crime be Alexander's murder?

More questions than answers. And only three days left to win his bet. His mind, frustrated and a little mortified by his defeat at Tibbs's hands, refused to concentrate any longer. The road being smooth, and the trap tolerably comfortable, he fell asleep.

He dreamed he was looking down from a great height on David Adams. Light blazed up at Adams from below. He was wearing a black robe and skull-cap, with a long grey beard half hiding his face. He lifted a hand and sent his voice soaring across the vast space: *Hath not a Jew eyes?*—

Julian sat bolt upright. "Stop!" he exclaimed to the driver. "Turn around! We're going back!"

# ✳ 23 ✳

## GHOSTS

In a matter of minutes, Julian was knocking at the door of Tibbs's cottage.

"Mr. Kestrel!" Tibbs appeared in the doorway. He had exchanged his worn gardening coat for an elegant frock coat of dark green wool. "Come in, come in! I little expected to have the pleasure of seeing you again so soon."

"I came back to beg your pardon."

"My dear Mr. Kestrel! Whatever for?"

"For having failed, even for a moment, to recognize Montague Wildwood."

A slow smile spread across Tibbs's face. He bowed, and Julian marvelled that he had not realized at once where Tibbs had acquired a bow like that: proud but subservient, courting applause and yet deeming it his due. "I saw you play Shylock when I was a boy. You were magnificent."

"My dear sir, you leave me speechless."

"Is that possible?" asked Julian mildly.

"A rare occurrence, but not unknown. Seriously, I'm quite overwhelmed that you should remember a performance so long ago. It must have made quite an impression."

It had. It was one of the few plays he and his father had ever attended from beginning to end. Ordinarily they had arrived after the third act, when the ticket prices dropped. That night they had been unusually flush. After the play, they had gone out for ices and explored the West End, with its rows of sumptuous houses, carriages adorned with glittering crests, footmen in brilliant plumage, ladies like goddesses in Grecian gowns. No, he was not likely to forget that night—his first vivid glimpse of what had once been his father's world.

"We must speak further," Tibbs was saying. "I have so little opportunity to conjure up the ghosts of those days. I was just going to sit down to an early luncheon, and I insist that you join me."

"Thank you, I should be delighted. We do have things to talk about."

"That has an ominous ring. But, never mind, we'll sit upon the ground and tell sad stories of—oh, anything you like. Actually, we'll sit upon chairs in the parlour—much more comfortable. Come with me."

A table had been prepared in the parlour, with the meal set out on a sideboard. Tibbs rang for the housekeeper to lay another place. They lunched on cold fowls, fresh Dorset cheese, and fruit from Tibbs's greenhouse, washed down with a bottle of first-rate Frontignac.

"I wasn't altogether deceiving you when I told you I was a tailor," Tibbs explained. "That was my father's trade, and I was raised to follow it. But the theatre captured my imagination when I stood no higher than this table, and nothing could break its hold. At fifteen, I managed to get work cutting and sewing costumes, and for the next few years I wheedled and struggled and schemed, till at last I had a chance to speak a line before the footlights. From there my career advanced— now by inches, now by dizzying leaps. Or I should say, Montague Wildwood's career. I thought I needed a more distinguished name. 'Tibbs' sounded—well, too much like a tailor. And my family had a horror of my vocation. Even when I became famous, they preferred not to have their name linked with the wicked world of the stage."

Julian reflected that Tibbs's relations had had some cause to be scandalized. Montague Wildwood was not only a brilliant actor but a notorious rake: hardly the sort of man a respectable tradesman's family would care to acknowledge.

Tibbs fell to reminiscing about his stage career. Julian listened with enjoyment; he was interested in the theatre, and Tibbs was a superb raconteur. After a time, though, he reminded himself that it was Tibbs's private life he ought to be investigating. Tibbs seemed to read his thoughts, for he said suddenly, "But I know it isn't my interpretation of Mirabell you wish to hear about—acclaimed though it was, if I may be permitted to say so. You want to know about Quentin and Verity. While I was making a name for myself at Drury Lane, my sister had the luck to marry a brewer who became quite plump in the pocket. They had one child, a daughter, for whom they were very ambitious. She was sent to the best schools and groomed to marry a gentleman. I only met her a few times and thought her a stuck-up, missish girl. But, there—I was only a rag-mannered actor and knew nothing about gentility.

"In due time, this exemplary maiden married a barrister named Clare—a brilliant, distinguished man, and quite as stuck-up as she. They naturally gave me a wide berth. None of their lofty friends had an inkling of the connexion between us. They obligingly sent me an announcement when their twins were born, and I obligingly refrained from embarrassing them by coming to the christening.

"When the twins were six, their parents were killed in a carriage accident, and they went to live with a distant relative of their father's. I was their only relation on their mother's side, and of course their parents wouldn't have dreamed of entrusting them to me. I wasn't easy in my mind about them—they were my only family, after all—and I wrote to the guardian asking if I could be of any assistance. But I wrote as George Tibbs, the twins' kindly, respectable great-uncle. It wouldn't have done to approach him as Montague Wildwood. You may be aware that my name had been linked to a scandal or two over the years?"

"I believe I heard something to that effect."

Tibbs's eyes danced. "At all events, he wrote me a disagreeable letter, making clear that the twins were a burden and all but begging me to take them off his hands. I was still thinking what to do about this when, not to put too fine a point upon it, Fate took a hand." He paused, then asked with a startling, quiet directness, "Of course you know why I left England?"

"Yes. Your career is famous not least for the way it ended."

"The greatest folly of my life. Because he was my long-time friend, you see. We were rivals on the stage, and sometimes in love as well, but we admired and loved each other. And our quarrel was about *nothing*. It ought to have come and gone like summer lightning. But we were in our cups, and he said —he said I was past my prime. I was fifty-seven, and that fear had been eating away at me of late. I couldn't bear to hear it spoken aloud. The dispute flamed up, and dawn found us at Chalk Farm with pistols in our hands. Mine was steady enough to hit him, but not steady enough to make it a trivial wound. I shot him through the right lung. He lived for a matter of hours.

"Of course I had to flee the country. But in my last hours in England, the thought of those children smote me. On an impulse, I turned up on their guardian's doorstep. I told him I was their uncle George, I was going travelling on the Continent and thought they might like to come with me. He was so glad to be rid of them, he didn't ask questions. An hour to pack their traps, and we were off. No one tried to stop us at Dover. It only occurred to me afterward that Quentin and Verity had saved me from capture. The Bow Street Runners weren't on the watch for a man with two six-year-olds in tow.

"The rest you know. I brought up the twins on the Continent in my character as George Tibbs: retired tailor, traveller, and student in the school of life. When they were old enough—which was quite soon, they were very precocious— I told them about my Wildwood days and my reason for leaving England. But I told no one else. I owed it to the twins not to associate them with the profligate I had been. Then, too, you'll hardly believe this, but I felt it was a kind of expiation. I'd killed my friend and fellow actor—*ergo,* I gave up the stage and all the renown that went with it. Montague Wildwood simply vanished. Not a bad way, really, for an actor to end his career. An audience, like a lover, ought never to be left quite sated."

"Why did you return to England?"

"I had a fancy to live out my last years here. Quentin was returning to study for the Bar, so I decided to come with him. Not to London, where I might be recognized, but to some quiet spot where I could make a home. I thought I'd have Verity with me, but that wasn't to be. Still, Quentin comes to lighten my solitude every so often. And I've discovered gardening, which is a positive delight.

> *"And this our life exempt from public haunt*
> *Finds tongues in trees, books in the running brooks,*
> *Sermons in stones and good in everything.*
> *I would not change it."*

This seemed to mark the end of the drama. Give Tibbs his due: he had succeeded wonderfully well at distracting Julian from the investigation—up to now. "Did your niece and nephew inherit any of your genius as an actor?"

"Verity did. We used to put on amateur theatricals—nothing elaborate or public, just a way to amuse the twins and some of our friends—and she showed a really remarkable gift. She could mimic anyone's speech and manner—all actors are part monkey in that respect—and she had an extraordinary grasp of character. She might have made quite a name for herself before the footlights, but that wasn't serious enough for her. She must needs read and have opinions and play her part on a broader stage." He smiled. "A regular Portia, in fact."

"And Mr. Clare—is there anything of the actor in him?"

"Nothing whatever. He's too shy to appear on stage, and too honest to assume any character but his own."

Julian took a turn about the room. "You must see, Mr. Tibbs, that your being the man you are reflects on him in this investigation. He was raised by a guardian who had to flee the country for killing a man—yes, I know a duel is different from murder in cold blood, but to an inexperienced young man, the distinction might blur. If Clare had a strong enough motive to kill Falkland, he might have felt justified by your example."

"So he might," Tibbs said genially. "Go on. What other blights have I laid on my unfortunate wards?"

"Mr. Tibbs, I have the highest regard for your former profession, but the fact remains that acting is deception."

"And you think my niece and nephew have deception in their blood?"

"I think that, in training them to act, you may have taught them to trifle with the truth."

"Will you permit me to say that you amuse me, Mr. Kestrel?"

"Gladly, if you'll allow me to share the joke."

"To hear you suggest that theatre in the blood can make one a liar and a murderer—! From another man, I might have let it pass. But, forgive me, it sounds a bit ludicrous on the lips of Julia Wallace's son."

Julian stared. In an altered voice, he asked, "You knew my mother?"

"To be sure I did. Not as well as I would have liked to—meaning no disrespect, of course. And I never trod the boards with her, to my lasting regret. She was Theatre Royal Covent Garden, and I was Drury Lane. And of course she was a shooting star in the theatre—blink, and you'd have missed her, her career was so short. But she did make an impression! I saw her as Lady Teazle, and she coaxed charms from that role I'd never known were there. It was like seeing a fan that had always been half furled, fully open in all its beauty." He smiled and added quietly, "You're very like her, especially about the eyes."

Julian came closer. "Tell me more."

"It was a kind of witchcraft, what she could do. She wasn't a beauty, but once she got to talking and laughing and spinning her stories, you forgot. Men who claimed they couldn't see anything in her one week were enslaved the next. Your father was the worst. He used to haunt the theatre at all hours whenever she was playing. He deluged her with letters, flowers, books—fancy sending an actress books! Wiser men sent jewels—and wiser men never got so much as the time of day from her.

"Frankly, no one expected him to marry her. She'd kept her character, which is no mean feat in the theatre, but still, she was an actress, and he was a young man of birth and prospects. So you can imagine how he confounded the cynics when he did the honourable thing. I heard his family cut up rough about it. Did they ever forgive him?"

"No," said Julian shortly. "They never did."

"Pity. They can't have met her, or she'd have won them over, I'll be bound." He added, "You never knew her, I suppose?"

"No. She died when I was born."

"Hard on your father."

"Yes. He'd sacrificed everything for her—family, property, connexions—and a year later she was gone, and in her place he had a screaming, helpless thing that would be dependent on him for years to come. Some men would have run mad with rage or regret, but not my father. He forgave me, wholeheartedly and completely, for the crime of having been born."

Tibbs smiled, not unkindly. "You might consider forgiving yourself one of these days."

Julian went cold with shock. He ought to have been more wary of Tibbs; he had known he could be dangerous. But he had let himself be beguiled, and the man had stripped off his skin.

He forced his voice level. "We've wandered rather far from the subject I came to discuss."

"Only a brief diversion—the scenic route, you might say. I merely wanted you to realize how much you and my niece and nephew have in common. You're all children of the theatre. Indeed, you show it, Mr. Kestrel. What is your fine self but a part you play—your clothes the costumes, your wit the lines? Society may puzzle over who you are and where you came from, but I make no doubt there are a few old cronies of mine left in the theatre who remember your mother and know whence you sprang. Don't worry—we wouldn't give you away. We count you as one of our own."

*One of our own,* Julian repeated to himself. And are they right? I wonder. I have no family, no property, no profession. Am I anything more than costumes and lines—a character in my own play?

The answer came back: Yes. Because a mere cardboard figure couldn't have solved two murders and be on his way to solving two more. Strange—I always thought I did this to amuse myself, perhaps to do justice to the victims. I never knew I was saving my own soul.

He said, "There's a crucial difference between me and your niece and nephew. I'm not implicated in a murder, and they are."

"No one could wish to clear their names more fervently than I. But I've told you all I can, and more than I ought."

"You do yourself an injustice, Mr. Tibbs. I can't see that you've given away anything to the purpose."

"On the contrary, I've said one thing that was unforgivably indiscreet. Don't ask me what it was; no power on earth can make me say it again."

"This is too serious a business for riddles, Mr. Tibbs."

"Too late." Tibbs sighed. "Because I've already set you this one—and I hope to Heaven you never solve it!"

# ✻ 24 ✻

## LET JUSTICE
## BE DONE

Julian returned to his inn in Yeovil and ordered a post-chaise for London. Finding Dipper in the taproom, he told him it was time to collect their things. They made their way through the tangle of corridors and stairs to Julian's room. On the way they passed a pretty chambermaid, who blushed furiously and scurried away.

Julian looked askance at Dipper. "I ought to keep you on a leash."

Dipper looked about vaguely, as if he supposed his master must be talking to somebody else. "She's a bit shy of strangers, sir," he offered.

"If there's one thing you're most unlikely to be to her now, it's a stranger. I feel a positive malefactor, taking you about the country with me. You're an egregious offence to the public morals."

"All by meself, sir?" said Dipper, impressed.

"Somehow I don't think this lecture is having quite the right effect. Come, I want to be on the road as soon as possible. I have a reckoning in London with Mr. Clare."

✻

Travelling at breakneck speed again, they reached London a few hours after midnight. Next morning, amid a clangour of church bells, Julian went to Lincoln's Inn.

Clare was not in his chambers and had left the outer door locked, indicating that he did not mean to return for some time. Julian looked in at the chapel, thinking Clare might be attending services there, but he did not see his fair, narrow head among the many heads bent over prayer books. He lingered a short while to listen to the music, then slipped away.

He next went to Bow Street. Vance was not there but was expected later. Julian hoped he was enjoying a little hard-earned leisure with his wife and children in Camden Town. He left his card, writing on the back of it: *"New developments. I am on my way to see Sir Malcolm & will call again when I return."*

He reached Sir Malcolm's house at about half past noon and was shown into the study. As he should have expected, Clare was there. He and Sir Malcolm had just returned from church and were looking up some point of law, their heads bent over a book.

"Mr. Kestrel!" Sir Malcolm came forward and wrung his hand heartily. "I was wondering what had become of you. I saw Vance yesterday, and he told me you'd left town on some mysterious mission."

"There's nothing mysterious about it. I went to Montacute to see Miss Verity Clare."

Clare's head came up from the book, his grey eyes dark in his white face.

Sir Malcolm was facing away from him and did not see. "Did you meet her? Did anything useful come of it? What did she—" He broke off, suddenly feeling the tension between Julian and Clare. He looked from one to the other. "What's wrong?"

"Miss Clare doesn't live in Montacute with her uncle," said Julian. "She never has. And I understand from the uncle, George Tibbs, that Mr. Clare knew that perfectly well."

"Where—" Clare moistened his lips. "Where did he tell you Verity is?"

"Why don't *you* tell me where she is? Then we can compare the two accounts and see which seems more plausible."

"Look here," broke in Sir Malcolm, "I see no reason to assume that Quentin is going to lie!"

"He's already lied, Sir Malcolm. He told us his sister was in Montacute, knowing full well that she wasn't. So I should be interested to know what story he means to tell now."

"What does it matter?" Clare asked, hardly above a whisper. "What has Verity to do with your investigation of Falkland's murder?"

"That is precisely what I'm trying to find out."

"But I swear to you, on my—my—"

"Honour?" Julian let the word vibrate in the air, then added more gently, "You can't say it. I'm not surprised."

Clare looked away.

"Why must you go on with these deceits and evasions—against your will, against your nature, against the law you aspire to serve? It isn't too late to make your peace with your conscience and tell us the truth. Where is Verity?"

"I can't tell you that."

"Can't, or won't?"

"Can't."

"Why not?"

"I can't tell you that, either."

"Did she kill Alexander?"

"No!" That word rang out almost defiantly.

"Did you?"

"No." Clare dropped his head in his hands.

"You're in a perilous position, Mr. Clare. Men have been taken up on suspicion for much less."

"I don't see any need to resort to threats!" Sir Malcolm said sharply.

"This isn't a threat," said Julian. "Refusing to answer questions in a murder investigation is obstructing justice. I feel rather absurd, having to point that out to two lawyers, but there it is."

"He's right, you know, sir," Clare told Sir Malcolm gently. "Mr. Kestrel, I can tell you nothing about my sister. If you think that makes me guilty of Falkland's murder, you may have me taken up. I won't leave London. You'll find me in my chambers, should you wish to send a constable." He turned to Sir Malcolm. "Under the circumstances, sir, the only honourable thing I can do is to break off our acquaintance. I won't take advantage of your kindness, when I can't give you perfect candour in return. Goodbye, sir. And thank you, with all my heart, for all you tried to do for me."

He bowed and went quickly away. Sir Malcolm stared after him. The next moment he ran out, calling, "Quentin! Wait! We must talk about this—"

He returned soon after, looking black as a thundercloud. "He's gone. I couldn't stop him. What do you mean by insulting him in that fashion?—a friend of mine, a guest in my house!"

"For God's sake, Sir Malcolm," Julian said wearily, "this is a murder investigation. I warned you—"

"Don't tell me again how you warned me your investigation might turn up shocking information. You haven't turned up anything shocking about Mr. Clare except that he won't tell you where his sister is. That hardly makes him a murderer."

"There's considerably more to be said against him than that. He wrote those letters to you in Alexander's name, and he won't tell us why. I think Alexander had some hold over him, and he can't reveal that without telling us what it was. If that's true, he had a double motive to kill Alexander: anger at being blackmailed and fear that the blackmail would continue, even grow worse."

"And what are you suggesting this blackmail was about?" Sir Malcolm demanded coldly.

"I should guess, about Verity. Alexander may have known some secret that would harm her if it were revealed. It's also possible he had a love affair with her."

"This passes all bearing!" Sir Malcolm strode about, waving his hands. "First you credit Adams's story that Alexander was keeping Mrs. Desmond, and now you think Verity Clare was his mistress as well!"

"It may be simpler than that. You're overlooking the possibility that Mrs. Desmond *is* Verity Clare."

"*What?*"

"They're both tall, slender young women with fair hair and light eyes, and they've both disappeared. I don't know why a strong-minded young woman who admires Mary Wollstonecraft should turn into a shallow light-of-love, who furnished her house like a brothel and apparently conducted it like one as well. But if Miss Clare chose to assume that character, she might well be able to carry it off. Tibbs told me she was a talented actress and could mimic any sort of manner or voice."

"This all sounds like the rankest speculation. But let's suppose there's something in it. Are you saying that Alexander had a love affair with Verity Clare and blackmailed Quentin about it, and Quentin killed him to stop the blackmail and protect his sister's reputation?"

"Perhaps. But you could equally turn the whole theory on its head. Alexander was blackmailing Clare about something that had nothing to do with Verity. Verity found out about it and arranged to meet Alexander secretly on the night of his party. She killed him to free her brother, and Clare knows it and is trying to protect her. In some ways, that makes more sense. Everyone says she's the bolder and less scrupulous of the twins."

"Oh, Lord!" Sir Malcolm pressed his palms to his head, as if he were trying to keep too much in it at once. "Suppose Verity *is* Mrs. Desmond: who was the driver of the gig—the gentleman who spirited a woman away from Cygnet's Court on the night of the Brickfield Murder?"

"Clare, rescuing his sister? Alexander, disposing of her? Some other man, running away with her behind Alexander's back? Whoever he was, he was mixed up in the Brickfield Murder. And I'll lay any odds that, if he wasn't Alexander, Alexander knew who he was and what he'd done."

Sir Malcolm said stonily, "I don't want Quentin taken up

on suspicion—not yet. I'm not prepared to believe in his guilt—not on the evidence you've mustered so far."

"I grant you, I'm richer in theories than in facts. I shall do what I can to remedy that. I don't think it's necessary to imprison Clare in the meantime. He won't run away."

"He's not a coward."

"He's not a fool."

"Why must you be so hard on him?"

"In part," said Julian thoughtfully, "because I'm wary of being too lenient. He does draw on my sympathies—and I don't like it. I feel I'm being taken in, and I don't know how or why."

"You trust Eugene, in spite of the evidence against him."

"I have yet to catch Eugene in a lie. If I do, I shan't show him any mercy."

Sir Malcolm waved his hand in a bitter, defeated gesture. "What does it all matter to you, anyway? If Eugene or any of the suspects should disappoint or betray you, it won't mean much. What's one person, one friend, to you, more or less? But I've lost my son, my chance of a grandchild, and everything of Belinda but the empty shell upstairs. Then Quentin came along, and suddenly it was all bearable. Better than bearable—I was happier than I've been in Lord knows how long. I wanted him—I needed him—and you've driven him away."

What do you want from me? Julian thought. Don't solve your son's murder. Adopt Clare in his place. Bury the truth under a load of sentiment, and be damned to the investigation. But you'll be haunted the rest of your life—not by Alexander, but by justice left undone.

He asked point-blank, "Do you wish me to give over the investigation?"

Sir Malcolm stared back at him and did not answer.

Dutton came in. "Peter Vance is here to see you, sir, with two young persons."

"Young persons?" echoed Sir Malcolm.

"Yes, sir. He said you'd wish to see them."

"We'd better have them in, I suppose." Sir Malcolm waited till Dutton was gone, then said, "I can't answer your question now. Ask me again after Vance and the young persons have gone."

The young persons proved to be a slender girl of about sixteen, with a small pointed face and large dark eyes, and a sandy-haired boy a year or two older, whose sun-baked skin, stubby, callused fingers, and vague odour of the stables told Julian he must be a post-boy or ostler. They were both dressed in their Sunday best: the girl freshly pretty in a flowered muslin frock, the boy ill at ease in a stiff, clean neckcloth and polished boots.

" 'Afternoon, sir!" Vance greeted Sir Malcolm. "Glad I've found you at home. And you, Mr. Kestrel—I got your note and hoped I'd be in time to catch you here. Sir Malcolm Falkland, Mr. Julian Kestrel, this here is Miss Ruth Piper, and this is Mr. Benjamin Foley. They came to Bow Street this morning in answer to the advertisement we posted about the gig and horse."

He took a piece of grimy parchment from his pocket and held it out. It read:

*PUBLIC OFFICE, BOW STREET*
*6 May 1825*
*50 GUINEAS Reward*

*Whereas, on the night of the* 22nd *April, Alexander Falkland, Esq. was foully and brutally Murdered, and whereas, on the night of the* 15th *April, a woman as yet unidentified was beaten to death in a brickfield southeast of Hampstead:—Notice is hereby given, that whoever shall give Information of the gig and horse described below, believed to have some connexion with either or both crimes, shall receive the above Reward by applying to the Chief Clerk at the Public Office, Bow Street.*

A description of the gig and horse followed.

"I got to the office just in time to interview 'em," Vance

went on. "Then I took 'em to see the gig and horse, and they recognized 'em straightaway. There was no magistrate on a Sunday morning to take their statements, so I brought 'em out here to tell you what they told me."

Ruth curtsied. Ben touched his forelock and shifted from one foot to the other.

"I'm very glad the two of you have come," Sir Malcolm said warmly. "You must have heard of the murder of my son a few weeks ago. We've been searching high and low for information that might lead us to his killer, and I shall be grateful for anything you can tell us that might light our way."

Julian was impressed. Whatever Sir Malcolm's private doubts and conflicts about the investigation, he could put them aside long enough not only to question these witnesses, but to woo them a little, put them at their ease. Julian could understand why he was so successful in court. He also saw clearly for the first time how much Alexander's famous charm had owed to his father's example.

Ruth curtsied again. "I'm sure we should like to help you, sir. But, sir, I can't believe the gentleman that drove the gig had anything to do with any murder. He was ever so kind. He wouldn't have hurt anyone."

Ben glowered at her. She lifted her chin and looked defiantly back.

"Perhaps we might begin at the beginning?" Julian suggested. "Where did you see the gentleman, and when?"

"It was the night of April the fifteenth," she answered readily.

"How do you remember that so precisely?"

"Because I keep a diary, sir. I wrote about the gentleman that night before I went to bed."

"You're an inestimable witness, Miss Piper," said Julian, smiling. "Now, where did you see this gentleman?"

"At the Jolly Filly, sir. It's my father's inn, in Surrey, just south of Kingston."

"Surrey," Julian mused. That was nowhere near Hampstead and the brickfield; in fact, it was on the opposite side of

London, across the river. What could have been the gentleman's business there? "Please go on."

"He came at about eleven, sir, or perhaps it was closer to half past. He left his horse to be fed and watered—Ben looked after it, he's one of our ostlers—and came into the coffee-room to have a warm. It was a damp, misty night. Later it rained dreadful hard, but that was after he'd gone."

"Yes." Julian nodded. "Now, this is very important: Was he alone when he arrived?"

"Yes, sir," said Ruth.

"Did he speak with anyone while he was there?"

"Only me, sir. When he come into the coffee-room, I asked if I might fetch him a drop of something. I help to wait on the customers, you see. He ordered coffee with curaçao, and when I brought it he talked to me—asked me how long I'd worked at the inn and whether I liked it. Then he—well, he flirted with me a bit—asked me if I had a sweetheart, that sort of thing. But he didn't mean anything by it—he was just passing the time while his horse was being looked after. He was kind. He made me feel—I don't know—as if I was the nicest girl he'd ever met."

Ben glowered more than ever.

Julian turned to him. "Meanwhile you were feeding and watering his horse?"

"Yes, sir. And it weren't much of a horse, for such a fine gentleman! A skinny old roan with a ewe neck, just like it says here." He pointed to the advertisement. "And his carriage was nothing but a shabby old walnut-shell. He ain't real quality, I says to Ruth—you can always tell a true gentleman by his cattle. But would she listen? Not her!"

"I told you," Ruth said impatiently, "that can't have been his regular carriage. He was incog—incog—in disguise. Just like a hero out of a novel!"

"Then why was he dressed so swell?" Ben retorted. "Driving a nag like that, and dressed in a fine black cloak and a topper! There was something wrong about him—I knowed it from the first. And when I seen this"—he waved the advertisement—"I brung it home to show Ruth, and I says, see, your gentleman friend's in trouble, Bow Street is after him. But she still don't believe it!" He lifted his hands as if calling Heaven to witness Ruth's obstinacy. "He's still guinea-gold to her!"

"Did the gentleman say anything about where he'd come from?" asked Julian.

Ruth and Ben shook their heads.

"Or where he was going?"

Another negative.

"When did he leave?"

"About midnight, sir," said Ruth.

"Did he seem nervous, or anxious to escape notice?"

"No, sir, not at all. But we hadn't many customers that night, so there was no one to take much notice of him, anyway."

Only one question—the most important—remained. It was Sir Malcolm who asked it. "What did this gentleman look like?"

Ruth and Ben exchanged glances. Ben said, "I only saw him outside, by the carriage lamps. He wasn't very old—about your age, sir." He nodded at Julian.

"But you saw him in the coffee-room, Miss Piper," Julian said. "There must have been enough light for you to tell what he looked like."

"Y-es, sir. Leastways, I know he was very gentleman-like, and had the most speaking eyes. But I'm not sure what colour they were, or his hair, neither. He was sitting in a corner, where there isn't much light of an evening. Candles cost so much, you see." She brightened. "I'd know him if I saw him again—I'm sure of that."

Julian looked at Sir Malcolm. "With your permission, I think we should all go into the library."

"Why?"

"Because I think it may simplify this enquiry."

"Very well, Mr. Kestrel, if you wish."

They went through the connecting door into the library.

Ruth and Ben gazed curiously around them. Suddenly Ruth gave a cry of pleasure. "There he is! That's the gentleman!"

She pointed to the portrait of Alexander.

"Oh, God." Sir Malcolm reached out and leaned his hand on a pillar to steady himself.

"I'm so sorry, sir," said Ruth. "Was he your son—the one who was killed?"

"Yes," Sir Malcolm said heavily. "He was my son."

"Do you recognize him, too?" Julian asked Ben.

"Yes, sir." Ben looked disappointed—probably at finding out the gentleman was not a criminal but a victim. He might have cheered up had he known that on the night Alexander stopped at the Jolly Filly, he had disposed of one woman, perhaps murdered another.

Julian took a moment to piece together the events of that night in light of this new knowledge. At about nine o'clock, Alexander drove the gig and horse to Cygnet's Court. Instead of driving in through the passage, he left the gig and horse with Jemmy Otis and went in on foot. He returned, carrying a sleeping woman wearing a cloak and bonnet and white slippers embroidered with gold thread. He put her in the gig and drove away.

When next seen, he was alone. He arrived at the Jolly Filly between eleven and half past and stayed till midnight, chatting with Ruth and resting his horse. He did not appear nervous or in a hurry—that suggested he had accomplished whatever task he had set himself. To take the woman somewhere, dispose of her somehow? But not by murder, surely—or, at all events, not the Brickfield Murder. He would not have had time to go all the way to Hampstead, then double back to Surrey on the other side of the river—let alone to carry out the murder and make himself presentable afterward.

No: if Alexander committed the Brickfield Murder, he did it later, after he had left the Jolly Filly. The murder accomplished, he returned to Mrs. Desmond's house, abandoning the gig and horse in Long Acre on the way. He cleansed himself of blood and brickearth at the washstand in Mrs. Desmond's room and went home at the fashionable hour of dawn. Well and good. But when and how did Mrs. Desmond's possessions disappear from Cygnet's Court? Who was the brickfield victim? And why did Alexander go so far as to destroy her face?

He realized he had walked away from the group and was standing before Alexander's portrait. Sir Malcolm joined him there. "You think he killed that woman in the brickfield, don't you?" he said in an undertone.

"The evidence points that way. But there may be some innocent explanation."

"Thank you for saying so. I don't believe it, and nor do you. We've already caught him deceiving me, deceiving his wife, dragging Quentin into his plots, and perhaps Adams as well. Alexander wasn't killed by footpads, or in a duel or an accident. Nobody stood to gain enough by his murder to make it worth the risk. I daresay we should have asked long ago what he did to make someone hate him enough to kill him."

Julian regarded him in compassionate silence. At length he said, "You told me to ask my question again after we'd spoken with Vance. Do you wish me to abandon the investigation?"

"No. We'll see it through."

"There may be more of these revelations about Alexander. We may find his murderer was someone close to him, and dear to you."

"So be it. The law has a saying in such cases: *Fiat justicia, ruat coelum.* Let justice be done, though the heavens fall."

# ✳ 25 ✳

# THE HOUSE
# WITHOUT WINDOWS

Sir Malcolm, Julian, and Vance held a council to determine what their next step should be. Julian explained his reconstruction of the night of the Brickfield Murder. "Of course it leaves a good deal unaccounted for. But I think we can safely make one assumption: the unconscious woman Jemmy Otis saw taken away in the gig was Mrs. Desmond."

"She don't fit the description of the brickfield woman," Vance pointed out.

"No. That's precisely why I think she was the woman Jemmy saw. It can't have been the brickfield victim Alexander took away in the gig. Assuming the Brickfield Murder happened after he stopped at the Jolly Filly, what did he do with the victim in the meantime? And why trouble to bring her all the way to Surrey, only to turn round and take her to Hampstead? Besides, Jemmy's unconscious woman was wearing gold-threaded slippers. That sounds like Mrs. Desmond rather than her maid—who also disappeared that night, and who does fit the brickfield woman's description."

"Didn't you say," Sir Malcolm asked, his voice heavy with repugnance, "that Mrs. Desmond brought other women to her house? That she—procured them—for Alexander? How do you know it wasn't one of those women he took away in the gig?"

"That's possible. But Alexander may well have had reason to be rid of Mrs. Desmond. She knew too much about him. She knew he was unfaithful to his wife, and he liked to play the devoted husband. Worse, she was involved in a plot with him against Mrs. Falkland. He had her dress up in her maid's clothes and lure Mrs. Falkland into Cygnet's Court. Whatever was behind that charade, it can't have reflected credit on him."

In reality, Julian thought he knew what was behind it. But no one asked him, which was just as well, because he wanted to keep that theory to himself for now.

"Supposing everything is as you say, sir," said Vance, "what's to be done about it?"

"We know Mrs. Desmond wasn't the brickfield victim: *ergo*, she may still be alive. Alexander was next seen in Surrey after he spirited her away from Cygnet's Court. He must have had some reason for going there. Perhaps she had relatives or friends there who could take her off his hands. So I suggest you draw up a new advertisement, to be circulated in the neighbourhood of the Jolly Filly, describing Mrs. Desmond and seeking information about her."

"Right, sir." Vance nodded. "And I'll send Bill Watkins to ask after her and Mr. Falkland at inns and turnpikes along the way. How will that be, sir?"

"Capital." But what am I to do in the meantime? Julian wondered. I've already lost a day on that infernal trip to Somerset, and I'm in no mood to cool my heels and wait for Vance's seeds to bear fruit. But where is the sense in tearing around aimlessly? Activity for activity's sake does no one any good.

He went home and occupied himself with going over all the information that had been gathered so far in the investigation. No new insights emerged. He sent Dipper out for newspapers and skimmed their latest stories about the Falkland case in the hope they might offer him a fresh perspective. But the papers were in the dark about the investigation, now that it had become largely a private endeavour of Julian's. Without coroner's proceedings or public examinations of witnesses, the reporters were finding it difficult to keep up. It was a sad state of affairs, the *Times* observed, when a serious criminal investigation was reduced to a gentleman's amusement. But *Bell's Life in London* revelled in Julian's role, coyly asking its readers what renowned nonpareil among dandies was leaving no stone unturned to solve "*the shocking and atrocious murder of a certain A.F., whose stylish entertainments all too briefly dazzled the* beau monde." Alexander had always been the darling of the society papers.

Julian dined out with friends at a hotel in Covent Garden, but declined their invitation to one of the neighbourhood nunneries. He was not in the mood for bought caresses. When he got home, he recalled Philippa Fontclair's letter lying neglected on his writing-desk. He took up pen and paper and began a response. He said nothing about the investigation—she had already been exposed to too much of that sort of thing last year, when murder had invaded her tranquil country home.

He thanked her for sharing the secret of her sister-in-law's condition and promised not to speak of it to anyone till she gave him leave. He added:

> *I shouldn't worry overmuch about not feeling like an aunt. I don't imagine it's the sort of thing one can feel in a vacuum. No man I ever knew could conceive of himself as husband till he had a wife, or as a father till he had a child. I'm persuaded that, once you have a flesh-and-blood niece or nephew, you'll get on famously.*

He blotted the sheet, then sat back in his chair, twirling the quill and wondering what it would be like to feel like somebody's uncle—or brother or nephew or cousin. You're blue-devilled, he told himself: discouraged about the investigation, and not quite recovered from Tibbs's vivisection. Finish your letter, and go to bed.

✳

He awoke soon after dawn in a completely different frame of mind. There must be something significant about the neighbourhood of the Jolly Filly, else why had Alexander gone there after carrying off Mrs. Desmond? He resolved to go exploring there himself. He would not follow any predetermined route—might not even stop to make enquiries. He would simply keep his eyes and ears open. Who knew, he might happen on something that Vance's conventional enquiries would miss. If not, he would be no worse off than he was now.

He rang for Dipper and told him his plan. By seven he was shaved, dressed, breakfasted, and on his way to see Felix Poynter.

Felix's manservant received him in some astonishment. "Mr. Poynter isn't at home, sir."

"No civilised person would be, at this hour. But my business is pressing enough to transcend courtesy."

"I couldn't take it upon myself, sir—"

"Then allow me to relieve you of the responsibility."

He went to Felix's bedroom door and knocked. There was no answer, so he knocked louder. At last a hollow voice called, "Come in—anything—only stop that rapping. My head feels as if there were two-score dragoons drilling in it."

Julian went in. Felix was looking blearily out through his green silk bedcurtains, his nightcap pushed over one ear. "Good morning," Julian greeted him pleasantly.

"My dear fellow!" Felix expostulated faintly. "Do you realize what o'clock it is? I haven't been in bed above an hour! What on earth do you want?"

"I came to ask if you would be good enough to lend me your cabriolet."

"Is that all? I thought war had been declared, at least."

"Nothing so dire. I'm going into Surrey on business connected with the investigation, and I need a carriage in case

I'm obliged to take anyone about with me or bring anyone back. So if you'll lend me your cab I should be very grateful."

"Really, my dear old chap," said Felix, struggling to sit up amidst a tangle of bedclothes, "this investigation is becoming a positive monomania with you."

"A monomania?"

"Yes, a monomania. Being completely mad upon one subject. From *mono*, short for 'monotonous,' and *mania*, meaning—well, 'mania.' "

Julian regarded him thoughtfully. "Why is it so important to you to appear stupid?"

"Why is it so important to you to appear clever?"

"But I *am* a little clever, I think, whereas I don't believe you're stupid in the least."

"This is making my head ache. Please don't take this amiss, because really, I like you excessively, and I count you among my dearest friends—but I wish above all things that you would go away."

"I know it's barbarous calling at this hour, but I'm rather pressed for time. I've bet de Witt five hundred pounds that I'll solve Falkland's murder by noon tomorrow, and to lose would be rather inconvenient, since, now I come to think of it, I haven't got five hundred pounds."

"You know," said Felix, plucking at the bedsheet, "you could always count on me to—"

Julian smiled. "My dear fellow, you're very good, but if I must borrow, it will be from one of the cent-per-cents, whom I can despise and resent with impunity. It's devilish confining to one's natural feelings, borrowing money from a friend."

"Well, if all you want is the cab, take it by all means." Felix brightened. "Take Alfred, too—my tiger, you remember. He'll be useful to look after the horse, and perhaps you might contrive to lose him in the countryside or have him stolen by gipsies. Find me pen and paper, there's a good fellow, and I'll write a note for you to take to the livery stable."

Julian went to Felix's little Louis Quinze writing-desk and rummaged through a litter of invitations, bills, fashion plates, racing calendars, lottery tickets, and French novels. At last he unearthed some notepaper and a steel pen enamelled with gold stars. Felix wrote a note authorizing him to take the cabriolet, then burrowed back under the covers. Julian thanked him and started to close the bedcurtains.

"You know," murmured Felix drowsily, "it's not altogether a bad thing you've come at this hour. Now you can dispel a rather nasty rumour that's been going about, that I sleep with—"

He was overcome by a yawn. Julian waited in some suspense.

"—my hair in curl-papers," Felix finished anticlimactically.

"I shall do all I can to nip that slander in the bud. Good morning—or, if you prefer, goodnight."

✳

After his frequent trips north to Hampstead, Julian found it a refreshing change to travel south into Surrey. And driving was a pleasure, especially a first-rate carriage like Felix's. Its cherry-red paint was too showy for Julian's taste, but in all other respects it was superb: light, elegant, and perfectly balanced. Once he had left the city traffic behind, he sped the horse to a canter and found the carriage springs more than equal to a fifteen-mile-an-hour pace. He would have liked to keep his own cabriolet, but it was devilish expensive. It meant buying, stabling, and feeding a second horse, renting space for the carriage, and hiring a groom like Alfred to look after them. He must face facts: his income did not permit him both to dress and to drive. And dressing was indispensable.

He decided to begin his explorations at the Jolly Filly and fan out from there. Following a tollkeeper's directions, he branched off the Guildford road between Kingston and Esher. He drove east past strawberry fields and flocks of sheep till he reached a long, low inn. It had a singularly angry expression, due partly to its jutting upper storey, which overhung the lower like a frowning brow, and partly to its bright terracotta front, which made it look red in the face. The swinging sign showed, not a cheerful little horse, but a sad-faced girl with blue eyes and gold ringlets. Julian guessed that, in some earlier incarnation, the Jolly Filly had been the *Jolie Fille.*

His arrival in the flamboyant little carriage caused quite a stir. Ben Foley took charge of the horse with a reverent air; this was clearly his idea of how a gentleman ought to travel. Alfred strutted about the yard, showing off his livery to the ostlers.

Julian went inside and enquired for Ruth Piper. She joined him in the coffee-room and brought him a pot of excellent ale. "There was a man from Bow Street here before you, sir," she said. "Mr. Bill Watkins. He come just after dawn, and there was a great to-do. Ben had told everyone how we went to Bow Street and identified the gig and horse, and how the driver turned out to be that Mr. Falkland who was murdered. And ever so many people came in from the village, saying they'd seen the gig and horse, too. They told *such* stories, you can't think! How they'd come in for a pint that night and saw Mr. Falkland do this or that, and what he said, and how he looked. Nobody really saw him for more than a minute but Ben and me—I'm sure of that, sir! But people must needs go putting their oar in. Pa says they just want a share of the reward."

"Rewards do tend to loosen people's tongues—sometimes to the point where memory gives way to invention."

"Well, I'm sorry for Mr. Watkins, because he's had to go and interview all those people, just on the chance they might really know something. Must you talk to them, too, sir?"

"No, I'm sure he's more than competent to deal with them. I should rather have a look about the countryside."

"What are you hoping to find, sir?"

Julian smiled wryly. "I wish I knew."

❋

A few hours of tooling about the neighbourhood, stopping occasionally to ask questions and rest his horse, left him no wiser about what he expected to accomplish. There was nothing significant to be seen. The villages, with their churches, inns, and little shops, could not have been more ordinary. The cornfields and hop-gardens, dovecotes and water mills, were pretty in the pale May sunshine, but of no apparent interest. What had attracted Alexander to this placid, pleasant countryside? Where could he have disposed of his mistress here?

Julian began to wonder if he was doing Alexander an injustice. Had he become so intrigued at finding flaws and vices in this young man everyone liked that he now believed him guilty of kidnapping and murder? He determined to see if he could concoct a theory in Alexander's favour. Alexander had taken Mrs. Desmond to Surrey, but not for any sinister reason. While they were there, someone had bought, borrowed, or stolen the gig and horse and used it to drive to Hampstead and commit the Brickfield Murder. That would account for the brickearth found in the gig—but not for the traces of it in Mrs. Desmond's house. Very well: after driving Mrs. Desmond into Surrey, Alexander gave her the gig—it was light enough for a woman to handle—and she drove it back to London, took her maid to the brickfield, killed her, and returned to her house to clean herself and remove her possessions.

That cock would not fight. There was no getting around the fact that when Alexander stopped at the Jolly Filly, he still had the gig and horse, and he was alone. If it was Mrs. Desmond who drove the gig back to London, where was she while Alexander was whiling away three quarters of an hour at the inn, drinking coffee with curaçao and flirting with Ruth? He had got rid of her successfully: that was surely the explanation for his carefree, unhurried air. But how?

Julian flicked open his watch. It was half past two. Why not return to the Jolly Filly and find some more sensible line of investigation to pursue? He turned the cabriolet about, smiling at his wish to keep his own carriage. That was no sort of dream for a man who would soon have to raise five hundred pounds.

He drew up at a fork between two roads, debating which to take. The wider and more well-travelled one would lead him back to the Jolly Filly, but by a route he had already traversed. A narrow track splitting off from it would take him through an area he had not yet seen. Catching sight of a smock-frocked boy trudging across a nearby field, he called, "You there! Can you tell me where this path leads?"

The boy gaped at him, saying nothing.

"Can you tell me where this path leads?" Julian repeated more clearly, thinking he might be slow-witted.

The boy shook his head and backed away. "I ain't allowed to go there."

"Why not?"

The boy went on backing, then suddenly took to his heels and lost himself behind barricades of hedgerows.

Alfred looked uneasy; perhaps he was afraid he might be asked to run after him and ruin his amethyst livery. But Julian merely shrugged. "We shall have to find out for ourselves."

"Begging your pardon, sir," ventured Alfred, "but p'raps there's a reason the boy ain't allowed to go down that path."

"Undoubtedly. And I mean to find out what it is."

They set off. Their pace was slow, for the road was bumpy and increasingly shadowed by trees. The horse might all too easily bruise a foot on the sharp stones. They saw no farms or cottages; perhaps this was a private road to some country manor. Sure enough, it ended abruptly at a high, grey-brick wall with a gate flanked by square stone columns.

Julian got out of the cabriolet and walked up to the gate. It was of thick wood and studded with nails. A brass plaque read: E. RIDLEY, PROPRIETOR.

He tried the latch. It lifted, but the door would not give; there must be a padlock inside. A bell was attached to one of the columns, so he rang. No one answered, and he rang again.

This time he heard footsteps shuffling toward the gate. A key scraped, then the heavy door opened a crack, and a man looked out. He had a red, wrinkled face and a bird's nest of grizzled hair. His coat was shabby and smeared with tobacco stains. "What's your business?"

Julian thought quickly. If he asked what sort of place this was, he might well be sent away with a flea in his ear. The old servant looked well able to dispose of inquisitive strangers.

He decided to try a little West End hauteur. "I wish to see the proprietor."

"Do you have an appointment?"

"I am not accustomed to needing an appointment."

The servant blinked and became a little more respectful. "I mean, sir, does Mr. Ridley know to expect you?"

"No. I was in the neighbourhood and thought I would call. Am I to be left standing in the rain?" For it had providentially begun to drizzle.

The servant hesitated. At last he drew open the gate, and Julian passed through.

Before him was one of the most forbidding houses he had ever seen. It was square, with a sharp little turret at each corner and a front door bound with iron like a prison's. No ivy, shrubs, or flowers softened the grey-brick façade. But the house's most chilling feature was that it had no windows. The openings where they had been could be seen, but they were all bricked up. Yet to judge by the house's commodious size and well-kept grounds, the owner could well afford to pay the window tax.

The servant took a heavy key from a ring on his belt and opened the front door. They entered a stone-flagged, rectangular hall, unfurnished save for two stiff little chairs. A window opposite revealed a grassy enclosed courtyard. Julian saw now why the house needed no outer windows: all the rooms looked inward to this courtyard for their light. A good way to keep out prying eyes—but why should the inhabitants turn such a dark, blank face on the outside world?

"What name shall I give Mr. Ridley, sir?" the servant asked.

Julian was about to reach for his card-case when he recollected that his name was publicly linked with Bow Street and Alexander's murder. If this Mr. Ridley were involved in anything hole-and-corner, he might well refuse to see him. He decided to try an experiment. "My name is Desmond."

The servant started, then looked at Julian narrowly from under thick grey brows. But all he said was, "If you'll wait here, sir, I'll see if Mr. Ridley's at liberty."

"Thank you." Julian walked away carelessly and affected to look out the window.

The servant departed through a side door. As soon as he was out of sight, Julian went after him. He listened a moment at the door he had left by, then drew it softly open. It led to a little dark winding stair. Hearing the servant's footsteps on the stairs above, he followed on tiptoe. When he was far enough up to see the man's dusty boots overhead, he stopped and flattened himself into the shadow of the wall.

The boots came to a stop before a door. There was a tap, then the door opened. "Yes?" called a fluty male voice.

"Excuse me, Mr. Ridley," said the servant. "There's a gentleman here to see you. Says his name is Desmond. But he ain't the same Mr. Desmond as was here before—the one as brought Number Twelve."

"Are you certain?"

"Yes, sir."

"Dear me," trilled Ridley, "this is most awkward. Who can he be?"

"I dunno, sir, but he's a very grand gentleman. Drove up in a swell carriage, with a boy in livery and all. I didn't know how to get shut of him."

"Tell him I'm engaged at present—press of business, and so on. Say I may find time to see him later, and meanwhile find out what his connexion is with Number Twelve."

"I'm afraid I haven't time to bandy words with your servant," said Julian, coming the rest of the way up the stairs. "I must insist that you see me at once."

The servant gaped. Ridley recovered his self-possession more quickly. He rose from behind his desk and held out a thin, yellow hand for Julian to shake. He was yellow all over: long, sallow face, lemony wisps of hair framing his bald head, and tawny, discoloured teeth. "How do you do, Mr. Desmond? Come in, come in. Welcome to my establishment."

Julian looked around the little office. It was fussily neat, with a knee-hole desk, two leather-upholstered chairs, a bookshelf, and a glass-fronted cabinet displaying all shapes and sizes of human skulls.

"You notice my little collection, I see," chirped Ridley. "It's been much admired by the phrenologists who come here. We get a great many of them, of course. It's extraordinary, what they can discern about human character by feeling the dents and bulges in the skull."

"So I've heard," said Julian politely.

Ridley sat down at his desk again, beckoning Julian to a chair opposite. "Now then, do please tell me what brings you here. How may I help you?"

Julian kept his answers short and guarded, so as not to reveal how little he really knew. "I'm looking for a young woman named Marianne Desmond."

"Ah." Ridley exchanged a glance with his servant, then rubbed his hands together. He wore a great many rings, though his dress was otherwise plain and business-like. "May I ask if you are a relation of the young lady's?"

"Was the first Mr. Desmond a relation?" Julian countered.

"I understood him to be her brother."

"You may understand me to be another brother."

"Indeed." Ridley smiled knowingly, as if he had a wide experience of young ladies and their "brothers."

In a faraway part of the house, there was a scraping sound, then a muffled thumping.

"Number Five," said the servant, frowning.

"I beg your pardon, Mr. Desmond," said Ridley. "Ordinarily nothing—distasteful—can be heard from my office, but Number Five is especially difficult."

From the same part of the house came a piercing scream.

"Go and see to Number Five," snapped Ridley, his voice dropping an octave. The servant touched his forelock and went to the door. "Oh, and Pearson," Ridley added more suavely. "Use the lash only as a last resort."

The servant nodded and went out.

Julian sat shocked into silence. He knew now what manner of place this was. "Shall we cut short these pleasantries?" he said at last. "I shan't ask you any questions—rather, I shall tell you what I believe to be true, and you shall tell me if I'm right."

Ridley inclined his head in agreement.

"The first Mr. Desmond came here about a month ago with a young lady he told you was his sister. She was blond, blue-eyed, and pretty. He was a gentleman of about five-and-twenty, medium height, slim and graceful, with auburn hair, brown eyes, and considerable charm. He said the young lady was insane and commended her to your care—with an ample remuneration, of course. And I rather suspect he urged you to leave her quite alone, not to have her examined by doctors or displayed to curious spectators, as some inmates of these private establishments are."

"He said strangers upset her," Ridley explained. "She has delusions of persecution, thinks enemies are plotting to imprison and abuse her. Curious, is it not?"

"Unaccountable," said Julian grimly. "So my assumptions are correct?"

"As correct as if you had witnessed it all yourself, sir."

"Mr. Ridley, I have come to collect that young lady. Be so good as to bring me to her at once."

"My dear sir!—"

"I warn you, if I leave without her, I shall return with a magistrate."

Ridley rubbed his hands together rapidly. "I've done nothing wrong. I took the poor creature in—"

"For a handsome sum, no doubt."

"That's my profession, sir—the care of those whose derangement will not allow them to care for themselves."

"By whose authority was she committed to your care?" Julian asked sharply. "Did any physician confirm that she was mad? Had you even any proof that this so-called Mr. Desmond was any relation to her at all?"

"I had no reason to doubt his word." Ridley's yellowish tongue darted out and ran around his lips. "He was a gentleman."

"I take leave to tell you that the gentleman you speak of is dead. No one will pay you anything further for Marianne Desmond's keep. The best you can hope for now is to have her taken off your hands discreetly. I am willing to do that. If you force me to go and return again, I shan't be so generous. Decide, Mr. Ridley. Which is it to be?"

Ridley beat on the desk with the flat of his hands, thinking hard. At last he rose, gathering the shreds of his equanimity about him. "Be so good as to follow me, sir, and I shall take you to the young lady."

"I should warn you, Mr. Ridley: my presence here is known. If I should chance not to return, my friends will know where to look for me."

"My dear sir! What can you be implying?"

"I think you take my meaning tolerably well."

Ridley came around the desk resignedly and took up a ring of keys. Lighting a candle at the grate, he ushered Julian out. They went down the winding stair and into a long, dark hall. Julian guessed it must run along the outside of the house, where there were no windows to light it.

The hall made a right-angle turn and continued along the side of the house. By the flickering light of Ridley's candle, Julian saw a row of heavy oak doors in the right-hand wall. Each was painted with a number, one through six. Sounds came from behind the doors: restless walking, banging, the clanking of chains. Voices laughed, muttered gibberish, sang songs. One woman wailed piteously.

Another right-angle turn, another dark corridor with numbered doors. Six, seven, eight, nine, ten, eleven. They stopped before Number Twelve.

Ridley drew aside a little wooden flap and squinted through the eye-hole behind it. "She's quiet today, but that may change at any moment. You're certain you wish to take responsibility for her?"

"Quite certain."

Ridley shrugged, selected a key from the bunch in his hand, and unlocked the door. Julian went in, Ridley following.

The cell was about ten by fifteen feet. It was lit only by one small window, too high to look out. There was a pallet bed against one wall and an earth-closet in the far corner. A damp, fetid smell hung in the air, though the floor was tolerably clean and covered with fresh straw. A young woman lay face down in the straw. When the two men entered, she lifted her head dazedly.

She was in her early twenties, with china-blue eyes and fair hair falling in a tangle over her shoulders. Her skin was chalk-white, her eyes ringed with shadows. Little bird-like bones stood out in her cheeks and the hollow of her neck. There was straw in her hair and a smut of dirt on her nose. She was wrapped in a grey woollen cloak, from which the tips of her feet protruded, clad in grimy white-satin slippers trimmed with the remnants of gold braid.

She sat up, staring at Julian. The next instant she flung herself at him and clasped him round the legs, nearly toppling him into the straw. "Oh, sir! I beg you, take me away! I'll go anywhere with you, I'll be your slave, only take me away, please, please—"

"Yes, Mrs. Desmond!" He tried to raise her. "I'll take you away. I've come for that very purpose—"

"*No!*" she shrieked. "You've come from *him!* He locked me up like this, and now he means to kill me!" She beat on his legs with her fists. "I won't go with you! No! No!"

"I did warn you, sir," said Ridley complacently. "She's in no fit state to be removed."

Julian turned on him, his voice dangerously quiet. "I should think anyone who'd spent a month immured in this cell with little hope of release would be in the same state. It seems you not only receive mad people—you create them."

He got hold of Mrs. Desmond's wrists, then dropped on his haunches so that his face was on a level with hers. "Mrs. Desmond! Listen to me. I've come here as your friend, in your service. Let me remove you from this place and offer you such protection as I can give, and you can honourably accept."

She blinked at him, torn between hope and fear.

"You don't wish to stay here, do you?" he urged gently.

"No," she whispered.

"Will you do me the honour to trust me and let me see you safely away?"

She caught her lower lip between her teeth and nodded jerkily.

He helped her to her feet. Her cloak parted, revealing a white silk evening dress, now grey with grime. The transparent tulle sleeves hung in tatters, and the flounce on the bottom of the skirt trailed hanks of dust, straw, and dead spiders.

Julian weighed the satisfaction of knocking Ridley down against the trouble and delay that would result, and reluctantly decided against it. Let the law deal with him and find out what other sane people he might have conveniently agreed to lock away. Julian's business was to look after Mrs. Desmond—and, of course, to find out what light she could shed on the life and death of Alexander Falkland.

# ✳ 26 ✳

## BEHIND THE MASK

Alfred gaped in amazement as Ridley's servant let Julian and Mrs. Desmond out at the gate of the madhouse. It was raining hard now, and the dirt road was dissolving into mud. Mrs. Desmond instinctively held up the hem of her skirt and trod delicately around the puddles, though it was hard to see what damage was left to be done to her gown and slippers.

When she saw the cabriolet, her eyes lit up, and she gazed at Julian with new respect. "It belongs to a friend," he explained.

"You've very fine friends, sir!" She ran her hand admiringly over the cab's sleek body.

"I ought to have introduced myself. Julian Kestrel, at your service."

"La, sir, it's I that should be at *your* service, after all you've done for me!"

Julian did not quite like the implications of this. "Hadn't we better go? The sooner we're away from this place, the safer you'll be."

"Oh, yes!" She caught his arm, glancing fearfully back at the madhouse. "Take me away, please, at once!"

He handed her into the cabriolet and jumped lightly up beside her. Alfred mounted his little seat at the back, and they set off.

"Where are we going?" she asked.

"I thought we'd stop at an inn not far from here called the Jolly Filly. The landlord's daughter can look after you and perhaps lend you a frock till you can find new clothes."

"I've ever so many clothes in town—gowns as fine as this one was." She plucked regretfully at her ravaged dress.

"Forgive me, but the circumstances of your disappearance obliged me to look into your wardrobe. Your clothes are missing."

"But not my jewels? He's never taken my jewels?"

"I'm afraid so."

"The bastard! The dirty, sneaking sod! I'll have the law of him, I will! I don't care a pin who he is, or what swells his friends are! He gave me the jewels, but that don't give him the right to take them back, does it? I earned them, Lord knows! Nobody'll ever know what I went through to get them! That son of a whore!—"

"I beg you, Mrs. Desmond, don't distress yourself. Your jewelry may turn up. Here." He gave her his handkerchief.

"Thank you, sir." She blew her nose, then cast him a side-long look and dabbed daintily at her eyes. Her accent took on a nasal, dubious gentility. "You must forgive me, sir, for the language I used just now. It's not my usual way of talking, indeed it's not. But after being in that dreadful place for days and days, with no hope of ever getting out again—"

"Of course. Anyone who'd been through what you have would be thoroughly overwrought."

"Oh, you do have a pretty way of putting things, sir! I *am* overwrought, something shocking. And when I heard my jewelry was gone—all I have in the world!—why, there was no bearing of it!" She added wistfully, "I don't suppose I'll ever get it back. The law won't help the likes of me—not against *him*. 'Spite of what he done—did—to me, shutting me up in that place, he's still Alexander Falkland, Esquire, son of a baronet, and what am I?"

"Mrs. Desmond, Alexander is beyond the law's reach, but not for the reasons you suppose. He's dead."

"Dead?" Joy blazed up in her eyes. "How did he die?"

"He was murdered."

She caught her breath, then clutched eagerly at his arm, causing him to jerk on the reins. "Who did it? How was it done? I hope it was painful!"

Julian explained briefly how Alexander had been murdered, and how he himself had become involved in the investigation. She hung on his every word. He told himself that her hatred of Alexander was understandable after what he had done to her, but even so, her unabashed delight was ghoulish. He suspended the conversation. She was buoyed up by nervous energy, but she needed rest and food before she could be questioned to good effect. He also wanted to be rid of Alfred, who had been listening avidly. So he drove on in silence. Mrs. Desmond soon succumbed to exhaustion, and her head drooped on his shoulder.

They reached the Jolly Filly at about half past three. Julian took Ruth aside and told her that Mrs. Desmond was an unfortunate young woman who had been wrongfully confined in a madhouse, and who had valuable evidence to give in the investigation. Ruth was obviously curious to know more, but she took her cue from Julian and asked no questions. An admirable girl, he thought—as capable as she was pretty. It crossed his mind that Dipper would have liked her immensely. He was glad, for the sake of her virtue and peace of mind, that he had not brought him.

While she took charge of Mrs. Desmond, Julian was shown to a private parlour, where he rang for a waiter and ordered dinner to be ready in an hour. Meantime, he refreshed himself with coffee and brandy and pondered what arrangements to make for Mrs. Desmond. He must certainly bring her to London: Sir Malcolm would want to meet her, and Bow Street would require her to swear out evidence. But where was she to spend the night? No respectable inn would take a young woman who had neither maid nor luggage. Bow Street would have no accommodation for her. She could not go to Sir Malcolm's house—not with Mrs. Falkland there. And Julian's landlady would not take kindly to her staying with him. She had once let Dipper's sister Sally sleep in her spare room, but Julian did not think she would extend the same courtesy to Mrs. Desmond. Sally, after all, was charming, warm-hearted —but this was no time to lose himself in reminiscing about Sally.

He could think of only one place where Mrs. Desmond would be comfortable and secluded, and where responsible servants could keep her under their eye. He did not trust her not to run away with the first man who dangled jewelry under her nose. David Adams, for one, could well afford to deck her out in diamonds, and he might have good reason to want her out of the way.

Julian rang for the waiter again and asked for a messenger to take a note to Hampstead. Then he sent for pen and paper and wrote a note to Sir Malcolm. He told him he had found Mrs. Desmond and proposed to bring her to stay at Alexander's house in London. He said they would arrive at about seven and asked Sir Malcolm to meet them there and to forewarn the servants.

Ben Foley, the ostler, appeared, saying he had got leave to carry the note. Julian guessed he had begged hard for the privilege. Boys his age tended to be fascinated by criminal investigations, and the clever ones made good allies. Julian gave him the note, together with directions and a generous tip, and sent him on his way.

Ruth brought Mrs. Desmond back after an absence of about an hour. She looked much improved. Her face still looked wasted, but at least it was clean, and hot water or assiduous pinching had coaxed a trace of colour into her cheeks. Her hair, though limp, had been induced to curl a little at the front and sides; the rest was twisted into a Grecian knot high at the back. Ruth had lent her the flowered muslin frock Julian had seen her in yesterday—surely her Sunday best.

"Thank you, Miss Piper," he said warmly. "You've been more than kind."

"I'm sure I was glad to do it for *you*, sir." She darted a scathing glance at Mrs. Desmond, who was admiring herself in the looking-glass over the mantelpiece. Julian guessed Mrs. Desmond seldom endeared herself to her own sex.

After Ruth had gone, Mrs. Desmond turned to Julian, patting her hair complacently. "I feel ever so much more myself now. 'Course, this trumpery frock ain't what I'm used to, though I s'pose it's good enough for the likes of *her*." She came up close to him, her china-blue eyes wide and melting. "I hate you to see me like this, sir—so pale and scarecrowish. Why, I'm just a wraith of my old self. You'd hardly believe it, but some men used to say I was good-looking."

"I can readily believe that."

"You *are* kind. I'll mend, I'm sure, now I'm out of that hell-hole—now that you've rescued me, I mean. I'm ever so grateful to you."

"There's no need to feel under the least obligation. I beg you won't think of it again."

"How can I help but think of it? When I was so cold and wretched and practically dying in that hateful place, and the most elegant man in London—in all England, I'm sure!—braves no end of danger to come and save me! There's nothing I wouldn't do for you—positively *nothing*. You've only to ask."

"Mrs. Desmond, I'm overwhelmed by your generosity, but I wouldn't dream of taking advantage of your vulnerable position."

"How you talk—so elegant and refined!" She brushed her fingertips lightly along the breast of his coat. "Do you think we might—"

To Julian's intense relief, the waiter appeared and began bringing in their meal. Marianne inhaled the aroma of hot roast beef and forgot everything else. She had taken so long over her toilette that Julian had not realized how starved she was. She eagerly devoured beef, bacon, salmon, potatoes, asparagus, bread, parsley butter, and trifle, washed down with bumpers of wine. Julian gave up hope of questioning her for the present—a meal like this would stupify her into sleep. But the wine had a temporary enlivening effect. For now she was disposed to talk, and with very little restraint.

"My pa was a wheelwright in Islington. I haven't seen him in ages. I don't know if he's alive or dead. I was so bored there, you can't think: sewing quilts, saying prayers, looking after the pig Ma kept behind the house. That's no kind of life, is it?—not for a girl that's young and lively and good-looking. I'd see coaches stop at the Angel—big and brightly painted, with shiny gold crests—and ladies inside, dressed in fine silk gowns and fur-trimmed pelisses. And I'd think, why shouldn't I have those things? I *could,* too, if only I wasn't stuck in this poky place.

"When I was seventeen, a troop of soldiers was quartered near my house, and one of them started making up to me. He said he'd marry me, but he didn't mean it, and I didn't care. We lit out for London and had some larks, but it was a hard life. He had to disguise himself when he went out, on account of being a deserter. They caught him in the end. I thought they would. I hadn't a rag left, so I went on the town. I had to keep from starving, didn't I? Any girl in my place would've done the same.

"I eked out a living, that was all. Dresses cost so much, and bribes for the watchmen. And the landladies stick it into you when they know you've nowhere else to go, because no respectable place will have you. But all that changed when I met Alexander."

She stretched luxuriantly and held out her hands to the fire. Julian prompted, "How did you meet him?"

"Through an introducing house. He told Auntie—the lady of the house, that is—the kind of girl he wanted, and she sent for me, 'coz I fit his spec'fications."

"What were they?"

She smiled a cat-like smile. "He wanted a girl that couldn't be shocked. Well, that was me, wasn't it? I'd seen 'most everything by then. He wasn't looking to set up a mistress, but after he met me, he changed his mind. He found me a house—it was monstrous stuffy, but I bought mirrors and paintings and things to smarten it up. He laughed at me and said I hadn't a particle of taste, but he paid for it all, so what did I care? He picked out my clothes and jewelry himself, though. Said he wasn't going to have me make such a fright of myself as I had of the house—not while he was obliged to look at me."

Julian hung fire briefly. He did not relish delving into her intimate relationship with Alexander. But she was the only person willing and able to open a window on Alexander's dark side, and Julian could not afford to be squeamish about the view. "You said he was looking for a woman he couldn't shock. Did he shock you?"

"No, not 'specially. He scared me a little at first, but once I understood what he wanted, I wasn't afraid anymore."

"What did he want?"

"To be himself. To say and do just what he liked. Sometimes what he liked was very nasty, but mostly it was just dull. He would talk—my eye, how he'd talk! He'd lie on the drawing-room sofa all evening and jabber about the great guns who came to his parties, the debutantes who were spoony upon him, the money he'd made with that Jew friend of his. How Lord Somebody had admired his house and Lady What's-Her-Name had admired his legs. He'd tell spiteful stories about his friends. And if he thought anybody'd slighted him, he'd run on about it for hours. He was a dreadful bore when he wasn't trying to be agreeable, which he never did when we were alone. 'Course, if there were other people with us— which wasn't often, he wouldn't let me have any friends—he was like one of those figures that come out of clocks and dance about or strike the hour. He had to be charming. He couldn't help it. Everybody must needs love him—though no one would ever love him as much as he loved himself."

"Why wouldn't he let you have any friends?"

"Didn't want anyone to know about me, did he? He made me live in a little dark court off the Strand, with no neighbours but that old cat Mrs. Wheeler, who was always peering out of

her windows at me. Stupid cow—hadn't she anything better
to do? I could hardly wait for Friday to come round each
week, because she'd go away for a day and a night and not be
poking her nose into my business."

"Why was he so anxious to hide his connexion with you?"

"Oh, he liked to make everyone think he doted on his wife.
That's a screamer, that is—she bored him into fits. But he
thought it romantic to dance attendance on her. And he told
me if he ever did own to having a mistress, it wouldn't be me.
I wasn't refined enough—I'd ruin his reputation for taste. He
wouldn't show me in public, any more than he'd put a close-
stool in the drawing room. Well, I didn't care a fig how he
talked to me, but I did care about being shut away with nothing to do. I says to him, What's the good of giving me fine
clothes if you won't let me show them off? Other gentlemen
give their lady friends boxes at the theatre and carriages to
drive in the park. He says, Then you'd best find one of those
gentlemen, hadn't you? I stayed. I could've done much worse.
Sooner or later I'd leave him and live as I liked on what he'd
given me. Meantime, I was willing to play his games and take
his gifts."

"What do you mean by 'games'?"

"Oh, I used to bring him other girls sometimes. He liked
fresh meat—girls who weren't hardened yet and could still be
shocked."

"I thought he was drawn to you precisely because you
couldn't be shocked."

"Yes, but I was different. He needed someone who understood what he wanted and could help him get it on the sly.
He hadn't much to do with me after he'd got me the house
—in the way of being lovers, I mean. I was more like—what
did he call it?—his accomplice."

"Wasn't he afraid one of those other girls would talk about
him—tarnish the image he was trying to preserve?"

"They wouldn't dare." She leaned toward him, sinking her
voice. "You don't understand how he terrified them. He knew
just what to do. He'd be kind and cruel to them by turns, till

they were so confused and scared, they'd do anything he asked. Often he'd blindfold them, so they didn't know what was happening around them or what he might do next. You'd be surprised how frightening that is."

"I daresay I would," said Julian, keeping cold command of his voice.

"He didn't hurt them—at least, not much. He was squeamish about bloodshed and bruises. That was the artist in him. He prided himself on not leaving scars."

Julian got up and took a turn about the room. Thank God Sir Malcolm can't hear this, he thought. With luck he can be spared the worst of it. Or can he? Suppose one of those young women Alexander tormented took her revenge on him through murder? Then this whole double life he led will be dragged out into the light.

He put that thought aside. Before he went looking for "Jane Noakes" among London's flotsam and jetsam of fallen women, he must try to exhaust more immediate possibilities. He sat down again opposite Mrs. Desmond. "Tell me about your maid, Fanny Gates."

"There's not much to tell. Alexander knew I'd need a servant to look after the house, so he set about finding one he could keep under his thumb. Because of course she'd have to know all about him and me, so he had to be sure she'd hold her tongue. In the end he sent me a mouse of a woman, fortyish, not a particle of style. She hadn't any references, and I expect she used to be on the town, but now she'd lost her looks, she was fit for nothing but cooking and scrubbing floors. Alexander would never tell me how he found her, but he said she was just the thing: no family, no friends, and couldn't say boo to a goose. She worked hard, I'll say that for her. She wouldn't dare do anything else. She knew Alexander would make it hot for her if she didn't."

"How?"

"Oh, he bullied her. Threatened her with the house of correction. He knew things about her I didn't. It's no use asking me what things, because I don't know. She was a deal of trou-

ble in some ways. She was religious. Some women get that
way once their looks are gone. They turn ever so prudish
about sin, once they've no chance to commit it themselves."

To hear her talk, growing old was something that only happened to other women. "How was her religion troublesome?"

"She disapproved of things Alexander did. She once came
into the drawing room while we were—while we had a guest.
One of those girls I told you about, you know. She got in such
a taking! After that Alexander used to lock her in her room in
the garret whenever we had company. Sometimes he locked
her in there just because her foolish face put him out of
temper—so he said."

Her face darkened suddenly. He asked, "Is anything
wrong?"

"I was just remembering that night—the night he brought
me to the madhouse. He locked Fanny up then—or rather,
he told me to. I didn't suspect anything. It was a quiet evening. We hadn't any company. Alexander was lying about on
the drawing-room sofa. He was peevish and sulky, because—"
She broke off. "Because we'd had a bit of a row," she went
on quickly. "When I came back from locking Fanny up, he
was drinking a glass of brandy, and he'd poured one for me.
I drank it, and he droned on about one thing and another. I
got very sleepy. Soon I could hardly keep my eyes open, and
everything was turning hazy around me. By the time I realized
he'd put something in my drink, it was too late. I don't remember anything after that, till I woke up in the cell where
you found me."

"This row you had with Alexander—what was it about?"

She looked away confusedly. "Oh, la, it's of no consequence. Just a lovers' tiff."

"If it caused him to shut you up in a madhouse, it can
hardly be of no consequence."

"Well, you see, I'd been making demands on him." She
stammered a little and looked at the wine decanter as if suddenly fearful she had drunk too much. "I wanted more
money, a better house, a life out in the open. He still wanted

to keep our relationship dark. We were always rowing about that."

"Mrs. Desmond—"

"Oh, you needn't say 'Mrs.' I was never married—I just thought 'Mrs.' sounded more genteel for a lady living alone." She added caressingly, "I wish you'd call me 'Marianne.'"

"Marianne, then." He was willing to give in on small matters. God knew, he was in no danger from her wiles. The thought of her with Alexander Falkland was enough to put a man off women for weeks. "If Alexander didn't want to accede to your wishes, why didn't he simply refuse, as he had in the past?"

"He—he couldn't. I threatened him. I said I'd tell—embarrassing things. Things he'd rather his fine friends didn't know about."

"What sorts of things?"

"Oh—the things I've told you about. My being his fancy woman and bringing him those girls." She flushed. "You needn't look at me as if I was lying!"

He sat back and surveyed her coolly across the table. "I don't think you're lying. But nor do I think you're telling me all the truth. You see—I know about you and Mrs. Falkland."

"Wh-what?"

"I know you approached her in the Strand, exactly a fortnight before Alexander put you in the madhouse. You were dressed in your maid's clothes, and you told her some story to lure her to your house. Alexander put you up to it and was there to make sure it went off all right."

"It—it was just a prank—I didn't mean any harm by it—anyway, it was all Alexander's doing!"

"Don't be frightened, Mrs. Desmond. The crime you and Alexander committed that day doesn't concern me, except insofar as it may throw light on his murder. I shan't even ask why you brought Mrs. Falkland to your house, because I think I know already. But tell me: do you know what took place after she arrived?"

"No," she said regretfully. "I don't know anything. I couldn't stay to find out."

Julian was inclined to believe her. Her frustrated curiosity rang more true than any show of innocence. "It was that episode you used to threaten Alexander, wasn't it? If it ever got out that he'd mounted such a conspiracy against his wife, his honour and reputation would be all to pieces."

"I wanted him to do right by me," she said defensively. "If he was going to drag me into his plots, he ought to make it worth my while."

Julian considered. "You said that on the night Alexander drugged you and brought you to the madhouse, he told you to lock Fanny in her room."

"Yes."

"Have you any idea what became of her after that?"

"I couldn't, could I? P'raps he let her out to help him take me to the madhouse."

"More likely to dispose of your clothes and other belongings. He wanted to make it appear you'd left of your own accord."

Her eyes lit up. "Do you think she has my jewelry? Oh, won't I just shake her, the scheming hag! Do you know where she is?"

"On the morning after you disappeared," he said quietly, "a woman of her age and figure was found dead in a brickfield near Hampstead, with her face smashed beyond recognition. And we've found traces of brickearth in your house."

"Oh, Lord," she whispered. "Alexander?"

"Very likely." Though how we shall ever prove it, he thought, the devil only knows.

"But—it don't sound like him. I told you, he didn't like shedding blood."

"I don't think the brickfield victim's face was destroyed for the sport of it. The murderer didn't want her recognized. Would Alexander be capable of smashing a woman's face, if it were in his interest?"

"Him? He'd do anything to anyone, if they were weak and

afraid of him. Fanny was both." She leaned toward Julian, plucked at his coat in her eagerness to make him understand. "To Alexander, Fanny just didn't count. She was ugly, and she was weak, and that meant she was just *nothing*. He wouldn't have stood a jot to kill her if she got in his way—leastways, if he could do it without being caught. It would be just like swatting a fly."

Julian moved abruptly in his chair. He had read a good deal about crime since he first took up investigating murders. *The Newgate Calendar* was full of the lives and deaths of hardened, heartless felons. But nothing had quite prepared him for this glimpse behind Alexander Falkland's mask.

"One more question," he said at last. "Did Mrs. Falkland's maid, Martha Gilmore, ever come to your house in Cygnet's Court?"

"Mrs. Falkland's maid?"

"Yes. David Adams says he saw her there."

"He must be off his head. What would Mrs. Falkland's maid be doing at my house?

Julian did not know. But nor had he any idea why Adams should have invented such a story. Martha's visit to Cygnet's Court was one of the most intriguing pieces in the Falkland puzzle, because it made so little sense as either the truth or a lie. Which told him there was much about this mystery he still did not understand.

# ✻ 27 ✻

## VERITY

As Marianne was growing sleepy, Julian thought he had better acquaint her with his plans for her accommodation that night. She was elated. "I'm to stay at Alexander's house? I've always wanted to see it! Fancy me being there to enjoy all his fine things and be waited on by his servants, while *he* lies under ground! There's some justice in this world, and that's flat!"

"Of course it will be only temporary, till we can find you suitable lodgings. And it will depend on Sir Malcolm's acquiesence. I've asked him to meet us there."

"Alexander's father?" She laughed. "What'll he make of me, do you think? Alexander always said he was a moralizing old stick."

"I don't think you need repeat that to him." Julian rose. "You'll come with me to London, then?"

"I'd go anywhere with you," she cooed. "Only—I won't have to go to Bow Street, will I?"

"I'm afraid you'll be asked to swear out evidence."

"But I don't want anything to do with the law! Who knows what they might ask me? A girl in my position has to be ever so careful—"

Julian murmured, "There have been some very substantial rewards offered for information about Alexander's murder."

"Oh! Oh, well—I'm sure I never meant to shirk my duty. If I've any useful evidence, why, I'll be glad to give it."

"I hoped you might see things in that light."

He rang for the waiter and ordered the cabriolet to be brought round. Meantime he paid the reckoning and persuaded Ruth to accept a generous sum for her gown. Then he and Marianne set off for London. She fell asleep almost at once and did not awake till they reached Alexander's house.

Leaving Alfred to look after the cabriolet, Julian gently roused Marianne and took her inside. She looked around her in awe and delight at the graceful Renaissance-style hall, the marble tables and gilt torchères, the glorious flying staircase with its ascending and descending bands of angels. She ran from one object to another, touching, inspecting, wondering how much each had cost.

Julian took Nichols, the butler, aside. "Is Sir Malcolm here?"

"Yes, sir. He's waiting for you and—the young woman—in the library. He asked me to have Mr. Eugene's old room prepared for her, and I've done so."

"Good." Julian smiled quizzically. "I'm afraid I'm embroiling you in a rather delicate matter, Nichols. I should be grateful if you would see to it that Mrs. Desmond doesn't receive any visitors, and that no one outside the house finds out she's here."

"You may rely on me, sir."

"Excellent man! Thank you." He went to Marianne and offered her his arm. "Come, I'll take you to Sir Malcolm."

✳

Marianne was sullen with Sir Malcolm at first. She apparently saw no point in trying out her charms on her lover's high-minded father. And indeed, his first reaction to her was an ill-concealed repugnance. But when he heard how she had suffered at Alexander's hands, his repulsion was lost in pity. She at once began putting on a show of feminine distress, speaking in a small, pathetic voice and making play with her handkerchief. Sir Malcolm's sympathy waned. Twenty years at the Bar would have inured him to crocodile tears.

Julian suggested she might wish to rest after her journey. One of the maids could assist her and lend her any garments she might need for the night. She went willingly, eager to see more of the house. Julian thought Nichols would do well to keep an eye on the more portable *objets d'art*.

Sir Malcolm hunted out a brandy decanter, and he and Julian downed a glass in silence. Finally Sir Malcolm said bleakly, "What can have possessed Alexander to turn from Belinda to *that?*"

"You wouldn't have done so, and nor would I. But she had something to offer Alexander. She told me he could be himself with her, and that must have meant a great deal to him. With most people he was constantly playing one role or another."

"But why?"

Julian shrugged. "He wanted everything: to be admired and loved and feared and hated, to have the credit for doing good and the pleasure of doing evil."

"I can't see any pleasure in consorting with a woman like that." He added, "Now you've met her, you can't still think she's Verity Clare?"

"It does seem far-fetched that she could be the young lady Tibbs compared to Portia for her fine, serious mind. Although he did say Verity was a formidable actress—"

He broke off, rose out of his chair.

"What is it?" asked Sir Malcolm, staring.

Julian began to laugh. "Sir Malcolm, we've been deaf, dumb, and blind!"

"How? What do you mean?"

*"The Merchant of Venice!* For the second time, that play's set me on the right road!" He went swiftly to the bell-pull and tugged on it. "We must go to Lincoln's Inn at once!"

"Why? What is it you suspect? Has—has Quentin been lying?"

"Oh, yes, Quentin Clare's been lying—brilliantly, outrageously! In fact, Quentin Clare may be the most accomplished liar it's ever been my privilege to meet."

Sir Malcolm passed a hand across his face, then rose. "All right. We'll go and see him. You be King's Counsel, and I'll be judge. Prove him a liar—prove him a murderer, if you can. And when you've done so, never ask me to believe in another human soul. Because if that young man is false, there's no truth in anyone."

*

Night had fallen by the time they reached Lincoln's Inn. The gates were shut, but the night-porter recognized Sir Malcolm and let them in. The inn was dark, save for the lamps blinking in staircase windows and a few candles smoking in upper casements, where clerks or conveyancers sat late over their work.

They entered Serle's Court. It was still and silent; their footsteps crunched the gravel with a sound like breaking glass. Midway across the court, Sir Malcolm halted and looked up at Clare's window, where a light burned dimly behind the blind. He had not spoken since they left Alexander's house and did not speak now. They walked on to No. 5, ascended the staircase, and knocked at Clare's door.

Clare opened it, a reading lamp in his hand. He looked white and sleepless, his neckcloth tousled, his pale hair spilling over his brow. He started slightly on seeing who his visitors were.

Julian looked at him intently for a moment, then smiled. "Good evening. May we speak with you?"

"Yes—of course. Please come in."

They entered. Clare closed the door and set the lamp down on a table.

"I'm sorry to disturb you at this hour," said Julian, "but my purpose wouldn't admit of any delay. You see, I know now where Verity is."

He and Clare exchanged a long, understanding look. Then Clare closed his eyes and turned slowly away.

Sir Malcolm sprang forward and caught him by the shoulder. "Wait a moment! I don't understand what any of this is about, but I want you to know—I trust you. No, don't turn away—I'm determined to speak, before Kestrel makes his case against you. I believe in you, Quentin. I know I believed in Alexander, too, but this is different. My faith in him sprang from ignorance of what he was, but my faith in you is born of knowledge and understanding. You've let me read your heart, and I know there's nothing base or evil there. I don't believe you killed my son or harmed any living soul. And what's more, I wouldn't believe it, even if you told me so yourself. So speak up, and don't be afraid. Where is Verity?"

Clare looked around at him miserably. "Verity is here. *I* am Verity."

"What?" Sir Malcolm jumped back. "What are you talking about?"

"I'm Verity Clare." Her voice began to slide into its natural higher pitch. "My brother, Quentin, died a year and a half ago. I took his place."

Sir Malcolm caught up the lamp from the table and shone it on her face. She met his eyes with an effort.

"Yes," he said softly. "I see it's true. Fancy Kestrel's seeing it before me!"

She coloured and dropped her gaze.

Sir Malcolm turned dazedly to Julian. "How *did* you guess? Am I mad, or did you say something about *The Merchant of Venice?*"

"Yes. When I went to see your uncle, Miss Clare, he told me at parting that he'd set me a riddle he hoped I would never solve. I thought back over our conversation, but I couldn't find the riddle, let alone the answer. Then tonight Sir Malcolm and I were talking of you, and I recalled how Mr. Tibbs had compared you to Portia—Portia, who also disguised herself as a man of law. Then everything fell into place. You and your brother were the same age. You'd been educated with him, even to the point of learning Latin and Greek. You had a formidable talent for acting and mimicry. You admired Mary

Wollstonecraft and shared her frustration with the narrow sphere of achievements open to women. You were said to be bold, even unscrupulous, in doing what you thought right. And finally, there were my own feelings toward you. I had a strong sense of your charm; it made me all the harder on you, because I sensed some deception behind it. Now I see the charm was perfectly real—the deception lay in veiling it behind a man's identity."

The compliment seemed to pass over her like a chill wind. Gallantries that were second nature to him were no light thing to her. He remembered Tibbs's saying she had felt imprisoned on a pedestal. Looking at her, pale and still in the lamplight, he had a vision of her being tied with ropes and hauled back up again—a renegade statue restored to its place.

"I feel abashed," said Sir Malcolm. "I don't know what I may have said in your presence—what words I may have let fall—"

"You mustn't worry, sir. You're one of the few men I've known who doesn't require a lady's presence to make him speak and act like a gentleman."

He looked at her in silence for a moment. Then he said gently, "Tell us, Miss Clare. Tell us how it all happened."

She moved behind the sofa and stood looking down, her hands resting on the back. Julian guessed she felt shy about showing her trousered legs, now that she had lost the protection of her male identity. There was none of the old diffidence about her silence; she was merely gathering her thoughts. He realized she had not only been playing a man, but a very different kind of person. There was nothing diffident about Verity Clare—unless it was in the realm of desire, where she was vulnerable and untried.

"You know that Quentin and I grew up on the Continent. We had an upbringing most people would consider very strange." She paused. "Mr. Kestrel, did Uncle George tell you anything about himself?"

"I know he was once Montague Wildwood and had to leave England after killing a man in a duel."

She nodded. "I didn't like to speak of that if he hadn't. I'm more than willing to tell you my own secrets, but it wouldn't have been right to tell his." Her face softened. "He was a wonderful guardian: loving and charming, and always respectful of Quentin and me as people, even when we were children. Conventional people would have told him he ought to settle down somewhere and not take us gipsying about Europe, learning languages and soaking up art and music and ideas. Those same well-meaning people would have urged him to send Quentin away to school instead of engaging a private tutor—and all for the silly, inconsequential reason that Quentin and I loved each other so dearly, we couldn't bear to be parted. Most eccentric of all, when he saw that I loved learning and could keep up with Quentin in his studies, he let me be educated along with him. I didn't realize then how lucky I was. I had no English misses for friends—I didn't know that, had I been raised here, I should have learned nothing but French, embroidery, and painting in watercolours.

"It was only as I grew older that I began to understand I was different from other women. The time came for me to put up my hair and go to dinner parties and balls, and I found I had no notion how to behave. Other girls' airs and graces seemed false and ridiculous to me. I talked of politics and philosophy, and men looked at me askance or laughed at me. I probably did say some silly things—I was over-confident and rash—but that wasn't why they laughed. They laughed because a woman was giving opinions on serious subjects. It was as if a horse had suddenly started talking—frightening to some people, absurd to others. Not all our friends thought that way, but the more respectable among them did, especially the English.

"As long as I had Quentin and Uncle George, I didn't much care what anyone else thought of me. But when Quentin and I came of age, he decided to return to England and read for the Bar. Our father had been a member of Lincoln's Inn, so he wrote to an old friend of Father's and asked him to sponsor his application there. He was accepted, and it was agreed he would arrive at the beginning of Hilary term—that is to say, in January of last year.

"I tried to be happy for him, but in my heart I felt such bitterness! Until then I'd followed him in all his pursuits, but this one was closed to me. And why, *why?*" Her eyes filled with bright, angry tears. "I had as good a mind as Quentin's. In education, I was just as suited to be a barrister; in temperament, much more so. There's no use dwelling on it: you know as well as I do the stupid, senseless prejudices that stand between women and any serious vocation. You may say, isn't it useful, admirable, to be a wife and mother? Yes, of course —but I had no future there, either. I wasn't pretty. I had no accomplishments. All I had was a head full of learning and languages, and an outspoken tongue that sent men running like startled hares. I felt trapped. Because I was a woman, my intellects must go to waste, and because I had intellects, my womanhood must go to waste as well.

"I didn't want Quentin to see how wretched I was. A few months before he was to go to England, we were invited to visit friends in Switzerland, but I persuaded Uncle George to take me to Vienna instead. Quentin went on alone." She paused, swallowed hard. "That was the last time I saw him alive. There was fever in the village where he went, and he caught it. When Uncle George and I heard, we travelled night and day, but we arrived too late.

"I was shocked. I felt as if a vital part of me had been hacked away. For days I walked about in a state of blind, insensible grief. Uncle George made all the arrangements. We buried Quentin quietly, in the little churchyard in the village. There seemed no reason to take him anywhere else. We had no home; there was no place in the world he really belonged. It was a peaceful, secluded place. I thought he would like to rest there.

"Afterward, Uncle George and I stayed on, lost and aimless, doing nothing. Finally Uncle George said, Verity, this mustn't go on. It's time we wrote to people about Quentin's death— putting it off won't bring him back. He said at the very least we ought to let Lincoln's Inn know he wouldn't be coming, so his chambers could be let to someone else."

She paused, as if steeling herself. "One thing you must understand: the idea was mine to begin with. I conceived it, and I alone should bear the blame. I knew even then it was monstrous. Quentin hadn't been dead a fortnight, and I was plotting to steal his life. But it wasn't entirely cold-blooded. It's true I wanted what he would have had: the chance to earn money, build a profession, affect people's lives on the world stage. But also, by becoming Quentin, I was keeping him alive. How could he be dead when people were sending him letters, lending him books, inviting him to dinner? Please don't think I'm mad—I knew it was only a game. But it comforted me—helped me to bear the loneliness of life without him.

"It was all made possible—compelled, it almost seemed—by a confluence of circumstances. I was so suited to impersonate a man. I'm tall and thin, and my voice is low; by keeping it a little husky, I could pass it off as a man's. And I'm so fair, no one would expect to see a stubble of whiskers on my face. I'd had a man's education; I knew Latin, Greek, philosophy, natural science. And thanks to Uncle George, I'd played breeches parts in amateur theatricals. He'd taken great pains to coach me for them. He said too many actresses were wholly unconvincing in their masquerades as men.

"Then there was the fact that Quentin and I had lived on the Continent since we were children. We had few English friends. I could be fairly confident that no one I met in London would know Quentin by sight. I fit his general description. And I would be armed with his papers, his belongings, my intimate knowledge of him.

"Uncle George was amused and delighted by my imposture. He groomed me rigorously for my 'part': made me practice walking, sitting, speaking, even sneezing. And he designed clothes for me that would conceal—that would make me look like a man. He'd been trained as a tailor; he first found work in the theatre sewing costumes."

Julian nodded. Tibbs had done his work well—rigged her

out in shapeless frock coats, loose-fitting trousers, and thick cravats, which lacked style but gave no impression of disguise.

"But, Miss Clare," said Sir Malcolm, "surely your uncle saw the risks, the dangers, the—the—"

"Impropriety?" she filled in quietly. "Deceit? He didn't mean any harm. He's a child in some ways. He didn't see it as lying—only as acting. *I* knew better, sir. So you see, the responsibility really does rest with me."

Sir Malcolm looked unconvinced but said only, "All right. Go on."

"Uncle George and I came to London, and I took possession of these chambers. By that time, I'd practised my masquerade in public and knew I could bring it off. I was a little nervous, but more exhilarated. For the first time in my life, I could go anywhere I liked at any hour: theatres, eating houses, walking or riding in the parks. At dinner parties, I stayed after the women had withdrawn, and I heard the talk turn to politics, foreign affairs, industrial inventions. Above all—I could study as much as I liked! No one worried that I was straining my mind or exposing myself to indelicate subjects. The freedom went to my head, till I hardly knew or cared what I was risking, or what principles I'd compromised. I told myself my imposture was justified: if the world denied women their rights, women must resort to desperate measures to obtain them. And Quentin wouldn't have grudged me my new life. We'd had a pact that each of us would do anything for the other. If I'd asked him for this favour while he lived, he would have granted it. Surely in death he would do no less?

"It wasn't so simple—I found that out all too soon. Do you remember the passage I marked in Mary Wollstonecraft's book, Mr. Kestrel—the one about the practised dissembler becoming the dupe of his own arts? That was I. I didn't have to adopt all Quentin's mannerisms in order to impersonate him, since no one in London knew what he was like. But I did all the same, because imitating him specifically was easier than imitating a man in general. What I didn't count on was that, having taken on his voice, manner, handwriting, habits

—I *was* Quentin now. I behaved like him even when I was alone. I really had kept him alive—he lived in and through me. And, through me, he looked with repulsion on what I was doing. He loved truth and honour above all things, and now I was using his name to live a lie. Such an endeavour couldn't have prospered, and it didn't. Something went terribly wrong."

Julian summed it up in one word. "Alexander."

"Alexander." She drew a long breath, then went on, her voice low but steady, "What I told you about how we came to know each other was true, so far as it went. We were both enrolled at Lincoln's Inn, and we dined in the same mess. Last Easter term, I was taken ill at dinner, and he offered to help me to my chambers. He hardly knew me, but it was like him—he was generous about small things. I tried to deter him, but it was no use. When we got to my chambers, I thanked him and tried to make him leave me. But he was curious now. He insisted—so graciously!—on coming in to look after me. I was too ill to fend him off. He urged me down into a chair and loosened my neckcloth, and the truth began to dawn on him. He—he forced off my coat, and—and—thrust his hand inside my shirt."

"The blackguard!" Sir Malcolm leaped up and walked about wildly. "The vile, contemptible scoundrel!"

"He hung over me." Her face was scarlet, her eyes wide and tearless. "He was fascinated. His eyes travelled all over me, with a look I can't begin to describe—"

"Oh, God!" Sir Malcolm broke in hoarsely. "Verity, what happened then?"

"Nothing," she assured him quickly. "I was sick. He fetched a basin and held it for me. Afterward I lay back, faint and almost beyond fear, and asked him what he was going to do. He smiled and said, I don't know yet. I'll come again tomorrow and see how you're getting on, and we'll discuss it, shall we?

"He did come next day. I was recovered and armed with a loaded pistol. I told him I would shoot him or myself—it hardly mattered which—so long as I need never feel his hands on me again. He could see I was in earnest. He always knew how far he could push people. If he saw a weakness, he would attack it, but a really determined show of resistance left him helpless. He had daring, but not courage.

"He said I'd mistaken his intentions. He assured me that a creature like me, neither man nor woman, had no need to fear she would be desirable to anyone. He said I had only one thing of value to offer: I was a drudge at my books. He hadn't time to study himself, but he wanted to shine in his legal career. He particularly wanted to impress *you*, sir." She looked at Sir Malcolm. "He hoped to go into politics and thought your backing would be useful. So he took it into his head to have me answer your letters. And he had me feed him insights about legal matters so that he could seem informed and clever in discussions in Hall.

"Of course, I hated being in thrall to him. But what if he exposed me? The disgrace would fall not only on me but on my uncle, and on my brother's memory. Uncle George might even be prosecuted for helping me. I would have faced all that sooner than—than yield to him as he first wanted me to, however he denied it afterward. But short of that, I owed it to Uncle George and Quentin to do all I could to keep my secret.

"I paid a high price. In spite of all he'd exacted from me, Alexander felt I'd somehow got the better of him, and he was always finding ways to take revenge. That's why he made such a friend of me. It was ingenious—everything cruel he did appeared so generous and kind. He kept me about him, made me attend his parties—and all so that he could keep me under his eye, set little traps for me and watch me struggle. He especially liked introducing me to women. People thought he was drawing me out, putting me in the way of marrying well. It amused him prodigiously. When we were in male company, he would slyly lead the talk into scandalous subjects. Then later he would come to my chambers and congratulate me on how much I was learning about—about relations between men and women. He soon found I wouldn't bring out the pistol again over anything he merely *said*. So he talked. He could talk for hours. I never knew till then that it was possible to be violated by speech."

Sir Malcolm closed his eyes for a moment. "My poor girl. How could you bear it?"

"I had one consolation, sir. Your letters." She lifted her fine grey eyes, with something of Quentin's old shy earnestness. "I hardly knew you when we began to write to each other. I'd watched you in court from the students' box, and I admired your knowledge and eloquence. But I was distrustful at first. Alexander was so thoroughly false—I was afraid you might be the same. I soon knew better. No one could doubt from your letters that you were thoughtful, generous, fiercely honest. I realized you and Alexander were worlds apart, and I couldn't bear to think how you would feel if you knew what he really was. So I made you another Alexander—one I hoped you might like and respect."

"I did, Miss Clare. I do still."

She looked away quickly, as if from too bright a light. "It was only when the truth came out, after Alexander's death, that I saw what a terrible thing I'd done. I'd deceived you, and I could never make you understand why. I had to see you and beg your pardon—and then, oh, sir, you were *kind* to me! After everything I'd done!"

Sir Malcolm had to smile. "That was your fault. You'd forged bonds between us that even your deception couldn't break. You can't win a man's regard and then turn it off like a spigot."

"If only that were the one deception I'd practised! Now you know my name is false, my sex is false, everything about me has been a lie—"

"Your fine mind? Your broad knowledge? Your compassionate heart? Could you have feigned all that? If you had, do you think me such a fool as to have been taken in? God knows, you were wrong to deceive us all this way—but it was a gallant wrongness, a wrongness more to be admired than most people's cramped and cowardly notions of right!"

"You're determined to be kinder to me than I deserve. And you must realize—"

"What?"

She appealed to Julian. "Tell him."

"I think," said Julian quietly, "Miss Clare means she's incriminated herself heavily in your son's murder."

"Rubbish!" said Sir Malcolm.

"It isn't rubbish," she said steadily. "I was his enemy. I hated him, feared him, longed to be free of him—"

"Did you kill him?" Sir Malcolm looked her straight in the eyes.

"No, sir. I swear I know no more about his death than what I told Bow Street. But I don't doubt Mr. Kestrel will need more than my word to absolve me."

"I wouldn't absolve any suspect on his word alone," said Julian. "But there is one circumstance that speaks in your favour. You were in a better position than any of the suspects to run away. You could have reverted to your female identity and confounded anyone who tried to pursue you. And yet you stayed."

"I was very torn about that," she owned. "Uncle George had always insisted I keep an escape route open, as he put it. When I first conceived the idea of impersonating Quentin, I wanted to pretend it was I who'd died—then we need never explain where I was. But Uncle George said I mustn't cut off my retreat—who knew when I might need to become Verity again? So in London I said Verity was living with Uncle George, and in Somerset he said she—I—was travelling abroad as a lady companion.

"After I wrote to him about Alexander's murder, he wrote back urging me to come and stay with him, which I took to mean, give up this masquerade, it's become too dangerous. But I was afraid of attracting suspicion if I left suddenly with the murder unsolved. And then, sir"—she turned to Sir Malcolm—"*you* befriended me, and how could I go after that? Everyone would have thought I'd committed the murder. You would have trusted first your son, then your son's friend, and both of us would have betrayed you." She finished simply, "I'd borne a great deal, but it was asking too much of me, that I should leave you."

Julian looked from her to Sir Malcolm. Rising, he murmured, "As I haven't anything more to ask Miss Clare, why don't I take my leave—"

"What can you be thinking of, Mr. Kestrel?" Sir Malcolm said sternly. "You can't mean to leave me alone in this young lady's chambers?"

"How can that matter now?" Verity smiled sadly. "After everything I've seen and heard, you can't suppose I have any delicacy left to offend."

Sir Malcolm strode up to her. "You must never say that again. I don't care what curses or ribald stories you've heard, or what poison my son poured into your ears. Do you remember what you said about the life of the mind being the only life you cared for? You've been living that life all these months, and it's left you as pure in thought and heart as the most spotless debutante that ever trod a dancing floor. And anyone who says otherwise will answer to me."

She said nothing, only took his hand and lifted it to her lips.

"Oh, really, Miss Clare," he stammered, "you mustn't do that. It's no more than any father would have said—and I'm old enough to be your father—"

"Oh, my dear sir." She smiled tenderly. "I could never think of you as a father."

# ✳ 28 ✳

## TROMPE L'OEIL

"What shall we do now?" Sir Malcolm asked Julian, when they had emerged from Clare's chambers into the secluded darkness of Serle's Court.

"I think I shall return to Alexander's house. There are several matters I'd like to pursue with Mrs. Desmond. I want to plumb every memory she has of Alexander's relationship with Fanny Gates. He invited so few people into that nightmare world where he turned from charmer to tormentor—why was she one of them? I also think we might as well get a description of Mrs. Desmond's late lamented jewelry. I can't imagine Alexander simply threw it on a dust-heap. He may have sold it or given it away, and perhaps we might learn something by tracing it."

"Do you ever stop and think," asked Sir Malcolm quietly, "that whoever killed Alexander did the public a service?"

"Do you mean that we ought to leave the murder unsolved?"

"No, no. Murder is always wrong, whatever the provocation. But if Alexander wronged the murderer, as he wronged so many people, it has to be made known. I won't spare his character—he hasn't deserved it. Let the murderer be punished—but let the punishment be tempered by consideration of what the murderer may have suffered at Alexander's hands."

"That's very just, Sir Malcolm, and very courageous."

"Tut!—it's only common decency."

"Common decency is rather uncommon these days."

Sir Malcolm waved his hand dismissively. "If I can't be any further use, I think I'll go home. Belinda is better, but I don't like to be away from her too long." He paused, looking up at the light in Verity's window. "In one respect, I bless this investigation. It's opened a whole new life for me—a better life than I ever dreamed of. You have to suspect her. I understand. But I know better."

✳

The clocks were striking eleven when Julian returned to Alexander's house. He reflected wryly that he was hearing the death knell of his five hundred pounds. Nothing short of a miracle would win his bet for him in thirteen hours.

Still, the murder had to be solved, however long it took to do it. He gave his hat to Nichols and asked where Mrs. Desmond was.

"She's in the study, sir." Nichols looked disapproving. "She wanted to see where the master was killed."

Julian went to the study. He found Marianne perched precariously on a lower shelf of one of the niches flanking the fireplace. With one hand, she clung to the edge of an upper shelf, while with the other she held up a candle so that she could peer into a row of Greek urns.

Julian hastened to her. "Here, let me help you down."

She resigned herself willingly into his arms. After he had set her down and relieved her of her candle, she leaned against him languishingly. "La, I feel so dizzy!"

"Allow me to help you to a chair."

"Oh, no, I couldn't move. I should fall down in a faint if I did."

"This sounds quite serious. I had better send for a physician."

"Oh, you're beastly!" She flounced away. "You might be a little kind to me, after everything I've been through."

He smiled. "Surely the greatest kindness I can show you is to treat you with respect?"

"Respect!" she cried indignantly. "That's a fine thing to say, *I* don't think!" Then she checked herself, smiling coyly. "But of course you're right—it's I that should be kind to you. You're my rescuer. I want to show you how grateful I am."

"Your word is enough."

"Not nearly enough." She came close, looking up at him through her lashes and playing childishly with his lapels. "I'd do anything you liked—and I mean truly *anything*, never mind what. Things a gentleman don't like to admit he fancies— why, that's just what I like best. And all I'd ask of you is a place to live—just till I've got on my feet again, you under-stand—and a few dresses. I'd be a credit to you, see if I wouldn't! I'd give the prettiest suppers for a gentleman's friends, you can't think—"

"I'm extremely honoured, Mrs. Desmond—"

"Because you could make me all the fashion, couldn't you? Everything *you* take up is all the rage directly."

"Mrs. Desmond, it grieves me to let your peculiar talents go to waste, but I'm so occupied with the investigation, I haven't time to do them justice."

"Well, if you ever change your mind, just tip me the nod." She plumped down in a chair. "Say, this house is a regular stunner, though! And to think he had his head smashed in, right here in this room! Where did it happen?"

"He was found underneath that window." Julian pointed to the left-hand window looking out on the back garden.

"The butler told me there was a party upstairs that night. So what was he doing down here?"

"If I knew that, I might be able to tell who killed him." He added curiously, "Why were you looking in those urns when I came in?"

"Oh, I got bored and thought I'd nose about. I had an idea I might find my jewelry hid somewhere."

"This room was thoroughly searched. If there'd been any jewelry, it would have been found."

"P'raps it wouldn't, then. Whoever searched the room might've pinched it."

"Either way, you're not likely to find it here. But if you want to go on searching, you needn't scale the walls. That cabinet opens into a set of stairs."

He pointed to one of the satinwood cabinets on either side of the door. Marianne frowned. "It looks just the same as the other one."

"Yes, I know. Alexander seems to have liked effects like that. He had a taste for symmetry—it certainly shows in this room. A niche on either side of the fireplace, a cabinet on either side of the door, a window on either side of the looking-glass. But he also liked his symmetry to be deceptive. So the cabinets aren't really the same—just as, in the library across the hall, there are bookshelves that look just alike, but one of them is a *trompe l'oeil*."

"A what-do-you-call-it?"

"A *trompe l'oeil*. It means 'to deceive the eye.' The bookshelf isn't real—it's merely painted on the wall. There's a similar effect in the supper room: the shutters are painted to give the illusion of a Chinese garden at night."

"Him and his little tricks," she sniffed.

"Actually, this house was the most honest thing about him. He was telling the world who and what he really was—and counting on the world not to understand. He was a *trompe l'oeil* himself: his vices made to look like virtues, his enemies made to look like friends—"

He broke off. His eyes travelled slowly around the room. Two niches, just alike. Two cabinets. *Two windows.* Alexander's body had been found beneath the window on the left. Suppose, in this house where nothing was what it seemed, there was something special about that window?

He went to it, candle in hand. The shutters were open, folded into the shutter-cases on each side. He looked out into the dark garden. The view was the same as that from the other window—nothing unique there. He examined the artfully draped white linen curtains, opened and closed the sash, and bent to study the window seat and the wainscoting below.

"What are you doing?" Marianne wanted to know.

"Nothing very useful, I'm afraid." The trouble was, it was far too dark for this sort of investigation. The pink-gold glow of the candle seemed to make more shadows than it dispelled. But he could not leave off yet—not while there was such an intriguing avenue unexplored. Because one thing about this window had been different when Alexander's body was found: the left-hand shutter had been closed.

He drew it out of its case and shone his candle on it, then on the shallow recess of the empty shutter-case. Both were painted pearl-grey and meticulously carved and joined. He closed the other shutter and compared the two. There was nothing to choose between them.

He turned back to the left-hand shutter-case. Pressing his ear to the inner panel, he tapped on it experimentally. Then he performed the same operation on the other shutter-case. Was it his imagination, or did the tapping sound different? He tried again. His musical ear, which sometimes tormented him by magnifying unpleasant sounds, served him well now. He could just make out a more resonant tone in the left-hand shutter-case.

Marianne came over to join him. "What do you want to go tapping on the windows for?"

"There's a hollow space behind this shutter-case."

"You mean, a secret cupboard? Just like in one of Alexander's horror stories?"

"That would be like him, wouldn't it—not only to turn fact into fiction, but fiction into fact?"

Marianne had no interest in metaphysics. "How can we get inside?"

"Break in, if we must. But there may be an easier way. An Italian friend of mine had a device like this in his house. The joining looked perfect, but if the panel were touched in just the right fashion, it would open. Let's have a try."

He set down the candle on the window seat and pressed his fingers against the inner side of the shutter-case. Nothing happened. He tried various positions, beginning in the centre and moving over the panel till one hand was at the top and the other at the bottom. He pressed yet again; there was a muffled click, and the panel swung slowly outward.

He caught up the candle and shone it inside. A dazzle of colour and brilliance leaped out at him. It was like the Arabian Nights stories he had read as a boy: a magic door concealing a secret treasure.

"My jewels!" Marianne gave a little cry, pushed past him, and thrust her hand inside. "Look, here's my emerald brooch with the feathers, my ruby comb, my cameo bracelet—What's this? Oh, this is Fanny's."

She tossed aside a small object. Julian picked it up. It was a topaz cross on a cheap, tarnished gilt chain. He held it up to the candle to examine it. What he saw made him reach for his quizzing-glass to take a closer look.

The chain was not tarnished, after all. There was some dark substance caked into the links. Julian worked a little of it out with his penknife. In the faint, fitful light, he could just make out that it was a reddish colour.

"Are you sure this is Fanny's?" he asked.

Marianne was pulling out handfuls of trinkets from the cupboard and hardly looked around. "Oh, yes. She wore it all the time. You'd think it was made of diamonds, she was so fond of it. Have I got it all?"

Julian shone his candle into the compartment. It was empty. Marianne gathered up her treasures and hurried to the looking-glass between the windows. "Light the candles!" she begged.

He illumined the candles on either side of the mirror. Marianne clasped on one ornament after another, the candlelight striking sparks of colour from the jewels as she turned from side to side, admiring herself in the glass.

Julian looked again at Fanny's cross—her one poor bit of jewelry. All at once a memory awoke in his mind. He walked back and forth, holding the cross like a thread that would guide him through a labyrinth. As, of course, it was.

✳

It was past midnight by the time Julian finished sorting his thoughts and laying his plans. Weariness had overtaken Marianne. She lay asleep in an armchair by the fire, all tricked out in necklaces, bracelets, and combs, like a little girl trying on her mother's jewelry. Julian did not have the heart to wake her. Her eyes had a bruised, exhausted look, and the firelight threw her wasted features brutally into relief. In her pallor and strain, she suddenly reminded him of Mrs. Falkland. Yet Alexander's mistress had one advantage over his wife: she lacked pride. The wounds his trickery, degradation, and abuse had inflicted on her would heal. He could not destroy her, as he had all but destroyed his wife.

Julian went to Alexander's writing-table and dashed off a note:

> *Sir Malcolm,—I've discovered something of importance. I shall call on you tomorrow morning at nine and tell you all about it. I'm afraid I'm obliged to bring Mrs. Desmond with me. I realize her presence under the same roof with Mrs. Falkland will be awkward, but I promise you, it's essential. Will you please ensure that the entire household remains at home, and that no one is informed of our visit in advance? I'm sorry to raise such a fog of mystery, but the matter defies explanation on paper.*
> *Your very obedient servant, Julian Kestrel*

He rang for Nichols and instructed him to have the note delivered as soon as possible. "And have one of the maidservants look after Mrs. Desmond—she oughtn't to be left in the study all night. Tell her I should be greatly obliged if she would accompany me to Hampstead tomorrow morning. I shall call for her at eight. May I leave Mr. Poynter's cabriolet in your stables till then?"

"Certainly, sir."

"Thank you. Have it brought round just before eight, will you?"

"Yes, sir."

Julian departed, taking Fanny's cross for safe-keeping. It was only a short walk back to his flat in Clarges Street. To his surprise, there was a light in the front basement room. Dipper looked out at the area window and made signs that he would come up and open the door. A moment later he appeared, wearing an apron and a pair of old leather gloves. "What have you been doing?" asked Julian, when they had ascended to his flat.

"Polishing the silver, sir—your dressing-case and the glim-sticks, and that."

"At one in the morning?"

"I thought they needed it, sir. They was getting in a bit of a muck."

"The devil they were. You've been playing mother hen, watching for me to come home. What did you suppose—that I'd vanished into an *oubliette?*"

"I dunno what that is, sir, but if it's some'ut you vanish into, it must be uncommon nasty."

Julian smiled. "I'll tell you all about my adventures, but in the meantime you'd better heat me a bath and get me to bed. I have to be up early tomorrow, if I'm to win my bet by noon."

✳

On his way to Alexander's house next morning, Julian reflected that it might be amusing to wake up Felix and ask to keep the cabriolet for one more day. But that would be beyond all bounds of cruelty, and besides, he did not have the time. Felix had not seemed in any hurry to get the cab back and surely would not mind if Julian used it to take Marianne to Hampstead.

It was waiting at the door when he arrived. Alfred stood holding the horse and craning his neck to watch a maidservant do up her hair in an attic across the way. Julian told him they would be leaving directly and went to ring at the door.

Marianne was waiting for him in the Turkish parlour. She had found a mauve silk dress of Mrs. Falkland's that was to be given to parish relief. It was too tight across the bosom, which did not seem to displease her. Julian suddenly remembered Luke's account of Mrs. Falkland's return from her visit to Cygnet's Court: *A silk dress the colour of lilacs . . . One of the sleeves was all but ripped away. . . .* Yes, there were traces of mending at the shoulder, so faint they would be noticed only by someone who knew to look for them. Still, knowing what he knew now, he could well understand why Mrs. Falkland had not wished to wear this dress again.

Marianne preened before the looking-glass. "Don't my amethyst brooch look well on this? And there's the sweetest shawl to match—I'm sure Alexander never gave *me* one half so nice. Where are we going?"

"To Hampstead, to call on Sir Malcolm."

"But why?"

"Because you are going to tell him who killed Alexander."

✳

Before leaving Alexander's house, Julian wrote a note asking one more person to join him at Sir Malcolm's. He gave the note to Luke to deliver, then set out with Marianne for Hampstead.

Sir Malcolm had been watching for them and opened the door without their having to ring. "Come into the library," he whispered. "I don't want Belinda to hear us."

"How is she?" Julian asked, once they were secluded in the library.

"Better. Still keeping to her room. She can hobble about a bit, but we don't encourage it. Eugene is with her. I haven't let her or anyone else know you were coming. Even if you hadn't enjoined secrecy, I would have done all I could to spare her an encounter like this." He looked at Marianne with a repulsion he could not conceal.

Before she could retort, the door opened, and Mrs. Falkland limped in, leaning on Eugene's arm. "I'm sorry," Eugene said helplessly. "I couldn't stop her coming down. She saw you from her window and said she'd come down alone if I didn't help her."

Sir Malcolm hastened to her. "My dearest girl, sit down—here, where you can put your feet up." He helped her to one of the leather sofas. "You ought not to have come here—it can only distress you—"

She said in a cold, quiet voice, "Was it really necessary to bring that woman here?"

"It ain't as if I wanted to come," Marianne rejoined. "*He* made me." She jerked her head at Julian.

"I beg your pardon, Mrs. Falkland," said Julian. "I would have avoided it if I could."

Mrs. Falkland looked at Marianne more closely and caught her breath. "She's wearing my dress!"

"What if I am?" Marianne tossed her head. "You'd thrown it away, and I haven't a stitch of my own. I had to get myself up respectable, didn't I, if I'm to be paying calls. Mr. Kestrel says I'm to tell everyone who killed Alexander—though I'm sure I can't think how, when I've been laid up in lavender for weeks and know less about the murder than anyone—"

"What's this all about, Mr. Kestrel?" broke in Sir Malcolm. "Do *you* know who killed Alexander?" He added eagerly, "And Belinda's accident: can you tell us now who you think caused that?"

"What are you saying?" Mrs. Falkland looked up swiftly. "Mr. Kestrel, who do you think was responsible for my accident?"

"I hadn't meant to speak of that yet. I don't wish to tax your strength too far—"

"You must tell me at once! I have a right to know! Who is it you suspect?"

Julian saw she was not to be put off. He turned to Marianne. "Mrs. Desmond, will you be good enough to leave us for a time?"

"I don't see why I shouldn't hear it, the same as her—"

"I'm afraid I must insist."

She pouted briefly, then slipped her arm through his. "Well of course, if *you* ask me, Mr. Kestrel."

He escorted her out. Seeing Dutton in the hallway, he beckoned to him. "Will you take Mrs. Desmond up to the drawing room? And, Dutton," he added softly, holding him back for a moment, "see that she remains there."

He returned to the library. "I'm afraid you must go, too," he told Eugene. "When you're needed—and you *will* be needed—you'll be called."

"But—" Eugene broke off, looked at Julian uncertainly, then nodded. "Yes, sir. I'll be in my room." On his way out, he stopped to lay a hand on Mrs. Falkland's shoulder. She closed her eyes briefly and covered his hand with hers, then motioned him to go.

Sir Malcolm stood beside her sofa and held her hand between both of his. She leaned forward tensely. They both gazed expectantly at Julian.

He drew a long breath. "Mrs. Falkland, you asked me who I believe caused your accident. If you must have an answer—"

"I must."

"Then I believe it was you."

# ✳ 29 ✳

## FAR ABOVE RUBIES

"What?" Sir Malcolm stared at Julian. "You must be mad! Belinda cause her own accident?"

"Yes. Mrs. Falkland drove those nails into her saddle. She was thrown because she wished to be."

"But that's preposterous! It's ludicrous! Belinda, tell him—tell him—" His voice trailed away.

She was looking up at Julian, pale but composed. "How did you know?"

"To begin with," he said gently, "you admitted you'd been to the stable to see Phoenix the night before the accident. That showed you had an opportunity to slip into the saddle room. Of course that would have meant nothing, standing alone. The idea of your inflicting such an injury on yourself, in your condition, seemed, as Sir Malcolm says, preposterous. And yet you were in the best position of anyone to arrange the accident. You knew your groom's routine, your horse's temperament, the contours of your saddle. You alone could determine whether and when you went riding, how you seated yourself on the horse, and when the girth was tightened.

"Still, I mightn't have thought to suspect you if it hadn't been for two other circumstances. The first was your refusal to countenance anyone else's being accused. You steadfastly absolved every suspect, declined to believe in anyone's guilt.

But more important, there was Eugene. After Alexander's death, you promised him he needn't return to school before the autumn. Suddenly, uncharacteristically, you broke your word and insisted on sending him away at once. After your accident, I saw why: he was the only person with a concrete motive for wishing Alexander to die childless. So he must go. But not back to Harrow—that was too close. People might say he could have returned secretly during the night. No, he must go all the way to Yorkshire. And when it turned out he hadn't gone after all, you were horrified—not because you feared he'd caused your accident, but because he'd thrown away the alibi you tried to give him."

She said quietly, "What a monster you must think me."

"No. I don't believe you did any of this with cruelty or indifference. I doubted your innocence, but never your grief."

"I do grieve. I knew I would feel pain, but I didn't expect such agony as this. I dream about it every night—the baby, I mean. I dream I'm holding it in my arms, and it clings to me and cries, and I say, thank God, it's alive, I can still save it! And then I wake up alone in the darkness, and I know that if I had it to do over, I should do exactly the same."

"Why, Belinda, why?" Sir Malcolm knelt beside the sofa, still clasping her hand. "What did he do to you—what did that devil incarnate do to you—to drive you to such a desperate act?"

"You know?" She looked at him in wonder. "You know he was a devil?"

"Yes." Sir Malcolm gathered her against his breast and looked up grimly at the portrait of Alexander. "So you needn't be afraid to tell us the very worst."

"You're so kind to me. I don't know how you can be. Whatever Alexander was, he was your son—his child would have been your grandchild. But you don't understand—I must make you understand—"

"When you're ready, my dear. When you feel strong enough."

"I'm ready now. Please let me go. I can't speak, I can't explain, if you hold me."

He brought over a chair and sat beside her. Julian sat on her other side, but a little way behind, where she could not see him. She would find this hard enough, without being reminded of the presence of a man she hardly knew.

"I became engaged to Alexander at the end of my first season. When you're eighteen, brought up as I was and not yet married, you don't know anything. You feel confident and ready to take on the world, but you don't know what the world is. You only see the parts of it that are considered fit for your eyes. I did know there could be tragedy even in the heart of fashionable London—that husbands could be weak or cruel, and wives could be made to suffer. My mother's second marriage, to Mr. Talmadge, had been very painful. But I was very young then, and Mama always took pains to make me believe I was safe and protected—that nothing like that could ever happen to me."

Her voice caught. She swallowed hard and resumed, "So when I met Alexander, I was proud and foolish. Being reckoned a beauty and a catch on the marriage mart had gone to my head. I was sated with admiration. Men told me they were my slaves, and I had contempt for them. What man of any worth would be a slave, even to the woman he loved?

"Alexander Falkland was no one's slave. He was charming, he was considerate, he made me feel admired and adored — but there was something elusive about him. He would laugh, and I wouldn't know why. He would look pensive, and I couldn't tell if he was thinking of me or of something a thousand miles away. And then, everyone admired him so, and how could I help but want what all the world esteemed so highly?

"He offered for me, and I accepted. I was happy at first, or I thought I was. We had a whirlwind wedding tour, then before I could draw breath, we plunged into our first season. You know what we became—how popular, sought-after, emulated we were. It was all Alexander's doing. He decorated our house, chose our servants, our guests, our menus. I wasn't his helpmate—I was merely one of his *objets d'art*. But I didn't understand that then. I was too caught up in the excitement of being one of London's foremost hostesses—at the age of nineteen!

"I never thought about how he could afford to pay for it all. I had an idea that the income from my property wasn't nearly enough, but I knew he had investments, and he was so clever, I thought he was more than equal to making us rich.

"I knew Mr. Adams, of course. Alexander introduced us and said Mr. Adams was advising him about his investments. We used to invite him to our parties—the larger affairs, not the dinner parties. Alexander said people couldn't be expected to sit down in intimate surroundings with such a person. But he was always gracious to Mr. Adams when they were together, and I took my lead from him. I was brought up to be courteous to people like estate agents and solicitors, and that was how I thought of Mr. Adams.

"This past March, Alexander told me that some of his investments had gone wrong. He sat beside me and held my hands and talked to me very earnestly. He said he was over head and ears, he owed thirty thousand pounds, and he hadn't the money to pay it. He couldn't legally sell or encumber my estate, and if he sold off smaller things, like paintings or furniture, the tradespeople would know we were in dire straits, and they would all begin dunning us. There might even be an execution in the house. And he told me over and over how sorry he was about it all.

"The strange thing is—I was glad. For a long time, without quite admitting it to myself, I'd felt a disappointment with our life together. The excitement and admiration were starting to pall. I was tired. I didn't care so much about being a celebrated hostess. And I hardly ever saw Alexander alone anymore. If we had to economize, we couldn't always be going out or giving parties. We would have to spend more time quietly at home—perhaps even retire to my house in Dorset. I suddenly realized how much I missed it.

"But I saw he didn't share my feelings. He loved our life—he didn't want any of it to change. All he cared about was finding some means to right our affairs. He said our obligations to tradespeople weren't of any account—it was only the thirty thousand pounds that threatened us with ruin. Then he told me Mr. Adams had bought up the debt. I said, But that's good, isn't it? You're on friendly terms with him—surely he'll be reasonable and give you time to pay?

"He said he had no power to sway Mr. Adams, but *I* might if I chose. I said, But I know nothing about money matters. What could I say that would have any weight with a man like Mr. Adams? Alexander said it wasn't my words that would move him, but my—my face, my—" She stopped short, forced herself to go on. "He used the most graceful language. He said I had only to look on Mr. Adams with favour, smile at him, have him to dinner. He made it sound such a trifle—the very least a wife ought to do for her husband.

"My mind kept rejecting what he said, *willing* me not to understand. When at last I couldn't mistake his meaning, I was horrified. I would have died sooner than dishonour him and break my marriage vows. And he wanted to barter me away! I didn't know if he was proposing an actual criminal connexion or merely a dubious friendship. But what did that matter? It was all one to me. I refused. I can't think what I could ever have said or done to make him believe I would do anything else.

"I ought to have left him then—either sought a formal separation or gone quietly home to Dorset. He wouldn't have dared to stop me and risk my telling people what he'd proposed. Even the most hardened profligates among his friends would be disgusted. But I stayed. I was proud. I couldn't bear people to know how he'd meant to humiliate me, *sell* me. I had better motives, too. I knew that Eugene admired him, and he'd had few people to admire. He was ashamed of his father—I didn't want to make him ashamed of his guardian, too. And, finally, there was you, Papa. You loved Alexander, and I knew you would be broken-hearted to learn what he really was."

"Oh, my dear——" Sir Malcolm shook his head. "When I think what you and Verity suffered at his hands, rather than let me be hurt or disillusioned—!"

"Who is Verity?"

"I'll tell you another time. Please go on—I didn't mean to interrupt."

"Alexander and I went on with our lives as before—outwardly, at least. I never saw him in private if I could avoid it. I didn't know what he was doing about his debts, and I didn't much care. We quarrelled once. I wanted to send Eugene back to Harrow, to remove him from Alexander's influence. He wasn't fit to be anyone's guardian. Alexander refused. He said he couldn't afford to maintain Eugene at Harrow when he was at low tide, and I wouldn't lift a finger to help.

"A few weeks went by, and it was the first of April."

She stopped suddenly, as if she had turned a corner and found a sheer drop before her. In a low, slightly shaky voice, she went on, "Alexander asked me to go with him to a hardware showroom in the Strand. I said I should have thought we couldn't afford to spend any money. He said it was all the more important to maintain an appearance of solvency. I agreed. He seemed to be holding out an olive branch, and though I wouldn't find it easy to forgive him or trust him again, it seemed my duty to try. Just before we left, he told me he'd invited Eugene to come with us, but he'd declined. I wasn't suspicious. Why should I be?

"We walked about the showroom arm in arm, and the shopmen fawned on us as people always did when we went out together. I missed the days when that meant something to me—when I took pride in admiration I hadn't earned and friendships I couldn't rely on. When we left the showroom, a woman came running up to us. She was young and blond and dressed like a maid-of-all-work, and she seemed upset. She asked me if I was Mrs. Falkland. I said yes. And she told me my brother had been kicked by a horse and was badly hurt. He'd been carried into her mistress's house and had told her mistress his sister was at a hardware showroom nearby, so her mistress had sent her, the maid, to find me.

"I never stopped to think about whether the story was true. All I thought was, Eugene had changed his mind and come to join us, and now he was hurt and in danger. Alexander was all commiseration. He asked the maidservant if a doctor had been sent for. She said no, and he said we must fetch one at once. I begged him to do so and let me go to Eugene.

"The maid said I would have to go on foot, as our coach wouldn't fit through the entrance to the court where her mistress lived. I said, that doesn't signify, only take me to my brother at once. If I'd stopped to reflect, I would have brought Luke with me. I would have expected Alexander to suggest as much. But in sudden crises, you don't stop to ask yourself if things are making sense. Why would anyone have invented all this? How could I have known it was a lie?"

"You couldn't have known, Mrs. Falkland," said Julian gently. "You did what seemed right at the time. Anyone of character and courage would have done the same."

"I wish I could believe that. I keep going over and over it —remembering, reliving, trying to sort out what I might have done differently. It doesn't do any good. I did do what seemed right at the time. And yet nothing will ever convince me it wasn't my fault.

"The maidservant led me through a narrow passage into a little dark court. Most of the houses were in disrepair, but one at the end had been refurbished. That was where she took me. She let me in at the street door and brought me to a back parlour. She stepped aside to let me go in first, and I found —David Adams.

"Everything was clear to me in that moment. Eugene had never been in the house. It was all a plot to leave me alone with Mr. Adams. And Alexander was behind it.

"I tried to get out, but I couldn't. The maidservant had locked me in. I pounded on the door and called to her, but she didn't answer. I said to Mr. Adams, I assume you have a key to this door. Be good enough to open it at once.

"He said he would, but first he must speak to me. He begged me to forgive him this deception, which had been his one means of gaining an opportunity to open his heart to me. He felt his feelings toward me had been misrepresented—he ought never to have trusted Alexander to convey them. Alexander was vicious, he cared nothing for me, he had no idea how to value me as I deserved. But he—Mr. Adams—loved me, he had loved me a long time, he would do anything for me. He said he asked nothing more of earth or Heaven than to be my champion against Alexander and all the world. If I would only believe in his love, he would lay at my feet his heart, his fortune, and his devoted service.

"Looking back, I think he was in earnest—that he exposed himself to me as perhaps he never had to anyone else. I may have known it even then. But what did it matter? I wanted no part of his love or protection. Protection! This man, who was all on fire to defend me against Alexander, had plotted with Alexander to trick and trap me. He was holding me a prisoner and trying to wrest from me the only thing of value I had left—the only thing Alexander hadn't been able to tarnish, because it was mine alone—my honour. They were both against me; I had only myself to rely on. And I felt, without thinking it out, that my only safety lay in utter, uncompromising rejection of his suit. If I stood firm against him, perhaps I could shame him into letting me go.

"So I was cold and disdainful. I threw his feelings back at him like rubbish I wouldn't deign to touch. It was disastrous. In proportion as he'd been gentle, he became enraged. He shouted at me. I was worthless, a gilt-paper angel, as shallow as the rest of Alexander's set. I let Alexander touch me—that proved I was no better than a whore. He despised himself for loving me. He cursed me, cursed himself. He took me by the shoulders. I cried out to him to let me go. He asked if I was ashamed to be touched by a Jew, if I would go home and wash myself to remove the contagion. I didn't care about his being a Jew—I cared that he wasn't my husband, he had no right to touch me. But I didn't owe him explanations. He was better than Alexander. He ought to have known.

"He didn't know. He pulled me against him. He—he—kissed me. Cruelly, without any love at all. I was shocked beyond imagining. He was so strong, and I was so helpless. I'd always thought of myself as strong, but I'd never been in a struggle like that with a man before. It was like trying to beat back the tide. I couldn't. I tried. Oh, Papa, I tried so hard—"

"My dearest!" Sir Malcolm held her close to him. "Please don't cry!"

"I can't help it. I'm so ashamed. He was right: I *am* a whore. There's nothing to choose between me and women who sell themselves in Covent Garden. Except that I cost so much more—thirty thousand pounds." She laughed, a little wildly. *"Who can find a virtuous woman? for her price is far above rubies."*

Sir Malcolm talked to her soothingly, cradled her against him, stroked her hair. At last she lifted her head from his shoulder. "I'm better now. I'm sorry to have taken on like this. But I've never told anyone about this before, and it seemed to bring it all back."

"He mustn't be allowed to get away with this!" Sir Malcolm fumed. "The brute must be punished—"

"Papa, you mustn't quarrel with Mr. Adams! I couldn't bear a public prosecution—it would splash what I suffered all over the newspapers, make it common gossip in drawing rooms. And he probably wouldn't accept a private challenge. Men of his class aren't accustomed to defend their honour with pistols." She went on more gently, taking his hands, "If he did fight you, he might hurt you, and I won't have you risk your life for me. Or he might simply stand there and let you kill him. I could imagine him doing that. And then you would be ruined, obliged to leave the country. And the worst of it is—Alexander would have won again! He would still be making a hell of all our lives, even from beyond the grave.

"I'll tell you something strange. I don't know if I can

make you understand it. After—after what happened at Mrs. Desmond's—I was too overcome at first to think about anything. I remember finding that the sleeve of my gown was torn and draping my shawl so that it couldn't be seen. Then I realized I would have to take a hackney home, and I was afraid I hadn't the money, and I would have to ask Mr. Adams for it. I kept searching through my reticule, and I couldn't seem to find any change. And all the while I wasn't looking at him, but I could hear him walking, walking. Finally I said I wanted to go home, and he fetched a hackney and paid the driver without asking me. I never looked at his face, but I saw his hand when he opened the carriage door for me. It was shaking.

"This is the strange thing, Papa. As soon as I could reflect at all clearly, I knew that I didn't hate him. I was afraid of him—more afraid than I'd ever been of anyone in my life. And I hated what he'd done to me. But I could understand something of what he'd felt—how I'd pushed him beyond endurance. I couldn't have done otherwise, but perhaps he couldn't have, either. It was like one of those Greek tragedies you talk of, Papa, where a god enters into a person and makes him or her do terrible things. Mr. Adams needn't be punished—he'll punish himself. What he did to me was unworthy of him, and he knows it. He'll know it all his life—he'll go to his grave knowing it. So it was as much a defeat for him as for me.

"I didn't hate him. I hated Alexander. He was my husband: he had a duty to protect me. When we were married, I thought he loved me; I knew now that was all a pretence. But even if he felt nothing for me, honour and decency should have compelled him to stand with me against a man who compassed my ruin! Instead he'd allied himself with that man. And then—but you shall hear what he did next.

"I didn't see him for the rest of that day or evening. Next day I asked to speak with him in private. I was very composed—or I managed to seem so. My worst feelings came to my rescue: pride, which wouldn't let me show how humiliated I felt, and revenge, which grudged him the chance to revel in his victory. I didn't tell him what had happened between Mr. Adams and me. He tried to goad or trick me into revealing it, but I wouldn't. I don't think he ever did know for certain, or he couldn't have resisted holding it over my head. All he ever knew was that his notes-of-hand were forgiven. It seems that Mr. Adams can be trusted to fulfill his business obligations.

"But I was telling you about our conversation that morning. I asked him for a legal separation and offered in return to say nothing of how he had tricked me into meeting Mr. Adams. Alexander didn't choose to make a public break. He said we both knew perfectly well I would never reveal what he'd done to me. If I did, I would savage my own reputation. Just having met with Mr. Adams alone would throw doubt on my honour. My whole story was improbable—people were far likelier to believe Mr. Adams was my lover, and we'd had an assignation at that woman's house. He said the woman would swear to it if he asked her. Then he would have grounds to divorce me by act of Parliament, and he would. He said, Is it really worth ruining yourself, bringing fresh disgrace on your brother? And my father—do you want him to despise you? If you and I told conflicting stories, which of us do you suppose he would believe?

"I knew I was defeated. I agreed not to break with him, on two conditions. The first was that he wouldn't—that we would be husband and wife only in name. The second was that Eugene should be sent away at once. Now that I understood fully what Alexander was, I couldn't let Eugene remain under his roof, in his power. Who knew how Alexander might corrupt him—take advantage of his youth and trust?

"So the next day we told Eugene he was to return to Harrow. Alexander made clear that it was entirely my decision, so all Eugene's rage and resentment fell on me. It was hard, his hating me so much, when I only wanted to protect him. And in the end all my efforts came to nothing: he made himself ill by staying out in the rain, so we couldn't send him away. Alexander had won again."

She looked suddenly at Julian. "I wonder what you're thinking, Mr. Kestrel? That our party happened soon after? That I retired with a headache so that I could meet Alexander in the study and kill him?"

He countered gently, "Why don't you tell me precisely what happened that night?"

"I suppose you've guessed the real reason I withdrew from the party. It's because Mr. Adams was there. I didn't know he'd been invited, and when I saw him I panicked. I don't know what I thought he could do to me among all those people. My fear of him went beyond reason. I only knew I had to get away."

Julian saw no need to tell her that Felix had revealed some of this already. After all she had been through, even such a well-intended betrayal of her confidence might pain her.

"I went to my room. I was sick at heart. What did he want from me? Why couldn't he make me the one reparation in his power and leave me in peace? Suppose he lingered after all the other guests had gone, and Alexander made me see him?

"I rang for Martha and told her I had a headache and wouldn't be returning to the party, but I wanted it to go on without me. As long as the guests were there, Alexander would be too distracted to think of me. Martha seemed worried about me, but she didn't say anything. She laid out my night-clothes and said she would be in her room if I needed her.

"I locked my door, but I still didn't feel safe. Alexander had keys to every room in the house. I couldn't rest, didn't dare undress, couldn't settle to anything. Before long I really did have a headache. I—" She stopped short, seemed to change direction. "I lay down on my bed and finally managed to sleep a little. The next thing I knew, I heard knocking. It was Martha, coming to tell me Alexander had been murdered.

"I lost my head. All I could think was that Mr. Adams had killed him, and now he was coming for me. I believe I expected him to burst into my room and carry me away. I thought he could do anything. That's why I screamed. It had nothing to do with Alexander. I was glad he was dead. And I wasn't surprised he'd been murdered. Who could come to know him intimately and not wish to kill him?

"From then on, I walled myself up in silence. I answered questions as briefly as I could. Alexander was dead—there was no reason to wring his father's heart by revealing the things he'd done. And I didn't want the murder solved. It kept me safe from Mr. Adams. He couldn't reveal his feelings for me without courting suspicion that he'd killed my husband."

She paused, lowered her eyes, and said quietly, "Now I can tell you about the child. You're both too considerate to ask, but you must be wondering who the father was. It was Mr. Adams. I knew, because Alexander and I were estranged both before and after—I was with Mr. Adams. I first suspected my condition before Alexander was killed, but it wasn't till after he was dead that I was sure. It was like a nightmare. I would give birth to a child everyone would think was Alexander's. People would lavish admiration and attention on it, and all the time I would know—I would know—" Her throat closed. "The worst part was, Mr. Adams might guess the truth, and it would bind me to him forever. He isn't a man to keep away from his own child. I believe the men of his nation cleave very closely to their flesh and blood. I would never be free of him, I would always be reminded—I couldn't bear it. I had to stop the child from being born.

"I thought of taking my life. It seemed more just. Why should I live, when the child must die? But two things held me back. I couldn't desert Eugene in the same cruel, contemptible way his father had. And—it sounds base, I know— but it galled me that people would believe I did it out of grief for Alexander.

"I had no one to advise me. People say there are herbal compounds, secret methods—I didn't know what they were. I tried drinking turpentine. Papa's housemaid keeps a bottle in her closet, for making furniture polish. It made me terribly sick, but it didn't bring about the result I'd wished. I was still recovering when you came to see me, Mr. Kestrel, the day you agreed to investigate Alexander's murder."

"Yes," he said, nodding, "I remember you were ill then."

"I had to think of something else—something that wouldn't give rise to suspicion that I'd miscarried intentionally. If that became known, the whole truth would have to come out. And I was afraid of what Mr. Adams would do if he knew I'd tried to kill his child. I had to think of some way to disguise what I was doing—to throw everyone off the scent.

"That's why I arranged the accident as I did. I wanted it to look as if someone had deliberately tampered with my saddle. I hoped people would assume the same person who killed Alexander had tried to kill me, or his child. I was sorry to make such a cruel use of Phoenix, because he's innocent and devoted to me and didn't deserve to suffer. But I couldn't think of another way.

"I did lose the child, but everything else went wrong. Eugene came back, after all the efforts I'd made to put him safely out of the way. And you turned up on the morning of the accident, Mr. Kestrel, when I'd made all the preparations, and it was too late to cry off. Other people might have drawn the wrong inferences, asked the wrong questions. You were too clever and clear-sighted for that. But did you know why I'd done it? Did you guess what had happened between Mr. Adams and me?"

"Not precisely. But I knew it was in order to throw you together with Adams that Alexander arranged for Mrs. Desmond to lure you to her house. That was on a Friday, the first of April. Fridays were the only days when Mrs. Desmond's neighbour, Mrs. Wheeler, was away. Adams told me he'd visited Mrs. Desmond's house once, early in April, and seen Martha there. When I asked him how he knew it was Martha, he said he'd seen her clearly by the sunshine streaming through the fanlight. Mrs. Wheeler said Alexander only called on Mrs. Desmond at night; if he'd paid a daytime visit or allowed Adams to do so, it must have been on a Friday, when he knew the inquisitive Mrs. Wheeler would be away. In short, Mrs. Falkland, I was convinced that you and Mr. Adams had been to Mrs. Desmond's house on the same day. The next day, Adams forgave Alexander a debt of thirty thousand pounds. And when you saw Adams at your party a few weeks later, you left precipitately. So I suspected Adams had taken some advantage of you. But I never doubted your honour, or saw you as anything other than the innocent victim of a base betrayal."

"Innocent? How can you speak of me so? I killed my own child!"

"Not in the eyes of the law," Sir Malcolm pointed out gently. "According to Blackstone, an abortion isn't murder if it takes place before the child has quickened in the womb."

She shook her head despairingly. "I don't know who Blackstone is, but I know he can't absolve me of the guilt I feel. Why haven't you accused me of killing Alexander, Mr. Kestrel? You must see I had every reason to want him dead, and if I could plot my accident, I could surely plot a murder."

"No, Mrs. Falkland. You didn't kill your husband. But I think you know who did."

"Wh-what?"

"You said you arranged the accident so that people—Adams in particular—would assume the same person who killed Alexander had attacked you."

"Yes," she said warily.

"How did you know Adams hadn't killed Alexander himself? How *could* you know—unless you knew who had killed him?"

She drew in her breath but did not answer.

"Are you willing to tell us who the murderer was?"

"No. No. I won't give anyone up to the law for doing what I'm glad was done—for ridding me of a husband I hated, and the world of an enemy to everything honourable and good."

Julian shrugged. "Then I shall have to submit my proofs."

He reached into an inside pocket of his coat and took out

Fanny's little topaz cross. "This belonged to Mrs. Desmond's maid, Fanny Gates. Mrs. Desmond says she wore it all the time." He described how he had found it in the hidden recess. "There was also some jewelry that Mrs. Desmond claims is hers."

"But what does it mean?" Sir Malcolm faltered.

"It confirms what we've suspected for some time," said Julian gently. "That Fanny was the brickfield victim, and that Alexander killed her. He must have taken the cross from her body after she died. The reddish substance caked into the chain could be brickearth or blood—perhaps both. After going to so much trouble to smash her face, obliterate her identity, he wouldn't have left her wearing an ornament someone might recognize as hers. But he must have felt it wasn't safe to dispose of it—or of Mrs. Desmond's jewelry, either—so he hid them in the secret compartment he'd devised when he designed the study."

Sir Malcolm held out his hand for the cross. Julian gave it to him. He gazed at it long and intently. It lay on his palm, a silent, remorseless witness. At last his fist closed around it. He lifted his head, and his eyes met the laughing eyes of the portrait of Alexander.

He flushed and came to his feet. Striding to the portrait, he tore it from the wall and smashed it against the mantelpiece. The frame cracked; Alexander's face dissolved in a burst of shredded canvas.

Mrs. Falkland gasped and fell back faintly against her pillows. Sir Malcolm spun around in quick concern. Flinging the portrait aside, he rang for Dutton and ordered him to fetch Martha. Then he dropped down beside Mrs. Falkland, chafing her hands and softly calling her name. Julian hunted out the decanter and poured her a glass of brandy.

Martha ran in, a smelling-bottle in one hand and a cloth soaked in vinegar in the other. She elbowed the men aside and administered the bottle to Mrs. Falkland's nose and the cloth to her brow. Her eyes flickered open; she sat up weakly.

Julian slipped out and went upstairs to the drawing room. Marianne was sitting on the sofa, amusing herself by going through Mrs. Falkland's work-box.

"I'm sorry to have left you alone so long," he said. "Will you come downstairs again?"

She pouted a little but went with him willingly enough. "You might tell me what's been happening. I can't think why you brought me here, if it was only to leave me cooling my heels."

"Grant me another minute or two, and I'll undertake to make everything plain."

They returned to the library. Marianne swept in with her nose in the air. "I warn you, I shan't stay if people aren't civil to me. That stuck-up wife of Alexander's has been perfectly horrid—"

She halted, gazing across the room. Martha was still bustling about Mrs. Falkland, plumping her pillows and tucking a rug around her feet. She looked up at Marianne without interest. But Marianne came a few steps closer, staring at her incredulously. "Fanny! Isn't it?" She turned to Julian in bewilderment. "You said she was dead!"

"She is. This is Martha Gilmore, her sister—and the murderer of Alexander."

# ✳ 30 ✳

## The Iron Weapon

Martha slowly straightened up. *So you've found me out,* her stolid gaze seemed to say. *What now?* The others stared in amazement—all except Mrs. Falkland, who looked sad but unsurprised.

Sir Malcolm came to his feet. "What—how—I don't understand—"

"The cross was what gave her away," said Julian. "If it hadn't been found, Alexander's murder might never have been solved."

"If I may speak, sir," Martha interposed, "it wasn't a murder. It was an execution."

"It wasn't for you to pass sentence on him," Sir Malcolm said gravely. "We all know what he was. Even I, his own father, admit he deserved to die. But who were you to be his judge and jury?"

"I was Fanny's sister, sir. That was judge and jury enough for him."

Sir Malcolm turned back to Julian. "But how on earth did you find that out? That Martha and Fanny were sisters?"

"Not merely sisters. Twins, and identical. It was the only explanation that fit all the facts." He looked thoughtfully at Martha. "You've puzzled me for some time. Suspicious circumstances swirled around you, but I couldn't link any of them clearly to the murder. First, there was your asking to speak with Alexander on the night he was killed, to tell him Mrs. Falkland wouldn't be returning to the party. Both Clare and Adams were certain you'd said nothing else, done nothing out of the common. But Clare said Alexander seemed disconcerted, and shortly afterward he went down to the study, where he was killed.

"Then there was Adams's story that he'd seen you at Mrs. Desmond's. I couldn't conceive why he should have invented such a thing. But you swore on your honour as a Christian that you'd never been there, and I didn't believe that was an oath you would take lightly. And of course it was the truth—but not the whole truth. You must have known it was Fanny, not you, Adams saw."

"I guessed as much, sir."

Julian nodded. "After I found the cross, I remembered Adams's description of you as he'd seen you at Mrs. Desmond's, then later at Alexander's party: same broad shoulders, same square face, *same cross around her neck*. I should have realized I'd never seen you wear a cross or any other ornament. But it was such a small detail, it passed me by.

"Now I see what must have happened. You'd been spying on Alexander, searching his rooms, and you came upon the cross. Somehow you pieced together that he'd killed your sister. On the night of his party, you put on the cross, then called him out of the drawing room on the pretext of giving him a message from Mrs. Falkland. That was how you disconcerted him—not by anything you said, but by wearing the cross he'd taken from his victim after he killed her.

"He knew, of course, that you and Fanny were twins. It probably amused him to give his wife and his mistress identical maids. It was another piece of *trompe l'oeil*—his cleverest and cruelest. When he saw you wearing Fanny's cross, he must ave asked himself, did you have one just like it, or had you und your sister's—the one thing in the world that could link ɔ to the Brickfield Murder? He couldn't rest till he'd gone m to the study to see if his hiding place had been disturbed. You lay in wait for him, and when he went to the shutter-case to open the secret cupboard, you struck."

"Is all this true?" Sir Malcolm asked Martha.

"Yes, sir," she answered calmly.

"Of course," said Julian, "you didn't count on being seen that night by Adams, who'd seen Fanny not long before. That was one clue that gave away your twinship. Another was your manner toward Mr. Clare. When I called here last week, I was struck by the way you spoke to him: gently, and with a familiarity very unlike you. I see why now: he'd been talking about his devotion to his twin sister, and that was something you could understand. In fact, you must have sympathized all the more keenly because your own twin was dead."

Martha nodded heavily. "Fanny and I were parted many years ago, and the Lord didn't see fit to bring us together again in this world. But I never forgot her or ceased to hope I'd find her. We came into the world together. She had my blood, my flesh, and even my face."

"Which is why Alexander destroyed her face," said Julian gently. "If anyone detected her resemblance to you, that might attract the authorities' attention to him, your employer. It was a slim chance, but one he couldn't afford to take."

They were all silent for a time, taking it in. Julian could have added one more proof of Martha's guilt, but he did not want to reopen the painful subject of Mrs. Falkland's accident. It had not escaped him that Mrs. Falkland had sent Martha away beforehand, just as she had banished Eugene. There was no reason she should have felt a particular need to give Martha an alibi—unless she knew Martha had killed Alexander and hoped, by absolving her of one crime, to mask her guilt for the other.

"Why did he do it?" Sir Malcolm asked bleakly. "What had the poor woman done?"

"Perhaps she simply knew too much about him," said Julian. "She saw Adams arrive at Mrs. Desmond's house and probably had a good idea what he'd come for. And she knew all about Alexander's life with Mrs. Desmond. It's possible she tried to blackmail him, as Mrs. Desmond did. But all we know of her suggests she wasn't bold or unscrupulous enough for that. All the same, Alexander may have felt it wasn't safe to let her live."

"But why did he go so far as to kill her?" Sir Malcolm spread out his hands in bewilderment. "He only put Mrs. Desmond in a madhouse."

Julian glanced consideringly at Marianne. "Mrs. Desmond told me that, in Alexander's eyes, Fanny was worthless—her life was of no account. He may not have thought it worth the trouble to find some ingenious means to dispose of her."

"But why in Hampstead?" Sir Malcolm wanted to know. "He'd taken Mrs. Desmond to Surrey. Why should he go all the way to Hampstead to kill Fanny?"

"I wondered about that, too. Then I recalled that he still had to dispose of Mrs. Desmond's belongings, to make it appear she'd left of her own accord. He needed a secure spot, far from both Mrs. Desmond's house and the madhouse where he'd left her. He knew Hampstead—he'd grown up there. It's the merest guess, but I shouldn't be surprised if Mrs. Desmond's things are at the bottom of one of those little willow-draped ponds on the Heath."

"I'll have the local authorities make a search," Sir Malcolm promised.

"Much good that'll do," grumbled Marianne. "It'll all be ruined by now."

"If Alexander took Mrs. Desmond's things to Hampstead," Julian mused, "he may well have enlisted Fanny to help him. She was terrified of him, by all accounts—she wouldn't have dared refuse. He killed her in the brickfield, drove back to London, and abandoned the gig and horse. Then he returned to Mrs. Desmond's house to clean himself and change his clothes. A very nearly perfect crime."

"But Martha found him out," said Mrs. Falkland, with a strange, quiet pride.

"Yes," agreed Julian, turning to Martha. "But you were suspicious of him even before the Brickfield Murder. You killed him exactly a week after he killed Fanny, and yet, according to Valère, you'd begun spying on him some days earlier. Why?"

"It was Fanny who warned me against him, sir. I had a letter from her, about a fortnight before she was killed. It was the first I'd heard from her in eighteen years. She ran away when we were girls. Our parents had died and left us each a bit of money. A man named Gates made up to Fanny and 'ticed her to go off with him—whether for her own sake or the money, I never knew."

"Gates is the surname she used at Mrs. Desmond's," said Julian.

"I wish I could believe she'd a legal right to it, sir," Martha sighed, shaking her head. "Anyhow, I tried to find her. She'd done wrong, but it was my duty to take her back and help her repent and atone. She was still my sister. But happen she was too ashamed, or she hadn't the money to come back—howsomever it was, I never saw her again. I don't know what she did all the years we were apart."

Marianne gave a little snort, as if to say that she for one had a good idea. "I know she'd no references when Alexander sent her to me."

"How can he have come to know her?" asked Sir Malcolm.

"I haven't a notion." Marianne shrugged.

"We can only speculate," said Julian. "Perhaps she found out Martha was in service with the Falklands and came looking for her, and Alexander saw her and was intrigued by the resemblance."

"That could be, sir," Martha agreed. "There are people in Sherborne, where we grew up, who could have told her I was in Mrs. Falkland's service."

"It's curious that, with all the descriptions we had of her, no one mentioned she had a West Country accent," Julian observed.

"She didn't, 'specially," said Marianne. "A country accent rubs off if you knock about the world enough—which she had, I make no doubt."

"Why was she willing to come to work for you?" asked Sir Malcolm.

"Why shouldn't she be?" Marianne retorted. "It was a good post, the pay was regular. 'Course, later she *would* snivel and beg to be allowed to give notice, but Alexander laughed and said, What do you propose to live on? Do you think you could earn a farthing in your old calling, at your age?"

Martha looked across at her fixedly. *"The dogs shall eat Jezebel by the wall of Jezreel."*

"What does she mean by that?" Marianne shrieked. "I won't be talked to so! It's enough to scare a person into fits—"

"Perhaps you might prefer to return to the drawing room?" suggested Julian smoothly.

"Oh, no," she said hastily, "that's quite all right, only she shouldn't fright a person so."

He turned back to Martha. "You said you received a letter from Fanny. When was that?"

"April the seventh, sir. I remember exactly what it said: *'Dear Martha, I am in great trouble. Will you forgive the past, and let me see you? I daren't come to you at home, or let you come to me. Will you meet me at St. Martin in the Fields at noon this Sunday? I can't explain until I see you. Whatever happens, beware your master. For pity's sake, don't let him see this letter, or I do not know what he may do to me.'*

"It wasn't signed, but I knew who it was from. I'd no idea where Fanny was, or how she knew the master, or why she was so afeard of him, but I meant to find out. I went to St. Martin in the Fields that Sunday, but Fanny never came."

"I remember that Sunday," said Marianne. "Fanny was wild to go to church. I usually let her, but that morning I was feeling a bit hipped and needed her to look after me. She made such a fuss! I said, All very well, Miss Imper'ence—we'll see what Alexander has to say about *you!* That brought her to heel quick enough."

"What can have prompted her to write at all?" Sir Malcolm

wondered. "She'd endured Alexander's tyranny so long, I should have thought she'd be resigned to it by then."

"Alexander and Mrs. Desmond had just tricked Mrs. Falkland into meeting Adams," Julian reminded him. "Mrs. Falkland was a respectable woman, and the employer of Fanny's sister. Perhaps it was simply too much for Fanny. Either fear or conscience drove her to confide in Martha and seek her help."

"She never wrote again," said Martha. "I didn't know if the master'd done something to silence her, or if she'd simply lost heart. I made up my mind to find her. I knew she'd been in London when she sent her letter, because it come by the two-penny post. I thought the master must know where she was, or she wouldn't be so afeard of him. There must be something wrong about him, and if I knew what it was, I might be able to find Fanny. I didn't let on I suspected him—he might do Fanny a mischief. But I watched him. When he went out, I made it my business to know where. And when he was at home, he was always under my eye.

"I wanted to have a look around his study, but it was hard to find a time when I could be sure nobody would catch me out. I knew I had no business there. My chance came the morning after Mr. Eugene stayed out all night in the rain. He come home at dawn, wet and cold as a winter Friday, and the mistress put him straight to bed and sent for the doctor. I wasn't needed, so I slipped into the study. The master'd been out all night, and I thought, if so be he comes home, he'll go straight to bed, or to look in on Mr. Eugene. Either way, he won't come here.

"I was wrong. He come home sudden-like and made for the study. I couldn't get out without him seeing me, so I hid behind the curtains of one of the windows. He came in and went to the other window, and I saw him press on the inside panel of the shutter-case, like this." She motioned with her hands. "The panel swung open, and there was a cupboard inside. He started taking something out of his coat pocket in handfuls and putting it in the cupboard. When he was done, he closed up the shutter-case and went away.

"I wanted to see what he'd hidden, but just then I heard people looking for me in the hall. Mr. Eugene was feverish, and my mistress needed me. The next few days I was kept so busy, I had no chance to go back to the study. But finally one night I crept in and opened the shutter-case, just as I'd seen Mr. Falkland do.

"I found a pile of jewelry, gaudier than anything my mistress would wear. I thought the master must've bought it for some fancy-woman he'd taken up with, and that was why he hid it—so my mistress wouldn't find it. I was just about to put it back, when I saw—" Her voice shook an instant. "I saw the cross.

"I knew it for Fanny's at once. She'd had it since we were girls. People joked that it was the only way to tell us apart—whichever one was wearing the cross, that was Fanny. There was something reddish-brown stuck to the chain—I couldn't make out what it was. I was sick with dread. I didn't know what to make of it all.

"I made up my mind to ask the master how he'd come by Fanny's cross, and where she was. Next day I heard he was alone in his study, so I went in to him. He was sitting at the table looking at one of his books about houses. He put up his brows and looked at me.

"I was a coward then. I'm ashamed to say it, but I thought of myself when I should have been thinking of Fanny. He was my master. If he dismissed me, I'd never see my mistress again. At first I couldn't speak—couldn't think what to say. Finally I managed to ask him if he knew what had become of my sister.

"He said, 'What should I know about your sister?' And he sounded so mild, and looked so puzzled, that just for a moment I thought I was all wrong, and he couldn't know anything about Fanny at all.

"Then I remembered he had Fanny's cross, and she'd

written to me that she was afeard of him. I was angry, and that gave me courage. I said I'd had a letter from her about him. He got up and came around the table. 'Where is this letter?' he wanted to know. 'I can't show it to you,' said I. 'Martha,' he said, smiling all the while and never taking his eyes off me, 'how can I help you if you won't confide in me?' He kept pressing me for the letter, till finally I blurted out that I'd burnt it, because Fanny was afeard of what would happen if it fell into his hands.

"He said, 'Then for all intents and purposes, there never was a letter, and I never knew your sister.' 'But there *was* a letter,' said I. 'I can swear to it.' And he smiled, as if he was talking to a child. 'You haven't studied law,' he said. 'I have. In law, truth is only what you can prove by evidence in court. You have nothing except your word, and I don't think anybody is likely to take that seriously, do you?'

"I just stood there and gaped at him. What he said was so wrong and wicked, and he said it so brazenly. I'd never heard the like of it before. He thought he'd won—thought I was silent for lack of an answer. He gathered up his papers and started toward the door. But all at once he turned around, mocking me with his eyes. He said, very low, 'Did you hear about that woman who was found dead in the brickfield? Tragic, isn't it?'

"After he'd gone, I stood there rooted to the spot. I'd heard of the Brickfield Murder—it'd been in all the papers the past few days. I didn't want to believe it, but I had no choice: that poor soul found in the brickfield was my sister, and it was the master who killed her. He was out all night on the night of that murder—I remembered, because it was the same night Mr. Eugene stayed out in the rain. Next morning I saw him come home and hide Fanny's cross. But what told against him most was that the woman's face was destroyed. I knew why now: because it was the same as mine.

"He didn't know I'd guess all that. I saw what he wanted me to think: that the brickfield woman might be Fanny, but

I'd never know for sure, and I'd eat my heart out over it the rest of my life. He didn't know I'd found Fanny's cross. I had no chance to tell him.

"I felt such a rage as I'd never known. I wanted to go straight to a magistrate and have the law of him for killing my sister. But then I remembered what he said about truth being only what you can prove in court. I didn't think I had enough of that kind of proof to make him pay for Fanny's murder. He was a gentleman, with titled friends and a famous lawyer for a father. He might explain away the cross, and who'd take my word against his?

"I asked the Lord for guidance. I closed my eyes and opened my Bible, and it opened to the Book of Job." She recited, staring straight ahead:

> "*Knowest thou not this of old, since man was placed upon the earth,*
> *That the triumphing of the wicked is short, and the joy of the hypocrite but for a moment?*
> *Though his excellency mount up to the heavens, and his head reach unto the clouds;*
> *Though wickedness be sweet in his mouth, though he hide it under his tongue;*
> *He shall flee from the iron weapon, and the bow of steel shall strike him through.*

"How could the Lord have made any clearer to me what I must do?

"You'll give me up to Bow Street, I expect. You must do what you think right. But I'm not sorry. As far as I could see, he brought misery on everyone. Hanging me won't bring him back. If it would, I don't believe any of you would do it."

She looked around at them challengingly. They were all silent.

"She won't be hanged, will she, Papa?" Mrs. Falkland urged. "Not when it's known why she killed him?"

"I don't know, my dear. We'll do all we can to present a

fair picture of her motives—after that, it's up to the judge."
He added, "Have you really known all along she was the
murderer?"

Mrs. Falkland looked at Martha sadly. "Remember how
you came to look in on me after I'd retired from the party?
You offered to make me one of your headache remedies, and
I said not to bother. But later I found I really did have a
headache. I didn't want to attract attention by ringing for you,
so I stole up to your room. That was at about midnight. You
weren't there. Later I heard you'd told the Bow Street Runners you were in your room throughout the time when Alexander might have been killed. I remembered then how, after
you told me about the murder, you held me and comforted
me and said everything would be all right now. And suddenly
I understood: everything was all right because you'd made it
so. I shall always be grateful to you, Martha." Her face crumpled. "And I shall miss you so much!"

It dawned on Julian how alone she was. She had had so
many friends as Alexander's wife—but the friends were all
Alexander's. And there was no substance to his friendships—
they were born of his charm, and they died with it. She had
no one left but Sir Malcolm, Eugene, and Martha. And now
Martha would be gone.

He murmured to Sir Malcolm, "I think you should send
for Eugene. I didn't want Mrs. Falkland to have to tell her
story in front of him, but she needs him now—all the more
because I think I hear Vance arriving. I sent a note to him
before I left London, asking him to join us here."

Sure enough, Vance was ushered in, his subordinate Watkins in tow. Sir Malcolm began explaining about the cross
and Martha's confession. For the first time, Julian spared
a thought for the clock. It was a little before twelve. Solved,
de Witt! he thought. And with four minutes to spare.

# * 31 *

## ENDINGS

After Martha's arrest, Julian collected his five hundred pounds and vanished from London for a fortnight. He wanted to avoid inquisitive acquaintances and journalists; besides, disappearing just when you were most in demand helped keep society in thrall. As Tibbs had said, an audience, like a lover, ought never to be left quite sated. From the seclusion of a cottage in Hampton Court, he followed the aftermath of the investigation through newspaper accounts and letters from Sir Malcolm, who was one of the few people who knew where he was.

True to his resolve, Sir Malcolm unflinchingly made public Alexander's imprisonment of Marianne and murder of Fanny. The solution to the Brickfield Murder all but eclipsed the news of Martha's guilt. Alexander made a far more romantic villain than Martha, and every organ of the press from society journals to ha'penny broadsheets resounded with his crimes.

Sir Malcolm's candour about his son's misdeeds stopped short of revealing anything that would shame or incriminate Mrs. Falkland. The whole story of her encounter with Adams at Mrs. Desmond's was suppressed, and the public was left in the dark about who had tampered with her saddle. Sir Malcolm's chief concern was to silence Marianne, who knew just enough about Mrs. Falkland and Adams to be dangerous. He struck a bargain with her: she would be paid a quarterly allowance on condition of her leaving England and revealing nothing about Alexander's plot against his wife. For the time being, she remained in London to testify against Ridley, who had been charged with false imprisonment and other crimes. There was a wave of protest about conditions in private madhouses; Sir Henry Effingham was to head a parliamentary committee about it.

In one of his letters to Sir Malcolm, Julian asked after Quentin Clare. Sir Malcolm reported briefly that Mr. Clare's health had broken down, and he had gone abroad to try to restore it. Julian drew his own conclusions.

When he returned to London at the end of May, he found a myriad of letters and invitations awaiting him. Among them was a card from David Adams, with a message written on the back: *"Will you give me leave to call on you? I ask nothing but a chance to talk to you. In God's name, please."*

Julian tapped the card against his hand. Finally he wrote a terse note stating that he would be at home tomorrow evening after nine o'clock.

✳

"Thank you for seeing me, Mr. Kestrel."

"You have nothing to thank me for, Mr. Adams. I feel a responsibility to the investigation to find out what you have to say. But for that, I wouldn't have received you."

"You know, then. About Mrs. Falkland and the thirty thousand pounds. She's told you?"

"She went through that humiliation, yes."

Adams passed a hand briefly across his eyes. He looked haggard—undramatically so, as if strain and lack of sleep had become a way of life for him. "I wondered. The newspaper accounts say nothing about it."

"You needn't be concerned. Everyone close to Mrs. Falkland knows the price she would pay for denouncing you. Her honour and peace of mind are more important than bringing you to justice."

"My God, is that why you think I came?"

"I have no idea why you came, Mr. Adams."

Adams's lips twisted into the old, ironic smile. "I suppose for the same reason I got myself invited to Falkland's party. The same reason I wrote Mrs. Falkland that letter warning her against her maid. The same reason I came to you after her accident and told you I'd seen her maid—or, the woman I thought was her maid—at Mrs. Desmond's. Because I was frantic with worry about her. Because I wanted to help her, protect her. Don't think I don't know how grotesque that sounds! I'm like a man who sets a house on fire, then rushes in to rescue the occupants after it's too late for them to be saved."

"What do you hope to do for her now?"

"This accident of hers—no one seems to know who was behind it. You can't mean to let it drop? If she's in danger—"

"She isn't in danger. We know who caused the accident, but we've dealt with it privately, to spare her any scandal."

"Who was it?"

"I can't tell you that."

"For God's sake, the child she lost might have been mine—"

"You have no rights in the matter, Mr. Adams. None at all."

There was a pause.

"How is she?" Adams asked quietly.

"Shattered. She'll rally, I imagine. She's very strong. She'll rebuild her life with whatever she has to hand. Between you, you and Alexander haven't left her very much."

"Kestrel, I didn't want to do it. I didn't mean to hurt her. I meant to hurt him. I loved her—almost from the moment I met her. I saw that she was as far above him as Heaven is above earth. I knew him: his greed, his vanity, his unholy craving for excitement. I knew that society's darling was a venal, vicious, diabolical child. But I stuck to him—not only because he was useful to me in business, but because I hoped he would ruin himself in the end, and I wanted to be there. And because of *her*—because I lived on the sight of her. It was hopeless. Even if she hadn't been married, her family and friends would never have let her throw herself away upon a Jew. But I couldn't root out my love. It lived upon nothing. It thrived in the face of all my mockery and her indifference.

"When I bought up Falkland's notes-of-hand, I didn't think to use them to get at her. I just wanted to have him in my power—make him beg me for more time, more lenient terms. Sure enough, he came to me, all charm and cajolery, wanting me to treat him like an erring schoolboy, instead of a grown man who'd all but beggared his family. It wasn't enough. I wanted to draw blood. I could pitch him into Queer Street— have the bailiffs into his house, make him sell off his precious toys and trinkets. But then I'd be branded the villain—the rapacious Jew fleecing a friend. No: what I wanted was to make him agree to the vilest terms I could think of—to prove there were no depths he wouldn't sink to, for the sake of his wealth and his vanity.

"I told him I wouldn't compound with him for the amount of the notes, but I might give them up to him, depending on what he would give me in return. I said I didn't care a twopenny damn about his paintings or his furniture or anything else in his showpiece of a house. He had only one thing I counted of any value: his wife.

"*What can you mean?* he said, opening up his eyes. I said, Why should you be shocked? I thought arrangements like that were common enough in the *beau monde.* I wanted him to resist, recoil—I wanted to see him squirm. No such thing. He approached the idea with a cool, easy, business-like logic that took my breath away. I'd meant to hold up a mirror to him, show what a contemptible thing he was, then make some arrangement about his notes and send him packing. But even now, he wasn't humiliated or abashed. He was merely showing his natural colours, and had no shame about them at all. I couldn't retreat while he was still triumphant. And suddenly I was tempted. To be alone with her, to declare my feelings—! Not to purchase her like a prostitute, as Falkland believed I meant to do, but to approach her free of barriers and distractions. Who knew—I might be able to make her love me. I had plenty of money. We could go away together and live somewhere out of England. Falkland was a fiend, he cared nothing for her. I would be doing her a favour, taking her from a man like that.

"You're probably thinking, was I mad? Did I know her so little as to think she'd fling away her honour, her home and family, for me, who meant no more to her than her servants —far less than her horse? I can only tell you, love like mine sends a man silly, blinds his eyes with moonbeams, drives numbing spikes through his brain. I was so crazed that, when Falkland concocted his plan to lure her to that woman's house, I agreed—even though I must have known that a woman of her pride and courage would never yield to a man who tricked and trapped her in order to plead his cause.

"Suffice to say, she scorned me as I ought to have known she would. She hurt me the way that ice, when it's cold enough, tears the skin from your hands. What I did—it wasn't because I thought I could win or conquer her that way. I did it out of despair. I don't expect you to understand."

"But you hope I will," said Julian quietly. "Or why should you tell me all this?"

Adams stared, wary and a little ashamed. "I'm not asking for your sympathy."

"No. I give you credit for that."

"Then you do understand, a little?"

"No. But I think Mrs. Falkland does."

"What makes you say so?" Adams caught his breath.

"The way she spoke of you." He paused, deciding how much it would be fair to her to repeat. "If I were to distill all she said into a few words, I would say that she doesn't wish to see you again, but she forgives you."

Adams drew a long, slow breath. "She forgives me." Then, with an emptiness that was part relief and part desolation: "It's finished."

"Yes. If you really wish to do something for her, you'll let her go."

"Oh, I'm a very bad hand at letting things go!" Adams laughed bitterly. "But you're right. You've helped me to my senses. I have duties; I'm an only son. I ought to marry some demure Rebecca or Rachel and continue the family line." He took up his hat and cloak. "Thank you, Mr. Kestrel. You've been very patient, listening to all this. Will you take a piece of advice, as the only return I can make?"

"What is it?"

"Buy railway shares. Someday these passenger railways are going to amount to something." He smiled his mocking smile and went out.

Julian looked after him for a time. He saw now why Mrs. Falkland could speak so understandingly of him, in spite of what he had done to her. They were two of a kind: proud, fierce, independent—cruel to others when duty demanded it, but cruelest of all to themselves.

It was a great love squandered—stillborn, like their child. They might have leaped mere social obstacles, but not the chasm that parted them now. They would never find their way back to each other. Not this side of Heaven.

# ✳ 32 ✳

## BEGINNINGS

Martha pled guilty to Alexander's murder, much to the disappointment of the public, which had hoped for a sensational trial. The judge was somewhat at a loss how to sentence her. In the end, he condemned her to lifelong transportation to the penal colony at Botany Bay, Australia. Julian heard from Sir Malcolm that Mrs. Falkland had wanted to bid her goodbye, but Martha had refused to see her. It would not be seemly, she said, for Mrs. Falkland to show any sympathy for the murderer of her husband.

Soon after, Mrs. Falkland wrote to Julian and asked him to call on her. He complied. He found her largely recovered in health, though thin, and strangely softer of feature, as if the decisive lines of a chalk drawing had been gently smudged. But what struck him most about her was her tentativeness: the uncertainty of a newborn creature finding its feet in the world. So many of her old assumptions and supports had been overthrown. He thought she had never looked less beautiful, or more appealing.

After they had exchanged greetings and courtesies, she said, "I wanted to ask you what I ought to do about Eugene. He admires you tremendously, and you seem to understand him better than anyone else. Should I engage a tutor for him, find another school—"

"Take him abroad," said Julian, without hesitation. "Expose him to music, art, fine cookery, elegant conversation. Don't take him among the bored and superior English expatriates—mingle directly with cultured, distinguished foreigners. He'll feel awkward, but he'll have an excuse, not knowing the language or customs. In time he'll acquire polish, confidence—affectations, probably, but a little gentle ridicule will cure him of that. I should be glad to provide you with a few introductions, if they would be any use."

"That's kind of you. But—do you think a tour abroad might be a dangerous influence on him?

"In what way?"

She dropped her gaze and said in a low voice, "Alexander travelled on the Continent when he wasn't much older than Eugene."

"Alexander did a great many things," he pointed out gently. "I don't think you can afford to live your life avoiding everything he touched. You needn't fear for Eugene. He's very promising material. And he has you. He can't fail to set an honourable course, with such a star to steer by."

"Thank you. You've been very good." She gave him her hand. "I want you to know—I don't blame you for anything. You did your duty. You helped Papa find out the truth, and I see now that he needed that more than he needed to believe in Alexander." She lifted her head resolutely. "I *will* take Eugene abroad. I can make it safe for him."

No, thought Julian, he'll make it safe for you. You'll take him to Paris, Venice, Rome, and he'll look at it all with wonder and delight and make you see it through his eyes. For his sake, you'll have to come out of your grief, entertain, make new acquaintances. There may even be a man who can make you see that there's still beauty in the world, and your life can't possibly be over at twenty—

If he ran on in this vein much longer, he would apply for the position himself. He bowed over her hand and took his leave. At the door he looked back for a moment. She was gazing into the distance, a little flushed, as if she could already feel the salt winds of the Channel on her face.

✳

Spring gave way to summer. London's whirl of balls, dinner parties, concerts, operas, and plays reached its height, then tapered off. In late July, the fashionable carriages began rolling out of London, bearing landowners away to country estates, young men to shooting lodges, and fair Cyprians to scout for new protectors in watering places and sea resorts. The courts shut down for their Long Vacation; trade languished in the Burlington Arcade and Savile Row. Humbler shopmen and their apprentices settled down to endure the heat and dust and the stench of sewage rising from the Thames.

Julian was strolling in Bond Street one afternoon when a coach drew up beside him and a voice exclaimed, "Why, Mr. Kestrel! How do you come to be lingering in this blighted landscape?"

"How can any landscape be blighted that contains you, Lady Anthea?"

"How charmingly mendacious. Seriously, I should have thought you'd be off to the grouse moors."

"I shall be, in a few days. How do you come to be still in London?"

"I have invitations from both my nephews, and I'm keeping them on tenterhooks about which I shall accept. A wealthy maiden aunt must have her little amusements— Oh!" she hissed. "Look! Or, rather, don't seem to look, but look all the same. Sir Malcolm Falkland and *that girl!*"

Julian glanced around discreetly. Sir Malcolm was coming out of Hookhams Library, accompanied by a pink-faced young man with a high collar, a mousy middle-aged woman, and a tall, slender girl dressed all in black.

"So that's Miss Clare," said Julian softly.

Lady Anthea nodded, her false black side-curls fluttering. "You know, the sister of that strange young man—no, one mustn't speak ill of the dead—that *unfortunate* young man who was so friendly with Alexander Falkland."

"I gather he died abroad some weeks ago?"

"Yes. I wasn't much surprised. He always looked rather frail. And I believe he was terribly attached to Alexander. The news of his being a positive *criminal* must have broken his heart. Then along comes this girl, his sister, and Sir Malcolm takes her under his wing, and the next thing anyone knows, they're inseparable! Everyone says he'll marry her as soon as she's out of mourning. Fancy such a sensible man turning spoony at his age! She could be his daughter!"

"I hope you're mistaken, Lady Anthea. I'm sure there would be legal complications."

"I didn't mean that, you wicked man. I meant she's young enough to be his daughter. Of course, I'm sure she's perfectly respectable. I was never one to believe that an eccentric upbringing *necessarily* gives a girl unsound morals. And she's not so *very* plain. A good modiste might do something with her—"

"I believe I'll take advantage of this opportunity to meet her."

"Do, by all means, then come and call on me and tell me all about her."

Julian inwardly resolved to be in Jericho first. "With the greatest pleasure, if I can possibly find the time before I leave town."

He stepped back to let her carriage drive off, then approached the group outside Hookhams. Sir Malcolm greeted him cordially and presented him to Miss Clare.

He bowed over her hand. "I've looked forward to this meeting."

"So have I. My brother told me how astutely you conducted the murder investigation."

"That was kind of him. I thought highly of him as well. I was sorry to hear of his death." He could not resist adding, "You look remarkably like him."

She did not even blink. "Yes, people always said we were very alike."

The resemblance was not as strong as Julian would have expected. Her face was framed so differently now: the starched white neckcloth replaced by a lace collar, the head encircled by a bonnet and a softening fall of curls. Not her own hair, surely—it could not have grown so fast—but far more convincing than Lady Anthea's sham ringlets. Julian detected the handiwork of George Tibbs, who, after all, had begun his career in the theatre making costumes. He had abetted his niece's masquerade as a man—now he was no doubt helping to ease her back into her life as a woman.

Sir Malcolm introduced Julian to the middle-aged woman, who was Miss Clare's hired companion, Miss Meeks. The idea of Verity Clare needing a duenna amused Julian mightily, but of course Sir Malcolm's future wife could not live in London unchaperoned.

The young man with the fearsome collar was a barrister named Pruitt, who had been having a legal colloquy with Sir Malcolm and was eager to resume it. "Of course, the essential difference between trespass *vi et armis* and trespass on the case lies in the immediacy of the injury."

"To be sure, Mr. Pruitt," said Sir Malcolm. "But do you really think this is the time and place—"

"But the principle is so difficult to apply in vehicular accidents. Logically, it oughtn't to matter whether a carriage that runs someone down was driven by the owner or his servant, and yet the court made precisely that distinction in—in—I can't think of the case—"

"*Reynolds versus Clarke,*" murmured Miss Clare.

Sir Malcolm's jaw dropped. He gazed at her with a mixture of pride and alarm.

"Why, I believe you're right, Miss Clare!" Pruitt exclaimed. "But how did you know?"

"Oh, my brother was forever talking to me about his studies. I couldn't help but pick things up."

"We're just walking over to Gunter's for ices, Mr. Kestrel,"

Sir Malcolm interposed hastily. "Would you care to come?"

"I should be delighted."

Miss Meeks peered anxiously at the sky. "I do hope it isn't going to rain."

"We may be tempting the gods," owned Sir Malcolm. "But I'm willing to risk it, if the rest of you are."

They set off, Sir Malcolm giving his arm to Miss Clare, Julian escorting a flustered Miss Meeks. "I never quite like to hear people speak of 'the gods' as if there were more than one," she confided. "It sounds so unchristian."

Sir Malcolm overheard and looked around at her. "I didn't mean to offend you. I'm afraid a lifelong study of the classics does give one a sense of capricious deities looking over one's shoulder, waiting for a chance to wreak havoc."

"Dreadful!" She shuddered. "How could anyone have conceived of that as religion?"

"Euripides might have agreed with you. He wrote, *'If the gods do evil, they are not gods.'* But he also portrayed them in a better light." He quoted some lines in Greek.

"That's very apt," said Miss Clare, smiling. "But Miss Meeks doesn't understand you."

Pruitt goggled at her. "You don't mean to say you read *Greek*, Miss Clare?"

"My brother taught me a little," she admitted.

Julian wondered how long she would go on using Quentin as a blind for her own achievements. Long enough, he supposed, for people to become accustomed to the notion of a baronet's wife who read dead languages and studied law. She was learning to compromise. But Julian felt sure she would always be tempted to leap boundaries and confound expectations. He remembered the inscription on the casket that contained Portia's picture in *The Merchant of Venice*: *"Who chooseth me must give and hazard all he hath."*

Sir Malcolm seemed happy to take his chances. Eyes alight with love and admiration, he said, "Why don't you translate for me?"

He repeated the Greek lines. She thought a moment, then

smiled and turned to Julian, inviting him to share a joke that only the three of them could fully understand:

> *"Zeus on Olympus dispenses many fates;*
> *The gods bring many things surprisingly to pass.*
> *That which we expected does not happen;*
> *A god finds means to bring about the unexpected.*
> *And so it happened here."*